The Journals of Aaron the White

Portal Jumpers # 1

The Journals of Aaron the White

J. Mikel Boland

Copyright © 2025 by J. Mikel Boland

All rights reserved.

No part of this publication may be reproduced, distributed, or transmitted in any form or by any means, including photocopying, recording, or other electronic or mechanical methods, without the prior written permission of the publisher, except as permitted by U.S. copyright law. For permission requests, contact J. Mikel Boland.

The story, all names, characters, and incidents portrayed in this production are fictitious. No identification with actual persons (living or deceased), places, buildings, and products is intended or should be inferred.

ISBN: 979-8-9929080-0-8 (Paperback edition)
ISBN: 979-8-9929080-1-5 (Ebook edition)

Library of Congress Control Number: 2025905268

Map by Sarah Caswell

Book Cover by Chloe K.

Illustration by Jacob Boland

Editing by Lisa Blackwell

Typesetting by Draft Works

https://Jmikelboland.top

Dedication

I would like to dedicate this book to the people in my life, without whom it would never have been finished, beginning with my wife, Melissa. Thank you for encouraging me to keep going whether it makes sense or not and for putting me back on track when I get discouraged. I would also like to thank my son Jacob for geeking out with me over some of my races and characters and creating things alongside me. To my friend Mark, who has been a terrific encouragement and asks about the books enough to help keep me going. To my sister Sarah, who dedicated a lot of hours making sure my world made sense, making maps, and ensuring my intermediate edits didn't break anything. To my editor, Lisa, whose contributions to the maturation of this book cannot be overstated, and to my critique groups and fellow writers in the TWA, thank you.

Table of Contents

Dedication 5
Table of Contents 7
I   WELCOME TO SORRA 11
    Preface 13
    Introduction Stories in the Darkness 14
    Chapter 1 A Beginning 23
    Bridge Revelations 34
    Chapter 2 Hunter or the Hunted 35
    Chapter 3 Fellowship 42
    Chapter 4 Teacher or Student 52
    Chapter 5 Tiiaan 55
    Chapter 6 Back to School 65
    Chapter 7 Playtime 74
    Chapter 8 Leaders of Tiiaan 78
II QUESTING FOR THE STAR GLASS 89
    Chapter 9 Fond Farewell 91
    Chapter 10 Back to the Wild 96
    Chapter 11 Things That Go Bump 107
    Chapter 12 To the Mines 119
    Chapter 13 The Welcome Wagon 133

    Chapter 14 Dark Travels 142

    Chapter 15 Thought Collecting 155

    Chapter 16 That Which Must Be Dealt With 160

    Chapter 17 Dark Decisions 172

    Chapter 18 Path to the Star 177

    Chapter 19 From Inky Blackness to Unbearable Light 186

    Chapter 20 … and Back Again? 191

    Chapter 21 Can We Stop and Ask for Directions? 196

    Chapter 22 What Exactly Is This Thing? 201

    Chapter 23 Avante! 208

    Chapter 24 Return to the Land of the Living 214

III   DEFENSE OF TIIAAN & ADVANCE TO BATTLE . 221

    Chapter 25 In Time? 223

    Chapter 26 Be Careful What You Search For 238

    Chapter 27 Racing the Storm to Tiiaan 255

    Chapter 28 Second Place Finish 268

    Chapter 29 War Counsel of Three Plus 277

    Chapter 30 Guinea Pigs and Dr. Aaron 287

    Chapter 31 Night Terrors in the Morning 294

    Chapter 32 Preparing Lemonade 301

    Chapter 33 Ready the Gear of War 322

    Chapter 34 Roses Amongst the Thorns 340

IV   WAR FOR SORRA & CONCLUSION 347

    Chapter 35 Marching To The End of Everything 349

    Chapter 36 Advance Preempted 358

    Chapter 37 Chasing a Ghost 367

Chapter 38 Great Start. But How Will the Day End?........ 385

Chapter 39 What Do You Do if the Ghost Catches You? 394

Chapter 40 Reunion.. 399

Chapter 41 Battle's End 408

Chapter 42 And Then?.. 411

Glossary.. 413

Main Character List 416

Author Bio 419

Sorra

1. Corrupted Bear Attack
2. TuskerKitty
3. Mental Bombed Bird
4. Corrupted Rock Piper Attack
5. Corrupted Tibbeus Attack
6. Shadowworms and Spinebeast Attack
7. Attack at waterfall
8. OasisAnts and Sludgemen attack
9. Corrupted OrOboid attack
10. Gathering

SeaWind Lagoon

Portal

Srake Peake Mines

SrakeKepp Mountains

Traveler's Respite

Crystal Castle

TownHold

Magic School

Tiiaan

Neslioth

I

WELCOME TO SORRA

Preface

"Be Welcome, Good Traveler," said a voice from the darkness that surrounded the sapphire glow I had walked through. A small brown robed, and cowled figure strode slowly into the dim moonlight. "Is this your first time across the Portal?" the figure inquired.

I collected my thoughts from where my fright had scattered them before replying, "If that's what just happened, then I've never done it before."

"Since you are new to this land then, let me offer you what assistance I may. You will need to understand this world if you are going to save it, so I will tell you of the people that inhabit this land, and some of their history."

Startled as I was by the sudden appearance of the man and his ghostly voice, I could tell that he meant me well and so I found a comfortable spot on the grassy earth and settled in to listen. I continued to cast glances at the portal as waves of unpleasant déjà vu assaulted me.

The remainder of this manuscript is what the stranger, Mikaal, spoke to me that night, recorded to the best of my ability. When I have finished recording what he told me I will leave the manuscript near the entrance to the portal with the hope that if I do not return, someone may find it. I have no idea what dangers or opportunities I might face. Not a single person will come looking for me. I have lived alone and so far from others for a long time, but one of the nature lovers that wanders the paths near my house could be drawn through the portal and have no strange little man to guide them.

Introduction
Stories in the Darkness

"This land, known to its inhabitants as Sorra, has a relatively peaceful past. All of the races that live either on the surface, or below it, lived in harmony for as long as anyone alive can remember. It seems that peace, or even our lives, is to be taken from us. If swift action isn't taken, I fear there will be nothing left of Sorra but stories. I'll explain what we're up against soon."

"I have seen twelve hundred and five seasons of rebirth... Spring I believe it is called in your land... Do not look so surprised! Time affects all races differently. Those of us with magic usually live longer than others of our race. I see the beginnings of doubt in your eyes, so I will go slowly and explain as much as I can."

"Let us see... Where to begin? I suppose I should tell you of the oldest of the races. They call themselves 'The Gathering' although most of us affectionately call them Critters. Critters vary widely in appearance. If you were to see one in its homeland it would be brown or black or perhaps a bright red. Critters live in the Wastelands. They are the only things that live in the Wastelands for long. There is no water there, only blasted rock and molten lava. If you were to go looking for a Critter at home, you would probably die before you found one. A single Critter by his or herself is usually no bigger than a gameball.... I see the look of confusion on your face; a gameball is about the size of your fist.

"Critters blend completely with their surroundings, usually taking the shape and texture of a stone. Sometimes they will blend with a flow of lava and roll slowly downstream. There is probably a Critter here with us now. If you were to examine every stone in this

INTRODUCTION

clearing, you would eventually find one that is not as heavy as it looks to be. Chances are you would be holding a Critter in your hand.

"The reason that Critters call themselves 'The Gathering' is fairly simple. A single Critter has little in the way of a mind as you or I would think of one, but when a group of Critters gets together, they link their thoughts and experiences. A Gathering of Critters in large enough numbers contains more knowledge than you or I could ever gather in our respective lifetimes. That same group would also have an incredible intelligence and could work through a problem infinitely faster than one of us.

"Critters usually live for several thousand years, and everything that happens around them is stored in their tiny bodies in the greatest of detail. Chances are that you will never see a Critter Gathering in your lifetime. It is a very rare occurrence, and I am one of the few people left alive to have witnessed one."

I knew when I walked through the shimmering void that if I survived the experience, I would likely be somewhere new, but what this shrouded stranger was telling me was hard to credit. I can't even see his features, though a campfire doesn't offer a lot of light. Maybe this is all some sort of elaborate hoax, but it felt real enough when I crossed over. I'll just listen a bit longer and reserve judgment for now.

Mikaal continued. "Off-worlders seem to find the OrOboid most fascinating. They are a tri-pedal race, most amazing to behold. They are impossibly slender, and their pale-blue flesh lends a very fragile air to their appearance. To describe the OrOboid is almost futile, as mere words cannot tell of the wonder that a person feels when they first lay eyes on one.

"They have no eyes or ears in the traditional way that you would think of them; instead, they have a thin translucent membrane that circles their small heads midway that serves them for sight, hearing as well as smell. Their mouths are at the apex of their skulls, and it is likely that you will never see them smile as they are generally in excess of twenty-five hands high when standing upright. They do not have a language of their own as all OrOboid are born with the ability to mindspeak. Necks only three thumbs breadth hold the head to the torso, which itself is maybe half the size of yours. The torso meets the legs at the largest part of an OrOboid body called the grundel, which is slightly bigger than your head.

"The legs of an OrOboid are similar in width to a horse or donkey but easily twice the length. Two arms that match the legs for width are placed on opposing sides of the torso. What makes the OrOboid so amazing to witness in action is that all of their joints are reversible. Each of their three legs, the single leading leg and the two trailing legs, have three joints. This allows them to fold their legs over double and leap great distances through the air like a spring. Furthermore, these wondrous creatures have the ability to walk in any direction and will at times turn their torso's and switch leading legs while in mid stride.

"OrOboid are extremely agile and graceful. Do not let these qualities distract you from their incredible strength though. Many an unwary traveler has lost life or limb by underestimating the power one of these spindly creatures contains and attacking them."

Right now, I am sure that this fellow is nuts. I can't imagine how something like these OrOboid could possibly live. If they do and I do spot one, I can't imagine trying to attack something so strange. He says they're amazing, but I have no interest in doing anything more than seeing them from afar. The really weird thing is that it feels like he believes what he's saying, so I feel compelled to continue listening. He was still talking, and I should probably be paying attention.

"Were you to find yourself near a crystal castle while venturing across this land you would be looking at the handiwork of the OrOboid. The only magic other than telepathy that the OrOboid possess is the ability to work crystal. They can make a small crystal fragment grow to the size of a peasant's shack in a matter of an hour. If they want the crystal to be useful, it would take them twice that long to coax the shard into growing into the shape they desire. Crystal is the building material used for every facet of OrOboid life from housing to tools to weapons.

"By some manner known only to them they have found a way to increase the strength of the crystal they work, if they wish it. A crystal spear created by a talented OrOboid would stand up in battle to a sword forged by a master smith and would weigh half as much. You can imagine that OrOboid weaponry is highly sought after and commands a very good price."

"OrOboids eat only plant matter as their tiny stomachs cannot deal with flesh, cooked or uncooked. This is probably the only weak spot in OrOboid anatomy. Because of their narrow builds, OrOboids are not able to eat a lot at any one time and must eat very often. They usually eat five times a day and cannot survive without food for more than two sunsets."

Speaking of food, I have almost nothing edible in my pack. I probably should have thought about that before I jumped willy-nilly through a hole in the middle of a glade. If this place is as different as Mikaal is telling me, I won't even know what is safe for me to eat. On the rare occasion that I hunted at home, I would have had my rifle. All I have with me is my father's sword and a wooden blowgun that I found in the attic and had decided to use to deal with a rodent problem. I wouldn't even have had the sword if that towny hadn't talked me into joining him for medieval roleplay the next valley over. Since the blowpipe could pass as a very short staff, nobody questioned that, but a rifle wouldn't have been allowed. If I don't march right back across the portal I'm going to have to figure out how to feed myself, and I don't want to wait even one more sunset to do so.

"Probably the most common of the races are the Garanth. They are bipedal and mostly humanoid, but you would probably still find them odd. Their feet are pointed in the opposite direction as yours as are their leg joints. When moving in a straight line they are incredibly speedy, and they can run for hours without tiring. Their midsections are similar in size to your own but four arms not two, spring from their bodies. Strength is not theirs in large measure, but their many hands are capable of incredibly complex tasks. Almost all of the mechanical devices found on Sorra are Garanth-made and they do have some truly marvelous creations.

"Their facial features are similar to yours with their noses being perhaps slenderer than your own. Most Garanth are dark brown or black in color, with hair generally a deep onyx color and worn long. As a race they are fairly strong in magic of all types and have created the only school for magic on the face of Sorra. They are mainly carnivorous and live on a diet of small prairie animals of various types, mostly chipchucks, hairs, and kittles. The Garanth are incredibly intelligent as a whole and are the only race that lives above ground that builds their homes completely by hand."

Garanth may be common here, but I'm going to have a hard time fitting in if I'm two arms shy of the locals. I sat here trying to envision a man with his feet and knees on backward and just couldn't. Why, oh why, did I think it was a good idea to come here? It is not as if strange shimmering veils have brought anything good into my life. And why was this person sitting here? That's a bit suspicious. He just keeps on talking. I guess I will just keep on writing, and we'll see if he runs out of words before I run out of paper in my notebook.

"I am a Noran. We are forest dwellers and are generally very elusive. As you can see, our faces are similar to what you are used to if a little smaller. What I have not shown you and will show you now, is that we have no jointed arms or legs sprouting from our torsos, only eight ropelike appendages that we name gaw."

Apparently, I jumped back without realizing it, as he continued.

"Sit down stranger, I have not tried to eat you yet, and I am not

INTRODUCTION

planning on it. Just because I do not look like you does not mean that I am going to try to hurt you."

I was thankful for the verbal reassurance, but the fact that the little man before me was really a land octopus of sorts kept me at least partially on my guard.

"That's better. Now as I was saying, our gaw are our primary means of locomotion as well as what we use in the way that you use your hands. We live far from the ground in nets made from vines woven into tree branches. We are generally considered to be average in intelligence, strength, and stamina. Our magic is what truly sets us apart though. Every Noran child is born with some magic talent, and overall we are the strongest of all the races in magic."

Great... and are the Sorran Squid race fond of luring interworld tourists here only to tell them long-winded histories until they pass out and eat them? Or if not, what do you people eat?

"We eat both plant and animal matter but prefer the flesh of birds that get caught up in our skynets."

Oh. Well. I am not a bird, or plant, and hopefully he means non-sentient animal, so—not dinner.

"Most of our bodies and gaw are colored in earth tones of brown, green, or black for camouflage. We can walk on the ground like you but find swinging from tree to tree to be a much more enjoyable means of travel."

"The last race I have to tell you about are also rather isolated, but more by their habitat than by purpose. They live burrowed deep in the sides of mountains and rarely venture out in daylight. The people of this race, the Moalean, are no more than ten hands high at maturity. The Moalean have developed a unique magical talent over the years that enables them to deal with the other races while at the same level, they can alter their physical size. A fully developed

Moalean can grow, in about one minute, to somewhere approaching your stature."

"Those of the Moalean race have four eyes, two of which they use when in complete darkness. This first set of eyes actually emits a faint light, which is what enables them to move about so freely in utter darkness. When there is a light source present, they will close their night eyes as they are extremely sensitive to light and open their daylight eyes. The second set of eyes, set slightly farther back in their heads, is very similar to your own in both form and function. If you were to see their night eyes you would notice that they are diamond shaped instead of rounded."

"The physical structure of the Moalean is very unique: They are covered completely with dark gray fur. Their heads are slightly conical with their primary eyes close to the front of their faces. Large noses take up the greater portion of their face, usually black in color, and round. The entrances to the nose are at the tip but have valves to protect against dirt. Ears are large and floppy, some reaching down to the thick neck. The mouth is small and houses flat teeth used for grinding the moss favored by this race as a food source."

"The trunk of the body is more rounded than your own and the arms and legs are joined to it more towards the front than yours. Hands are not very adept at grasping or elaborate motions but are very strong and excel as weapons. Feet are made up of extremely long and agile toes with which the Moalean perform intricate magical carving rituals. Primarily these creatures walk on all four limbs, sometimes using the long, curved nails of their hands to dig through rock and dirt. They can stand upright though it pains them to do so for long periods. Physically they are weak, but have good stamina, incredible hearing, and excellent magical abilities."

Mole people, tree squids, tripods, talking rocks, and four-armed bipeds. This would be a lot easier to swallow if he had pictures or something, but I guess the fact that he isn't human should prove that I'm no longer in my own neck of the

INTRODUCTION

woods. What else does Mr. Mikaal have to throw at me? Any more weird people groups? Perhaps one that has a single leg and hops like a pogo stick? No. Oh goody he's moving on to a new subject. Maybe he will enlighten me as to why I am here, what the threat is, and what he thinks I might be able to do about it.

"As I have said, Sorra's history is a relatively peaceful one. All of the races gain something from the others and have reached a level of mutual understanding. Of course, no land and no group of people are perfect, and so we have had tensions and difficulties. Small groups have arisen from among the races and tried to wrest power from the current leadership or convince others like them that their race is superior to all others, and anyone unlike them should be under their power. On occasions when food supplies have run low because of a drought, there have been raids and disputes over hunting grounds or borders. In the memory of most of the creatures alive on the face of Sorra there has not been war, deadly famine, plague, or any other thing that might threaten the races."

He paused, shrinking into himself with a sigh borne of regret or perhaps weariness before rallying and resuming his story.

"Now though comes a danger that no one expected, a peril so dire as to threaten the very existence of every living being on Sorra. Cold, dark shadows have fallen on a land that has known only the light of day for time immemorial. A spirit has been loosed on the land, a spirit viler than we could have imagined. Those of us versed in the lore of magic have tried, without success, to find out from whence this being came. We can only conclude that this spirit…this presence can only have come through portals from another world."

I scratched my chin, trying to keep my thoughts from reaching my face, apparently unsuccessfully. Why do I keep feeling this weird déjà vu around portals? How can something be both familiar and unfamiliar at the same time?

Another thing… because the menace is something evil they're not familiar with, it had to come from another world? How many portals does this world have, and how many visitors does Sorra get, anyways?

"You do not believe me. Come here. In this first cage is a chipchuck, small, furry, and for the most part harmless. In this cage is a chipchuck that has come in contact with the malignant spirit. Do not get any closer. This is what the vile presence does. It takes what is good and wholesome and perverts it. Just a moment under the influence of the corrupting being turned this innocent woodland creature into the slavering beast that you see before you."

"Every night that falls sees the influence of the spirit increase. Only a small part of the land has fallen as of now, but if we do not find some way to turn back the blight, all will be taken. This beautiful land will be lost forever. I fear that, by ourselves, we cannot stand against this threat. You see, the races have become complacent. In response to this terror, do you know what is being done in our defense? Nothing! All anyone on Sorra knows is peace. The leaders of the races tremble and fall away. Instead of trying to find a way to contain or repulse the invasion, people simply pack up and run!"

"I have done what I can by myself, but it is not enough. I will now seek others who may be able to help. Most of the people in the southern portion of Sorra are even now not aware of the danger that faces them. Believing as I do, that the threat comes from another world, I first came here to the Portal to seek help from afar. I spent several hours in meditation preparing the enchantment that I would use to enlist the aid of the person who would best be able to assist me against this foe. Across the portal I sent my magic, searching out a hero. I felt my magic make a connection, and I slept. Now you have come at last."

That's the way I remember this conversation going. Mikaal was so dramatic at the end.

Chapter 1
A Beginning

"I am Aaron the White. I have not always been called this. I have always kept a journal, and I will continue to do so as it seems more critical now than ever. However, I have crossed over from one world to another; I am beginning a new life here and so I will record it in a fresh journal. This is the record of my life on Sorra."

I did not believe Mikaal at first. Nothing of what the strange little cloaked Noran said made sense to me. He said that he called to me with his magic. I did not believe in magic. Yet I couldn't deny that recently I had been drawn to the Portal, compelled even, until I had found myself here. Only his strange appearance gave credence to his words. If it were not for the shape of his body, I wouldn't have believed that any of the other races existed. Truly, I was in for the shock of my life as the little man's words were proven to be both true and inadequate.

A wiser man than I might have turned and left back through the Portal as quickly as he had come. I won't lie and say that the thought didn't cross my mind. I just couldn't turn my back on these people if there was something I could do to help. I didn't see what I could do. I had only what fit in or was strapped to my backpack of supplies and my blade at my side. I did not possess any magic, if magic truly existed here. From what the little man had told me of the races that inhabit this world, all were better suited to fighting off some unknown menace than I was.

Still, somewhere in the back of my mind I knew that I had to make the attempt. Maybe it was boredom. If that was the source, it was my own fault for keeping myself secluded. I could have had a 'normal' life, but after losing so many people I loved, I could not bring myself to try. Or maybe I saw in this a challenge unlike any I had faced in my life across the Portal, but I couldn't leave.

It wasn't like anyone was going to miss me. The first person who would notice my absence would be the tax collector next month when I didn't send in my payment. I had a phone but couldn't remember the last time it rang. It had been decades since my parents were lost, and years since I'd had any family. Maybe, just maybe I could make a difference here.

Darkness had fallen just before I stepped across the Portal, and by the time Mikaal had finished his account it was well into the night. I pulled my travel blanket from my pack and found a spot to rest. Mikaal made a droning noise from deep in his body and walked a circuit around me. When he was finished with whatever it was he was doing, he looked at me and smiled and was suddenly gone. No, he hadn't really vanished; he somehow was hanging from a tree branch several feet above my head. This unnerved me slightly but as he said, if he was going to do me harm, he could have done it before now.

I rolled over and tried to sleep, but the burning eyes of the corrupted chipchuck appeared to torment me. I calmed myself and mentally pushed the image from my mind. I slowed my breathing and quieted my thoughts until I was asleep.

I awoke just before dawn with a sense that something important was taking place. I kept my body still but opened my eyes ever so slowly. I took in every detail of the land around me that was within my field of view. Nothing seemed amiss that I could see. The hairs on my arms were all standing at attention. My fingers closed around the hilt of my blade of their own accord, and I tensed my muscles.

A Beginning

With all the speed I could muster, I threw aside my blanket and rolled to a standing position as close as I could to where I'd slept. I took quick stock of my surroundings and was still unable to locate the source of my distress. I looked up to the spot where Mikaal had been last night, and he was still peacefully hanging from a large limb. As I looked back down, my heart froze in my chest.

There was a shimmering in the air above the stone circle that comprised the Portal and then it winked out. Not just the shimmering, but the entire Portal. For the first time since I arrived, I found that I could sense magic. The realization hit me when I felt the magic of the Portal disappear. I panicked. I ran towards where the Portal had been-and slammed into an invisible wall.

When I awoke again, Mikaal was standing beside me with an understanding look on his face.

"I am sorry. I thought you knew," he said.

"Knew?" I replied.

"That the Portal is not stable here," Mikaal said with sorrow in his voice. "It will be back, but no one knows when or for how long it will stay."

"What did I run into?" I queried.

"My protective barrier. I put it up both to protect us and to make sure that you didn't wander off and get hurt last night. You are still unfamiliar with this land and its dangers, and I was concerned for your safety. I did not dream that I would cause you harm by trying to protect you. I apologize."

So, I was here to take down a foreign evil that's trying to destroy the land, but first I had to survive the good intentions of my friends not knowing what I'm capable of. Fabulous!

"I'll live. I was surprised by the Portal's disappearance, but I never really considered that I would return right away. Let me pack my things, and I'll be ready to travel. Answer me this though. In the past, when the Portal vanishes does its magic disappear with it?"

"I do not understand," Mikaal said.

"When the Portal vanished, I felt the magic drain away at the same time. I just want to know if this is usually the case."

"I am afraid that I cannot answer your question, Aaron, because no one on Sorra has ever claimed to be able to sense the presence of magic."

"Oh. Well, I didn't know that I could do that until now myself."

"Amazing. Truly, you must be the hero that I sent for. I am even more sure of it now."

So, if I wasn't the right hero he was going to what, move to the next portal and send another 'call Hero' spell? I'm not sure where I would have ended up in that scenario. Now that he was convinced, he could help me to overcome my unbelief.

I put my travel blanket in my pack and strapped my blade to my side. As I did this, I heard Mikaal making the same droning noise as he had the night before. I closed my eyes, and I could feel the barrier around us pop like a bubble. I shivered slightly and opened my eyes. Mikaal was looking at me with curiosity.

We began our journey, Mikaal and I, by walking towards the growing daylight.

"Why are we going east?" I asked.

Mikaal looked confused. "We're not. We're going south, why?"

"Wait, does the sun rise from the south here?"

"Indeed it does. I take it the world works differently where you are from?"

I thought for a moment before answering. "I'm used to it rising in the east. I guess I have a lot to learn about Sorra. Way more than I thought."

A Beginning

We lapsed into silence, so I took the time to study the world around me. Things looked basically the same. Trees looked like trees, mountains like mountains, rocks like rocks, but the coloring was different. It wasn't so drastic a difference that I noticed it right away. Most of the leaves on the trees, while shaped similar to what I had always known, were a slightly lighter shade of green. The trunks of the trees were several shades darker so as to appear almost black. The growth on the forest floor was varied in color with flowers being the usual assortment of colors, but most of the stems were darker than I was used to. Sorra really was beautiful. The colors contrasted strikingly, and for the first time I began to realize that I was in another world, not just in a dream or talking to someone's idea of a joke.

I grew lost in my thoughts until I almost didn't notice when my guide stopped. I froze and listened to the sounds of the forest. The sounds that reached my ears didn't sound out of place, but I had no way of knowing what was normal in this world. I turned slowly, trying to discern what could be causing my guide's hesitation. Still nothing that I saw or heard caused me any reason for alarm.

I sensed a bit of magic flow from Mikaal off into the woods behind us and then swiftly return to my new friend's body. The little Noran sprang into action; all of his limbs seemingly moved at once to propel him behind and to the left of me. The deep droning sound that I had heard last night as a precursor to Mikaal's spellcasting began just a split second before I heard a horrendous noise from the forest in the direction we had been traveling from.

It wasn't long before I saw the source of the noise. A blackened hulk came into view, holding the lower half of a tree in its gaping maw. If it had been up to me, I would have passed out, but my body wasn't listening. I had never seen anything in my life so terrifying as the beast that stood in front of me. It stood seven feet tall even hunched over as it was, and it took me what seemed an eternity before I recognized that this vile monstrosity must have at one point been this world's version of a bear. It had stopped when it saw us standing there and looked at us. I can only assume that it was sizing us up, maybe as foes or maybe as food.

It broke the standoff first by grinding the tree in its massive jaws and then spitting it at me. The makeshift missile hurtled toward my midsection, and I jumped higher than I ever imagined that I could. The jump was almost high enough. The tree hit the curve between my shins and my feet and spun me head over heels in the air.

Miraculously, I spun a complete circuit and was mostly upright by the time my feet hit the ground. I touched down and thought for sure that both my feet had been taken clean off, but the bones were not broken. My balance was off though, and I did a mad hop-step a couple of feet backward until I regained my footing.

The beast opened its maw wide and let out a sound that I can only assume was meant to be a laugh. When the racket died down, the bear-thing cracked the most hideous grin I had ever seen and began to come towards me. I saw its luminescent eyes change from orange to red and followed their gaze to my hand. I realized then that the beast had come after me first because I'd instinctively taken up my sword. Better safe than sorry.

The pain in my feet was unbelievable, but I knew that if I was going to live, I had to kill this thing before it did me any more harm. I took a faltering step forward before Mikaal's first spell took effect. A ring of fire appeared around us, and for the first time our enemy seemed uncertain. I felt a slight touch on my ankles, and Mikaal's second spell was complete. The pain and swelling that had been nearly overwhelming faded away almost instantly to nothing.

I thanked my friend and looked back to our foe. I saw in the distorted face fear and madness struggling for control. Madness won. Whatever was left of the instincts of a natural creature was consumed completely in swirling Chaos. It stepped into the magical fire and howled its pain and insanity into the bright daylight. Still it came.

Put yourself in my shoes. Even with Mikaal's helpful Cliff Notes about what to expect, I never envisioned this. Sure, I had a sword, but it wasn't made with massive, evil-corrupted bear monsters in mind. This was no afternoon strolling around a Renaissance Fair.

Where once there had been paws there were now mammoth talons that gleamed metallic ebony. Brown hide had given way to burnt and singed skin in some places and hardened bone plates in others. The fangs, several times larger than normal, were set in a jaw that unhinged like a snake. I was certain that if I cared to look between the teeth closely enough, I could see the beast's stomach. No sane person would want to get that close to this thing though, and I was holding on to my sanity very tightly at this point. The flaming bear demon was only a few feet away from me now, and I had to act.

I tensed to spring at the creature, but just before I leaped, I was distracted by the sound of an arrow in flight. The sound was swiftly followed by the reality of an arrow striking home. Deeply embedded in the vile thing's chest was a smoking shaft. The creature howled in frustration at the unexpected attack, yet it continued its approach toward me. I wasn't sure where that had come from, but I was grateful for our unexpected source of help. As I danced lightly out of its path, I noticed that the place where the arrow had stuck was hissing and steaming. Of course! The friendly archer must be using magic or acid or some kind of caustic substance on their arrows.

The beast, more enraged than ever, turned and came at me faster than before. I waved my blade in a repeating pattern to keep the things attention while backing up quickly but carefully. I was trying to keep myself as far out of harm's way as possible while keeping the monster between the archer and the magician. I was momentarily blinded as lightning arched from somewhere to the left, courtesy of Mikaal, into the flank of the beast. I heard another arrow strike home into our foe's other side. The stench of burning flesh was almost beyond my ability to withstand. I could only marvel at the amount of damage that was being delivered, and the beast hadn't even slowed. I decided that the time had come for me to get my blade wet, so I took a chance that I was faster and smarter than the thing that I faced.

Kicking off of a nearby tree, I reversed my momentum and rolled beneath the reaching claws and between legs larger in diameter than some of the older trees. I stopped my roll just on the other side of the beast's legs and sank my blade as deep and hard as I could into the nearest one. I was hoping to open up a large blood vessel that I guessed would be located somewhere near where I had struck if the animal was anything like the ones on my world. The blood did begin to flow quickly, but I had no time to see if I had disabled the creature.

I scuttled off into the brush as quickly as I could and hoped that I was not seen as the dark form turned. We had rounded a bend in the path through the forest, and when the brute turned around, it saw only empty forest. I soundlessly searched for a stone on the ground around where I lay. My hand closed around a small rock, and I flung it through a hole in the foliage so that it passed behind my confused foe before striking a tree and bouncing off into some undergrowth.

When the beast turned its back to me, I leapt up from hiding and drove my blade into its neck almost to the hilt. A scream of anguish tore through the forest and my skull alike, but I held on to my blade as I was lifted off the ground. I turned my blade in the wound as well as I was able to given my limited leverage. The misshapen mountain began to pitch backward, and I shoved off, drawing my blade from the living scabbard as I flew. Unfortunately, I was unable to gauge my direction and slammed into a tree, hard. As my consciousness slipped away, I thought that I hadn't been a very good hero and wasn't likely to become one.

I awoke an indeterminate amount of time later and was able to discern two shapes standing over me through the haze that blanketed my vision. As the sunlight lifted the fog from my head, I realized that the one with eight appendages must be the Noran, but the other one

A Beginning

appeared to be human. No, not human, but not very far off. The main difference, of course, was the color of the skin. Truly amazing! A woman whose flesh was the shimmering color of the ocean. It was like staring into the vast depths of the sea and seeing a wave break away to take on human shape. I was speechless. I could hear Mikaal asking me if I was all right, but I couldn't respond because I was truly captivated. After a moment I was able to come back to myself enough so that I realized there might still be danger.

"I am fine, Mikaal, but where is the thing that attacked us?" I asked.

"You finished it all by yourself! Took its backbone clean in two," he excitedly replied.

I breathed a sigh of relief and sat up.

"How long was I unconscious?"

"I don't think that you were out for more than a minute. We didn't see you when we got here. When we saw that the dark beast was dead, we began to look for you. The sharp eyes of the archer picked you out after only a few seconds. I had to work a minor healing upon you as you had cracked your head bone on the tree. You flew pretty far."

I turned to the woman who seemed even more beautiful somehow as my sight cleared. "And I assume you're the archer?" It seemed obvious as soon as I said it, but it was hard to think while looking at her. "Thank you," I stumbled on. "Mikaal, you never mentioned a race like hers. Why?"

"Because I thought there were no more beings of her race left alive. I have not seen any SeaWinds for over five and twenty years. Tell me child, how many of your people remain?"

I bit my lip hard enough to draw blood when I heard her speak. Her words were normal enough and easily understood, but her voice was the sound of a stiff breeze through marsh reeds. It was as if she was singing all parts of a song by herself, harmonies blending and changing within the confines of her single voice. Every emotion that

I had ever experienced in my life rolled over me now, and I almost wept. More so because the beauty that flowed from her like rain from the sky was tempered by an almost infinite sadness. When I recovered from my shock, I comprehended what she had said, and I understood the melancholy I had sensed.

"I am the last." She said, "My name is Coral, and I have been looking for those who would stand up to the darkness."

"It would seem that you have found what you are looking for then." I said, while rising to my feet slowly on uncooperative legs. "You're more than welcome to join us."

When Mikaal said nothing, I looked to him. He was standing there, looking up at me with a crooked grin on his lips and respect in his eyes. It occurred to me then that this Noran was in some ways very childlike for a man of over 1,200 years, and I had to wonder if all of his people were that way.

"I accept your proposal. May it be that we can prevent any further species from suffering the same fate as my own." She replied with a light shiver. "My bow and magic I offer to the cause. Where were you headed?"

"To consult with the leaders of the Magic School in Tiiaan," Mikaal answered.

He hadn't actually told me this, but I didn't have any context anyways, so I had to trust that the being who called me knew what our likely next steps should be.

My eyes shifted focus slightly, and I saw the carcass of the monster that I had killed. I walked toward the form lying still on the ground, stopping only to retrieve my blade from the ground where it had been knocked from my hand on impact with the tree. The body was on its side, and I saw at once that the faint illumination that had emanated from the creature's eyes had been put out. I walked around to examine the wound that had stolen the glow. If I was going to be coming across any more of these things, I wanted to know how best to stop them. I didn't need to have taken any medical courses to figure out that I had severed its spinal column. *Ok, fine. To kill a mindless beast, you just had to rip out its spine without getting dead. Simple enough.*

My resolve to save this beautiful world flickered wildly. I was willing to go to great lengths to help these people and Sorra, but I had no experience taking life in this way. The monster I killed had at one point been an innocent woodland creature and hadn't asked to become what it was. I sighed deeply, cleaned my blade on some dried leaves, put it in its scabbard, and retrieved my hatchet from my pack.

I saw my two companions looking at me with mild curiosity, and so I told them that I was going to build a pyre to consume the body. The Noran turned and began searching the area for large stones to place around the corpse as a base for the bonfire, and Coral began gathering deadwood for tinder. I turned to the tree nearest where the fire was going to be and began to climb. When I was far enough up, I used my hatchet to cut branches that would most likely be over the blaze. When I was done with the first tree, I climbed down and went on to the next closest tree.

An hour passed in silent preparation. Mikaal lit the pyre by touching it with a glowing gaw, and we stepped far enough away to avoid most of the smell. We remained close enough to watch the blaze and prevent it from getting out of control. The fire lasted far longer than I expected. When the last embers had been put out it was approaching midday. We were all hungry but wanted to put some distance behind us before we stopped to eat. I am sure that I was not the only one thinking how glad I was to still be alive.

Bridge

Revelations

The march resumed with Mikaal the magician swinging from tree to tree, and Coral and I hoofing it and trying to keep up. I got into a steady rhythm and put my body on automatic so that I could think. I had to be honest with myself now. There was almost no chance that I would ever return to my world. I accepted that with little hesitation. There was little that I would miss about my world of origin. It might be strange to never drive my father's truck again, but it has been harder to find parts for it, so I'm not sure how much longer I would've been able to. I didn't dislike the world that I was born into, but I wasn't attached to it either. This place though, Sorra, I could get used to. All I had to do was keep myself alive long enough to understand how things worked here.

It worried me a little how quickly I was adjusting to the changes. I had never believed in magic before, but now I did not, could not, doubt it. Outside of normal fright I had not even been surprised by the monster that had attacked us. I realized that I had wordlessly taken command earlier and more disturbingly that this had been at least a part of the source of Mikaal's glee. I had never shown myself to be a leader before. I had been in this world less than one full day and already I was becoming somebody else, someone whom I did not recognize. So far, the changes were all for the better, but I wondered if I would recognize myself in the mirror in a week's time.

Chapter 2
Hunter or the Hunted

I remained lost in thought for so long that I didn't notice when the trees that had been close around us began to thin out, and the ground started to rise. The path through the woods had been fairly level and clear, so I was surprised when I tripped over a stone. I caught my balance and almost fell but it was one of those embarrassing moments where you grit your teeth and hope no one saw you. A quiet giggle from Coral told me that I had not been that lucky. I straightened myself and kept on moving ahead.

Now that my attention had been drawn outside of myself, I looked around to see that we had left the forest proper and that we were now traveling in the foothills of an extensive mountain range. Either the canopy of trees had blocked my view of the mountains, or we had traveled much farther than I realized.

"Mikaal. I think we should stop to hunt before we get too far away from the forest," I suggested.

"Then we'll probably have to camp here for the night," Coral added.

"We have to get to Tiiaan as soon as possible, but you're both probably right. I'll set up camp while you two hunt." Mikaal offered.

I wasn't sure about Coral, but neither Mikaal or I had eaten anything all day, so I pulled the last of the jerky from my pack and split it between my companions to keep up our strength against the unexpected.

I watched the Noran start off south in search of a defensible location and then turned around to speak with the archer, but she had already slipped silently away. I had no idea what types of wildlife I would encounter around here or what plant life would be safe to eat, but I set off in the direction that seemed most likely just the same.

I had my blowgun strapped to the outside of my leather pack that was well suited to bringing down small game, and I readied it as I walked. I spotted some animal tracks just a short distance from where we had been. The tracks didn't look like any beast that existed where I came from, and I could only hope that it would make a tasty dinner.

I followed the tracks for what I guessed to be twenty minutes before a crashing in the brush ahead sent me dodging aside. The animal that charged me looked like a cross between a boar and a wildcat and was remarkably quick to turn around. I fired my dart at it as it passed and scored a hit on its shoulder. That seemed only to irritate the animal, and I narrowly avoided getting gored. I hoped that the tranquilizing agent I had treated the darts with would at least slow the thing down.

I dropped the blowgun at my left foot and took out my blade with my other hand. I saw my dinner rake the ground with its great furry claws and charge me again, and I decided to try a new strategy. The kitty-pig was almost on top of me when I leaped, but not to the side this time. I jumped straight up and centered all my weight on my weapon as I came down. I missed all the vital organs and succeeded only in pinning its hindquarters to the ground. That was one mistake that I have never repeated to this day.

This particular animal is much more flexible than I gave it credit for. It gave an enraged squeal and turned on me. When I came down, I had landed with my upper body driving the blade into the back part of the animal. The bottom half of me had hit the ground, and it was this that proved to be my undoing.

The angry piggy didn't have a good angle to use its tusks on me, so it improvised. It opened its mouth and clamped onto my right butt cheek. This was the first time I had ever been bitten by my food, and now it was my turn to squeal. I had absolutely no idea what to do. If I removed my blade in order to strike a killing blow, the animal would be free, and I would be at a disadvantage. In the meantime, however, I had a wild animal masticating my buttocks.

I yelled and tried to wriggle free of the painful teeth but maintained my grip on the handle of my blade. My attempt failed spectacularly. I was beginning to think that I was going to spend eternity locked in a death struggle with this strange animal when it suddenly slumped to the ground. I figured that the loss of blood and the tranquilizer had knocked the animal out. I let go of my blade with my right hand and reached behind me to extricate my hindquarters. A yelp and then a sigh of relief escaped my lips, and then I pulled myself to my feet. Quickly I dressed my kill and prepared to drag it back to camp.

The trip back was painful but uneventful, and I saw that Mikaal had a fire burning brightly. Coral had not yet returned. Mikaal looked up at me when I appeared and said with delight, "Good, good. You have managed to kill a TuskerKitty. Impressive. Usually it takes a group of hunters to bring one in."

I could only reply with sarcasm. "Now he tells me."

Since I wasn't bleeding from the bite, I allowed my pride to keep me from saying anything about my discomfort.

Daylight was in short supply when Coral returned. I could tell that she hadn't had good luck in her hunt by the expression on her face. She confirmed the fact by laying down a handful of roots and herbs. Mikaal and I had only just finished cleaning the kill, and so we decided to make a stew. Mikaal produced a bag from somewhere inside his cloak and pulled a kettle much too large and heavy for him to have been carrying around from its depths. I just raised my eyebrows and started placing meat inside.

A brook ran swiftly a little to the east of us, and I went to fetch some water for the stew. When I arrived at the running water, I was surprised to find that the brook seemed to emit light on its own. I dipped my hand into the water and brought a few drops to my face. It didn't smell strange, and so I tasted it. I tell you that I had never tasted anything so pure and so refreshing in all my life. I put my face into the brook and tried my best to empty it in one draught. The water here was full of energy, of life. I didn't know if all water on Sorra was like this, but I hoped so.

I filled the containers that I had brought and made my way back to the campsite. I passed one of the containers to my companions and filled the kettle with the other containers. I settled down by the fire to stir the stew as it cooked. My curiosity got the better of me, and I asked Coral what had happened to cause her to become the last of her people. I was immediately sorry that I had when I saw the look of pain that crossed her exquisite features. I was going to apologize and tell her not to talk about it if it was too painful when she began.

"My people have never been very large in number. Over the course of many decades, the SeaWind as a people grew apart from one another. As a result, there were fewer pairings and fewer children being born. Five and twenty years ago, my father the king, sent out a call to our people. We were to gather in a lagoon far to the north of here. King Anemone's idea was to keep all the remaining SeaWinds in one place in the hopes that we would grow in number again. The very next year saw more children born than in the five years before that. My father's plan was working. My parents met in that lagoon, and less than two years after my people moved there, I was born."

Coral stalled and took two deep breaths to control her emotions before continuing. Whatever happened was, if her expression told the tale, horrifying to her. I clamped down on my natural instinct to comfort her and waited patiently for her to resume.

"In the last year my father had begun to rely on me, his only child, to renew our bonds with the other races. It was for this reason that I was away when the darkness engulfed my people. When I returned four days ago, I saw my parents and all my people had been changed, and I was forced to flee from the creatures my family had become and my home.... My father often told me stories when I was a child. I loved listening to his stories and knew most of them by heart. My favorite stories were the ones of his time with the 'crazy old wizard' Mikaal."

"By The Gathering!" Mikaal interrupted, "I am not crazy!"

"No. Just eccentric," I replied. "Now settle down and let Coral finish her story."

"My father loved you, Mikaal, like you were his own father. It was only through your influence that my people finally began to use our natural magical abilities. You would have been proud of your student and all that he had accomplished since he became king."

Tears began to fill the young woman's eyes, and despite my personal fears and inhibitions I went to her and put my arms around her. She didn't push me away, and in a second she had buried her head in my shoulder and was sobbing uncontrollably. I could tell that this was the first time she had allowed herself to express the loss of her family, and so I let her go on crying until she was too tired to cry anymore. When she finally pulled away, her eyes were puffy and a darker shade of blue. She smiled at me sheepishly, and I could tell that she was a little embarrassed.

"I apologize for losing control. You are the first people I have spoken to since I escaped from the lagoon."

"I'm sorry you've had to suffer all of this alone, Coral. You're very strong to have come this far with no support. I know what it is like to lose everyone you love. I know the pain and feelings that you should have done something more or different. I will do everything in my power to keep you from having to feel that again," I said, meaning it, but not knowing how I would pull it off.

Mikaal had completed the cooking duties while I had been comforting Coral, and it was now time to eat. The diminutive Noran placed bowls into our hands at just the right moment to distract Coral from her discomfort.

I took my food and moved a little bit away but watched her as we ate. I tried not to peer too intently at her, but I noticed that her delicate hands held semi-transparent webbing between the fingers, and her ears were slightly swept back and pointed. Her build was petite, but in a way so that she seemed taller than she was. I thought that most SeaWinds had probably been thin so as to facilitate their movement through the water. I wondered how they breathed underwater and resolved to ask the magician later.

Coral's facial features were almost frightening in their perfection, and she reminded me vaguely of a China doll. Her eyes were the deepest blue I had ever seen, like the color of deep water just before sunlight gives way completely to darkness. Her hair was very fine in texture and colored similarly to her skin, blue and green intermixing in shimmering waves, but slightly darker in hue. She was dressed in a fairly modest equivalent of a bikini made from woven seaweed. I had to remind myself to breathe after looking at her. She was truly the most stunning thing I had ever encountered.

When we had all eaten our fill, Mikaal simply made the dishes vanish. The tricky little magician threw a cold spell at the kettle containing the remainder of the stew and stuffed it back into the bag that he had taken it from. Now that we were out of the heavy tree cover the wind had begun to pick up. This close to the mountain some of the breezes had developed a bite.

I asked the others if they used tanned animal skins in this world. Blank looks are apparently universal. I explained the process as simply as I could to Mikaal and asked him if he could work up a spell to achieve the desired result. I had set the animal hide over a tree limb that was close by, and I retrieved it.

Most of the skin would be needed for my first purpose, and so I cut the pelt carefully to the desired size. I gave this first and largest piece to Mikaal and asked him to do his best. The funny little man used four of his appendages to hold himself up and the remaining four to hold the skin above him. I heard him begin his chant and felt the power rise within him, and then a flash of smoke and an acrid smell rose from the pelt. Mikaal looked quite pleased with himself as he handed the new blanket to me. I looked it over and had to admit that he'd done an amazing job given my less than stellar description. I called Coral over and wrapped the blanket around her. She gave me a bright smile and thanked us both, curled up on the ground, and was asleep in minutes. Mikaal and I shared a chuckle at how such a simple gift had pleased her.

I took the remaining bit of hide and again explained what I wanted done with it to the spellcaster. A moment later I was holding a fine leather jacket. I placed this in my pack before pulling my blanket out and preparing for bed. The Noran cast his little protective circle and crawled up into his tree. I bid him a good night and fell asleep quickly myself.

Chapter 3
Fellowship

I awoke before the others, due in part to my decision of places to sleep and my injury coming together to point my face towards the sunrise. I packed up my blanket and walked the perimeter of our camp. My newfound ability to sense magic kept me from walking into Mikaal's defenses again for which I was very thankful.

I was enjoying the fresh morning air and taking in a deep breath when a brown form landed on and enveloped my head. I got the impression it was nearly as big as I was, but it weighed a lot less… perhaps as much as my neighbor's Rough Collie. Confused and surprised, I slapped at it ineffectually before I thought to use the invisible wall to free myself. I pointed my head towards the barrier and, bellowing mightily, tried to bash my attacker senseless. I felt the magic of the shield vanish just as I was about to hit it. My confusion turned to irritation as the brown bundle clinging to my head began laughing uproariously.

Embarrassed, I pulled the cackling magician from his perch atop my skull and flung him at a nearby tree, where he merely latched on and continued to roar his mirth into the still morning air.

"You scared me to death Mikaal! I thought a giant arachnid was going to be munching on my face any second! I'm glad you like jokes. Hopefully you like them as much when they are played on you."

I turned to see Coral rolling on the ground, clutching at her sides. Unable to help myself, I joined them in their laughter.

Even though I was embarrassed, it was admittedly a good way to start the day. I hadn't laughed like that in I can't remember how long. I vowed internally to get Mikaal back, but I knew myself and I probably wouldn't really.

When we had all regained our composure, we set off, Mikaal in the lead. I filled my containers from the brook as we passed it and realized that the water glowed even in the daylight. The little Noran set a brisk pace, and I tried to keep up without showing a limp, but I was very bruised, and it didn't take long before I began to fall behind.

For the record, TuskerKittys are normally vegetarians and so don't have exceptionally sharp teeth. However, their preferred source of food is tree bark, and because of this, they do have very strong jaw muscles. When it was discovered that I was in pain I was forced to recount my battle with our dinner and another bout of laughter began. Mikaal healed my incredibly swollen glutes, and we began anew, this time making much better speed. I decided that I would be much more careful today and try to avoid further embarrassment if possible.

We passed a fruit tree and picked ourselves a hearty breakfast. Mikaal said that both the tree and its fruit were called Spirals. I laughed aloud when I saw the tree. It looked like a barber pole that had sprouted limbs. Spiral fruit was quite tasty, tart, and sweet at the same time. The world of my birth held nothing even remotely similar to this unique tree or the fruit it bore.

The next few hours passed uneventfully and saw us out of the foothills and to the base of the mountains proper. While we walked, I asked Mikaal if there had ever been another human in this world. He did not know for sure, but he believed I might be the first. I hesitated before asking my next question. I wanted to know whether I could perform magic while in this world. I didn't know whether I would be bothered more by a positive or negative response.

When I finally did ask the question, I was more surprised by Coral's reaction than Mikaal's. She beamed me a bright smile, looked at the magician, and offered him a wink. Mikaal caught her wink and threw one of his own back at her and then suddenly looking solemn he asked me if I really thought I should learn. I felt more than a little left out, but I couldn't answer the question honestly and so I lapsed into silence.

A few minutes later I had the incredibly powerful sensation of being watched. The feeling came not from anything that I could sense in our surroundings, and I didn't realize what was going on immediately. I looked at my friends to see if they felt it too. Neither of them showed any outward signs of anything being wrong. I turned my face back to the path and tried to calm myself. I felt a tickle in my mind and knew something was going on.

I instinctively clamped down all my mental defenses and felt the tickle disappear. I looked again at Mikaal and then Coral. The magician seemed normal, but the archer had become extremely pale. Suspicions danced in my mind which brought with them anger. Coral had been in my mind! I was outraged.

My anger spent itself in a fraction of a second and was replaced quickly by curiosity. I calmed myself and cleared my mind of anything but the view in front of me. Slowly I released my tight grip on my mind, and then I waited. The tickle came again in a moment. I memorized the path ahead of me quickly, closed my eyes, and continued walking. I searched out the tickle in the depths of my mind, and then I followed it back to the source. I was able to reach Coral's mind, but she had her defenses wrapped around her tight.

I went back to my mind and tried a new tactic. I spoke to the tickle. I heard a mental sigh, and then the tickle disappeared. My interest piqued; I wasn't going to give up so easily. I again took a mental image of the path ahead, closed my eyes, and retraced my steps to Coral's mind. Her defenses were still up, but I wasn't going to turn back just yet. I conjured up a mental fist and lightly rapped my knuckles on what I believed to be the door to her mind. I heard a sharp inhalation from the physical Coral.

"Who is knocking at my door?" she giggled.

"It is I, your student, Aaron."

"Good. Now open your eyes while you walk, before you trip."

I would never have believed how difficult it was to focus on two things simultaneously. I think that I almost fractured my consciousness on that first attempt. I had to stop, take a tighter mental rein on myself, and tell my body to open my eyes. Irritated, I pulled back wholly into myself. This could not be the right way to go about this. Coral was more in control of her body than I was when she mindspoke. I didn't realize it until I heard a knocking that I had drawn my defenses tight around me when I had retreated back into my body.

I tried opening a window where I had heard the knock.

"Who is it?" I asked.

"It's Coral, Aaron."

I cleared my mind of debris before adding a door beside the mental window.

"Please come in."

"Why did you draw back?" she asked as she entered.

"I tried to open my eyes like you said, and it nearly broke me. I'm not sure what I'm doing wrong. I went back in to get control of myself and figure out why," I said still someone shaken.

"Why did you stop moving?" Coral asked. "We were making good time and then all of the sudden you stopped in mid step with your left leg off the ground. It looked like you were going to fall."

I had no idea that I had done this at all and laughed at the thought of the three of us standing, still as statues, in the middle of the road with both of them looking at me like I was crazy.

"I didn't realize I did. I guess I need to figure that little issue out before I get clobbered in the middle of a fight."

She was about to say something else when I felt someone coming in the window. Before the intruder could cross into my mind completely, I slammed the window on them. Mikaal yelped like a kicked puppy.

"Mikaal, is that you? Why are you being all sneaky and creeping in a window?"

"Ow, Ow, Ow. I was checking to see if you had sufficient defenses against someone trying to get in and cause you mental problems. You do! You really do! Now will you please release me?"

I opened first the window and then the door. When the Noran limped into the confines of my mind, I destroyed the window.

Coral had been keeping Mikaal up to date on the status of my training and was impressed with the strength of my mental defenses. She had told him that I had thrown up a wall that she would never even attempt to break through. Apparently, SeaWinds are among the strongest mindspeakers. No one could keep an adult SeaWind from their mind. I was now the exception to that rule. Compared to the races native to Sorra, I was mentally very strong. I needed to gain experience and finesse. Together we set about trying to discover why I was finding it nearly impossible to contact someone and keep my body under my power concurrently. We decided that Mikaal would stay in my mind and watch me try to speak to Coral.

There was a more important matter that they wanted out of the way first. Sorran Mindspeakers know that every person has a distinct mental flavor. When trying to contact an individual in a large crowd, it is almost impossible to find someone without knowing how they 'taste'.

"If you want to be able to contact someone, no matter where they are, you need to get a taste of each other. You should only do this with people you trust." Coral began.

"A long time ago I was spending time with a nephew and was teaching him. We needed to talk from far away, so we exchanged tastes. Unfortunately, he ended up being an insomniac chatterbox and he nearly drove me insane talking to me all hours of the day and night." Mikaal added.

"So, Aaron, do you trust me?" Coral asked.

This was perfectly normal to her, but I'm sure my face flushed bright red when I answered yes, and I fervently hoped that my desire to exchange mental tastes with her did not come across the link.

"Alright, just stand still a moment," she said.

Coral's non-corporeal personification strode up to me and touched me gently. I couldn't help laughing. The sensation was like having my brain massaged.

"Now if you want to taste someone else, you get close to them and gently overlap your image and theirs. They should be expecting it, or things might go poorly."

Every part of this experience was new and exciting. I followed her instructions and briefly touched Coral's mental projection.

Incredible! Tasting someone was like getting a fuzzy picture of that person's personality. In a fraction of a second, I gained a complete overview of Coral. When viewed as a whole, the information was clear. If I tried to focus on a part of her, the edges blurred. The instant I broke the mental touch, Coral disappeared into her mind.

Mikaal was still present via projection in my mind and said, "Now, if you'll will allow me to taste you too, you can practice again on me. Then I want you to contact Coral by scanning around you for her flavor."

"Sure."

Exchanging tastes with the Noran was less intimidating, probably because I wasn't attracted to him. It was still intimate, but more like getting years' worth of friendship distilled into a moment.

That done, I created a mental radar detector and set it to look for Coral. I could see why people preferred this method. I was knocking at her door in an instant. Before she could answer, I was snapped back into my body. Mikaal's mental self was gone from my head. Both my friends had stopped walking. Mikaal's dark brown skin had gone almost white, and Coral's blue-green skin was mostly green.

"Yo-yo-you left your body," Mikaal said.

"What else would I have done?" I asked.

"We just send out a thought to talk to someone. You actually removed your inner being and flew through the air with it!"

I paused. "Was that why I couldn't seem to get my body to respond to me?"

"Since you only left the finest thread of self connected to your body, I would say yes."

"Guess I need more practice then?"

The exasperated Noran's eyes grew large. "Yes, yes, yes. That could be extremely dangerous. If you lost the thread holding you to your body, you would die."

"Oh," I said, dumbfounded.

"You know, Aaron," Mikaal said, suddenly thoughtful. "Every time I think I know how you're going to behave; you change."

"Thank you." I said grinning.

"Why does that make you smile?" Coral asked, intrigued.

"When I was little, before I lost my parents, my mother would talk about keeping the mystery alive. I never fully understood what she meant, but my father told me once to always keep people guessing. I'm not sure they both were talking about the same thing, but between them I learned to always say and do the unexpected. I'm a bit out of practice because I've been alone so long, but it's good to know that I can still surprise people." I answered.

Coral smiled at me, but Mikaal just shook his head, bemused.

The direction of the morning light had changed little while I was occupied with my lessons, so I decided to keep practicing. I withdrew into my mental living room again, but this time I tried to alter the direction of my thinking. I opened a large window on one wall and mentally connected it to my physical eyes. This way, I could be withdrawn but still pay attention to what was going on. I didn't know if the natives had to take all these extra steps to mindspeak successfully, but I was human and had different experiences to draw on. I would do this the best way I could, even if I had to relate to things differently than others.

In my mind, I tried thinking of Coral and directing the thought to go to her. I watched my thought take flight and go toward the wall. The thought flew into the wall and vanished with an inaudible 'poof'. I was starting to grow impatient with my progress. I took a deep breath to calm myself and created an outgoing message slot just to one side of the door. Then I realized that the door had remained where I had placed it, even when I had stopped focusing on this imaginary room. So, if I got everything set up just the way I liked it, it would remain that way. Good.

I spawned another thought-message and sent it on its way to Coral. When I concentrated, I could follow the thought on its flight to Coral without leaving my mind. The thought went right through the wall of Coral's mental blockade. I was starting to get the hang of this!

A short span of time later, a thought appeared in my head. I reached out to take hold of the foreign thought, and it dissolved into me. Coral was pleased that I had been able to send her a message. Ok, now I understood better. I brought another thought into being, attaching a tiny mental thread to it before sending it out. The message flew true to its destination. This time I could hear Coral's response. I had established my first two-way link. We spoke for a few minutes longer before I snipped the message thread and banished the space in my head to temporary non-existence.

Mental exercise was more draining than I'd ever imagined, not that I'd imagined something like this in my wildest dreams. I had spent merely a few hours learning the basics of silent conversation and was already exhausted. I asked my traveling companions if they minded stopping for an early lunch. I was weak and ravenous. I think that the two native Sorrans realized how much the training had taken out of me. We were walking a rough path that bisected the mountain range and a suitable place to stop was easy to come by.

Mikaal led us to a small cave just a little ahead of where we were. Within the cave, someone had placed four stone chairs. Gratefully and without question I sank into the nearest one. The chair was hard, but I was so worn out that I didn't even notice. A small area cut into the rock on one wall was covered in soot and ash. Mikaal produced some wood from I know not where and quickly had a fire going. He pulled the remains of our stew from the magic bag he carried, knocked the ice from it, and set it in the fire. Coral sat down across from me and just watched me. I gave her a weak grin; all I could muster at the moment and closed my eyes.

What seemed to me to be only a second later, a steaming bowl of stew and a piece of bread were shoved into my hands. I came alive quickly and emptied the bowl, wiping it clean with the bread in record time. Almost before I had finished the first bowl, a second took its place and I finished it off almost as quickly. When I had finished my meal, I looked up. Mikaal and Coral stood side by side looking at me with concern. Mikaal spoke first.

"You will learn to store up mental energy soon enough. Most children born on Sorra learn the techniques in their first years. You took to your training so quickly that we assumed you knew how already."

Coral added, "We would tell you how you should store this energy up, only it is different for every person. You will have to make your own method."

"Does every form of magic take this much out of the person wielding it?" I queried.

"Some more, some less," Mikaal acknowledged,

They told me that I had slept for the greater part of an hour. We put out the cookfire before we left. My mental faculties were restored; the cave now seemed strange to me. I asked about it and was told that it was a traveler's respite. It had been put there mainly to avoid people freezing to death in the harsh snows that covered the mountain paths in winter.

    I spent the rest of the day discovering ways that I could contain and store energy as we traveled. I was even able to begin to funnel a trickle of mental strength into my reserves before we stopped to camp for the night. We had made remarkable progress both in my training and in our travels that day, and we were on the other side of the mountain before it became too dark to travel.

    I followed Coral when it came time to hunt, and she showed me some plants and berries that were safe to eat. We dined on peasant that evening, a rare bird on Sorra and utterly tasty. When I lay down to sleep, I directed all of my remaining inner stamina into storage and was unconscious immediately.

Chapter 4
Teacher or Student

I awoke the next morning ravenous. My two companions were up for the first time before I was, but I didn't even notice. All I could think of was my angry stomach. By pure instinct I located a large bird flying nearby and sent it a mental command to come here. When the bird was directly above me, I sent a bolt of concentrated thought jarring into the tiny brain of my unwitting prey.

I stepped back, and the bird flopped in front of me, dead. I sent a thought to Mikaal requesting that he cook the bird quickly using his magic. As consumed as I was by my hunger, I didn't notice the look that crossed my companions' faces.

Mikaal did as I requested in the blink of an eye. I ripped a large chunk of flesh off the fowl and devoured it immediately. Coral and Mikaal ate in silence beside me. With my hunger satisfied, I could see how strangely I was acting. What had I just done?

"Mikaal… Coral…. I'm sorry for acting strangely just now. When I woke up, I was so famished that I couldn't think at all. It was like animal Aaron was in charge."

I don't know how I expected them to react to either words or my actions, but Coral's "What did you just do?" certainly wasn't it.

When I explained, I thought she was going to faint and the Noran with her. In the history of Sorra, with all of the diverse mental magic that existed amongst the races, no person had ever killed with a thought.

I began to worry that I might wake up and find no easy prey and cook one of my friend's brains by mistake. Mikaal asked me to recount what I had been doing mentally before going to sleep. I told him that I had siphoned off all my remaining power into storage so that I would generate more during the night. He said that this was likely the root cause of my hunger. It seems that storing all one's strength places a large drain on the body. The body will generate more power but will need large quantities of food to do so. If food isn't readily available, the body will begin to feed on itself. The gnawing hunger I had felt was my body telling me that it was preparing to devour itself.

After our impromptu breakfast, we resumed our trek. Conversation was almost nonexistent, and I knew my friends were thinking deep thoughts. I hoped that they weren't regretting meeting me. I allowed the silence to stretch for what I judged to be an hour before asking what was wrong. I expected Mikaal to speak up, but Coral spoke first. She wanted me to teach them how to destroy an enemy's mind.

At first, I didn't get why they were hesitant to ask, and I said so. Mikaal said that if they had the power to kill so easily, the temptation to use it might be too great. My new friends had to be sure that they would be up to the responsibility. So now the teacher had become the student.

I struggled at first because I thought of the process in terms of the world I came from, things that neither of them had ever experienced. What I had done to kill the bird wouldn't work on a creature with a much larger or more complex brain, but I was confident that I could adapt the method for something as mentally complex as a man.

The trick, as I thought of it, was to create a package of thoughts that the creature on the receiving end couldn't handle. Random thoughts of a fully self-aware being would be incomprehensible to a bird or other small creature. A being of greater intellect would have to be hit with something substantially more complex. In my mind, this was a mental bomb. Neither of these people had ever experienced a bomb, and so this was the best way I could explain it to them.

After several unsuccessful attempts to destroy the brains of innocent creatures, Coral finally mindblasted a carrion bird. The bird made one squawk and spiraled to the ground. The bird's comrades had picked the bones clean by the time we got to the body.

I looked from the carnage back to Coral to see how she reacted to her success. She started out with a beaming smile, complete with a joyful leap that turned into the Sorran version of an end zone dance. Her celebration cut short abruptly. She stopped, tense, and muttered to herself that she should not be happy at killing an innocent creature. Mikaal was still practicing when we came to the city.

Chapter 5
Tiiaan

We crested a hill, and there spread below us was the largest city of the Garanth. Tiiaan wasn't a city by the standards of my world. There were suburbs with more land area and probably people as well. There was a significant wall around it, but the gates stood open. No building was larger than four stories high and most were only one. Still, it was marvelous.

A tower stood near the center of town. It wasn't very large, but every inch of its surface was covered with gears and springs and coils and other mechanical gizmos. I realized that the side of the tower that faced northwest was a clock of some sort, but the northeast section was a mystery to me. Most every building had a sign or symbol that twirled, rotated, bounced, jounced or otherwise moved. The notable exception was the large single-story building that was set aside from the others. I pointed this one out to Mikaal, and he told me that this was the Magic school.

We decided to find a place to stay the night before we began looking for ways to combat the darkness. We looked for a building with a bed mounted to a spring high in the air and headed towards it.

Before we entered the town proper, we had developed a silent following. In this city of the Garanth strangers were not unusual, but as Mikaal had said, Norans were not greatly given to travel and so were unusual except for a few in the magic school that kept mainly to themselves. Coral was the first SeaWind that anyone in this part of the world had seen in twenty-five years, and no Garanth would have ever seen a human.

As we walked, people dropped what they were doing and followed us. No one seemed openly hostile, only curious. I didn't want to be the one to break the silence so I established a mental rapport with my travel-mates so that we could converse as we went. I was growing slightly nervous at all this attention and asked Mikaal what we should do to dispel the crowd. He seemed bemused by the suggestion that we should do anything about the crowd. Coral didn't say anything but edged closer to me.

We made it to the main street of town without incident. There must have been close to ninety natives following in our wake. I was shocked to see that the streets of Tiiaan weren't packed earth as I had imagined, but a substance that looked vaguely like concrete but had a slight springy feel. The roadway was clean of debris and trash, and I could see that these people were intelligent, responsible, and proud in the layout of the buildings and the care and attention paid to them. So wrapped up in sightseeing, I nearly missed seeing the child that stood in the middle of the road, blocking our way ahead. We pulled up just short of the little girl and waited.

"Who are you?" she asked us innocently.

I couldn't help taking her question personally as her wide young eyes were glued to my face. "I am Aaron. This is Coral and Mikaal. We're just looking for a place to stay. Who are you?"

"I am Neilia. I am six years old."

"Where are your parents?" A Garanth woman broke free of the crowd at my question and scooped Neilia up.

"Cute kid," I said to the newcomer.

"Thank you. Welcome to Tiiaan. My name is Estrall. Please forgive us for following you. None of us mean you any harm; like my daughter we are curious. It is just that none of us has ever seen a being like you. Would it be too impolite of me to ask where you are from?"

I chuckled. I didn't get offended easily—maybe I was a little oblivious even--but I didn't have anything to hide. "My people are called humans. I came through a portal from another world."

"Then you are trapped here! All portals are closed now. Were you planning on staying on Sorra or were you taken by surprise?" Estrall questioned excitedly.

"I had not really intended on coming to Sorra, and while I was surprised when the portal that I came through closed, I am not disturbed at the thought of being stranded here. This is truly a lovely world. We will probably be here for a few days, and I will be happy to answer more questions later. We should be moving along now though."

I could sense that Mikaal was itching to say something to these people about the impending darkness closing slowly but inexorably on the planet. Before he could speak, I mindspoke to him that this was not the time nor the group of people to be making proclamations of doom to. People could be motivated to band together and fight, but that was best left to their leaders. If we came into town spreading rumors of danger we might cause a stampede and brand ourselves troublemakers. He didn't say anything to the Garanth or to me, just shot me a mixed look and followed behind me as the crowd that had ringed us while I was talking parted to let us pass. Most of the Garanth interest abated after hearing me speak, and we were accompanied no farther.

Just before we reached the inn we had seen in the distance, I realized that I had no money or even an idea of how local currency might work. I mindspoke to both of my associates and suggested that someone other than I take the lead.

At first they hesitated but when I explained my lack of knowledge and funding Coral stepped slightly ahead of us as we passed into the building. She immediately addressed the innkeeper, and I tried to follow the bargaining process, but I was distracted by the contented muttering that was coming across the mental link I had left in place between Mikaal and I. Something like… good leader knowing when he didn't know… coming along nicely. I didn't know whether to be flattered or irritated that I was being judged on my performance.

Before I could decide how I felt, Coral had our rooms arranged and was already to the stairs. The little magician grabbed my arm with one of his many gaw as he passed me, nearly jerking me from my feet. We were forced to pay for two rooms, more to keep the appearance of decency than for any other reason. I was more than a little disappointed that Coral was going to be out of my sight, but I understood the reasons.

We placed our equipment in our rooms and cleaned up for dinner. I was speechless that the Garanth had even developed running water. This was the first time that Mikaal and I had been alone since Coral had joined us. I still wasn't entirely comfortable with mindspeak, and I wanted to ask Mikaal about something for a while.

"Mikaal, how do SeaWinds breath underwater? I don't see any gills on Coral."

With a twinkle in his eye, the Noran turned. "Why do you not ask her? You like her? Are you embarrassed to want to know more about her?"

"Yes and yes. Will you answer the question, you little fiend?"

"Very well. SeaWinds do have gills. The reason you have not seen them is because they are on the soles of her feet. There is more than a passing reason for the placement. When Coral goes underwater a valve changes position in her throat. The valve prevents water from entering her lungs and channels it instead to her gills. Instead of swimming and opening her mouth and letting the water flow through her body like a fish, she opens her mouth and breaths in constantly. Large volumes of water flow into her mouth and out of her feet. She propels herself in this manner as well as swimming as you would."

"Wow! Coral is jet propelled!"

"What?" Mikaal asked, perplexed.

"Nothing. Never mind."

Mikaal had been getting ready for dinner while we talked, but I'd been too involved in my questions to prepare, so when we heard a knock at the door, he was the one to answer it. There was no bathroom set aside in our room; instead, there was a privacy curtain set around the privy and water trough. I heard Coral's voice as she was let into the room but didn't see her because I had the curtain closed while bathing. It felt very good to be clean, even if there was no shower. This wasn't like any civilization I've ever known, but after spending the last few nights in the wilds, running water and a bed were heaven to me.

I had one fresh set of clothes left in my pack, and I pulled them out now. I would see about getting my other clothes washed after dinner. I pulled back the curtain and walked toward the sound of voices. I had said hello to Coral through the curtain when she came in, but when my eyes finally landed on her I landed on the floor.

In the short time since I had known her, Coral had been wearing the same clothing. Sometime during her dealing with the innkeeper, she must have arranged to get some new clothes. She was wearing a dress that came down to just above her knees. The straps that went over her shoulders and crossed over her back were thin, and the neckline was cut enticingly low. Overall, more of her was covered than had been before, but she was even more stunning than ever. Her freshly cleaned hair was unbound and flowing freely about her shoulders.

From where I sprawled, I could smell the fragrance she was wearing. She smelled like sunshine after a hard rain, fresh cut grass, hundreds of varying flowers in a field, and citrus fruit all at the same time; like all the good things in nature found her as delightful as I did and clung to her.

She ran to me when I fell over and helped me up, and I gave her a sheepish grin for thanks. Through my embarrassment I could barely hear Mikaal chortling and snorting behind Coral. I stated that dinner would probably not wait for us and pointed the Noran towards the exit to our room.

There was a catch that held the door shut but no lock that I could see. Mikaal said that most guests didn't feel the need to lock their doors in Tiiaan as there were no criminals, and the few that did worry after their belongings usually locked the door with magic. He was getting ready to cast a spell to do just that, but I stopped him and told him that I wanted to try something.

The first thing I did was create a mental motion detector and placed it on the inside of the door to alert me if anyone did successfully enter our room. Next, I set up an active suggestion field. I hadn't done it before, but all things here were new to me. Anyone who attempted to enter our room would either have a subconscious urge to move along placed in their mind, or if they persisted, a very powerful command to get lost.

Another guest of the inn stepped out of his room about this time, probably heading down for dinner as we were. I stopped him and asked him if he would assist me. I said that I had a method for keeping people away from a room that I did not want them in without hurting them. I wanted to prove to my friends that it worked and would he please try to enter my room.

This man didn't seem at all put off by my being from a race he had never encountered and agreed to try. He reached out his hand to flip the catch that held the door. Just before he made contact his eyes widened then narrowed; he blinked twice and walked calmly away. Coral seemed as if she understood, but Mikaal was perplexed.

"How does that prove anything?" he asked. "The fellow did not even touch the door and just walked away like he had never spoken to us."

"That's the point, Mikaal," I said. "I placed a suggestion in his mind that he shouldn't go in, and he obeyed it."

"That is not going to help unless you are planning to stand here and watch the door."

"Try to go in, Mikaal."

The magician reached toward the door and felt the suggestion take hold. He caught himself before he walked away. He frowned at me for a moment, and then I could see comprehension on his face like sunlight breaking over the horizon. He said no more to me, just smiled and led the way.

The volume level in the crowded common room fell noticeably when we entered. At first, I thought that people were looking at me because I was human. Some were, but most everyone's eyes were on Coral. She smiled at the room and people started talking again, though I think that a lot of the conversation revolved around her. I offered her my arm and led the three of us to a table against the wall that was not being used.

The four-armed serving wench came out with a steaming platter of some animal that looked faintly bovine but was about as big as a German Shepard. Whatever they called it, the smell was fantastic. The girl set this on our table and went back into what I took to be the kitchen. She reappeared shortly with three large wooden goblets, three large plates, and two prodigious bowls. One of the bowls turned out to contain a vegetable mix while the other was used to fill the goblets.

I took a quick survey of the young Garanth's appearance. She was clad in a white blouse covered by a gray apron and a long flowing skirt colored several shades of red. With the skirt covering her legs, her extra set of arms were all that kept her from looking human. I glanced around the room briefly before looking back to my friends. Coral's face showed a flash of something and then it was gone.

I mindspoke to her and asked her if something was troubling her. She said that nothing was, but she didn't sound convincing. I continued to send her smiley face mental notes until she laughed. I asked her again what had upset her. She admitted that she had not liked the fact that I had been watching our server. I blew her a mental kiss, and she blushed dark blue. I terminated our contact and resolved to talk more to her later to see if the feelings I think I'm reading from her are true or just wishful thinking on my part. Just now the food that sat in front of me deserved my attention.

When we had eaten our fill and the remainder had been cleaned away, we set about making plans. The greater part of the day was behind us, and so we decided to wait until the morning before contacting the city leaders. Tonight, we would go to the magic school and consult with the headmasters about ways to combat the corrupting cloud.

Before we left the table though I asked them to give me a rundown of Sorran finance. It seemed that sometime in the distant past, (before Mikaal was born at least) the races on this world had agreed on a single monetary system. The basis for the currency wasn't gold or any other precious material as I would have expected, but time.

A day on Sorra has thirty hours, each hour consisting of fifty minutes. Each minute was sixty ticks long. The primary unit of the Sorran monetary system was called a Patun. One Patun was the equivalent of one hour of work. The Patun was broken into smaller pieces called Hasmut that are worth ten minutes of labor. There are of course five Hasmut in a Patun. It did not take very long for them to explain the system to me. There were really no set prices for anything. Every purchase made involved haggling. Simple enough. Mikaal handed me a few Patun to keep on me in case we became separated.

If the Sorran Patun was tied to an hour of work, I was really wishing that I had brought a watch or at least had any idea what time it was when I arrived. My best estimate since I took the position as resident hero and protector of the

Tiiaan

world meant that my first paycheck would be north of 80 Patuns tonight. I wondered if they had taxes, but not enough to seriously ask about it.

We left the inn and began to make our way across the city towards the magic school. Tiiaan hadn't seemed that big at first but when viewed from the inside it could be quite intimidating. On foot it would take us around a half hour to arrive at our destination. The owners of some bird-driven carts offered us rides-for-a-price, but we decided to walk.

As we walked through the city, I was in awe of the sights, but I was still thinking about my newfound powers. I knew there were other forms of mental magic that worked here, but I hadn't seen any evidence of mind over matter yet. I decided to give it a try.

I took a coin from my pocket and held it in front of me. I reached out with my mind and tried to grasp the coin. After a few tries I was able to make a connection. A grin stole across my face. If I could hold the coin with my mind, then surely I could move it. I held the coin steadily in my mental grasp and slowly lowered my hand. The coin remained in the air in front of me. I flipped the coin up in the air and caught it in my hand.

Suddenly I ran into the back of Mikaal. He turned and looked at me and asked me what I had found so funny. I hadn't realized until just that moment that I was laughing like an excited child. I asked Mikaal and Coral if either of them had ever known anyone who could control physical objects with their mind. Both shook their heads no.

I held out the coin in my hand again. Mentally I grasped the coin, more quickly this time than before. I pulled my hand away quickly, and the coin was floating in air. Coral gasped and Mikaal gaped. I sent the coin rolling end over end and then made it fly a figure eight around the two stunned Sorrans.

After a moment, Coral reached out and plucked the coin from the air and began to examine it closely. I let my hold on the coin go and tried a different target. There was an open field, which I took to be a park just off the side of the road where we had been walking. I spotted a large flowering bush and sent my mental hand out. I took a flower by the stem and pulled. The flower broke off, and I pulled it quickly toward us. Coral had just passed the coin to Mikaal to allow him to inspect it as well when the bloom flew up. I held it just out of her reach to allow her to see it and then placed it gently in her hair.

I turned my attention back to the Noran and to the coin, which he was still examining, and pulled it from his gaw. He sputtered and backed away but watched the coin return to me and fly into my pocket. A triumphant smile stole across my face as I resumed walking toward the now not-so-distant magic school. I heard my two friends following, and I didn't need to look to know they were trying the trick for themselves. Neither the SeaWind nor the Noran were able to lift a coin before we arrived at the magic school.

Chapter 6
Back to School

The magic school was the only building in Tiiaan not covered in gadgets. The gates at the courtyard entrance were ornate and gave the place a sense of seriousness not found elsewhere in town. Before Coral could spin the handle on the gate bell a tiny face appeared. The face looked down at us for a moment and then began to descend. I was able to recognize the creature as it approached. It was another Noran, and this one's gaw were as black as the metal of the gate. When it was only a few feet away, it spoke.

"I am Jixxell, keeper of the Gate. For what purpose do you come here?"

Mikaal answered, "Greetings, Jixxell. You are growing into a fine young lady, aren't you? Well, it has been a long time, I suppose you don't remember me. I am Mikaal, and these are my friends Coral and Aaron. We are here to speak with the headmasters on a matter of some urgency."

"Master Mikaal, I am sorry that I did not recognize you. Please, you and your companions come in."

With that, Jixxell opened the gates with a spell and followed us inside. We were ushered into a waiting room where the young Noran girl sent a runner to alert the headmasters of our presence before returning to her post. Evidently, Mikaal's name carried some weight here. We didn't wait long before a young Garanth appeared from thin air and asked us to follow him to the meeting hall.

The room was dark as we approached, and our guide bowed and left us before we crossed the threshold. I don't know if this was meant to intimidate us or not, but for me it was pretty unnerving. When Mikaal, who was in the lead, crossed into the meeting room, glass globes began winking to life one by one down the length of the room and back. I heard Coral make a startled noise, and I was glad that I was not the only one startled by the sight. This place was humming with magic, and I could feel it pulsing around me, through me, into me, and back out again. This wasn't so much the feeling of magic in use though but the potential for magic. With the amount of power that I sensed in this building, I wondered again what use I would be against the corrupting force attacking this world.

As the last globe flared bright, four figures stepped out of alcoves lining the walls. Two of these were Garanth, one old and one appearing middle aged, one was Noran and one was a creature that I had not seen before. I recognized this being from Mikaal's description as Moalean. I assumed that these were the headmasters that we had come to visit, and I made a formal bow. They all bowed in return.

One by one they introduced themselves to us. The ancient Garanth was the leader and went by the title Mackta but gave us no name. The second Garanth asked that we call him Glanoot. The Noran was Notrus, and the Moalean, a female, went by Maegen. Mikaal introduced Coral and me as his friends before asking that they secure the room against listening ears. The Mackta made what looked to be a dismissing wave, but I watched, wide-eyed, as an enormous amount of magical energy leaped from him to cover the room.

The old man saw my reaction and without a word hobbled over to stand before me. He was shorter than me by a good six inches, but I felt small as I looked down on him. The man exuded an incredible sense of power, and I thought that he might be the exception to Norans being the most powerful magicians on Sorra. The elder said nothing to me for well over a minute but continued to stare and scrutinize me. I was getting ready to ask him what he was looking at just as he spoke to me.

"You are stronger than you look, Aaron. You also have talents not seen on this world before. I could tell by your reaction that you can see and feel magic, and more, that you are becoming increasingly sensitive and perceptive to it. I do not know what other skills you possess, but I am glad you are here."

Mikaal spoke up. "Then you know, great Mackta, about the enemy that destroys our world?"

"I have known about it far longer than you, child."

From somewhere behind the impossibly imposing old man, I heard the other headmasters questioning one another, trying to determine what was being talked about.

"What are you doing about it then?" Mikaal asked.

"There is nothing I may do to affect the outcome of the situation. You have heard rumors that I can see the future?"

"Yes."

"To a small degree I can. I was born with this ability, but it is not something I share with others often. I suppose that it is needed now. I sensed the presence as soon as it arrived on Sorra. I spent the next three days and nights looking for answers in every way I knew how. All my attempts seemed to prove was that we were not going to survive. The fourth morning the futuretrance came upon me. I could see a stranger stepping in from another world. I knew that I was not the one who called him. This stranger would be brought to me. Then the trance ended. I slept that night and was at peace. Now Mikaal, my student and friend, you have brought us a hero."

"So that little dance with the future didn't tell you what I was supposed to be doing here, did it?" I asked, slightly vexed.

"No, Aaron, I have few answers for you on this journey. The best that I can offer to any of you is my knowledge and perhaps a point in the right direction. I wish that I could do more. Huff... If only I were younger, I would join you." The Mackta did seem truly displeased to be left behind.

We adjourned to a large circular table to talk and plan. The junior headmasters decided that the best way to learn what we all apparently knew was to listen, for they had all fallen silent. Mikaal and the Mackta had both attacked the all-consuming cloud at one time and both had concluded that Sorran magic had little or no effect on it. If the darkness kept its pace, we had only twelve days before it overtook Tiiaan. The old Garanth headmaster did have a few ideas though. He had bent all of his considerable power recently towards discovering the nature of our enemy and what could be done to stop it and learned much.

The dark cloud making its slow but determined way ever outward was not alive as had been suspected. Through methods that he would not describe, the Mackta had learned the nature of the thing.

"It is one of a few kinds of Chaos Cloud, known as an unbinding. It is not a living thing as Mikaal and I first thought."

I was sure the blank look on my face showed that I had no idea what he was talking about. Thankfully he continued.

"When an unbinding comes into contact with anything living, it will break links inside of the being, both physical and mental. This is what causes the effects we have seen. When an unbinding touches non-living items, these things are undone as if they never were, are perverted, or destroyed.

"Unbindings are usually caused by one of only a select few things. There are two known types of beings capable of creating and maintaining a cloud of this size."

From his description, either one would have been considered a demon where I had come from.

"I have eliminated the possibility that the smaller of the two creatures was the culprit. That particular demon could not exist outside of its home realm for more than a week. This began eight days ago."

Logic is alive and well in Sorra I guess.

The Mackta explained that the greater being was especially cruel and used several variations of Chaos Clouds to destroy worlds, but it could be fought and killed.

"Another possibility is that a magic user from this world had called up what he believed to be a weather spell and got more than he bargained for. In this case, we would simply have to locate the magic user, who would have been corrupted by his creation, and kill him."

"That also seems unlikely, Mackta. None of the races are given to frivolous use of magic. In fact, I'd say that would be more likely to happen here at the school than anywhere else." Maegen suddenly chimed in.

The Mackta nodded in sage agreement before continuing.

"There are one or two worlds where Chaos Clouds are a natural phenomenon. It is possible that the phenomenon found its way through a portal randomly. These worlds have methods for dealing with rogue unbindings if they are not being maintained by a living being."

"If this is the case," Mikaal offered, "we would simply make contact with people from that world and obtain a solution from them."

"Finally, it has happened that a magic user, traveling through the portals, came upon a world which had been destroyed by an unbinding. If this magic user were to be a person of cruel intent and sufficient power, they could harness the cloud and take it with them. Then they could find a world they like, unleash the unbinding for a time, demand the surrender of any people that remain, and rule there. Of course, it could be none of these or something in between, but only you will be able to tell for sure."

I looked at him and realized that the you he meant was me.

"Oh, right. I'll just use my unbinding origin tracking tool to find out and we'll know what to do next." I said sarcastically.

The Mackta made a face, realizing I was joking, but Glanoot didn't catch my sarcasm. "How helpful that you came equipped for the task."

"Glanoot, right? I was kidding. I have no idea how I would be able to tell the origin of this Chaos Cloud, and I'd never heard of one before coming here."

"Oh," he said, chagrined.

"There is an artifact of great but peculiar power," the Mackta said solemnly. "It was said to have been lost in the mines of the SrakeKepp Mountains."

The name was familiar—maybe the mountains we passed by on our way here. I should have paid attention, but my mind was on not getting munched by another TuskerKitty.

"The Star Glass can alter and even enhance the natural and magical abilities of its possessor," the Mackta said with a long look at me. "No one could say what effect it might have on you, so that must be your first mission. Find this precious artifact."

At least this guy is coming with ideas instead of sitting here in his school complaining that doom is coming to get them all.

"No one knows how the Star Glass got into the mines. The last time the artifact was seen, it was in a convoy that was bringing it as a gift to the OrOboid leader. The device was locked in an enchanted chest said to be completely resistant to magic or physical damage."

The Mackta paused for an extended breath, making me think he was done.

"The key to this chest had been discovered in the belongings of a powerful Garanth magician upon his death. When the key was discovered, it was sent to Tiiaan to be protected here at the school. Many adventurers have entered the mine in search of the Star Glass. None had found even a trace. Some were never heard from again."

The Mackta brought the key from somewhere in his clothing and held it aloft for our inspection. It was exquisitely carved and ornamented crystal, covered with markings that I assumed were magic symbols of protection. I sensed a very faint magic pulse from the key. I had been beginning to wonder why they thought this was so important that we should stumble around in the dark looking for this artifact that had been lost well over a hundred years before. Suddenly it made sense. Secluded in the mines, away from any other magic that might interfere, I could easily use my newfound ability to detect the Star Glass.

"So, you think I will be able to succeed because I can see Magic," I asked.

"It does seem our best avenue for success, yes."

"I'm not sure if it will work or not, but I'm willing to try." The Mackta had placed the key on a silver chain and ensorcelled the chain for strength and to keep it securely around my neck. I felt the magic take hold when the old man clasped the chain at the back of my neck.

The headmasters decided they were going to tell the pupils at the school about the Chaos Cloud the next day, just as we were going to talk to the leaders of Tiiaan. We hoped that by telling as many people as possible, people would begin to work together for a solution to this problem. Much time had passed in conversation, and it was getting late. We said our farewells and took our leave. The headmasters would see us out of town tomorrow and would be providing us with mounts and supplies.

When we got back to the inn, dinner was already underway. Mikaal and Coral took seats at our table from this morning. This time our server was a man, and I caught Coral looking at him. I was annoyed by the white-hot flash of jealousy that ran the length of my spine. I couldn't tell if she was attracted to this man or if she was trying to judge my reaction, but I had to say something to her.

In mindspeak, "Now who is looking at the server?"

"Do you care?"

"Would it please you if I did?"

"Perhaps"

"Well, I can't change what I felt when I saw you looking at him. I've never been the jealous type but apparently, I am now."

The only response that I got was a glorious smile, but that was enough for me.

When the meal was completed and the dishes, platters, cups, and bowls had been cleared, people began to push their tables and benches against the walls. A moment later, a door swung open and three Garanth men came into the room. Each man had a musical instrument of some design or another. When they were seated in a corner they began to play.

This was my first time hearing music since I had arrived on Sorra, and I wasn't disappointed. Like most everything else here, the music was beautiful. The oldest of the men was playing a small wind instrument that produced two tones at the same time. He led the melody, playing slowly and with great feeling at first and then picking up speed until the music reached a fevered tempo. I have never to this day heard anyone better with the Twinpipe than that old man was. The voices of his instrument danced together, intertwining tantalizingly before pulling apart and singing in counterpoint.

The Garanth to the left looked to be the first man's son. This man had a stringed instrument, which was alternately strummed and plucked. The Bannam, as I later learned it is called, had remarkable range. The son played his instrument with a maddening fury that threatened at times to snap it in two. It was easy to tell that these two men had been playing together long as they balanced each other perfectly, the Bannam player usually taking the low notes but occasionally sneaking up to offer its voice to the twin singers of the pipe.

The third and final player had carried a strange looking miniature drum set into the room. When the pace of the song began to quicken, it became clear that this musician's job was to bring the youthful exuberance of the son and the mellow feeling of the father into perfect synchronization.

The inn patrons waited and listened to the music for most of an hour. Some unseen signal must have passed through the room because everyone got up at the same time and began to dance. Unlike the modern dances where I was from with everybody doing more or less their own thing, the dancers here moved in pairs. Each couple was somehow part of the greater whole, moving and flowing in and out of each other. The steps were not complicated if you watched those who were already on the floor. It vaguely reminded me of the frivolity and fun of a barn dance I saw in an old movie as a kid, but without any of the camp or corniness.

How easy to forget the danger that was even now moving against us in the face of such innocent revelry. I could not help myself. I grabbed Coral's hand against her protests, and we swung out into the dance. She looked scared for a moment but was soon laughing and cavorting with glee. The dance went on for two hours, and we didn't stop until the musicians did.

When the music stopped, we headed upstairs. No one had even attempted to enter our room. I unbound the suggestion from the door and the tripwire as well. I was asleep before my body hit the bed.

Chapter 7
Playtime

I felt more rested after sleeping in an actual bed than I had felt since before I had come to Sorra. I left my eyes closed and reveled in the safety, before stretching once and breathing deeply. When I did open my eyes, I found that Mikaal was still sleeping, dangling from the headboard. I got up, attended to the call of nature, and bathed.

On a small table, there was a basket of bread, fruit, and cheese that hadn't been in the room last night. The door was secured from the inside by one of Mikaal's spells, so I decided that the innkeeper must keep a magic user on staff to transport the basket to the rooms in the morning. I must have been awakened when I sensed the spell take effect. The Mackta had been correct; my ability to sense the presence of magic was growing stronger.

I didn't recognize any of the fruit in the basket, so I tried one that was shaped a little like a banana. It was very good but tasted nothing like it looked. It had a slightly meaty flavor to it. I finished up the fruit and chased it with a cheese sandwich and water. Mikaal still wasn't awake, so I tried to occupy myself.

I'd been able to lift a coin from my hand and make it fly... I would practice this talent and see what else could be done with it. There was a fairly large window in the room. Since we were on the second floor of the inn, the windows were big enough for a person to sit on the sill and even to crawl out of them. Only a small metal latch on the inside secured the window. I reached out my mental hand and unlatched and opened the window.

Then I tried to think about this mind over matter stuff from a different perspective. Instead of envisioning a hand and then controlling it, I tried exerting my will directly on my surroundings. I focused on the ground beneath my feet and pushed away. The floorboards began to groan and bend beneath me, and I quickly stopped. OK, I could directly affect things without the mental hand.

I tried exerting my will on a piece of fruit that was in the basket. The fruit moved, but not as I expected or would have wished. The entire basket lurched suddenly into the air and began to fall. I formed a flat barrier in the air below where the fruit was and caught the basket and its contents before it hit the ground.

I thought I should try to push myself a little farther and try to do two things at once, so I continued to hold the basket aloft and summoned my mental hand. I righted the basket and then put each piece of food back into it before placing it back onto the table. There. I had successfully done two things at once. Not too bad. The barrier had wobbled slightly but not too bad for a first attempt.

I was about to dismiss the barrier to oblivion when another idea came to me. I walked over to it and touched it. I didn't think anyone else could see the things that I created in my mind, but the objects were undeniably real and solid. I turned and sat on the big floating square, Indian style. Amazing! I was defying the law of gravity, holding myself aloft just by the force of my own mind. I grabbed another piece of fruit from the basket with my invisible hand and fed it to myself. That wasn't as easy as I thought it would be. I had to clean my face with a cloth after I finished eating.

I knew what I wanted to try next, but I was more than a little frightened. I could hurt myself badly if I lost control. I centered all of my thoughts on the mental magic square beneath me and moved it slowly forward. I did not slide off. So far, so good. I tried to turn myself to the left and go between the beds. Again, shaky but successful. I raised the platform to where my head was nearly touching the ceiling. No problem. This was getting easier. Not perfect, but I was doing pretty well. Now came the real test as I pushed my little square out of the open window.

When I left the window, I flew straight up and hovered over the rooftop. I didn't want anyone on the ground to see me if I could help it. The biggest surprise of all was that I wasn't using very much energy. I flew two laps around the roof and then settled on my next target. I flew over the edge of the roof and down, straight to the window of Coral's room. I didn't sense any movement from within.

I hesitated only a second before pulling the window open further. I floated through the window and over to the bed. She was sleeping soundly. So beautiful. I floated above the bed and watched as each breath made her chest rise and fall ever so slightly. I smiled as I wondered what I would have done if I could have looked into the future before I came to Sorra. Probably signed myself into a mental institution.

I widened the barrier so that I could lie flat. I hovered down until I was just inches from Coral's face. I had never met a woman whose breath smelled sweet in the moments just before she woke up, but this beautiful SeaWind's did. I was floating back up when her eyes opened. I half expected her to scream, but she only smiled at me as if it were perfectly natural that I should be floating above her early in the morning.

Great work, genius, I said inwardly. Now she's going to think you're a creepy stalker type. Time to say something intelligent and reassuring. Think of something clever!

"Good morning," I stammered quietly.

Smooth, Aaron. Very smooth. I would have facepalmed, but I couldn't lying on my stomach and with less than an arm's length between us.

"Yes. A very good morning," she replied. A shiver went through me at the sound of her incredible multi-tonal voice.

"Are you cold?" she inquired.

"No." I closed my eyes before continuing, "The sound of your voice is delightful to my ears. I shiver with happiness and excitement."

Ok. That was super corny. But she's not screaming. Maybe I don't frighten her? Maybe they don't have stalkers here... A surprised "oh" and then another came from her. The second gasped "oh" as she discovered that she was awake and I, who owned no magic that should allow me to do so, was levitating.

"You are really here?" she asked with a gentle shake of her head. "I thought I was dreaming."

"I was in your dreams?" I asked in shock.

"Um…" she said quietly. I could feel, but not see, her blushing. *Be chill, Aaron. Do something clever.*

I raised myself up another foot or so before, with my eyes still closed, retrieving two small magenta fruits from the basket behind me and flying them into my right hand. I opened my eyes and looked into Coral's. She was surprised, but not afraid. I brought the first of the two fruits to my lips and bit. Sweet juice flowed down my throat. The second fruit I fed to Coral. Seconds passed. I flew slowly to the bedside and tilted my flying bed so that my feet were almost touching the ground before stepping off. Coral had turned and sat up. She was wearing a nightgown of elegant design, and this reminded me of something I hadn't really considered. Coral was a princess. Sure, maybe her kingdom was gone but she had been raised as royalty. She was used to nice things. Pushing self-doubt aside, I gently took her delicate fingers into mine and kissed her knuckles one by one. Then before she could respond, I stepped back onto my barrier and flew out the window.

Chapter 8
Leaders of Tiiaan

I flew to the window of the room I shared with Mikaal and slipped lightly inside before dissipating my transport panel. I latched the window closed by hand. I really didn't feel that I had used much of my stored energy, but I thought I should be a little more cautious for a time.

I could hear through the walls and floor sounds of the other guests of the inn rising and beginning to move about. Mikaal was still asleep, and I gently shook him.

"Mikaal. You should get ready to talk to Tiiaan's rulers."

"Hmm spag werd?" he stirred, not awake enough to make sense.

"You know, world ending danger heading our way…. Time to call up the King or Princess, or whatever they have here."

"Counsel of Three."

"Ok. The Council then."

"Nope. Not Council… Counsel!"

"I know you are sleepy, but you're not making any sense."

"I'm awake now, Aaron. You are mistaken. You are talking about something that doesn't exist. The Counsel of Three aren't a governing body like you're thinking of. They are the Three wisest people in the land, and everybody listens to their Counsel. Get it now? The Counsel of Three."

"Uh… sure. I'm not sure how you were determining the spelling of the word by my voice, but I get you now." (I rolled my eyes silently.)

"I heard that!"

"Heard what? Uh. Can you release the door so I can check on Coral?"

I decided to stop talking and check on Coral before Mikaal somehow 'heard' my thoughts about having just been in her room.

Once the magic was lifted, I made my way down the hall where I couldn't be easily seen if Mikaal was to decide to leave the room. I sent a telepathic message to Coral to let her know that I was supposed to be checking up on her and to make sure that she didn't need anything. About fifteen seconds passed before I got her response. She said that she was getting ready for the day and appreciated that I respected her privacy enough to contact her by mindspeak so she didn't have to answer the door partially dressed. Her reply caused a very pleasant mental image, and I quickly walked down to the common room to avoid temptation.

There were few patrons in the common area this early in the morning. Most likely the baskets that were provided were more than enough to satisfy most guests. I spent a few minutes looking at the sparse decorations on the walls of the inn before becoming bored and wandering outside.

I noticed a small group of people standing in a knot a short distance away from the inn, and I was feeling curious, so I went to investigate. The group was mostly older women. All attention was focused on one very animated middle-aged woman. I was trying to be nosy without getting caught, so I only heard bits and pieces of what was being said. What I heard was enough to make me realize that I had been seen while flying around this morning.

I quickly turned and tried to get back to the inn before I was spotted. I was lucky that everyone was standing so close about the woman who had watched me learn to fly. Since I was the only human in town, I was probably pretty easy to spot. I just hoped that I wasn't being made out as a criminal or demon or whatever else a middle-aged Garanth woman worried over.

When I made it back to the room, Mikaal had already finished getting cleaned up and was finishing his breakfast. There were several pieces of fruit left, and the bread and cheese were mostly untouched. I grabbed a fruit that I hadn't sampled and bit into it and suggested that Mikaal stash the remainder of the food in his magic bag for safekeeping. The little man threw a preservation spell over the whole basket and shoved it into the bag hidden in his clothes. It was amazing, not to mention humorous, to watch a large basket disappear into the little Noran's clothing without leaving so much as a bump or wrinkle to mark its presence.

Just then, a knock sounded on the door. I was closer, so I opened it. Coral stood in the doorway looking, if possible, more stunning than the day before and wearing a secret smile that complemented her new forest green dress. She walked in, and before I could close the door, the innkeeper was standing there. He looked vaguely surprised to find the door open and me standing in the doorway but proceeded with his business anyway.

"One of the townswomen that lives close by noticed someone flying around near your window early this morning. I just wanted to be sure that everything was all right, and that no one had been bothering any of you. Any problems?"

My stomach dropped in alarm. I thought I'd been cautious enough, but apparently not. I guess people flying around was as unusual on Sorra as my own world. I doubted I would need to be reminded after this.

I replied, "No." I said, feigning heavy thought. "Nope. I can't think of anything strange." Turning to my friends I added, "Either of you?"

Mikaal and Coral replied in unison, "No."

"All right." The innkeeper seemed a little let down. Maybe he was bored and wanted to pick a fight? Who knew? "If anyone bothers any of you, please tell me so that I can take care of it."

All three of us answered in the affirmative, and the concerned Garanth man made his way to the door of the next room. We wanted to get to TownHold (home to the rulers of Tiiaan) early so we could be finished quickly and leave on our mission. We packed up our gear and started towards the Capital fortress. I was more than a little afraid that the woman was going to see me and start screaming about a flying demon, but we made it away from the inn without incident.

After fifteen to twenty minutes had passed, I finally relaxed. Mornings were beautiful on Sorra. Interestingly enough, if you get up early enough on Sorra, the sun can be seen glowing blue instead of orange. The buildings in Tiiaan are architectural marvels, covered with a plethora of whirling, clicking, clanking wheels and gears. This was truly a place worth saving. I was really floored at the way people treated one another here as well. I hadn't seen one fight or lost temper during my visit. The Garanth seemed to respect each other and even outsiders, in a way that humans never had. When the woman who spied me flying this morning had spoken with the innkeeper, he hadn't called her crazy. He had taken her at her word and checked on his guests. He hadn't accused any of us of wrongdoing, just made sure that everyone was ok.

The buildings seemed to get taller and closer together the farther we got into the city. TownHold was in the oldest part of Tiiaan. Businesses and shops seemed to crowd around closely like eager little children, and when there was no more room to expand out, they had expanded up.

We approached the complex. I tell you truly that I had never seen anything like it. The entire edifice was composed of mechanical pieces. All the buildings in Tiiaan had some form of mechanical decoration, but this massive structure was completely made of metal. Every part of TownHold was in motion. Sections would break away from where they were sitting and move to another spot to attach themselves there. Amazingly, there was almost no sound accompanying the motion. If it were not for the hiss of steam being vented from numerous points of TownHold, I would have thought the movement was the result of magic. I couldn't begin to reason out why this building was the way it was any more than I could figure each mini-building's purpose.

One thing did strike me. TownHold was an appropriate name for the building. I couldn't even begin to imagine a way to attack this place. Magic might be able to take it down, but I doubted it; partially because of the way the building was put together, and partially because this city housed a school for magicians who would undoubtedly have been commissioned to erect magical defenses.

I expected a line of people waiting to enter and was surprised when we were shown directly inside by a guard. We were shown to an office where an attractive young Garanth lady sat at a desk. This was where the line was, though it was still much shorter than I would have expected. We waited for what I guessed to be ten minutes for our turn to be called to the desk.

The walls of the office were unadorned with hangings of any sort. I thought that was strange at first, but then I felt the building shift beneath me, shuddering mildly, and decided that there was good reason for this. A vase of fresh flowers that was secured to the clerk's desk was the only source of color in this room. When the room finally settled back into place, the clerk stood and showed the visitor to the door that we had entered from. When the door was open I caught a flash of a hallway strikingly dissimilar from the one that had been on the other side of that door when we came in.

I looked around briefly, and the building started making a lot more sense. There was only one door in this room. A series of levers built into the clerk's desk controlled the placement of this small building based on where the visitor needed to be. This would also serve to keep people from coming through the front door and having a straight walk to the city's rulers, especially in times of war.

The last person remaining before us was called and, after a brief conversation with the clerk, the building began moving to its new destination. The young clerk waved us over as soon as the door was closed.

"I am Cairna, one of the Clerks of TownHold. Why have you come today?"

I took the lead again. "I am Aaron, and this is Coral and Mikaal. We've come to warn the people of Tiiaan of a great danger approaching the city. We would speak with the City Leaders."

"You must understand that I cannot let everyone who approaches and asks to see the Counsel of Three pass. Most people seem to overestimate the importance of their problems and can be helped just as well by someone else. Would you tell me of this danger so that I can judge?"

"I would prefer to tell the Counsel and let them decide how they want to break the news to the people of Tiiaan. I will tell you though that unless something is done, Tiiaan will not stand twelve more days."

The obsidian-colored skin of the Clerk's face went nearly white. "You must tell me the nature of this danger."

I looked to Mikaal who nodded slightly, then took a deep breath and continued. "I will tell you, but first I will have your word that you will not speak of this to anyone, until the Counsel has made the announcement."

"I will say nothing. You have my word."

"There's a cloud of utter darkness making its way across the face of Sorra. It's called a Chaos Cloud. It can't be stopped by magic or by physical force. Anything that it touches, living or non-living, is changed, corrupted almost beyond recognition. We three are leaving today in search of an artifact that will help us in the fight against the Chaos."

Disbelief flickered across the Clerk's features. Before she could dismiss us out of hand, I mindspoke to Mikaal, suggesting that he might produce some proof. Mikaal spoke for the first time since we left the inn this morning.

"You have seen a chipchuck before?"

The clerk jumped at Mikaal's voice but answered, "Of course."

"Look at this then."

Mikaal took out the Magic bag he had hidden in his clothing and produced from within the small cage containing the corrupted animal he had shown me when I arrived in Sorra. The clerk drew a sharp breath as if she was going to scream, but Coral's hand clamped over her mouth before she could give voice to her panic. When we believed she was no longer going to yell, Coral released her hold on the woman. Cairna looked frightened but stared closely at the contents of the cage for a short time before reaching to her desk and pulling two levers.

"You are correct. The Counsel must see this," she said.

When the floor stopped shaking, Cairna pointed to the door, and we left.

We found ourselves in a long, dimly lit hallway that smelled of oil and metal, with only one door visible at the far end. I stepped ahead and heard my friends following behind. I arrived at the simple wooden door and turned the handle, but the door wouldn't budge.

I heard the click of a latch opening behind me and turned in time to see an elderly Garanth man step out of a hidden door halfway down the hall. His delicate steps brought him to us, and he reached for the same door that I had just attempted to open without saying a word. I saw him make an intricate gesture with his left hand just before the door opened. Locked by magic, of course.

He waved us in before walking over to a group of low couches sitting in a square a short distance from the door. This room was anything but bare; handcrafted books lined the walls on shelves designed to keep them from flying to the floor and getting damaged with the motion of the building. The floor was covered with a thick cushioning foam that had been dyed in whirling patterns, and small tables dotted the area, each set with an OrOboid-made crystal vase holding fresh wildflowers.

The old man sat in the center seat of one of the couches and bade us sit opposite him on another. Seconds passed; the only noise in the room was the creaking of the oldster's leather skin as he smiled at us. When I thought I could stand no more of this nonsense and opened my mouth to say so, I stopped without saying a word. A tapping noise had begun from behind one of the bookcases on the far side of the room. The noise resolved itself into the sound of a cane hitting the floor in a steady cadence. The noise announced the entrance of the remaining two members of the Counsel of Three.

Whereas the old man that sat in the room with us seemed only old and senile, the man who entered was grizzled and rough to the point that one would assume just by looking at him that he had been though several wars. At his side was a lady who appeared perhaps half his age, which is to say she looked as if she still had some spark of life left in her.

These two joined the first old man on the couch facing us. The silence stretched for what seemed an hour, and I began to grow impatient again. Maybe the old thought they had eternity to sit in silence, but we had a mission waiting for someone to speak.

"I assume that you are the Counsel of Three," I said finally.

"That would be a correct assumption, young man," said the woman who would apparently be the speaker for this group. I thanked fate that I wouldn't have to wait for either of the men to finally wake up enough to speak. I made introductions on behalf of our group before lapsing back into silence to wait impatiently for her to respond in kind. I believe that I would have waited the remainder of the day had I not spoken up again.

"Forgive me if sitting in silence is how urgent news is received here, but we are here to warn Tiiaan of danger. There isn't any time to waste. Are we waiting on someone else, maybe someone alive, or should we get started? This city is amazing and worth saving, but we do not have the time to waste in foolish games or protocols that I don't understand."

"Go ahead," the first old man spoke out of the blue.

I sputtered my irritation and continued, "A darkness is growing to the North. It creeps across the land, devouring everything that it touches. It is called a Chaos Cloud. It can't be harmed by magical or physical means. In eleven days, this Cloud will overtake your city. Nothing will survive unscathed. Even the imposing structure we stand in now will be blown away like sand in a dust storm. We don't know of anything that will stop this abomination for sure. We only know that we must prepare in the hope we can prevent this from happening. The Headmasters at the magic school have been alerted and are telling their students today. If everyone in Tiiaan were to work together to find a solution to this problem...."

"Have you any proof?" the woman asked.

Mikaal placed the cage full of proof in front of the Counsel. I suspected that the shock would have killed at least one of the Counsel members, but they didn't even flinch. The first sign of life from the remaining Counsel member came when the caged chipchuck beast appeared.

"So, it is true," he said in awe. "I have heard stories of animals twisted beyond recognition, but I did not believe it."

"You will excuse us for a moment while we confer?" inquired the female Counselor.

Before I could frame a reply, the woman's hand raised and magic sprang to life around the three ancients. They all became more animated than I would have suspected them capable of as they discussed what was to be done. Each Counselor glanced several times at the cage during the course of the discussion. They were finished before I had time to become impatient again. A gesture from the woman and the shielding spell was removed.

The woman said to us, "We will do as you have suggested and warn our people of the danger. We would ask a small favor though. We would like to keep this beast you have brought to us so that we might study it."

"As you wish," I replied. "There will be many more animals that have been touched by the Chaos Cloud where we are going."

I felt an almost imperceptible current of magic disappear from the room. When I looked at the Counsel again, I did not recognize any of them. Where the three old Garanth had stood, a woman no more than five years older than I was flanked by two middle-aged and powerfully built Garanth males. I struggled to keep surprise away from my face and doubted my success.

"We are the Counsel of Three," the taller of the two men said. "I am the Senior Counselman, Athious. This is Clanus, and the lady is Breauus. We apologize for our appearance on your arrival, but we needed to ensure that you were who and what you told Cairna you were."

"I understand. We must start out on our quest now. Good luck."

"Good luck to you and your fellows, Aaron. If the city still stands when you return, please visit us again."

"I would be delighted."

The door we had entered through swung open. Mikaal and Coral reached the door just ahead of me. The long hallway was gone and had been replaced by a white room, similar to the Clerk's office but a fraction of the size. We stepped inside and shut the door.

The floor shifted underneath us as the room began to move. This room was apparently very speedy for we were walking out into the sunlight before I knew it. Outside of TownHold, a small contingent of mages waited for us. They bowed to Mikaal and offered us the reins of several animals. I hesitantly took the reins offered me before inquiring of the mageling what the beast was.

Used as transportation and pack animals by the Garanth, Rhinodons have six legs, which connect to a body longer and thicker than that of a horse. The massive neck holds up a head of equally mammoth proportions. Rhinodons have a single tusk protruding from their bony upper lips, which matches the single eye set in a deep socket high on the long head. The beast was imposing to say the least, but after I pet it a few times it seemed to warm up to me.

The student-mage who gave the beast to me showed me the storage flaps built into the thick hide behind the saddle and told me what supplies were packed inside. The magic school had provided us with enough food to last eight days so that we didn't have to stop to hunt. I was told the commands used to control my Rhinodon, Pakky, and to keep from being thrown from my seat. Within fifteen minutes all three of us were mounted and we were heading towards the eastern city gates.

II

QUESTING FOR THE STAR GLASS

Chapter 9
Fond Farewell

When we reached the eastern gates, the Mackta and his fellow headmasters were waiting. They had brought a gift for each of us. For Mikaal, a new cloak to replace his worn and tattered one. This cloak had been imbued with a defensive spell which activated when danger was present so that he could cast spells unhindered. Coral was given a bow created by the students. It required no arrows as it fired energy bolts that drew from her stored energies.

The Mackta personally presented me with two gifts. The first was a crystal spear made and strengthened by the OrOboid. It was light, strong, and fast but had no magical properties. The second gift was a pair of shoes. Made out of animal hide, they were closer to slippers in design than shoes. They were very comfortable and protected my feet much better than I would have imagined. The Mackta himself had cast the spell that made these shoes special. The shoes lightened gravity slightly for me. This had the effect of making me much quicker and more agile, as well as giving me the ability to jump long distances and carry heavier loads.

We thanked the Headmasters profusely and were about to depart when we heard the first scream. I thought at first that the scream had come from one of the Garanth ladies grouped together behind us. I was quickly disabused of this idea. The scream sounded again, closer this time. I looked to the source of the noise—the sky.

The beast that flew into view above the city was a horrifying sight. I didn't know what kind of bird this had been when it was born, but I was confident that nothing like it existed in nature. When it had been farther away, I thought maybe it was a dragon if they existed here. This was no dragon.

The body of the creature was at least as big as a single-story house with a wingspan of three of Tiiaan's city blocks. It was mostly feathered, but in places the feathers had fallen away to reveal scales like that of a fish. The neck and legs were much too long for the body; the four-toed feet were little more than claws. The head that perched atop the sinuous neck was long and exceptionally narrow. The beak was longer than my blade and easily as sharp. I could see the gleam race along the edges in the sunlight. Venom dripped from a hole just below where the neck met the thing's body, splattering to the ground and steaming and hissing where it fell. It was gray as stone in some places and green in others where its scales showed through.

One of the lesser headmasters shouted out a long string of words, of which I understood enough to get the idea that this had once been a small hunting bird called a Rock Piper. Streaks of light tore from the ground and flew towards the abomination. Only one out of forty or so hit the beast as it blew by unimaginably fast, and that one did no more than singe a small patch on its underbelly.

As the Rock Piper monster turned for another pass Coral decided to play with her new toy. She loosed a bolt from her bow and a battle cry from her lips. The bolt flew straight and true (and amazingly quickly) into the beast's right wing. The beast screamed its anger and raked the air with its claws. When it was over the city it sprayed its venom and ripped two buildings from the ground, one per foot. Several people were covered in the acidic bile, screaming their torment as they died.

The onslaught was met by another volley of fireballs and energy blasts from the magic users of Tiiaan. Mikaal exhorted them to keep firing as he bounded up the side of a building to get a better vantage point. Smoke began to rise from the belly of the beast, but the battle was not going in our favor. Before it got out of range Coral fired another bolt. This one hit the beast in its tail feathers, causing it to lose some maneuverability. A plan began to form in my head.

I took the spear I'd been given and ran into a nearby building. I climbed out the window and onto the roof. On the beast's next run, it came in low so it could rip more buildings from the ground. I jumped as high as I could and launched my spear at the thing's heart. The new shoes allowed me to get great air, but my throw should have still fallen short. I was expecting this, however.

As the spear left my hand, I reached out with my mental hand and carried the spear the rest of the way to my flying target. I heard a solid 'thunk' as my missile hit home. The bird-thing's wings faltered slightly, but it continued to stay aloft. I couldn't tell if my aim had been off, or if the creature had no heart.

It turned, more slowly this time and began coming back at us. I sent out my mental hand again, questing for the shaft of my spear where it protruded from the murderous beast's flesh. When the enemy was directly above, I pulled the spear free and flew it back to my hand. Another shot from Coral landed beside the first tail hit. There were almost no feathers left on the thing's tail now, and it was having a hard time keeping itself in the air. I could also see that it was losing a lot of blood from the spear wound.

I called out to everyone nearby to aim for the thing's head on the count of three. As soon as it turned around again, I began my count. At two, Mikaal appeared on a rooftop closer to the monster's approach and threw a wave of ice particles into its face. At three, a baker's dozen fireballs and bolts flew from the mages around me straight at the face of Tiiaan's attacker. Seven of the projectiles hit the mark this time, one of which took out an eye. The neck of the beast snapped up abruptly and then it fell from the sky.

I was concerned, with good cause, that it would hit the city walls when it went down. As fast as it had been going, it managed to skid to a stop less than an inch away from the West Gate. The monster struggled to rise but was beaten down by a thick rain of magical projectiles. The beast was mostly cooked by the time the city mages stopped firing at it.

A loud cheer rose from the city. A group of City Protectors rode out to make sure that the beast was dead and not just wounded. Then the cleanup work began. Crews began to form around the city to help the injured, remove rubble and remove the twisted body of the creature from outside the city walls.

I watched as several of the nearby Garanth slapped each other on the arms in congratulation and joy. With the plethora of arms available, many were heartily pounding multiple others at a time. The din was wonderous. Coral and I had become separated in the final few seconds of the fight, so I went in search of her. I stepped around a building and found her searching for me as well. Out of habit I smiled and held my hand up for a high five. She walked up grinning and looked from my face to my hand a couple times.

"Why are you holding your palm towards me, Aaron?"

"High-five?" I said sheepishly, feeling foolish.

"Five what?"

I took her left hand in mine, counting her fingers aloud, before I brought her hand to my own with a soft but firm slap.

"Where I come from, this is how we congratulate each other when something goes really well."

"I see," she said with a giggle. "Let me show you how we show that we're happy to have survived…." she said, brushing my cheek with a kiss.

"Your way is better."

"I agree" Mikaal said, dropping from the roof above us to the ground. "I doubt that her way was for everyone though."

Coral and I looked at each other, winked, and grabbed Mikaal together, both of us planting a chaste congratulatory kiss on his cheek before falling to the ground in a heap. We sat laughing in relief and elation at being alive for a few moments.

This episode only reinforced to us that haste was needed, so we made our rapid goodbyes to the Mackta and the other headmasters. I cleaned my spearhead, and we urged our mounts forward. As we passed through the crowd near the gates, everyone stopped what they were doing to watch us go. I feared that the Tiiaanians thought that I was the cause of the attack because I was different; but this was not so.

A few people had seen me make an impossible throw with my spear and the word had been traveling through the crowd as we were talking with the Headmasters. Others recognized that I had led the final attack that brought down the beast. Amidst the rubble shouts broke out, people asking for my name. I only grew embarrassed and ducked my head, but Coral's unmistakable voice rang out strong and clear like a chorus of trumpets.

Once the people knew my name, a chant began quietly and picked up volume as we rode. The chant was simply: "Aaron! Aaron! Aaron!" repeated again and again. At that moment, I fervently wished I had developed the power to become invisible in this world. I held my head as high as my unease would allow until we passed through the gates and out of the city.

We traveled in silence for quite some time after we left the city. I doubted that we would have heard each other even if we had spoken. Pakky and his friends were marvelously fast but also very noisy. Rhinodons have feet instead of hooves, comically large two-toed feet that made slapping noises when they hit the dry earth of the path. The three animals together sounded like I imagine a Garanth mother in a room full of naughty children.

Chapter 10
Back to the Wild

When the sun had passed its zenith, we stopped our mounts for a rest and lunch. I slid out of my saddle, and Coral echoed my grunt of pain. None of us were frequent riders. Mikaal was better off than the two of us as he had no thigh muscles to bother him. We walked around for a few minutes to free the kinks in our legs before dipping into Pakky's storage compartments and retrieving a bit of food.

I realized that I was still wearing my travel pack, so I took this opportunity to store it. While I was chewing my food, I decided to have a little fun. I summoned up a mental hand and picked some fruit from a nearby tree. I brought the fruit into the area between my friends and myself before summoning another mental hand. This was the first time that I had tried controlling more than one hand, but it wasn't much different than controlling a hand and a barrier.

Slowly at first, I began to juggle the fruit. The animals didn't seem to enjoy the sight, but Coral laughed and clapped her hands like a child. Juggling must not exist here I decided. I sent the fruit twirling in a few other patterns before slowing them in the air and feeding them to our mounts. I looked at Mikaal who had not made a noise while I was brain juggling and sensed a bit of disapproval. I asked him why he looked displeased.

He felt that I would need all of my strength for the tasks ahead, and I shouldn't use my power for something so frivolous. I called him an old sourpuss and told him that when the end of the world was staring at you, you had to keep your spirits up if you wanted to make it through. He lightened up a little, and when I said that I needed the practice anyway, he gave in and threw me a smile.

When we finished eating, we mounted back up and continued on our way. I was bothered by the thought that our only plan for stopping the unbinding was that I would try to push my gifts through some artifact and hope something happened. Everyone looked to me for their salvation, but I had no idea what to do or even where to begin. I'd never even seen the thing I was supposed to be fighting. More than anything I was afraid of letting my friends down. I thought that I would be able to find the Star Glass, but everything beyond that seemed too much for me to handle. I fought to calm myself. I just had to take this one day at a time and hope that I was up to the challenge.

I decided to practice my magic hunting skills before we got to the mines. I closed my eyes and pushed the sounds of travel far from my mind. I could see Mikaal even in the darkness, and his magic shone like a beacon to me. Coral had a lesser glow around her. I searched the immediate area for magic, not surprised to find none. Looking back towards the city, I could see the immense blaze even from here.

I turned my magic sense back in the direction we were traveling and was surprised to see a brightly glowing spot in the road some distance ahead. I sent a mental note to Coral and Mikaal to be ready for trouble and continued to watch the magic glow creep closer. When we seemed to be right on top of the glow, I opened my eyes and slowed my mount.

No person of any race was on the path so I began to scan the area again in hopes that I could locate the source. I mentally called for a halt. We all dismounted and tethered our animals to a tree just off the road but away from where the unknown creature had passed before continuing to watch the glow. The road was very wide and whatever I was seeing was off to one side of us. We had stopped, but the source of magic continued to make its way towards us undaunted by our presence. It was moving slowly, but enough that I could mark its progress.

I was so focused on tracking the thing that I was surprised to realize that I was looking straight down. The magic was passing directly below me. I had begun to turn so that I could track it further when I heard a groan and the earth beneath me gave way. I was given little chance to protest this fate as the dirt road that I had been standing on and I exchanged places. Buried alive!

I fought to control my panic, finally pushing it away. I wasn't helpless in this world. I formed a mental barrier just above me and pushed upward with all my remaining willpower. I heard a whoosh as air rushed in to take the place of the lightly packed earth and a surprised yell as my two worried companions were showered with dirt.

Freed of my makeshift burial vault, I was able to move around. By the squalid daylight filtering from above I made out a small underground cavern. I sent some brainmail to Coral and told her that I was ok and was looking for the cause of the cave-in. She sent back that she was glad I was not hurt and to be careful. I caught a whisper of Coral's voice as she passed the message along to Mikaal.

The dirt had shifted in the collapse, and I had to dig a hole big enough for me to squeeze through, and even then it was a close fit. The being that I was following was either not very big, or else it felt more comfortable in enclosed areas than I did. The cavern was big enough to allow me to crawl instead of slithering on my belly like some underground snake. I quickly looked around with that thought, but I was blind in this darkness. I wished for some gift that would allow me to see in darkness.

When no such gift manifested itself, I began crawling towards the receding magical glow. I bumped into rock formations more than once on my journey across the dark passage. I was still making progress, and even gaining a little bit on my quarry, when I ran hard into a solid rock face. Frustrated, I clawed at the rock, moving left and right in an attempt to bypass this latest obstacle. It became quickly apparent that this was the end of the line for me. The cavern had ended.

I moved back over to where I thought the creature should have come through. After fumbling around in the darkness for a few minutes, I found a hole that had been cut into the rock. This hole was only a little larger than my thigh. I was beginning to wonder if this tiny digger was sentient, or if it was just a magically enhanced animal. I could still see its glow moving slowly away from me. I didn't want to take the chance that I might hurt my friends by pushing through to the surface, but I couldn't find my way back to where I had fallen with no light to guide me.

I contacted Mikaal and Coral and told them to watch the ground around them before forming a very small barrier and pushing upwards. When my barrier reached the surface, I asked them if they were able to see the soil that I had disturbed. They didn't see anything at all, so I must have been a good distance away from them. I formed another barrier above myself, large enough that I would be able to pass through it on my way to the surface. After I had moved this load of terrain to the surface, I flew myself upward and landed on a freshly made mountain of sorts.

I used my mental hands to scoop large amounts of earth back into the hole I had made. When I had patched up my escape route, I yelled, hoping to attract the attention of my companions. I heard them crashing through the brush a short distance to my left. I turned my magical vision back down to where I had last seen the creature. I was surprised to see that it had started up towards the surface.

My physical eyes were just coming back into focus when a dirt-covered Coral slammed into me, taking us both to the ground. I never had a chance to say anything. As soon as we slid to a stop, Coral began kissing me. I was completely out of breath before she broke the kiss. I breathed in deeply and looked at her in surprise.

Salty green tears fell from her eyes to land softly on my chest. I freed my right hand and after wiping most of the dirt from it, used my thumb to wipe the tears from her eyes. I brought my thumb to my mouth and tasted her sorrow. She had obviously been sobbing as her breaths were coming in gasps that could not have been caused by the short run from the road to me.

"You frightened me, Aaron!" Coral gasped breathlessly. "After you told us to look for you to come up, we didn't hear anything else from you. We looked everywhere and listened for any sign of you. It was really quiet, and I tried to reach you. After so long without a word I thought you were lying crushed somewhere and we'd never find you."

I held her close, whispering in her ear, "It will take more than that to keep me from you."

I sensed that Mikaal had gone off to one side after seeing Coral's emotional display and thanked him silently for the consideration.

I loosened my arms around Coral and took her face in my dirty hands. Tear tracks in the earth that dusted her face made her more attractive than ever to me because I knew her tears were for me. I kissed her then, pouring out all of my stored-up feelings for her through my lips. It wasn't as long a kiss as I would have liked because I was very conscious of the fact that whatever had nearly killed me was still nearby. I broke the kiss and looked at her for a second, searching her eyes for a hint of the depths of her feelings for me. I formed a barrier between my back and the ground and lifted us to a standing position.

When we were upright, I spoke to Mikaal, who had his back to us. I still had my arm around Coral, but she pulled away when she saw Mikaal's eyes go wide and realized that I was bloodied in several places from my ordeal.

"Huh...'tis but a scratch, or maybe a few," I exclaimed in my best mock British accent, forgetting they wouldn't have any context.

"Then it won't take long to heal," Mikaal replied tartly. "Stand still please."

"Thank you for letting us be sure," Coral added, brushing the dirt away and inspecting the wounds as they vanished.

When he finished his repairs, I let my focus slip into magic mode and started looking around again. I saw that the glow was much closer than before and traveling above ground. We made our way back to the path and waited for our guest to arrive.

A small furry creature came into view around the base of a tree; its size and big floppy ears making me think it was a rabbit. It neared us and I watched in amazement as it grew from no bigger than the height of my knee to standing just below the bridge of my nose. My magic sight revealed that only a small part of the power this woman carried was within her. She carried a satchel at her side. I couldn't tell what was inside, but whatever it was, it was very powerful.

After all I had been through, I was expecting some crazed and tormented animal to come tearing out of the brush at us. Seeing a perfectly healthy young Moalean stride up to us was certainly a surprise. The only other Moalean I had seen to this point was Maegen, one of the Headmasters of the Magic school. Maegen had worn clothes, so I naturally assumed that this was the norm for the species. The female Moalean that stood in front of me wasn't wearing any clothes, and her thick fur was caked with dirt from burrowing through the ground. Apparently, they only wear clothes when they are among the other races and it is expected of them.

"Explain yourself!" I said.

The young woman started at my tone and stood for a moment looking confused before answering, "You are not a digger, yet you follow me through the earth and then command me to explain myself. I would think that you are the one that needs to explain yourself."

"I followed you only after you caused the road to cave in and bury me. Why did you attack me?"

The young woman looked truly mortified. (If I was reading her expressions correctly. Moalean faces are so different from any other race.) "I did not mean to bury you, sir. I was simply trying to hurry and was careless. I went right through a bit of stone that must have been holding up the road where you were standing. I heard the collapse behind me, but I did not know you had been harmed, or I would have returned to help. When I heard you following me and getting closer by the minute, I thought you were a Rigglewerm interested in having me for dinner, and I fled as fast as I could. When you reached the surface and called to your friends, I heard you and realized you were intelligent and came to investigate. I have never seen anything like you. What are you?"

"I am human. I have come through a portal from another world in answer to a summons by this Noran."

As often as I have to 'splain myself, I wished I had this as a recording I could just play. Maybe something fun, like in the voice of Lucille Ball.

The Moalean woman's claws flashed, and she growled as she said: "You must be the bringer of the darkness that is destroying our homes!" She tensed to spring but was interrupted by the energy bolt that seared into the ground between us. Coral strode towards the woman with her bow drawn back and said, "Aaron would do no such thing. He was called to help us stop the darkness from spreading. We are on our way now to locate an artifact which may help him defeat the Chaos Cloud and whatever is causing it."

Maybe I needed a big neon sign over my head that reads "Not the bad guy!" while I'm at it.

The woman sheathed her claws. "I am sorry," she said. "The Cloud you spoke of overtook my mate-to-be in the night, changing him into a monster. He tried to kill me, and I had to flee. That is why I was in such a hurry. I know that the Cloud had to have come from another world, and I assumed...."

Coral lowered her bow.

"I understand. No harm, no foul. Let's start again. I'm Aaron. The archer maiden is Coral and this," I said pointing at Mikaal, "is Mikaal."

"I am Junean," she said, with a confused look.

"Good. Junean, how far was your mate-to-be behind you?"

"Not very far. He must have heard the sound of our voices by now. I would expect him to be here soon."

"Mikaal, do you have a spell that will freeze him in time?"

Mikaal responded, "Yes, Aaron. I will prepare to cast it." His gaw flashed madly, and he was hanging from a nearby tree.

"What do you want me to do?" Junean asked.

"Hmmm. Are you any good at making protective shields?"

"Yes."

"Good. Place one around you and our animals, then make another one to keep the animals from harming you if they try to bolt. Be sure that the shields won't allow him to get to you underground."

"He is my responsibility; I should not be hiding behind a shield while you three risk your lives!" Junean said excitedly.

I said in my most soothing voice, "I understand how you feel, but this is where you can do the most good for my plan to work. You must trust us."

She simply nodded and moved off towards the animals.

"What is his name?" I asked Junean.

"Tibbeus" she replied.

"Alright. Coral, you and I will flank Tibbeus as he comes after Junean. If he comes at you, Coral, I want you to run. Nobody hurt him unless you have to. This is the first intelligent being altered by the Unbinding that we have faced. So, let's be extra careful. Mikaal, are you ready to cast that spell?"

"Yes. It should work. What will you do with him when we have him?"

While I was talking, I had been looking for the presence of magic. I saw it now. Tibbeus was here.

"No time to talk. Tibbeus just arrived," I said.

I was the only one who could see him because he was too far away, but that didn't last long. Tibbeus was the size of a child when I first saw him. Within two minutes he was taller than the few trees around us. He came on slowly, sniffing at the air. Most of the fur that had covered his body was gone, metallic skin gleaming in its place. It looked as if iron had been leached from the ground to coat him from head to toe.

The long, curved nails that graced the hands of the Moalean had grown longer still and had somehow been straightened. Each nail was as long as my blade and had taken on much the same form. Tibbeus' nighttime eyes were open now, contrary to his normal instincts, and bright light poured from them, swinging back and forth as he surveyed our positions. Stone antlers had grown at the peak of his head and a foul stench nearly knocked us all senseless when the wind shifted towards us. A sob escaped Junean when she saw Tibbeus, but she bit it back quickly.

My plan wouldn't work if I couldn't get him to shrink himself back down to normal size. I racked my brain as the beast-that-was-Tibbeus advanced on us. Coral fired a few weak blasts at it as it came closer, drawing its attention, popping up to fire, but hiding and moving quickly to another spot. When he was close enough for his horrific odor to fill the air, I came up with a plan. Coral's quick thinking bought me critical seconds I needed to enact it.

I searched quickly until I found a mammoth rock off in the distance near the mountains. Working as quickly as I was able, I sent my invisible hand out and strove to free it from where the elements significant weight had cemented it to the ground. The Tibbeus creature was almost on top of us when I got the rock close enough to act. I waved the giant rock in his face a couple of times and then flew it straight at him. He ducked to the side. I brought it back around and hit him on the side of the head. Not hard enough to cause serious damage or to break my stone but enough to get the thing's attention.

I struggled to keep the boulder at the same height as his head. Tibbeus snarled at the rock and swung at it. I moved it out of his range and then back in to clobber him on the opposite side of his head. My rock crunched into his right antler, bending it. We went back and forth a few more times until finally instinct took effect. I flew the big rock directly at his face, but by the time it got to where he was it flew directly over his head. Yes! Due to a dislike of being clocked with a boulder, he was shrinking himself. He was still just a little bit too tall for my liking, so I pressed on.

I sent out my other mental hand and broke the stone in two. The sound of the stone splitting caught Tibbeus' attention just as he was getting ready to take a swing at Junean and the animals. I brought the twin stones down to his level once again and set them to spinning. I swirled the rocks around Tibbeus' head, dipping them into his range enough to get him to swing at them and then back out again several times. Then I brought them together when he was off balance to knock him on both sides of the head at once. As I pulled them away, I crashed them into his antlers trying to disorient him even further. He didn't play the game nearly as long this time before he shrank himself again. Now he was only a little taller than I. Close enough.

Before Tibbeus could test Junean's shields, I told Mikaal to cast his spell. He had anticipated the request. The spell went off almost at the same time I told him to cast it. Before the first blow fell against us, Tibbeus froze. I looked at him with my magic sight. The only glow that showed was the glow of Mikaal's spell. Tibbeus himself had no aura of magic now.

We all met down by the statue that Tibbeus had become. When I inquired, Mikaal said that his spell would last indefinitely. I asked Mikaal if we could put Tibbeus in the magic bag that he carried in his clothes. The little Noran burst out in a fit of mirth. Junean looked hurt until he explained that he was laughing because I had come up with a perfect yet simple solution that had eluded him.

All of us together were able to get the bag over Tibbeus. When we were done Mikaal handed the still empty seeming bag to Junean. He then pulled out an identical magic bag and told us that the one we had put Tibbeus in was an empty spare he had on him in case of emergency. Junean was pleased at how we had handled the situation. More than that, I offered her some hope, however slim, that we might be able to restore her lover.

"Do you think Tibbeus will ever be the same again?" Junean sniffled.

"I can't promise anything other than that I will try, and that we stand a better chance together. I know about losing loved ones. If I can prevent you that pain…"

"If anybody can do it, I believe Aaron can." Coral said firmly, gripping my hand.

"So, we will face the unimaginable, with someone who does the impossible. I will travel with you." The digger lady announced.

Junean had been returning to her home, the cavern city called Fellinat, to report on a series of tests she and Tibbeus had been conducting on the Chaos Cloud and to report the loss of Tibbeus. Since she wouldn't be returning, she needed to send a message to her father in Fellinat. She surprised me by pulling out a small stone carving of a Moalean man with wings, speaking to it briefly as if it were her father, telling it to "Go to Innean," and throwing it into the air. I was even more surprised when the tiny rock wings of the statue began pumping in the air. The statue was out of sight before I finished gasping my astonishment. I had thought that nothing in this world would surprise me after the events of the last few days. Wrong again.

Chapter 11
Things That Go Bump

We turned our attention to the animals, who were all understandably shaken up. We made soothing noises while sending mental waves of calm. Pakky was eating out of my hand, literally, in two minutes. The problem of having one less mount than we had riders was solved quickly and without fuss. Junean shrank herself down to her natural size and found a spot to ride standing on the supplies in one of the storage flaps of Coral's Rhinodon. Quickly we were on our way to the mountains again.

Three more hours of Rhinodon-powered travel brought us to the foothills of the SrakeKepp mountain range. We decided to set up our campsite before trekking farther into the mountains. The temperature had already begun to drop, and the sun had not completely set. We tethered the Rhinodons to the largest tree we could find, hoping it would hold them through the night. This close to Srake Peake, the oldest and highest mountain, trees were scarce. The few that did grow were gangly, scraggly things.

Pakky began to graze as soon as his legs stopped moving. Junean grew to our size when we began to unpack food from the animals. The provisions given to us by the magic school were packed for each of us based on our preferred source of food. Mikaal, Coral, and I ate very few vegetables, and I worried about Junean until she produced another magical stone carving from the bag slung at her side. It was shaped like a tree leaf and hinged. Each time she opened it up it held a goodly sized piece of infinitely light green moss. We all set about the business of filing our bellies. No one spoke. In the shadow of the mountain, we all felt small and helpless against the darkness rushing towards us.

Coral began to shiver as she leaned against her mount. I turned and fished through the pouch in Pakky's flank for my pack and then once again as I searched for the leather jacket Mikaal had made me when we first met. I grunted in triumph when I found it. No one was really looking at anyone else, and so as I moved slowly around the Rhinodons and out of view I wasn't noticed. I moved without sound as I slipped around the tree holding the animals and right up behind Coral. Her skin looked more like waves than usual because the gooseflesh gave her skin texture.

I placed the leather jacket around her bare shoulders, and she leaned back into me as I did so. I wrapped my arms around her, and we stood there together unnoticed for several minutes before I slid noiselessly back to where I had been standing.

The final meal of the day transitioned into preparations for sleep. Mikaal put up his defensive barrier as always, and Coral and I each pulled out our respective blankets and spread them on the ground. Junean simply shrunk herself to child size again and loosened up the soil beneath her. She was snoring contentedly before we had even laid down. Mikaal had no tree near enough that would support his weight, so he reached into his magical pouch and pulled out a large cushion.

I was the last person to fall asleep. I kept staring out into the night and wondering if the Unbinding was a natural occurrence that slipped through from another world, or if something had created it and was now controlling its path. I wanted to think that this was just a really bad storm that had gotten really far off course, but something in the way it was moving made me believe that there was an intelligence behind it all. Finally, I drifted off.

Things That Go Bump

I was woken two hours later by screams. I rolled off to one side, ready for action, before I realized that Junean was dreaming. Not wanting to risk her sharp nails, I reached out with a mental hand and shook her gently. She clawed at the air in desperation and terror. I would have lost a hand had I tried that with flesh instead of energy. I called to her and shook her again, less gently this time, and she came out of her dream with a sharp intake of breath.

I was amazed that none of the others were awakened by the din. Perhaps I was a lighter sleeper or maybe it was the rock I had apparently been sleeping on that kept me nearer consciousness.

Junean sobbingly told the story of what happened.

"When Tibbeus and I...." she faltered as the sobs of someone who had cried long and deep shook her. "When we reached the edge of the Chaos Cloud, we set up camp and began our tests. But after an entire day using all our skills, nothing we did had any effect."

They decided to try again at night in the hopes that it was powered by the daylight. After waiting through the day, talking and relaxing in preparation for the long night ahead, they readied themselves as the sun fell.

When the first magical item came out of the bag Junean carried at her side, the ground began to rumble. The Cloud wall began to throb as far as they could see in both directions. A wail, like the sound of eternal sorrow and unending hunger echoed across the forest. The Cloud rippled outward and began to grow—straight toward them.

"Hope vanished in that moment, and we ran for our lives."

Coral startled me when she crawled out of the darkness and put a steadying hand on Junean's arm.

"We ran far and fast before...." She struggled against emotion to continue. "Before Tibbeus tripped over a fallen tree. The trunk had been balanced atop a stone, and the impact was enough to start the tree rolling. When the dust settled, Tibbeus legs were wedged under the tree trunk.

"I did everything I could think of to save him" she whispered. "I was prepared to stay with him to meet the cloud together." Tibbeus pleaded with her to run, eventually convincing her that the best thing was to save herself and try to find a way to restore him later.

She had watched him change as she ran. Now the memory of that terrible sight had come back to haunt her in the night. We calmed her as much as we were able before returning to our sleep.

I wasn't able to sleep right away. I seemed to have too much pent-up energy. This had always been a figure of speech to me. Now I really did have too much energy. Since I was storing my energy instead of wasting it, I noticed that I produced far more energy than I seemed to need. Flying boulders around for several minutes hadn't even put a dent in the power that I had generated today. Seeing magic seemed to be more of an innate talent and did not require any power.

I went inside my mind and looked at the storage area that I had created. The mental door was closed, but it was bulging out, loose energy spilling to the floor. I created another room beside the first one and transferred some of the energy over. This alleviated some of my restlessness, but I was still feeling like a teapot that was getting ready to boil over. The only thing that I could think of that would burn off energy was to fly. Even that took very little effort and therefore little power, but maybe it would be enough to take the edge off and allow me to sleep.

I lifted myself, blanket and all, off the ground. I lay there in mid-air for a few minutes before having a brainstorm. If I needed to burn off some energy and flying took only a little bit of energy, maybe I could burn more if I lifted everyone else. I decided to start with Pakky. I placed a mental barrier below the sleeping animal and began to lift. Once he was on a level with me, I lifted the next animal. I continued this way until only Mikaal remained on the ground. I was able to lift three animals and three people (including myself) all on separate mental platforms! I was getting better at this.

I tried to form another barrier beneath Mikaal and almost dropped everyone. Strong as I was becoming, I couldn't create that many barriers at once just yet. I set the animals back down one at a time and banished the barriers that had held them; then I created one big barrier below the three of them. This proved to be much easier to handle.

I turned my attention back to Mikaal and was just forming the barrier beneath him when the shadow appeared. It seemed to be a thing with little or no substance, but I could see it when it moved, and I knew it was both real and dangerous. I only saw the one at first, as it appeared where I happened to be looking, but lightning quick Mikaal was covered with them. I lifted him from the ground as quickly as I was able without dropping the rest of us. The shadow creatures moved along the ground and didn't seem capable of flying or jumping up to us on our invisible platforms.

I brought Mikaal closer so that I could try to help him. I could see that several of the shadows remained attached to his gaw. Dark patches had begun to grow on his skin near the creatures. I had not tried to directly touch any corrupted creatures with my mental hands before and worried that I might lose control of the platforms if anything unexpected happened. Nevertheless, I had to act quickly.

Stretching my gifts to the limit, I reached out with a phantom hand and grasped one of the shadows. I did not feel any mental assaults, so I continued. Pulling gently but firmly, I was able to remove the shadow from Mikaal's flesh. I held it out away from my friends and squeezed it until it popped before going back to remove another one.

When I held the last of the mental creatures in my disembodied hand, I brought it close, studying it to see what harm it had done so I could undo it. I turned the thing over several times before I recognized it.

It was, or originally had been, some form of earthworm. The Shadowworm, as I dubbed it, was as thick as my forearm and seemed to be able to vary its length. Even looking at it as closely as I was, the worm seemed to be continually blurring at the edges. I sent a message to Coral telling her that danger was near and to wake up but not to move. Incredibly quick, she was alert and sitting up. Coral was a true hunter and always slept with her bow beside of her, and I asked her to begin shooting Shadowworms. I was starting to develop a splitting headache from the constant concentration required to keep us all aloft.

Less than a minute after she regained consciousness, Coral had cleaned the area of the threat. I sent a message to Junean to wake her up as well before lowering first the animals and then the rest of us to the ground. My headache receded a little when my flying mental barriers disappeared.

Mikaal luckily slept through the whole thing. I had a suspicion that the Shadowworms were some of the worst foes we had seen yet. While not particularly deadly, the marks on Mikaal looked a lot like the flesh of some of the creatures that had been altered by the Unbinding.

On the upside, once the Shadowworms had been removed, the dark spots didn't continue to grow. Mikaal's gaw were the only thing the Shadowworms had attached themselves to. Since his gaw were the only part of him that had remained uncovered while he slept, this seemed logical. With a discarnate hand at the ready, I woke Mikaal.

He seemed to be in his right mind, but with his gaw caught between their natural state and something completely unnatural, he was incapacitated by incredible amounts of pain. Junean pulled a figure out of her bag in the dark and spoke to it. I couldn't make out the shape, but its eyes began to glow, and as she placed it beside Mikaal his pain seemed to lessen. None of us, even Mikaal, had any way of repairing the damage done, but I had to try something.

I pulled into myself to think. Some distance outside my head I heard the twang of a bowstring as Coral shot a straggling Shadowworm. So far, I had been able to handle most challenges by creating something in my head that I was familiar with from my birth world. I hoped that this tactic would work again.

I sat there thinking to myself: What could I create that would help Mikaal now? There were no Unbindings or Shadowworms in the world I had been born into. No form of technology had ever been invented to deal with this situation. If I could only see what had been done to him. Then it came to me.

I brought a microscope into being within my mind. The twin windows in the room of my mind that I had connected with my physical eyes were still where I had placed them. I brought the microscope to the window connected to my right eye and told my body to close my left eye. I focused the microscope on one of the dark spots on Mikaal's gaw.

This was actually working! I was able to see the individual cells in his skin. The cells in the dark spots looked similar compared to the cells farther up Mikaal's gaw where the Shadowworms had not been able to do any damage. What I needed to do was to look at Mikaal's DNA.

I guessed that only an electron microscope could accomplish that, but maybe my mental reconstruction wasn't bound to the exact same rules as the physical models in my birth world. I turned the magnification power dial on the bottom of my microscope to a level that would allow me to see what was really going on.

I focused on a healthy area of Mikaal's skin and looked at his DNA. There was no possible way that I was going to be able to remember every minute detail of what the healthy DNA looked like when I was looking at the corrupted DNA. I thought about the problem for a minute before creating an instant camera with an attachment for the eyepiece of my microscope. I quickly clipped the camera into place and took a snapshot. When the image resolved itself, I set it on the sill of the window and moved the microscope to where I would be able to look at one of the darkened areas.

The Journals of Aaron the White

"Aaron?" Coral's voice, but I wasn't sure whether I was hearing her or it was mindspeak.

"Yes?"

"We haven't seen any more of those worm things for a bit now. You've been sitting there for several minutes staring at Mikaal's gaw while he writhes in pain. Can you help him? Can we help you help him? Junean is still trying to take away his pain. I thought about trying to heal him but wasn't sure if that would mess up anything you might be doing."

"I'm so sorry. I have an idea to help that I'm hoping will work. I should have said something before I started. I hope it won't' be much longer. I know being a lookout isn't much fun but keeping us safe is something I can't do right now. I need to focus on trying to help Mikaal."

"It's alright. We'll keep watch over you as long as needed," she said warmly.

After removing the camera, it took me half a minute to refocus the microscope. When I placed my inner eye to the microscope, I gasped in astonishment. Every section of the DNA had been twisted or replaced entirely. No wonder Mikaal was in such pain! His skin was literally tearing itself apart. I didn't know much about DNA, but I realized that Mikaal's body was looking at the altered skin as foreign and had begun to reject it. I had to do something quickly.

I brought my mental hand into being in the air beside me. I concentrated hard and the hand began to shrink. I continued to shrink the apparition until it was no longer visible. Then I sent it into the eyepiece of the microscope. I looked into the eyepiece, which was only partially blocked by the phantom arm, and guided my mental hand to the DNA chain. I closed the hand over it and began to pull it back through the microscope.

As my hand and the payload it carried came out of the eyepiece, they grew. I looked closely at the DNA chain and at the picture on the window cell and began to rebuild each link, moving bits around by hand until it looked the same as the picture. Uncounted minutes passed as I worked. When I was finished, the picture and the chain I held at least looked the same. I wasn't going to be able to help Mikaal if I had to rebuild each DNA chain that was damaged. I decided to create chains identical to the one I now held and replace the damaged ones. I hoped that his body would be able to repair the damage from that point.

I made a copy of the DNA chain I now held and carefully compared this new chain to the one that I had repaired. As far as I could tell, they matched. I realized that I would have to make these small enough to be effective if I wanted them to do Mikaal any good. First, I created a syringe at the base of the microscope and focused on it. Then I took the twin chains in my mental hand and forced them back through the microscope. The mental hand was no longer needed, so I caused it to fade to mist.

I knew that I would have to bend the laws of reality that I was familiar with for this to work, but that hadn't stopped me so far. In fact, it sounded like fun. I looked through the eyepiece and began to rapidly create replacement DNA chains until the syringe was almost full. When I finished this task, I pulled my eye away from the microscope and closed the syringe. As a precaution, I mentally added to the syringe a virus that would destroy only damaged chains and replace them with my altered chains. I didn't want to accidently start a zombie Noran pandemic on top of the current crisis. I shook the mixture well and went to the window. I hoped that this creation of my imagination would be able to help my friend. I re-created my mental hand and with it, took the syringe from my physical hand. I went to the window and sent the disembodied hand and the imaginary syringe through it. I began injecting the virus into the affected areas of Mikaal's skin. When I was done, I pulled out of my mental room back to reality to watch Mikaal and hope. For once I was glad for the experience I had giving shots. Between giving my grandmother injections and taking over from the Vet when he was too frail to wrestle our stubborn mule at vaccination time, I had gotten pretty adept at it.

The night was deadly quiet except for the whimpers coming from the little Noran. Coral and Junean stood nearby taking turns watching over us and searching the darkness for danger. I smiled weakly at the two of them before returning my attention to Mikaal. His whimpers turned to tears as the virus began attacking the rogue DNA. Even Junean's little Aspirin statue (that is the way I thought of it anyway) wasn't much help against the pain caused by having your DNA scrambled and unscrambled. I hoped that what I had done was doing some good. Every sound of pain that came from Mikaal burned into me. I could not think of anything that I could do to ease his suffering. If the magic statue wasn't able to help....

We sat with Mikaal for an hour before his pain-wracked sobs finally decreased in intensity. When I looked, it seemed that Mikaal's gaw were returning to their normal color before my eyes. When the dark spots were only a few shades darker than the surrounding skin, Mikaal sat up. He took hold of the Aspirin statue and handed it back to Junean, thanking her for her help. Then he turned to me.

"What did you do?"

"I found what was broken and fixed it."

"How?"

"I used knowledge and ideas from my world that I barely understand, and I did my best to recreate them in my mind and use them here in Sorra."

I could tell that Junean was ready to burst, thinking that I could do the same thing for Tibbeus. I didn't wait for her to ask. I couldn't let her get her hopes up too high.

"I'm sorry, Junean. The only reason that this worked on Mikaal is because he wasn't completely changed. Maybe sometime in the future, I will be able to find a way to restore Tibbeus. I am sorry. Right now, I just do not have the power."

She lowered her head and in a strong voice said, "I trust you and I believe that you will find a way to set things right again."

"Thank you."

I bent over and took one of Mikaal's gaw in my hand, looking at the coloring and making sure that it seemed ok. The skin was darker than it had been, but it seemed mostly normal.

"How do you feel?"

"Tired. My gaw still hurt a little bit, but I think they are back to normal."

"Can you move them normally?"

Mikaal wiggled his gaw slightly and tried to stand up. He took a few steps and turned around, quickly returning to his sleeping cushion.

The night was only half over, and we all were desperately in need of sleep. I had certainly used up enough energy that I no longer felt restless.

"Before we sleep, we need to understand how these Shadowworms had gotten through Mikaal's barrier," I said to the group at large.

I looked around us with my magic sight and saw that barrier was still up. I looked at the ground until I located the place where the worms had churned the earth. When Mikaal had created the barrier, he had formed it to protect us from burrowing creatures as well as those who walked on the ground. I went to my knees at the worm tunnel and began to dig.

A few feet down, I ran into the barrier. When I cleared enough dirt away, it was easy to see that the barrier had been eaten through. Large holes matched the tunnels in diameter. I could only conclude that Shadowworms shared the Chaos Cloud's ability to destroy magic. We would have to do something to protect against worm bites.

I had Mikaal re-create the barrier and asked for suggestions as to what we could do. Coral had little in the way of skills to deal with burrowing creatures. She was from the sea and had never even seen diggers except for a few Moalean. Junean however had a solution. She reached into her satchel and pulled out a thin stone disk carved with intricate spirals. She breathed once on the disk, bent over and buried it flat in the ground.

"This should keep anything from approaching us from below. If they get within twenty hands of the disk and are not repelled, the disk will make a loud noise to alert us." Junean explained to us.

Feeling almost safe once again, Mikaal and the women tried to sleep. I walked over to see to the animals. They were all shivering with fear, and I spent several minutes calming them. I walked back towards my travel blanket, which was on the far side of our campsite from the animals. I stopped when I got to Coral and sat down beside her.

I loved looking at her. I could sit still and watch her for hours and never grow tired of the view. Her shimmering skin caught the faintest light and sent it dancing in every direction. Her close-set eyes showcased her every emotion, and the light of life burned brightly in them. Her cute, tiny little nose was more perfectly suited to her face than any person I had known before. Her small mouth was framed by thin dark-blue lips that begged to be kissed. Every inch of her skin was smooth and free of blemishes. She was simply the most feminine woman that I could imagine. I would save this world for one of her smiles.

Sitting there, I finally allowed myself to realize that I had fallen completely in love with this woman. I didn't want to wake her up, but I wanted her to know how I felt. I didn't know if she knew how to read, or if the way I had learned to write would be understood here. I decided to send her a mental note. As soon as I sent the message to her, she smiled. I thought that I had woken her up. Mortified, I mentally lifted myself off the ground and flew myself to my blanket as quickly as I could. I looked at Coral's form lying on the ground. She hadn't moved, but the smile on her face never dimmed.

Chapter 12
To the Mines

The rest of the night passed without incident, but we awoke bleary-eyed and haggard. I had my back to my companions and was rolling up my bedroll when I heard Mikaal grumpily ask Coral what on Sorra she was smiling about. She had no answer for him; she just knew that she woke up happy. I did not feel very rested either, but when I turned around I had a rather large smile on my face as well.

"Come on Mikaal. The sun is shining. We survived the night. Brighten up! Are you still in pain?" I said.

"I apologize. Yes, Aaron, I still have pain. I will try to work a healing on myself."

Mikaal sat down on the ground and began a low chant. I could sense the magic building within and around him. Rings of light blue appeared around his gaw, moving slowly away from his torso. I moved closer to Mikaal and magnified my vision again so that I could watch his healing take place. I was amazed that nothing visibly changed as the magic took effect. When the magic had finished its work, Mikaal breathed a sigh of relief. Well, I guess I wasn't really much of a healer. Maybe with practice and more imagination I would be more effective.

"Feeling better now?" Junean asked.

"Yes. The pain is gone."

We put together a quick breakfast of bread and cheese from the supply packs. The bread was the most recognizable thing I had eaten since being on Sorra. Not only did it look like what I was familiar with, it actually tasted much the same. The cheese was a different story. Mikaal called it Sal Cheese. It was probably the strongest tasting thing I had ever put in my mouth. Sal Cheese tastes like fresh garlic but leaves no noticeable odor.

I decided to scout around and make sure we did not have any more surprises. I created a mental platform, stepped on, and lifted myself slowly two inches into the air. Without moving my feet, I turned in midair and spoke to my companions: "I am going to take a look around. I won't be long. Mikaal, will you remove the shield please?" I felt the magic that surrounded us vanish.

I had begun to raise the platform when I felt Coral step on beside me. The platform shifted only slightly, but I had to enlarge it a bit so that she had a decent space to stand. She whispered in my ear that she wanted to go with me. I took us up and sent a mental message to Mikaal to let him know that Coral was with me.

When we were out of visual range of the campsite, Coral stepped closer to me, and I wrapped my arm around her. We flew in a circle around the camp, saying nothing to one another, just searching the morning for danger. I flew as slowly as I was able, and we made two complete circuits. Having seen nothing that looked dangerous, I reluctantly turned the platform and started back. The camp came into view too soon for my liking. Coral smiled sadly at me as she pulled away.

The morning air was hushed and motionless as we approached. I saw that Mikaal's shield was back up but didn't think anything about it until I felt several projectiles bounce off the barrier beneath us. Instinctively, Coral and I both went into a crouch. The platform that we flew on was transparent to Coral, but I couldn't see through it. The errant thought skittering through my consciousness that she must trust me greatly to step onto something she couldn't see and leave the ground. I had to push it aside so that I could focus on the problem at hand.

I increased the size of the barrier outward and upward as well so that nothing on the ground would be able to harm us as long as we were crouched. We were no longer moving because I couldn't see what was going on, and I didn't want to run us into one of the few trees in the area. I asked Coral if she could see our attackers. Neither of us had been looking straight down when we had been attacked, and so we didn't know where the enemy was.

I linked myself to Mikaal and asked, "What the heck is shooting at us?"

Mikaal's mental voice came back almost too quiet to understand. "You two were barely out of sight when something tore the bark off the tree and covered me with it. I threw up a barrier as quickly as possible, but I was too slow. Coral's Rhinodon screamed as the shield took shape."

"Are you and Junean safe?"

"Yes, but healing her mount took too much out of me. I tried to tell you, but I guess I didn't have enough energy to reach you that far away. Neither Junean or I were able to see our attackers, so we just waited and hoped you would be back soon. We were sure the two of you would be able to get us out of this situation."

"Tell Junean to take over shield duty. If you're struggling, you need to rely on us to help you!" I ordered before I broke contact and set about trying to decide what to do.

Since we stopped moving, we hadn't been attacked. I tried to make the platform invisible to myself but only succeeded in nearly dropping us. Coral suggested that if we moved, the unseen attacker might fire at us again, and she might be able to locate them. Coral's suggestion gave me an idea. I suggested that if Coral would create a link that would allow me to see through her eyes, I could fly us around again. She agreed to try.

After several minutes of silence, I felt her send a link. Neither of us had ever shared our vision with someone else, and it took several tries before we got it right. When the link was established and I could finally see, I began to move us forward slowly. We both saw the dart-like missiles fly out of the brush directly below us and collide with my barrier/platform. When they hit, I could sense that turning them away took some of my energy. No wonder Mikaal had been so drained. If they had been moving about the campsite when they were attacked, they would have drawn the enemy's attention, and his shield would have sustained multiple hits.

I lowered us slowly so that we could take a better look. Whatever was down there wasn't as tall as a man or we would have been able to see it. When the next group of projectiles thudded against the barrier, we noticed that they came from another location. Either there was more than one attacker, or it was incredibly fast. I stopped our downward motion and started towards the campsite again. Through Coral's eyes we were able to see a tail lift out of the brush below us. The spikes were coming from that tail.

"It must be a Spinebeast," Coral exclaimed. "Normally they never attack unless provoked, but we've seen what the Chaos Cloud does to any creature unlucky enough to touch it."

Her description of the creatures sounded like porcupines with much larger teeth and the ability to change colors to match its surroundings. When threatened, Spinebeasts will grip up to four of their poisoned quills in their tails and throw them at their attacker. Judging by the size of the tail and the quills we had seen, these were much larger and more aggressive than normal. Considering the other creatures we had encountered, I didn't want to get close enough to see what other changes exposure to the Unbinding had wrought.

I shifted my weight slightly, and another round of quills thudded into my barrier. Sensing my movement Coral looked at me and I nearly lost my mind. Seeing myself through someone else's eyes was a shock that I had not been prepared for. I had to break the link with her so that I did not lose control of the platform and drop us.

She saw my distress and asked what had happened. When I told her what was wrong, she went almost white and began to tremble. I told her that it was not her fault and not to worry about it. We had other problems now. My face as seen through her eyes flashed though my mind again, and my only thought was that I needed a haircut and a shave. I smacked my head into the side of the barrier to clear it of the vision. My skin had darkened, and my hair seemed dull due to being outside constantly. I was grateful that I'd never been prone to sunburn. The green of my irises were brighter than I remembered. I wasn't sure if I looked different or this was just how Coral saw me.

I had to figure out some way of allowing us to attack without putting us in danger. Coral had her old bow with her, but I didn't want her to stand up and take the chance she would be hit. Several minutes had passed and I was beginning to lose hope when I finally discovered a way. I asked Coral to link me with her eyes again but to remember to look only towards the ground. As soon as I was looking though her eyes again, I set my plan in motion.

Giving her a warning to hold on, I began moving us swiftly towards the ground where I had last seen that tail. The beast below us fired its quills again seconds before I crushed it beneath my barrier. Coral made a gagging sound as we both saw the beast's innards through her eyes. Not the most pleasant way to fight, but I saw no alternatives. Coral regained control of her stomach before she lost her breakfast.

I took us up again in case there were more of them close by. The sound of metallic quills bouncing off the side of my barrier proved that there was at least one more. Luckily, animal innards don't stick to psychic barriers, and we were still able to see. I flew us in several different patterns before we were able to determine where the remaining beast was. The second beast was no more difficult to kill than the first. Since Coral knew what to expect this time, she had no digestive problems. We flew around for half an hour in widening patterns to ensure that there were no more of the creatures before returning to camp. When we were safely on land again, and I regained the use of my own eyes, I noticed that Coral was more green than blue.

Mikaal was crumpled on the ground looking about half dead. I kneeled beside him and asked him if he was all right. He said that he was but that he had no energy left. I brought him some food, which he ate slowly. The food seemed to help some, but he was still very lethargic. All the use of my talents in the last day had used considerable energy but I still had plenty to spare. When I looked at Mikaal with my magic sense, his aura was almost nonexistent. I nearly choked as the light surrounding him flickered and almost went out completely. Mikaal was dying and I had to do something! I paced back and forth beside him until a thought came to me.

Quickly but quietly, I asked Mikaal to lower his mental defenses. Going back into the room in my inner mind, I opened the door to one of my energy storage rooms. Pulsing yellow energy stood as tall as I was right up against where the door had been. I pushed my hands into the gooey stuff and began to knead it like dough. When I felt the energy was malleable enough, I twisted off a large piece and rolled it around in my hand. When I was finished, I had created a ball of pure energy.

I closed the door with my foot and walked to the window of my inner eyes. I took the energy ball in my non-corporeal hand and sent it out the window to Mikaal. His mental defenses were lowered as I had asked, and I pushed the energy ball into his mind. I pulled back out of my mind and into reality and watched Mikaal. A pained and confused expression crossed his face I could see him struggling and sweat began to pour from him. Several minutes passed this way. I wondered if I had done him more harm than good until I saw color slowly returning to his face. The expression of intense concentration and pain faded and was replaced with calm. His eyes flickered a few times as the sweat dried into salty trails down his face. His eyes finally opened, and he took a deep breath before sitting up.

"How did you do that?" he asked me.

"I don't know. I just did it. That helped, did it?"

"Yes. I do not think I would have survived otherwise. The damage that was done to me last night prevented me from generating any energy. Once I finished the healing that you began, I was too exhausted to be able to recover. Your gift of energy allowed me to set things to rights within myself."

"Good. That means you'll be around to save us later. Are you strong enough to walk?"

"Yes. Though I am sure I will not be overly fast." Mikaal sounded almost like his old self. "When did you learn to fly?"

I hadn't really thought of it that way, but it must seem that way to others. "Not really flying," I said. "I just knew I could move other things, and I made an invisible barrier that could hold me up too."

Silently, so as not to cause tension, Mikaal said: "I noticed that Coral knew about this talent before this morning."

I said nothing, just turned away. I am sure that the redness of my face and neck spoke volumes.

An hour later found us on the trail once again. We had decided to continue on until we reached the mines. We traveled through midday, eating as we rode. The few trees and scrub brush that had surrounded our campsite thinned out, eventually becoming nonexistent. There was no movement on the rocky land we traveled through. The only excitement we saw during the day was when a small bird dove at us, losing feathers all the way. We didn't have to get a good look at it to know that it had been corrupted. Coral blasted it from the sky almost as soon as it appeared. The energy bolt that she fired destroyed the little body almost completely so that there was nothing to examine.

The students at the Magic school in Tiiaan had repeated the directions to the mine several times to each of us, so when we got to the carved stone hand in the center of our path, we knew that we were getting close. Only two hours remained of sunlight. We pressed ahead with as much speed as our tired animals were able to muster and stood at the entrance to the mine just as the sun sank into the horizon.

We set up camp in front of the sealed doors to the mine. The entrance was cut into the side of the mountain. The only access was the path we had come in on. Jagged rocks rose straight up above the doors, and the path was lined on each side by a steep cliff. Anything or anyone who toppled over the edge of the path would land, horribly broken, on the rocks far below.

We had been warned that the doors of the mine were protected with a spell. As much as we all wanted to end our travels this day inside the mine, Mikaal needed at least one more night of sleep before endeavoring to break the spell and gain us entrance. Within a few minutes of stopping, we had the animals tethered to an outcropping of rock as close to the center of the path as possible. Junean went to work to provide us with a barrier, and Coral and I retrieved food for Mikaal and ourselves from the animals.

We ate quietly but with barely contained excitement. All of us were looking forward to exploring the mines. We all tried to forget, if just for tonight, that we were on a mission to locate an object to oppose the darkness and tried to imagine that we were here for no other reason than to investigate the Star Glass's whereabouts. Even Mikaal, exhausted as he was, still fairly glowed with anticipation.

Junean was the only one of us that seemed oblivious to the excitement. She just clutched the bag containing her future husband to her as she ate. I looked at Coral out of the corner of my eye and imagined how I would feel if I saw her get overtaken by the Unbinding. Junean was handling it much better than I would have. I walked over to Junean and knelt down beside her to whisper in one of her big floppy ears.

"He will be whole again soon. I promise."

She just sighed and gave me a faint smile.

With my sleeping area prepared, I walked over to the edge of Junean's shield-barrier so that I could take a look at the doors of the mine. We were several feet away from them, but I was able to make out a decent amount of detail. Each door was made from a thick slab of stone with wooden inlays. The wood was held to the stone with ornate metal bands. The metal appeared to be copper treated in such a way (probably magically) that it did not corrode. Each band was twisted and woven masterfully so that the eyes could not follow a single strand for long. Precious gems gleamed at intervals on the door, mostly in shades of red and yellow. No hinges were visible, so I assumed that the doors swung inward. The handles that stood out of the face of the doors were carved from the same stone as the doors themselves and wrapped with the copper banding that held the wood in place. I imagined that it took several craftsmen many days to create the doors. They exuded a sense of artistry and pride. I hoped that there was more such craftsmanship inside of the mine.

I didn't hear Mikaal walk up beside me, so his words made me jump. "What are you thinking, Aaron?"

"I was just looking at the door and wondering what was behind it. I wish that we had time to explore this place freely. What's on your mind?" I responded, looking away from the challenge and toward my friend.

"My thoughts are similar to your own." Mikaal paused, picked up a stick from the ground with a gaw without bending over and scratched idly at the dirt before continuing. "That, and worrying whether we will be able to find the Star Glass quickly enough for you to have time to try to learn to use it before Tiiaan is overrun."

"I can see nothing past the magic of the doors. I can only hope that will change and I will be able locate it once we're in the mine." I held out my hand to Mikaal, who put the stick he was holding into it. "Not that. Your gaw," I chuckled at him, dropped the stick and examined the appendage. "Are you feeling any stronger?"

"Some. I think by the morning I will be more myself."

I turned back to stare at the mine entrance. "What are we going to use for light when we're inside? I know that Junean doesn't need light," I waved my hand in front of my face, "but I can hardly see anything even now."

"I will be able to supply some light." Mikaal's robe rose, exposing a faintly glowing gaw. "Would you like me to teach you a spell?"

"Please."

Make Soran magic lights and shields, how to carry lots of stuff in a small bag... there are a few things I wouldn't mind learning and that could make a huge difference. I wonder if I'll have to ask him to show me each one of them.

Mikaal spent a few minutes instructing me in the proper gestures to use while casting this simple spell, and after a few tries, I was able to reproduce the motions to his satisfaction. Then he bade me watch him as he spoke the words of power and brought forth a light. As soon as he spoke the first word, I could see the magic gathering in his fingers. Each of the short syllables that he uttered increased the glow until with the last word and the accompanying gesture the magic glow leaped from his hands into the air to create a ball of visible light. The ball floated to his shoulder, just behind his head and stayed there as he walked around.

He allowed the ball to illuminate the area as he had me repeat the words of the spell over and again until I had mastered them. Mikaal doused his magical light before he instructed me to try the spell on my own. I did as I had seen him do, chanting softly the words of the spell while making the hand motions. I could see the magical glow faintly at the tips of my fingers as I began the spell. I don't know what I was doing wrong, but it took me three tries before the magic I had gathered would leap into the air. The faint ball of light was nowhere near as bright or as large as Mikaal's had been, but it did respond to my mental commands and move around where I told it to. I placed it over my right shoulder as Mikaal had.

Faintly winded, I said to Mikaal, "That's not as easy as the other type of magic."

"No, it takes much more practice and requires much study. It can be very powerful though. Mental magic, such as you have been using up to now, takes its power from within you. The type of magic that I have just shown you, Spirit Magic, takes only a tiny portion of power from its wielder. Most of the power used by Spirit Magic is drawn from the world around us. That is why your light is so faint and why you had difficulty casting the spell; you have only a weak link to the magical power that flows around you. With practice, you should be able to more easily control the magic of this world. Be glad that you are able to at all. Since you were not born here, I did not know if you were going to be able to control it."

The little Noran bowed slightly and walked to his bedding. Before my back was turned, he added his snores to the ones already coming from Junean. I stared at the door for a minute more before turning towards the animals. There was little or nothing for them to eat here, so I needed to find some plant life. I stepped over to the glow of the shield where it neared the animals and looked at it. I didn't want to wake Junean just to have her lower her barrier. I brought out my mental hands and poked Junean's shield. Where my mental fingers touched the surface of the barrier it dimpled outward. I tried pinching the barrier in each hand and pulling it apart. The barrier yielded to my touch almost like parting a curtain. While holding the shield open for myself, I stepped through. I closed the barrier behind me and flew off in search of food.

Higher up the mountain, I found several small shrubs clinging tenaciously to the rocky soil. I collected several of these as well as some moss that was clinging to the underside of a projection. I almost felt bad for killing these plants who fought so hard for survival, but Pakky needed to eat. I took this meager bit of Rhinodon food back to camp.

My mental hands were full of vegetation and when I reached the shield surrounding our camp I brought my physical hands up without thinking. Fiery pain lanced through my fingertips and brought me to my knees. I hadn't realized that the shields we used for protection were so violent. Several minutes passed before I was able to stand normally. I had to create a flying platform and load the plants onto it so that I could open the barrier with my mental hands. When the shield parted I stepped through and brought the Rhinodon dinner flying in behind me. I closed the barrier back and sent the food the rest of the way to the animals without me.

Dispelling the platform and my mental hands, I reached out hesitantly to touch the interior wall of the shield. When I ran into the inside of Mikaal's shield, I'd only smacked my head, not shocked myself. I breathed a sigh of relief as I laid my hand flat against Junean's shield.

When I turned around, Coral was standing behind me. She had a funny little grin on her face that disappeared as soon as I saw it.

"What were you doing?" she asked me.

"Being curious. What are you up to?"

"I was looking for you. I searched everywhere inside of the shield and didn't see you. I was getting ready to wake up Mikaal and Junean when I saw you appear out of the darkness. That was nice of you, going out in search of food and not waking anyone up. How did you get through the shield?"

"I pulled it apart with my mind and walked through it."

Coral's eyes grew large. "You made a hole in Junean's shield without her knowing?"

"Yes. Why?"

"I have been led to believe that Moaleans who can create and maintain a shield like this one would know if a feather fell from the sky and touched their barrier. Now you say that you have walked through Junean's shield twice without waking her up."

"Maybe she could sense that it was me?"

"Perhaps. I will ask her in the morning. Come on. Let us get some rest. We have a long day ahead of us."

Coral took my hand and lead me back to where Junean and Mikaal still slept soundly. The night air was quiet and chill. A faint breeze crossed the path where we slept, deepening the chill to a biting cold. Apparently, Junean's barrier didn't offer protection from mountain winds. There was no wood nearby for a fire, and I was worried that some of us might not last the night.

The animals didn't seem troubled at all by the cold, their thick hides and large amounts of stored body fat keeping them warm. Junean was covered with fur and was in no danger. Mikaal didn't look even the least bit cold, and I decided that his magic must keep the cold at bay. Coral's flesh was a deeper blue than I had ever seen it, and the waves that washed over her skin seemed to crawl as if the water in her body had begun to thicken. I wasn't in very bad shape right now, but I did not think that I would remain that way through the night.

Coral had placed her leather blanket less than a foot from my machine made one and was wrapped in it now shivering. I didn't want to wake up our other companions, but I wasn't crazy about the idea of freezing to death. I laid down on my own blanket and asked Coral to lay down beside me. She looked a little bit shocked at first but did as I asked. She was cold to the touch! I unwrapped her from the leather blanket and used it to cover both of us and then wrapped my travel blanket around us as well. Coral was shivering uncontrollably. I put my arms around her and held her close.

Several minutes passed this way. Slowly her body began to absorb the heat from my body, and she shivered only slightly. Coral looked into my eyes, inches from her own. She didn't say a word. Then she leaned into me and kissed me. It seemed to last forever. As we kissed I felt her knock on the door to my mind. I opened the door to her, and she walked in. Her mental projection was wearing a gown of incredible beauty. Every inch of the fabric was formed from a drop of water stuck by sunlight. She truly glowed. She walked towards me and held out her hands. I took them in my own.

"I want to tell you something," she whispered.

I nodded to her but didn't say a word.

"Last night as I slept, I could feel you. I had a sense of love from you that I have never felt from anyone else. I do not know if that was only a dream but… Aaron, I love you." Coral vanished from my mind.

I opened my eyes and realized that we had never stopped kissing. I broke the kiss as gently as I could. Neither of us had breathed for at least a minute, and as we both struggled for air our breath came in unison. When we were breathing more normally, Coral opened her mouth to speak. I kissed her again. When I pulled back, she had tears in her eyes.

"I want to tell you something now, Coral." I took a breath, preparing to pour out my heart and pushed away the fear of sharing too much too fast. "Last night I was walking to my blanket, and I stopped to look at you. I watched you breathe. I traced every curve of your face with my eyes. Then I looked into my heart and realized that I was in love with you. I wanted to tell you then, but I didn't want to wake you up, so I told you with a mental letter. That is why you felt me. Now with you in my arms I'll tell you again. Coral, I love you. Every second that we are together is bliss."

Her eyes had closed as I spoke. She looked as if she was absorbing my words as completely as she had absorbed my body heat. Tears flowed freely from her, but they were happy tears. I clutched her to me and kissed her neck. Moments later we were fast asleep.

Chapter 13
The Welcome Wagon

The sun was just peeking over the horizon when I awoke. Coral was still in my arms and the feeling of her breath on my neck made the morning shine. A shadow fell across our prone forms, and I turned to see Mikaal looking down on us.

There was a merry twinkle in his eye as he said, "If you were cold, you could have told me."

"Where is the fun in that?" I replied.

The diminutive magician chuckled to himself as he walked away.

"Coral. Wake up."

"Mmmmm. Good morning."

It was more than that—it was the very best morning there had ever been. The words escaped me though, and we shared a quick kiss before rising and preparing for the day.

Mikaal had Junean on her feet by the time Coral and I had our blankets stowed away. We all searched the morning air for signs of attackers before Junean released her shield. The excitement we had felt last night spread even to Junean this morning. No one spoke of eating; we were all too excited.

We gathered around the door as Mikaal began tracing glowing letters in the air. I looked at Mikaal with my magic sight and was pleased to see that his strength had returned in full. The Noran magician spent half an hour creating a convex wall of magical writing around the door.

When he finished, he turned to us and said, "Good. Now I may begin."

The air huffed out of me. I believed that he had been attacking the magic of the door all along. In a sense that was true. Mikaal explained to us that the magic he had wrought was meant to drain the strength of the door's magic. It couldn't destroy the spells that bound the door shut completely though. Mikaal would have to fight the spell or spells that remained one at a time. The door had been warded so long ago that no one really knew what type of spells might protect it.

I asked Mikaal if there were likely to be any physical attacks from the door. He didn't even know that for sure, but he thought it likely. Before he began attacking the spells in earnest, I brought the animals close behind us and made a mental wall of force to protect us. The shields that Mikaal and Junean could create were effective against magical attacks but wouldn't allow the magical attacks from people within either. The wall of force that I was able to create seemed only to be effective against physical things. So, Mikaal would be able to attempt to open the door by magical means, but if the door responded by throwing large rocks at us, we would be protected.

With our defenses in place, Mikaal began his assault on the door. Mikaal began by throwing a fireball at the door. The fireball streaked from Mikaal's upthrust gaw and struck the door with a hiss like an angry cobra. Fire engulfed the door for perhaps five seconds before the door responded. Its response was not what we expected. The fire was simply sucked into the center of the door. There was no evidence that the door had ever been attacked. The luminescence of Mikaal's magical wall of text intensified. The door had converted the fire into magical energy! If Mikaal hadn't created the draining wall around the door, his attack would have strengthened the door's magic.

The Welcome Wagon

Mikaal decided on another test. He reached down with two of his gaw and picked up a large stone. He spun twice in a circle before heaving the rock with all his might at the door. The door was quicker to respond this time. Before the sediment projectile reached it, a beam of energy lanced out from one of the yellow gems on the door, turning the stone to powder.

With the rock destroyed, the gem turned its fiery eye on Mikaal. I almost tackled Mikaal to get him out of the way, but I would have been too late anyway. The beam was weakened as it passed through Mikaal's draining wall of words, but my barrier did not hinder it in the least. The beam had been aimed at Mikaal's head, but the little Noran had his gaw up and caught the beam. It didn't burn him but seemed to strengthen him instead. Mikaal was using the door's trick against it. He was absorbing the magical attack.

Mikaal stood in that position until the beam faltered and died. The yellow gem that had sparkled in the sunlight a moment before went dark and fell away from the door. Mikaal lowered himself to the ground and began waving all eight of his gaw in the direction of the door. I heard his droning chant begin as his eyes closed. I assumed that he must be done with his tests and be trying to attack the core spell that powered the door's defenses.

I was watching so intently that I didn't notice Coral walk up behind me until she pushed food into my hand. My reverie broken, I accepted the fruit and bread she offered me and sat down to eat. I broke off some of the bread and offered it to her, but she said she had eaten already. She sat down beside me and watched Mikaal as intently as I had been.

"Coral, I can tell this is fruit, but I don't think I've seen one of these before. What is it?"

"Probably not. Grooverfruit are very hard to find as they only grow in high places rich in magic. They are my favorite. I danced when I found them, and not because of the side effects…" Coral broke into giggles.

I frowned in confusion until I looked at my feet. Without realizing it I was doing a very poor imitation of the king of pop from my world.

"What the heck?" I asked her. "Mhmm. Side effects, huh?"

Coral just grabbed her sides and nodded.

I had just popped the last of my grooverfruit into my mouth when the door began to rumble. I moonwalked toward Mikaal for a better view. The rumbling was accompanied by the gems that remained on the door winking out and falling away. The twisted metal bands uncoiled themselves from the surface of the door and began raining blows on my barrier like thousands of whips. My dance ceased and I staggered under the force of the blows. I didn't feel any pain, but each blow that fell was very powerful and weakened my barrier slightly. I had to keep feeding my barrier more of my stored energies to keep us safe.

The door's wooden inlays slid down to reveal pointed metal tips. Those weren't just decorative inlays; they were spears! One by one they fired at us as if by an invisible hand. They didn't fly straight though. Each spear arched as it flew to strike at us from different angles. My barrier kept us safe once again, but I was starting to tire under the force of so many blows. I had plenty of energy to spare, but this barrier was also an extension of my will. Constant mental attention was required to keep it active.

One of the spears slammed into my barrier as I was weakening. It smashed into the ground mere inches from where Coral was standing. That sight was enough to strengthen my resolve and prevent any more attacks from getting through. One by one, the whip-like bands of metal began to shatter like glass as they hit my barrier. I was breathing hard, but my mental shield didn't falter again.

After several more minutes of the whips attacking and shattering the door finally shuddered and was still. Mikaal stood up, and I crumpled to my knees and then fell over on my face. My three friends were with me in an instant. They turned me over, and Coral

The Welcome Wagon

produced a cloth and a water container and began to bathe my face. As soon as I was able to talk again, I assured them that I would be fine. I had just drained myself and needed to rest for a few more minutes.

"I am glad you were here, Aaron. I do not think I could have defeated that door by myself."

"Is it finished then?"

"Yes. We should be able to open this door like any other now."

"Very good. Let us hope that the rest of our voyage in the mines is not so difficult."

Coral brought the water skin to my lips, and I drank. She followed this with a bit of dried meat and more water. I was able to sit up about two minutes after, and in ten more I was able to stand and walk normally. The first place that I went once I was able to walk again was to the door; or more precisely to the rubble at the foot of the door. I began to rummage through the sharp bits of metal and broken spears with the point of my blade. I wasn't immediately able to find what I was looking for.

I was at the point of giving up when I found the first of the darkened gems. I sheathed my blade and began carefully retrieving the little jewels one by one. I had uncovered eleven gems on my first try, and a little more poking around with a broken spear brought me to the first gem that had fallen. One dozen dark gems. I smiled to myself. When I turned around my friends were staring at me.

"What?" I asked.

"What are you doing?" Mikaal asked me in return.

"Watch."

I pocketed all but one of the gems. This one I held up in front of my face and stared at it gravely. The look on my face, of course, was all for the benefit of my friends. I'd gone into my mind to get a bit of energy from one of my storage rooms. My newest room was empty. I hadn't realized that the fight against the door had drained me of so much energy.

I went to the door of the other storeroom. This one was still three quarters of the way full. I reached into the glowing mess as I had done the first time for Mikaal and created a small ball of energy. I didn't want to use too much in case this didn't work. When the ball finally took shape, I walked to the windows of my mind's eyes. I created a non-corporeal hand and used it to send the small energy ball to the yellow gem in my hand. When I returned to my body, the gem had begun to glow. It wasn't nearly as bright as before, but it definitely had power.

"Mikaal. Prepare your defenses. When you're ready, throw a stone at me."

Mikaal looked annoyed but did as he was asked.

The stone that he threw never made it to me. It exploded in a shower of dust just as the stone Mikaal had thrown at the door had done, and then it turned its beam on Mikaal as soon as it finished with the rock. Mikaal caught the energy beam just as he had done when he was attacking the doors.

Before Mikaal could drain the gem again, I put my hand in the path of the beam. The gem somehow sensed my wishes and stopped attacking Mikaal. Luckily, my guess was correct, and the beam had gone out before my hand had been damaged. Junean and Coral gasped at this display. Mikaal only shook his head in amazement, whether at my guessing the gem's nature or risking my skin to stop the beam I don't know.

I spent a few more minutes picking out three more yellow stones and recharging them. When all four were glowing brightly, I turned again to the pile of rubbish. Using a mental hand, I grabbed some copper from the ground. Into my mental room I went. I decided it was time to make a new room. One wall in my mental room held the door that led outside of my mind. The wall that I thought of as the front held the windows that looked out of my eyes. The west wall held the twin doors to my energy storerooms. The south wall stood vacant, so I added a double door there.

On the other side of this door, I created a workroom. I lined the walls with benches and tool racks. The back wall of this new room became a forge and anvil. I took the copper there now. A fire blazed impossibly hot in the forge. I brought the mental hand full of copper bits into the fire. Seconds later the copper was molten. I created another mental hand and four small thin molds. I poured the liquid metal from my hand into each of the molds. I let the metal cool enough to take a basic shape before I proceeded. Three of the molds I placed near the forge to keep them malleable. The fourth mold I took in my mental hands and began to braid. I worked the metal until it became too cold to work and then reheated it. I worked as quickly as I possibly could, conscious as I was of time passing. I had always wanted to have a torc, ever since my Arthurian legend phase as a kid, but there weren't many places that made them. In my favorite series, the nobles and kings always wore the decorative braided metal bands around their neck like an open fronted necklace. It was after my favorite of the drawings in the first book that I copied.

It took me approximately one hour to complete the designs. I set the strands of copper on the workbench to cool and went into the main room to retrieve the gems. I had to tell my body to move my physical hands into view so that I could grasp them. Once I had the gems inside my mind I took them back to where the newly completed torcs waited. When I was forming the metal I left a small opening in the front. It was into these openings that I now placed the gems. One gem for one Torc. One Torc for one friend. I bent four copper pins down to contain each gem and then began to polish the Torcs.

When my mental focus returned to my body, I was holding four defensive magical Torcs. As soon as I moved my friends surrounded me. Mikaal was closest to me, so he was the first to receive his Torc. I placed the Torc around his throat and clasped it behind him. I did the same for Junean and Coral and handed the last Torc to Coral so she could put it in place around my neck. When I looked back at

Mikaal, I found him staring at me with a look of admiration. He gave me a little nod and turned towards the doors that led to the mine.

Mikaal had his gaw on the handle of the door when the rest of us, with animals in tow, caught up with him. He waited until we had taken up defensive positions around him before he pushed. First one door and then the other was pushed back to reveal... nothing. The mine entrance was dark and dusty. Nothing stirred in the shadows.

Mikaal took a few hesitant steps into the gloom before calling up his Magelamp. The glowing ball of light appeared just above his shoulder, just as it had the night before. Mikaal was getting ready to move forward again when scrabbling claws behind him brought him up short. He looked relieved when he discovered Junean to be the cause of the noise. With her ability to see in the dark and her knowledge of the underground, she wanted to be the first in. She would be able to locate danger more easily than we could. Mikaal graciously, and perhaps gratefully, stepped to the side to let the young Moalean woman into the narrow tunnel passage. No light marked her passage into the mine. She simply stepped forward and was gone from sight.

We waited impatiently for Junean to step back into the light. When Junean disappeared, Mikaal stepped quickly back into the light. We stood, each of us near our Rhinodon, and peered into the darkness. I had turned my eyes away from the darkness for only a second when she returned.

"Come. There is no danger that I could find. There are stables where we may leave the animals only a few minutes' walk inside. There is only one passage beyond the stables for at least as far as I could see. The first intersection has four paths diverging from the first one. I followed one of these paths for a short time and was greeted with more choices not very far in. It is a virtual maze down there. It is a good thing that we have you to find where we must go, Aaron. Without tearing through walls, even I could get lost in this place."

The Welcome Wagon

No one said a word in reply; we just followed Junean into the heart of the mountain.

The air was still, save what was created by our forward progress. The passage was cooler than it had been outside and had a faintly musty odor. Mikaal's Magelamp floated as high as the passageway allowed, which was about twice my height. This allowed us visibility only two to three steps before and behind us. Our little group drew closer to one another as the weight of the mountain rested on us more with each step forward.

We walked in silence until we reached the stables Junean had told us about. Each stall was easily big enough for two of our Rhinodons. I couldn't help but wonder what mighty beasts the miners had kept here. While I was settling Pakky into one of the large enclosures, it struck me that we had no food for the Rhinodons.

Junean seemed to have read my mind. She stepped into the stall as I was removing the final pieces of Pakky's gear and pulled a statuette from her satchel. She took this item to the large trough set into the wall and began to chant softly to it. She repeated the half-heard words several times before twisting the statue's head off and turning it upside down. Grass, grain, and leaves began raining from the statue into the trough. When the container was full, Junean placed the head back on the statuette and moved into the next stall.

By the time I had transferred enough food and supplies from Pakky to my pack, Junean had provided enough food for all three animals to survive much longer than any of us were likely to live. Water for the animals was provided by the miners of old. A circular container was set into the corner of each stall. Just above these containers was a hole in the stone that dripped fresh water from an unseen mountain river somewhere above us. The Rhinodon trio was munching happily when we walked from the stables and back onto the main tunnel. Mikaal's Magelamp followed us, and I heard a bleat of alarm from Pakky as they were left in the dark. We paused long enough for me to create a battery powered lantern that would hopefully last a few days, before continuing on our way.

Chapter 14
Dark Travels

Too little time passed before we reached the first fork in the passage. Eager as I had been to start this underground expedition, I was now equally as nervous. Without my talent for sensing the presence of magic, we had no hope of finding the Star Glass before the Chaos Cloud overtook us. My friends were counting on me… trusting me…to steer them down a twisting path that only I could see the end of. One wrong turn could mean a fate worse than death for all of us.

I had to ask them all to stay several paces behind me, partially to ensure that their magical auras did not interfere, but mostly just so I could calm myself enough to begin. I also made sure that they took my magical torc with them when they left and had Mikaal banish his Magelamp. Junean would lead them with her glowing night eyes.

I waited until their footsteps disappeared, closed my eyes, and took several deep breaths. When my heart no longer felt like a frightened rodent scampering around in my chest, I opened my eyes to the search. For several minutes I could see nothing. I had to turn around and locate the glow of my friends to reassure myself that I was still able to sense magic at all. Alone in the dark, I began to panic. The words 'This is never going to work' echoed in my mind so loudly I was sure that Junean's large ears would surely hear them. I closed my eyes against the feelings, though in the perfect darkness that surrounded me, there was no real difference. That was when I sensed it.

I had been looking for an aura that was strong enough to be seen, but I was so far away and there was such a large volume of stone and dirt between where I stood and my target. The object I was looking for would have needed to be more powerful than every person at the magic school in Tiiaan combined to put off that kind of aura. I smacked myself in the head at my own stupidity. My senses had still been attuned to magic when, in the midst of my panic, I had closed my eyes, and I heard the slight hum of a powerful magic in the distance.

Keeping my eyes closed, I turned left and right until I was able to discern the direction of the sound. Slowly and carefully, I took a step forward. I followed that step with another, and one more. I put my arms out to the sides, and when I didn't feel anything I brought them forward. I fully expected to slam into a wall at any moment. After several more hesitant steps the fact that I was still upright and conscious led me to believe that I had entered one of the tunnels.

I sat down, being careful to keep myself pointed in the same direction I had been walking. I was just about ready to send a message to my friends to join me when I heard their footsteps behind me. The faint illumination coming from the gems around their necks and the light from Junean's eyes were visible before they entered the tunnel. When they had caught up to me, I rose without a word and, closing my eyes again, continuing on my way.

I followed the magical hum for about an hour, and the echoing footsteps behind me were my companions' only contribution. I was able to tell by the echoes when I had entered a new split in the path. When the volume of the echoes died down I knew to slow down and make sure that I was going the right way. Just after I made the eleventh turn I heard a loud growl from behind me. I tensed for an attack and ducked to the side of the corridor. The sound of laughter let me know that everything was all right. The growl was Mikaal's stomach. He was the only one of us who hadn't eaten yet.

The four of us pulled close together in the tunnel, and Mikaal created a light for us to eat by. Coral stepped out of the shadows behind me, startling me. She placed my Torc back around my neck, and I hugged her when she was finished. The rations that we had brought with us when we separated from the animals consisted mostly of dried meat and hard rolls. We didn't bring any fresh fruit, not because we thought it would spoil, (Mikaal had explained to me that the students had cast spells of preservation over all our food supplies) but because we didn't want the fruit to get ruined if we came into trouble in the tunnels. Between bites Mikaal asked me how sure I was that I was leading us correctly. My answer to his question came with my head bowed.

"When you first left me in the tunnel, I began to panic. I kept looking around for the Star Glass and couldn't find it. Once I closed my eyes I was able to feel the magic faintly. I am taking us to the only source of magic that my senses are able to find inside the mountain. Anything more than that we'll have to wait and see."

I was surprised when Junean spoke up and said, "That is all any one of us can ask of you."

"I do think we're heading in the right direction. As we get closer I should be able to tell more about what I am sensing."

Excitement was still running though our blood like fire. None of us was paying overmuch attention to our surroundings, and I nearly had a heart attack when the jewel on my neck suddenly spat forth a beam of light. The sudden intensity blinded us all, and I put my hand in the path of the continuing beam as I tried to cover my eyes. The light winked out and we were left in complete darkness once again.

Mikaal, in his surprise, had lost control of his magic light, and it had gone out. Without my eyesight the only thing that I could tell for sure was that something larger than a house cat moved away from us quickly. The dim glow coming from the Torcs around our necks wasn't even visible to me for several minutes.

When my vision finally returned, Junean was standing in the midst of us, holding something small and squirming aloft. She stepped back and threw the creature to the ground. The pathetic looking bundle squeaked when it hit and bounced slightly. I grabbed the thing in a mental hand before it could escape.

By that time Mikaal had created another light globe, and I was able to see my attacker. From its misshapen head to the end of its gnarled toes, the creature was no more than two feet tall. Lightly furred wings were attached to its body on the side, not on the back where I would have expected. Its legs were placed normally but its arms exited from the front of its torso. Other than its wings the creature was hairless and naked. Small bony protrusions on the top of its head reminded me of horns that had just begun to grow.

I walked closer to get a better look and the little beast struggled to get away. Suddenly the things demeanor changed, and it lunged toward me. Since I was holding it in the air, it didn't get very far. It began clawing the air and spitting at me. My Torc lit up and began blasting the flying spittle from the air. When there were no more projectiles, the beam turned towards the creature. I placed my hand in the path of the beam before it could do more than singe the little monster. When the beam struck the creature it screamed loud enough to deafen all of us.

The creature regained its composure and turned a baleful glare on me.

"Torment me no longer human," the pathetic beast whined at me.

"Human? Why would you call me that?" The question escaped my lips before I had time to restrain it.

"I have seen your world, human! I know a man when I see one!" In its anger the creature began raising its tone.

"Who are you?" My voice, soft and low so soon after its outburst, caught the creature off guard.

"I cannot answer your question," the creature, whining again, answered.

"You will answer me… or would you prefer that I take the answer from you?"

Hatred flickered in the thing's eyes and was quickly replaced by fear. Seconds passed. The beastie breathed deep several times and finally answered me in an almost human voice, "You did not understand me. I *cannot* answer your question, whether I want to or not. There is a compulsion spell placed on me which prevents me from giving my name to anyone."

"Why would someone do that to you?"

The creature winced visibly before answering, "Some beings can be controlled by those who know their true names. I am one of those beings. Many years ago, so many that I have lost count, I entrusted my true name to one that I thought worthy. I am now a slave of that person. My master, whose name I am also prevented from uttering, told me that if I killed you, he would set me free. He has no reason to do so, but he probably thought that I would try harder if I had some incentive. I did not want to kill you, but I cannot go against his wishes. I never wanted to kill…."

The tiny creature's last words were a whisper, but I heard them. I believed that this was truly a creature in distress.

"I cannot let you return to your master. You will have to travel with us." I said slowly. "We have to call you something, I will call you… Granalis."

The name had no sooner left my mouth than the air around us shimmered and shook violently. Granalis screamed, but this time with surprise. His excitement was a nearly tangible thing as his voice, more human than it had been, cracked as he spoke. "My name! How did you know my true name?!"

How did I know his name? What was I even thinking about when I pulled that out of the air? I can't remember! Knowing things I shouldn't have any way of knowing would be really useful. I have to remember to try to figure out how that happened and if I can do it again, but not now.

"I'm not sure. I was trying to think of something to call you and it just popped into my head."

"You have set me free! You all felt it too, didn't you? Oh, after all the thousands of years I am finally free of HIM!"

Each of my friends had a smile on their faces that seemed somehow to force back the darkness. When I looked back to the newcomer, the smile I was wearing slid right off of my face. The flesh on Granalis' body was crawling, and his bones and limbs were breaking and reforming themselves in new patterns. His mouth was open in a silent scream. Agony and ecstasy took turns dancing across his quickly changing face.

Once my astonishment faded I tried to think of something that I could do to help him. I tuned my eyes to see magic and looked at Granalis. I was trying to discover whether this was a magical attack launched by his former Master. The aura that was created by magic had always been blue to me. Granalis' body was lit with a red glow so powerful that I had to close my eyes against it.

When I reopened my eyes I realized that I still held Granalis' tormented form aloft with one of my invisible hands. Quickly I laid him on the ground so as not to cause him any more pain. I heard the low droning of Mikaal casting a spell and shouted at him to stop. He looked confused but did as he was asked. I hadn't been certain what had been going on until I heard Mikaal casting.

"Wait. WAIT. I don't think is an attack!" I was thinking out loud at this point, trying to convince myself as well as Mikaal. "Granalis' body was changed by his former master. When I broke the spell that bound him to the service of our enemy, the spell that changed Granalis was broken also. His body is returning to its natural state. He's in pain! Junean, the statue you used on Mikaal, get it, please."

Junean had the statue in her hand almost before I finished my sentence. She placed it on the ground beside the writhing figure and stepped back. Granalis continued to be remade before our eyes, but he didn't seem to be struggling so much now. This was all we could do for him. We hadn't finished our meal, but none of us had the heart to eat much. Mikaal and I nibbled at our food but quickly gave up and began to pack our supplies. I estimated that a half hour had passed while Granalis continued to change. I decided to walk farther into the tunnel and try to scout out our route.

I did not leave my Torc behind again. If this unknown, unseen foe was sending his minions against us, I wanted to be as prepared as possible. Since I was listening for magic instead of looking for it, the aura of the Torc didn't interfere with my search. Each magical item seemed to make a slightly different pitched sound. I walked on for several minutes, taking one turn after another. I was becoming more confident in my ability to locate the artifact that we sought. The longer I searched, the less attention I paid to my surroundings. Coral's mental call, when it came, startled me enough that I lost my footing and fell. I hit my head on something hard and did not wake for some time.

When awareness returned I was back with the group, but I had no idea how I had gotten there. I was seeing my friends, but it was different somehow. It was as if I was seeing the entire scene at once from all angles. When I focused on Mikaal, I could see him from both sides, above, and below all at once. How was this possible? What had happened to me? It was when I tried waving my hands in front of my face that I got a clue. No hands. No face. Nothing to move. Where was my body and why was I not with it? I was trying to think of the last time I had a body when I was distracted by the actions of my friends.

Granalis' body finished its transformation. Coral immediately tried to contact me mentally. When I didn't answer, she began calling aloud for me. She told Mikaal, who was examining the unconscious Granalis, that I was missing. Mikaal stood, wrapped the still form in a thin cloth he pulled from his cloak, picked him up, and handed him to Junean. He began chanting quietly, his gaw circling slowly in the air as if they moved through a sea of molasses. A pinprick of light appeared in the air before him. This new light moved in circles and swirling patterns as if it had a life of its own. Mikaal spoke to it, and it raced off into the darkness. Just before it went out of view, it stopped and began its spinning dance in the air. Mikaal set off after it with no word to the others. Junean and Coral were right behind him though, Coral stopping only to retrieve my pack. I watched them walk away. I did not realize what had happened until I was pulled along behind them. I tried to plant my feet firmly to stop the motion, but my feet and the ground were no longer on good terms. My toes slid through the dirt like it wasn't even there.

"I am dead!" I said wordlessly to myself. I tried to increase my speed and was able finally to catch up with my friends. I tried to fly ahead and catch up with the floating light but was pulled up short before I could catch it. Somehow, I had become tethered to one of the group! I didn't understand how this could have happened. The only idea that I could come up with was when I died, my love for Coral had drawn my spirit to her.

I flew back over to her and tried whispering in her ear, but she couldn't hear me. I shouted. I pleaded. I flew back and forth in front of her face. Nothing I did seemed to work. It wasn't until I gave up entirely that I found a way to communicate. I simply stopped moving. I had, of course, been in front of Coral when I stopped and she, oblivious to my presence, kept walking. When she reached where I was floating, I found myself pulled into her mind. I was not even conscious of myself for some time. I was a part of Coral in a way no one had ever been before. My self was scattered across the landscape of her mind.

I don't know how much time passed before I regained my sense of self. I began pulling myself together one bit at a time. An eternity and a second passed before Coral found me floating lost in her mind. She pulled me into a part of her mind the equivalent of my inner room. Coral's mental "inner sanctum" was a small clearing in a sea of trees. There was a stone table in the center of the area surrounded by ornately decorated seats carved from the living trunks of trees. Close to the edge of the clearing was what appeared to be a birdbath.

Somewhere beyond the trees I heard the sound of waves crashing against a rocky coastline. I was finally surrounded by something approaching reality, and I was able to get a firmer grip on my mind.

Coral appeared in front of me. Her eyes were tear-stained as she looked at me.

"What happened to you?" she asked.

"I think I fell and hit my head. The next thing I knew, I was floating around you."

"I almost lost my mind when I felt you enter my head. Mikaal said that I screamed and fell to my knees. They thought that I had been attacked. Mikaal tried to heal me while Junean went looking for an enemy. They finally had to wait until we regained ourselves to find out what had happened. Now that Mikaal knows that you are…" Coral could not continue, she broke into wracking sobs.

"Dead," I finished for her.

She nodded her head slightly and tried to compose herself enough to speak.

"Mikaal went to search for your body. Junean and Granalis are guarding us."

"I had hoped to die in a slightly more noble fashion."

"This can't be the end…." Coral began sobbing again.

I wanted to hold her, but I had no body to do so. Without thinking, I created a mental hand and tried to pat Coral on the back with it. The hand passed right through her. Finally I realized my error. Coral wasn't really there. This was her mental projection. Then it hit me. If I was dead, I shouldn't have any more power. I was apparently drawing from Coral's stored power. I was about to say something to Coral when she disappeared. She reappeared several minutes later.

"Mikaal is back with your body," she told me.

"May I use your eyes?" I asked.

"Of course, my love."

Coral led me to the bowl sitting on a pedestal that I had taken for a birdbath. She looked at the still water, and I saw Mikaal. I was confused until I realized that this was Coral's mental link to her eyes. She looked down to where my body lay. There was a line of blood across my forehead where my skin had split when I had fallen on the rock. My skin had taken on a slight bluish cast. I turned back to Coral.

"Tell Mikaal to try to cast a healing on my body."

Coral, still crying, shook her head and disappeared.

Several minutes passed and Coral reappeared. I was watching the bowl and didn't even notice until she spoke. "He said that he would try." Even as she spoke the words, I saw the glow of magic surround my body. I gathered my mental self and leapt from Coral's mind.

Still outside myself, I saw the skin on my head bulge slightly as the fracture in my skull was knit back together. I was still tethered to Coral's body, so I still had her power to draw on. I used this ability to create some mental hands again. Time to make another wild guess, wrap it in a leap of faith, and pray things worked the way I hoped. Not that I had a choice in the matter. If I didn't try something, there would be no chance of success.

I willed the mental hands to become as insubstantial as I myself was and plunged them into my own chest. I created a pair of comical x-ray glasses for myself so that I could see into my flesh. I sent a message back to Coral to tell Mikaal to continue casting the healing spell. I did not want to try to return to my body and have to live with brain damage.

That taken care of, I placed my mental hands, one around my heart and one around my right lung. I placed a breathing pump over my mouth, like the ones I'd seen paramedics use on TV in my past life. I willed my mental hands to become solid only where they touched my heart and lung. I did not want to destroy my body by materializing the entire hands inside of my chest.

Then I began to squeeze first my heart, then my lung, then the pump to refill the lung. Seconds passed and I heard Junean and Coral gasp in unison as normal coloring returned to my body. Between my efforts and Mikaal's healing, my brain started responding and began breathing and pumping blood on its own. I dispelled all of my mental creations, steeled myself, and jumped back into my body; or rather through my body. I began to panic again. My body no longer accepted me!

I returned to Coral's body, my non-corporeal head hung low. When I entered her mind she began to cry again. I explained what had happened and asked her to let Mikaal know that he could stop casting the healing. Coral sniffed and nodded and was gone.

She appeared several minutes later with a smile lighting up her face. She was about to tell me why she was happy when I felt my world ripped free of its anchor. I was sucked from Coral's mind so quickly I couldn't even scream. When the world finally ceased its movement, I opened my eyes. There before me was.... I didn't know what it was; I'd never seen anything like it. Just then something struck me. I was seeing... through my own eyes. Somehow, I had been placed back into my body.

I struggled to sit up, finally succeeding. With the change in perspective I realized that the reason I wasn't able to identify what I was seeing was that it was too close to my face. Granalis, or what I assumed was Granalis, was standing over me. Mikaal was standing to my right, while Coral was leaning heavily on Junean, both of them smiling.

"What happened?" was all I could think of to say.

The fluffy form on my chest spoke first, though I was almost unable to understand it because of a heavy accent.

"You were dead. That much you know. When you and Mikaal restored your body, I was able to use my talents to restore your spirit to where it belonged."

"Thank you for my life." I said softly.

"I think that we are even, since you just saved my life too. I owe you my thanks as well."

"Still, you didn't have to help me, and you did."

"Maybe, but I would not have been able to live with myself if I had not done what only I could do."

"What will you do now?" I asked Granalis.

"Well.... Since our enemy has used his power to close all the portals in this world, I cannot go anywhere else. I do not wish this world to be destroyed. It would seem that I should stay with you. That is, if you will have me."

"You are more than welcome to join us. Whatever talents you have may just tip the balance in our favor."

"Thank you. Just please don't go dying again. I can only reattach a spirit to its body one time."

"You have my word that I will be more careful. Being dead is an experience that I don't wish to repeat until I have lived to a ripe old age."

Coral suddenly broke free of Junean and, stumbling slightly, made her way to my side. She said nothing, just clung to me. I held her close to me and buried my face in her hair.

Curiosity drew my eyes back to Granalis. This was the first time that I had really looked at him since he finished his transformation. I couldn't believe how much our enemy had altered his body. In his natural state he was just as beautiful as he had been ugly before. The fur that covered his body was the brightest white I had ever seen, and it was as fine and soft as silk. He still had wings, but they were on top of his back now. He was not really any bigger than he had been, but now he was longer than he was tall.

In his current form he walked on all fours. I looked at what I thought would be his front paws and saw that he had hands. His six fingers were well articulated, and his thumb was, other than being furred, just like my own. Granalis' pupils were orange, but despite the odd color his eyes showed only kindness. His eyes rode low in a long face, which reminded me of a cross between a horse and a dog, at least in size and shape. His movements were almost painfully graceful.

I kissed Coral's hair and tried to regain my feet. We were both weak, me from being dead, her from my use of her energies, and it took us three tries to get standing. Coral wouldn't leave my side, and we ended up leaning against the wall together. Conscious as we were that an abundance of time had passed, we weren't going to make very good time in the shape we were in. I asked Mikaal and Junean to get us some food and closed my eyes to try to locate our target again.

Being dead didn't seem to have affected my abilities any. I found the faint hum of magic in the distance and locked its position in my mind. When I opened my eyes Junean was standing in front of me with concern on her face. When she saw me open my eyes, she handed me some dried meat and a container of water. I chewed the meat slowly and thoughtfully. After a few minutes, I could feel some of my strength returning. I looked down at Coral and saw color returning to her face.

We set off again in the direction of the Star Glass. With Mikaal's Magelamp to light the way, we traveled for hours uneventfully before finally stopping for the night. By the time we stopped, Coral and I were so exhausted that we collapsed in a heap on the ground and didn't wake up for more than half a day.

Chapter 15
Thought Collecting

Coral woke before I did and, when she found out how long we'd been asleep, grew very concerned about me. She tried to wake me with a kiss, by shaking me, and finally by knocking on the door of my mind. Finally, she managed to bring me around, and everyone shared a sigh of relief when I opened my eyes.

It was early in the morning by our reckoning. We had spent a full day in the mines already. We had less than eight days remaining before the Chaos Cloud would reach and destroy Tiiaan. I had never been given much to worry or stress, but then I'd never had the fate of an entire world depending on me. Now that our momentum had been halted, I found myself nearing panic at the enormity of what we were trying to do. I decided to fight my rising panic by asking questions.

"How many towns and cities, of how many different peoples are north of Tiiaan? How many will have been destroyed already?"

Coral recoiled as if hit by my question and began sobbing softly. I had not thought about how my question would have reminded her of her still very recent loss and pulled her closer to me gently, apologizing for my foolishness mentally to her.

Mikaal sighed briefly and responded, "Thankfully, the northern part of Sorra is sparsely inhabited. The land there is hard and barren for many days travel in any direction. The few exceptions were the lagoon where the SeaWind were rebuilding their kingdom and a few small OrOboid and Moalean settlements. Most of those who were in the path of the Dark Cloud saw corrupted wildlife attacks first and, after understanding their source, fled south to what they hoped would be safety. It is from those who sought sanctuary near where I was traveling that I learned of the impending disaster. As far as I can tell, the Chaos Cloud first appeared slightly north of the SeaWind lagoon. They never had a chance to learn what was coming before it was on them."

Junean added quietly, "Tibbeus was from one of the northern families. He and a few of his brothers and sisters were among those who were forced to leave their homes. He came to my father's Cavenheld to both seek a place and warn us of what was coming. My father's advisers asked Tibbeus to test the wall of death that had destroyed his home to learn how it might be defeated. I was determined to keep him safe and not lose him, so I volunteered to go with him."

Understanding just how much pain my friends had endured, my desire to save this world and its people swept away my fears. I rose, determined to continue our search. I gave Coral a final squeeze and mental apology, and she wiped her eyes and stood beside me.

"Oh," she began. "Junean. I meant to ask you before we entered the mine. Is it true that a Moalean shield will alert its maker to even the smallest of impacts?"

Junean swelled up to her full nine and a half hand height at the recognition of her people's strength and answered, "Yes. We can tell if a single raindrop falls on our barrier. Why do you ask?"

Coral realized that this was an accomplishment that the little Moalean and her people held dear and delicately asked, "Have you ever heard of someone being able to walk through such a shield without waking its owner?"

Junean's reply was sharp. "I have never heard of it and would say that it was impossible. Why do you ask?"

I winced. "She's asking because she knows that Moalean shields are sensitive, but I didn't. When you were sleeping before we entered the mine, I split your barrier to go get our mounts some food. Coral saw me returning and told me that she didn't understand why that hadn't woken you," I offered.

"Aaron doing the impossible again," Junean breathed. "Let's hope he can keep doing that." With that, she hoisted her gear and began walking down the rough tunnel in the direction we had been heading. The light from her night eyes faintly illuminated the walls, and we quickly moved to follow her. Granalis was perched on my pack and stayed in place when I shouldered it and began walking. Coral and Mikaal fell in beside me as we hurried ahead.

"How did you come to be in the human world" I asked Granalis. I heard the opening and closing of his small mouth several times before he answered.

"As much as I would like to tell you about that, it appears that the spell of constraint which kept me from talking about my former master remains intact."

"Hmmm. Let's see what we can learn anyways." I spoke my thoughts aloud. "Can you tell us about your world?"

Granalis huffed once lightly and began. "I will tell you as much as I can. Even as I am much smaller than most of you, so was my world. I say was, because so far as I know, I am the only one of my kind to still be alive. We were the only race on Cuméform that was self-aware. I don't even remember now why we had a name for our world, since we weren't aware of any world but the one on which we lived. We had never thought of anything beyond our day-to-day peaceful existence. We weren't very numerous, maybe a few thousand of us living off of the land and the few creatures native to our world. I remember vividly hunting the herds of barleystalkers that roamed the plains near the tree village in which I was hatched. I've never seen another world in which the plant life was able to roam at will like they did at home."

Granalis stalled, lost in remembrance, shaking himself physically to break his reverie.

"One day I was out hunting. Several of my hatchmates were helping me herd a group of strong young barleys toward a cliff in which we had prepared a net to ensnare them. I heard a noise as we walked toward the edge of the precipice like the beating of many leathery lettucewings, but I couldn't look away from my prey for fear of the incredibly quick beasties darting past me. We reached the edge, and the barleys began falling into our trap, when all of a sudden the darkness of the canyon rose up in front of us. All of my friends who were tending the nets below the drop were swallowed up in the impenetrable wall of malice as it rose into the brightly lit day. Daylight began bending and then warping around the edges of this undulating formless mass, and the day dimmed as if the light was being absorbed more quickly than our sky could provide it."

Terror and hurt, even dimmed by an unknown amount of time, radiated off him nearly as clearly as if I had the ability to see emotion as well as magic. Coral sensed it too and ran her hand through his soft fur in consolation.

"Then, from within the mass came a howl and shrieking laughter. The darkness was rent by a mass so black as to be indescribable except to say that it made the maelstrom pale in comparison. The sound of laughter came from within this new void. I looked into this place, and it looked back at me with eyes of imperial purple. I could not look away from the sight and words began forming in my mind. My body filled with agony and who I was, I was no more."

His tiny body shuddered with the force of the memory, and his mouth worked silently for a short time more before he stopped and closed his orange eyes. I thought for a moment that he died from grief, but I could feel his breath deep and even on my neck.

As he had been speaking, we had been walking. Even weak as I was, I felt more strongly with every step the pull of the artifact we sought. What had been incredibly hard to locate at first now seemed to be singing out, not calling my name exactly, but perhaps blending with the rhythm of my heartbeat.

We kept descending into the maze of cross corridors and branching paths. Most of the time I didn't even need to pause before moving forward. The last two turnings had us walking down steeper inclines. The walls grew closer around us, and moisture twinkled in the many crevices in the now rough-hewn walls. Questions formed at the edges of my mind and vision about who and what had lived and worked the mines, but the pulsing sing-song of our target quickly drove them from my mind. The soft soles of the shoes I had been gifted were quite comfortable, but now there were sharp edged rocks at intervals in the path. I was glad that I'd saved the workman's boots that I had been wearing when I arrived in Sorra and took a moment to swap them out during a short break.

Chapter 16
That Which Must Be Dealt With

The corridor following our last turn seemed to go on for an eternity, narrowing twice before opening up into a larger rotunda carved out of the deeps of the earth. We were getting close now but still had a significant way to go. I began turning slowly, surveying each of the five evenly spaced paths before us. Foreboding began to wash over me as the sound calling us onward seemed to come from all of the paths equally.

I had completed two circuits around the space when the light above Mikaal's head bobbed once, then twice, then condensed into a smaller, brighter ball before haring off down the leftmost pathway and colliding with a wall before exploding into tiny shimmering stars. The stars blinded all of us but Junean, who had the advantage of two sets of eyes. I heard her make a very unladylike battle cry as the dim lights from her eyes struggled to illuminate the form crawling from the opposite tunnel on the far right.

Coral recovered more quickly than the rest of us as her eyes were also used to the darkness of deep waters. A dripping, sucking noise from that dimly seen form preceded another blinding flash as Coral's bow sung out an attack that appeared as if lightning had been called forth from thin air. Her attack hit something hard and bounced further into the tunnel. Whatever it had bounced off of wailed its displeasure and started moving towards us more quickly.

"This is not good." Junean's voice rang out in the near silence of the heart stone we stood in. "This is not a creature turned by the cloud. It is a natural enemy of my people, known for being nearly unstoppable. It is armored nearly everywhere and feeds on the despairing spirit of those it encounters. Once it has a bellyful of spirit energy, it will turn to drinking the lifeblood out of each victim while injecting the most painful poison known on Sorra. It is such an old creature that its name is lost in time." Even as she spoke, she was pressing us backward away from the creature.

"What happened to your Magelamp, Mikaal?" I asked.

"I've never known of anything that can control another person's light, but suddenly it was as if my globe was drawn away from me, and nothing I did could stop it."

Not knowing what I was facing, I drew my spear and held it toward the ceiling where the sucking, slurping, and wailing noises continued toward us, even as Junean urged us around the edges of the space we had to work in. I decided to trust my friends to keep my body as safe as possible for a moment and retreated into my inner room.

Light seemed to be what I needed most to be effective, so I started with that problem. I didn't think another light created by Sorran style magic would help, so I again drew on ideas from my world. I crafted the brightest light I could imagine, with a strap for my head, and launched it from the windows that represented my eyes using a mental hand.

I quickly exited my mental sanctuary and reached up with my left hand to switch on the headlamp I had just equipped myself with. Bright white light lanced out from my head, illuminating the brown and gray of the walls and ceiling. Just a few paces forward and above us was a hideous monster. It had a face like a human child, but larger and yet shrunken at the same time. Where a mouth would be were large pincers that clacked together and sent out a screech when my light hit the faceted eyes. The body was segmented like a centipede, but with thick layers of armor plating overlapping one another. Instead of legs at each segment there were tentacles encircled with sucking cups from which a smelly goo was dripping onto the floor.

The monstrosity shrank back when I trained my headlight at its face and squealed its displeasure loudly enough that the room vibrated. I kept my face pointed directly at its face and it stopped moving forward. I heard a petulant "go away! Go AWAY!" from somewhere, right before something flew over my head near enough to part my hair for me, followed by something crashing and splintering on the wall behind me.

Sharp shards bit into my clothes from behind. I heard the same voice hiss, "Leave here!" and shouted at my friends to duck and scatter, before taking a couple quick steps to the right, still trying to keep my light shining on the strange face before me. If any of us had been one second slower, someone would have been skewered as another barely seen missile slammed into the wall.

"Did any of you hear that voice?" I asked as they all struggled to regain their footing (or gaw'ing for Mikaal).

Coral, Granalis, and Mikaal had heard something but didn't understand it. Junean had heard nothing. It occurred to me then that I wasn't sure if I had heard with my ears or my mind. It further occurred to me that I'd never heard Junean mindspeak. The babyfaced centipede monster began inching towards us again despite the light, and Coral pulled back her bow while a red glow began to build around Mikaal. I felt like I needed to do something but attacking didn't seem the right thing.

"Go away!" skittered across my mind again and as I yelled a warning and stepped where I hope the attack wouldn't be, I mentally shouted "Why?" back towards the source of that thought.

This time I was able to see the projectile leave the maw between the pincers, but the stony arrow dropped harmlessly to the ground in front of us. The babypede stopped moving again, and I thought "Why do we need to go away?" at it. Nothing happened for a second,

That Which Must Be Dealt With

but I could feel the tension in both Coral's bow and Mikaal's spell nearing release.

"Don't attack!" I said aloud. I wasn't sure if everyone said "What?" at exactly the same moment or not, but they held their fire.

"Makers say no one can come," the voice said again.

"I think I can talk to it," I said out loud, unsure of who could hear the mental conversation.

"But why?" and "Who are the Makers?" I thought at the creature. It clacked its mandibles together quickly, and I thought I had angered it, but it did not attack.

"Makers are Makers. Why you come?" the babypede thought out slowly.

"We are trying to save life." I struggled to convey much meaning with few words. I was still new at talking in this way, but the mind I was hearing did not seem all that smart.

"You not 'fraid?" it asked me.

"Too much to save to fear," I thought.

"Little digger 'fraid."

"But she wants to help too."

Aloud I said, "Try to be brave. This may not have to be an enemy."

The mandibles clack, clacked again for a few seconds, and then "Digger fear going" came to me stronger than before. "You are here. Now I go."

The babypede's face turned away toward a blank wall and down to the floor. Then it began gathering itself into a ball. It stayed still for what seemed a very long while before I realized that it was becoming transparent. Slowly the menacing monster seemed to evaporate into the air and soak into the floor at the same time. And then it was gone.

I banished the headlight I was wearing with a thought as it was starting to make me slightly woozy as it moved with my head.

We all breathed a sigh of relief; Junean's sigh was disproportionately loud given her small size.

"I thought that was the end of us," she quavered. "I've never heard of a Moalean facing that creature and living before."

Mikaal quickly attempted to cast another Magelamp, and it seemed nearly blinding. We assessed ourselves for damage and found nothing more troubling than a few bruises and scratches from the shattered rock darts that had been fired at us. We were still taking stock and adjusting our eyes when Granalis (whom I had almost forgotten about due to him sleeping on my pack right behind my head through the entire ordeal) hissed for us all to be quiet.

At first none of us heard anything, but Granalis dropped to the floor and put his animal-like ears to the floor, so we kept listening. So slowly at first that I wasn't sure I was hearing anything, a vibration came followed by a long, deep scraping sound. Seconds later it repeated, slightly louder.

Everyone seemed to be holding their breath until each noise finished, until the next began. It was coming from the central pathway directly across from where we had entered. At every repetition the sound came a little louder and a little sooner. Mikaal's gaw began weaving an intricate dance that I couldn't follow with my eyes, but coupled with his droning chant and the red tracers following his movements I knew he was ready to attack. Hopefully whatever was coming was either an enemy or very forgiving. I couldn't blame him for attacking.

"Something large is coming towards us. It appears to walk on two legs and is dragging something heavy. I'm guessing it is a tail. It will be here very soon," Granalis said.

"Wait until I tell you before attacking. There is a bend in the tunnel ahead and it won't hit anything," Junean instructed, standing beside the crude entry before us with her night eyes trained toward the sound.

That Which Must Be Dealt With

There was another eternity of waiting before Junean's cry to release, and then Mikaal's spell shot forward with a fiery blast before veering abruptly and violently to the left. It shot over Junean's head, singeing her slightly before rocketing down the left pathway to smash into the same wall that destroyed his earlier Magelamp. Thankfully the globe of light over Mikaal's head remained in place for now.

"It is a large lizard shaped creature walking on its hind legs, but I can't see it breathe," Junean offered us. "I think it might be made of stone."

A few more steps forward and I could see it too. It was vaguely like the pictures of a dragon I'd seen in my home world but with no wings. Its mouth was large and full of more than one row of evenly spaced teeth. Its front arms were shorter than its hind legs, and I could barely make out the thick tail dragging in the shadows between each step. Its eyes were big and dead and looking right at me.

Suddenly it quickened its steps and began a lurching run straight at me. As it entered the space with the rest of us, it blew past Junean. A bolt from Coral launched from beside me and took off a tiny chip of the lizard-thing's shoulder, but it paid no attention. I shifted my stance to be able to dodge and bellowed for my companions to scatter. Granalis flew up from behind it and landed on its head, gripping its eyes. It had no effect at all. I feinted to the right, and the rockdragon turned that way.

It was almost on top of me, and it reacted much faster than I feared. I rolled forward and to the left, hoping to escape by surprise and daring. I failed. A glancing blow from its right leg knocked me several feet away towards the magic-eating hallway. I heard the creature slam into the wall and rebound while I tried to stand and shook stars out of my vision. I heard Coral and Junean asking if I was alive, and I made the most reassuring kind of noise I could with no air in my lungs.

Granalis had jumped away before the impact and was now circling the area above us, looking for a way to help. I wondered if my abilities would be sucked away by the magic sinkhole beside me, or for that matter what my abilities even were. While thinking, my left hand reached for my OrOboid spear.

This second attacker was moving again, and I could see where it had slid along the wall to slow itself and turn. So, it was big and heavy and reacted quickly but couldn't turn all that well. Good to know.

I contacted Mikaal mentally and instructed him to get behind it and try to attack it when it was between him and the place where his spells were going anyways. His Magelamp rose above us to illuminate the room the best it could while I saw him edging forward behind the living rock that was after me.

Being this close, each step our attacker took shook the air and echoed all around us. Junean, moving faster than I'd thought her capable of, barreled toward the enemy and leaped onto its tail. She then scrabbled up the back of the granite Gila monster and began gouging away at the base of the long thick neck. Her long claws raked impressive furrows, especially given her small size. This was the first attack that got any reaction from it, and so we were all surprised when the tail lifted from the ground and flicked Junean up into the air as if swatting at a fly. Thankfully Granalis swooped down and caught her. He wasn't big enough to hold her aloft, but he was able to slow and guide her fall so she wasn't damaged further.

It was coming for me again and picking up speed. Coral fired three more bright streamers of light into the same spot that Junean had weakened, each time sending splinters of ore careening into the walls. I was really hoping that one of their attacks could divert its attention even for a second to give me a chance to act on the glimmer of a plan which was coming together.

Almost as if the hope gave birth to it, Mikaal fired a blast of cold into the growing fissure of mineral-zilla's nape. It took two steps closer to me, and he followed that with an old-school fireball. Cold

That Which Must Be Dealt With

stone and fire met in an impressive explosion of stony shrapnel. The great head snapped toward the ceiling, and a deep grating roar reverberated down every passageway and echoed back to us. Ichor like lava poured from the wound.

Before the head could come back down, I snapped my spear down into the ground below me and angled it towards center mass. One more step brought it straight into this unexpected impediment. As I feared, the base of my spear, even buttressed by my boot, dug a great trench as the serpent automaton's inertia pressed me back. We were almost to the passageway that had swallowed Mikaal's spells. I had no interest in being crushed between a rock wall and this thing pressing me ever backward. I was just barely out of range of its clawed arms, and they began reaching for me with the intent to maim and destroy. Time to be somewhere else.

I jumped up and hit the spear with both feet, using it as a springboard to hopefully escape over and around the awful arms and tearing teeth. My weight on the spear pushed it deeper into the earth and the great chest, slowing it slightly, and I vaulted up onto a mental platform I had prepared.

I was almost away when I felt a crushing tug at my foot. I almost slid off my platform as my boot was ripped from my foot. It felt like my foot was going to go with it. Then things got worse. It used the same attack on me that it had used on Junean. The great tail shot up and tried to spear me into the ceiling. If I hadn't been lying on a psychic barrier, I would have been so much meat skewered down the center. As it was, I was slammed upward so hard I would have bounced, but the tail kept me pinned in place.

Once again, I saw stars and realized I wasn't breathing. This time, however, it was due to the amount of pressure it was exerting on me. If I lost consciousness, I wouldn't be able to keep the platform between me and certain death. I tried to push down with my mind, but the beast was stronger. Fortunately, I had ended up where I could see past the edge of the platform. I retreated into the maker space in my mind and did the only thing I could think of. I created two diamond-edged saw blades and sent them spinning as fast as I could imagine in my mental hands.

Hoping I didn't hit any of my friends, I sent them close below where I lay and began cutting away at the spiked rear-end of death. I felt a chunk of it fall away and got half a breath before the remainder slammed me again. I heard my friends below yelling and attacking. The little bit of air bought me a few more seconds, and I continued cutting away with my twin blades. I saw the golden curtain of unconsciousness creeping at the edges of my vision and was starting to give up when I heard a crack from below, and I dropped about six inches. This was enough for me to take some gasping breaths and push back into full awareness.

I tried to fly to one side or another and only managed to wedge myself in a new location. I went back to sawing and wished I was helping the people below who believed in me instead of trying to stay alive. A few more cuts and I was floating free again. I got out of tail space and turned to assess. The chamber seemed large when we first entered but was too small for a battle of such scope. I had only a forearm's length between my head and the roof. There were perhaps six paces from the abbreviated tail to the opposite side of the room where Granalis, Mikaal, and Junean fought. Coral was trapped between the wall and the teeth of the amazingly still connected head. Mikaal and Coral had done significant damage, but this thing wasn't alive. How were we to stop it? If we cut it apart, would it just keep attacking?

I had to keep trying. Mikaal was still behind the thing with a much dimmer glow as he prepared to cast again. His robes were smoking, and he looked dead on his feet. I still had the blades I'd created, and I pressed on hacking the beast's head from its body. I lowered myself to the ground and compacted the square I had been riding on into a smaller and more dense area before sending it careening into the opposite side from my blades.

Coral was trying to press herself further into the wall to keep from being chewed up when suddenly the chomping muzzle snapped away, dropping teeth. I could feel its senses circle around. It knew where I was now, and it tried to back itself off of the spear to get to me. The stump of a tail waved wildly, nearly smashing Junean who was still struggling to her feet. Coral took that chance to break away and circle toward me. My bladed mental hands kept cutting away while the platform that had become a brick smashed its face once more.

It was able to back off the spear and take a step towards us before our combined attacks culminated in an earsplitting crack, like a tree being hit by lightning in an enclosed space. Molten goo spewed from its wound as the neck broke off and its head fell away from the body. It took one more step, pitched forward, and ceased moving.

There was a minute of absolute silence, save for the ragged breathing of overexerted adventurers as we waited for movement or an attack. When nothing came at us each of us walked toward the only area clear of debris from the battle and began checking on the others. Coral and Granalis were in the best shape, having only minor scratches. Mikaal was swaying on his feet after emptying his already strained magical reserves into the attack. Junean had a nasty bump on her head near one floppy ear and was struggling to stand due to extreme dizziness.

I probably looked the worst. I felt like I had one or more cracked ribs, and my left foot was bloodied and uncovered. Luckily the metal toe of my boot seemed to have prevented me from losing any toes, but it had caved in and gouged a layer of skin off the top of my foot up to the first joint of my middle toe.

In order to conserve Mikaal's little remaining strength, I created a battery-powered light fixture in my mind and used a non-corporeal hand to drive it into the highest point in the subterranean rotunda, before telling Mikaal to banish his lamp. I instructed Granalis to keep a lookout and Mikaal to eat something while Coral began attempting a minor healing spell on Junean.

This left me to try to put myself back in order. I didn't have magic healing spells so far as I knew and wouldn't know how to cast one if I did, so I created a first aid kit and a new boot and gingerly started bandaging my foot. This was made even more difficult by the fact that every breath and every motion sent waves of agony through my midsection.

Coral had Junean looking significantly healthier by the time I was finished with my repair, and so I stood up as they approached, trying and failing to suppress a gasp of pain. Coral rushed to me and asked how I was hurt. I told them what I thought was wrong, and Coral frowned her dismay.

"I don't have any spells strong enough to mend bone," she explained.

Junean thought for a moment before digging in her satchel and producing the aspirin statue and another figure that I hadn't seen. The second figurine was birdlike, with a very sharp beak. The moment she placed the former of the two in my hand I could feel the pain lessen and my breathing ease. Then she had me point to where I thought the damage was, and I wished I hadn't. She asked Coral to hold my shirt up and then jammed the bird's beak into my ribcage quickly and unexpectedly. This seemed to surprise Coral as much as it did me... or maybe it was the unmanly squeal I let out at this new turn of events.

Seconds passed and she removed the beaky figure slowly from my skin. The skin seemed to return to normal as the statue left my body, and my pain was, while not gone, much reduced. I wish I could say that I was more macho the second time she stabbed me, but knowing it was coming really didn't keep it from sucking.

Within a short time, I was able to hand back the aspirin statue and move around relatively easily. I could tell I was still damaged but was on the mend. "Thank you," both Coral and I said nearly in unison, and then I knew what she looked like when she blushed. Even in this poorly lit area I could see the skin of her cheeks brighten like sunlight peering from behind the clouds and illuminating the ocean as the tides pulled away from the shore. Junean's smile in return was glad, yet wistful.

Deep in darkness, I had no idea what time it was outside, but we were all running on fumes. With no immediate sign of danger, we began to discuss setting up camp. And then just as we reached a consensus, the need to choose was abruptly taken from us.

Chapter 17
Dark Decisions

One minute it was our merry band of five alone in the heart of a mine, the next saw a shining being walk out of the aperture which I had thought to contain only a magnet for errant spells. The light emanating from this vision was not terribly bright, but it changed color at irregular intervals. So too did the face and body meld from one person into another and back again. Now it was a yellow glow surrounding the small body of the oldest Moalean I could imagine; lines blurred and hues shifted, and the person I saw before me could have been Coral's mother bathed in aquamarine light; yet again I looked and a young looking Noran man stood there in all his tentacled glory with the verdant glow of the deep forest. Several others melded before me, a Garanth or two in shades of metallic silver, and my first glimpse of an OrOboid, tall and surrounded by facets of shimmering white.

Somewhere in the cacophony of faces and shades I heard a voice. I couldn't be certain if I was hearing with my ears or my mind, but it didn't really matter. It said something once, —transition— and again in a new voice, —transition— and finally on the third repetition the question broke through my awestruck reverie.

"Why are you here?" the voices said, together and yet distinctly alone.

"I...we, are here because Sorra is in danger," I stammered. "Perhaps it is already too late, or we are insufficient to the task, yet we must try to save her."

They seemed to absorb my words and coalesce together before the next face spoke. "That is an admirable reason to have come. —transition— Yet are you strong enough to make the difficult decisions? —transition— Can you choose whom will live and who will not?"

I had no idea who or what this being was. The sense of being in a mine deep in the earth had been replaced with a feeling of gravitas and purpose. I thought to Coral and Mikaal and asked if they were seeing the same thing I was and if they knew what was going on. Awe-filled acknowledgement of what we were seeing, and a sense of being confounded by the proceedings, was all I got.

"We will seek to save everyone we can..." I began, only to be interrupted by a deep bass note from a face and body from no race that I was aware of existing here.

"We are/I am the Sorran Conclave of Magic!" The voices seemed to blend together on the first two words. "Our essences were stored here to protect the most powerful artifact we have ever known. —transition— I/we did not ask all of you these questions. The question is to the leader of the quest. —transition— You were called/sent here for a purpose. You are the champion!" —transition— The final words belonged to a creature that looked and sounded reptilian and was delivered in a high-pitched shriek. "Aaron. Who will live? Who will die?"

The voice rebounded around the circular room, swirling around us in a vortex that rose to a powerful wind. The wind became so urgent that I could see its intensity. First it was a tornado filling the room, and then it split into two funnels without losing apparent size or strength. Before I could react, the first vortex seized Mikaal. When I turned to help him, my heart stopped as I heard Coral's voice scream out her fear behind me.

The wind was whipping around each of them at speeds that made me woozy, but Mikaal and Coral spun lazily around within. For the first time since setting foot on Sorra, I panicked as my friends were carried away from me towards the two remaining passages where attacks had not originated. I could not lose either of my friends like this. It would be my fault! I could not stand by and lose another family like I had at home!

My fear paralyzed me until the heat of my regret burst through. I would not fail a second time!

"Junean and Granalis. Follow and save Mikaal!" I shouted to my remaining compatriots tersely. "I'll go after Coral." And to the undulating form standing ahead I said, "I reject your options! I will save everyone that I can regardless of the cost to myself."

The Moalean and the flying alien shot off after Mikaal at my command. I leapt into the air and landed on a wing of my creation that was visible only to me and raced after Coral. My source of light was quickly left behind with the echoing laughter of the ancients emanating from the malleable mannequin behind me. I dived back into my mental workshop to quickly craft a pair of night vision goggles. I could see the maelstrom carrying my Love away from me and see her shifting slowly within. I was quickly catching up to her, but I could also tell that this trail also came to a deadly end. Coral was careening toward what appeared to be a mouth comprised of stalactites and stalagmite teeth which were gnawing and smacking in anticipation of the end of the SeaWind race.

Now that I could see the danger, I had little time to react. This had to be a creation of magic for me to have seen it visibly. The beings that had left a piece of themselves to defend their great treasure probably didn't know of anybody with my talents. I hoped that was enough to win the day.

I was close enough to act, so I dropped myself to the ground as if I was stealing a base and used the wing I was riding as well as two others to surround the unnatural weather pattern. I brought each of them closer to the center where Coral was held as quickly as I dared to avoid hurting her. As she spun, I saw her launch a physical arrow back up the way she had come in an effort to anchor herself and prevent her being carried away. Her aim was incredible as always and I had to pivot my slide and kiss the wall to avoid being impaled yet again.

My trio of wings began to shear the wild winds away from Coral and lessen her progress, but not quickly enough. I had to exert every ounce of will fighting this storm. The ferocity of the wind increased as I shunted the force away from my Love and into the walls through which she passed. I feared that I wouldn't be able to save her, much less be able to help Mikaal as well if needed.

At the last possible second, I turned all the wings so that the force of the wind was propelled directly toward the danger. This allowed for enough slowing so that the leading fangs merely ripped the cloth of her satchel rather than tearing her apart. I rushed in and pulled her to safely as the storm and the mineral choppers tore one another apart.

I wanted to stop and hold her close, but I had another friend in deadly peril. I pulled a telekinetic carpet under us and carried us back towards the rest of our compatriots as quickly as possible. We burst into the light with a whoosh of displaced air and began to turn to where Mikaal, Junean and Granalis had vanished.

To my great relief, Junean was larger than I'd seen her before and was pulling herself along the wall by her great claws. Granalis was engulfed by a bright sorcerous glow and was scaling the wall on the opposing side. His wings were gone, and he instead had two additional muscular, gripping arms, similar to Junean's front arms. Between them was a lightly glowing net, containing one bedraggled and sheepish Noran wizard. It appeared that the magic that had attempted to end his life was still actively trying to do so. I created a concrete wall in my mind and placed it directly behind the trio, and the vacuum behind them ceased.

I sought and found the Conclave with my eyes and walked towards them, never letting go of Coral for an instant.

"No one's dying so long as I'm alive," I informed a small purple Noran, just before it was replaced by another OrOboid.

"So, we see," it responded brightly. "You avoided a fight where it was not needed. You fought where there was no choice and triumphed. Finally, you led your team of diverse races to support and protect one another."

—transition— "You are worthy to defend Sorra. —transition— You are worthy to direct the Star Glass."

Following these words there arose a rubbing, grinding sound from the leftmost path, where Mikaal's magic had been pulled. The wall that had been at the end of this passage split in two and began retracting into the sides of the passage. Our way ahead was clear again.

A figure appeared suddenly before me which was cast in orange and tangerine and appeared more substantial than the others had. I was unready for the tall, catlike, androgynous form to grab my arm physically and pull me close.

"Below you will find that which you have sought. Still, you do not understand how difficult the journey ahead will be and what will be asked of you before it is complete. Have you not wondered how you understand what is said to you here on a world so unlike your own? Are there not many languages where you come from? Does it not occur to you how unlikely you would journey to a world where you could communicate and even find friendship so easily and quickly? Aaron… you were called for by Mikaal truly. You were also called from among many lands and many peoples and offered up to help the people of this place to live. Ponder these things and do your best for Sorra."

I opened my mouth to ask questions and found that nothing remained of the feline humanoid but a tickle in my throat reminding me I was allergic to cats.

Chapter 18
Path to the Star

"Is everyone ok?" I asked, retrieving my spear and shaking my head in confusion.

Granalis growled out that he was fine, but his voice indicated a great deal of pain. I looked over and watched his body reverting to its normal form. Changing shape seemed excruciating.

Coral didn't say anything and just pulled my arm tighter around herself. Junean and Mikaal were helping each other up from the ground and indicated they were well. Junean took the netting from the floor with her feet and deftly wove it into a small tight ball but left two threads free. I was guessing that would prepare it for quick deployment again at need. She then stowed it back in her bag of goodies.

"If it is all the same to everyone, I'd like to move down past the doorway that just opened up and get some distance between this area and us before we rest," I said.

All nodded their assent, and we began picking our way gingerly toward the path we hoped would lead us finally to our goal.

As we reached the place where the wall had been I was astounded that I could see no traces of where it had been. The Sorran Magicians of the Conclave must have been incredibly skilled at their craft. They also appeared to me to have been slightly insane to have created such traps. Who knows how many people of different races had met an untimely demise down here.

As we moved ahead the light I had placed before was left behind, so I stretched out my internal arm and retrieved it. I held it near the ceiling and slightly ahead of us to light our way. We travelled until we rounded a natural curve in the tunnel and could see a long straight section before us and then a bit further until we could see a good distance straight both before and behind.

When I suggested we stop the little Noran seemed to sink into the ground. He kept moving forward and was snoring soundly almost immediately when he stopped. Unwilling to be caught unaware again, we decided to take turns sleeping, leaving one of us alert at all times. Junean volunteered to sit the first watch and as the others settled in, I planted the light in the wall low enough that she could reach it and showed her how to turn it off and on. I was concerned that her excitement over a device that seemed to her to be magical and from another world would cause her to be distracted, but she calmed quickly once I told her it was a device like a Garanth might make. Moalean are fond of magical devices, but care little about mechanical apparatus.

She bundled herself up beside the light and waited for me to pull my blanket around me and settle in next to Coral before flipping the switch. The darkness that enwrapped me was complete and, to someone not used to being underground, stifling. I was beginning to allow myself a panic attack, but Coral's hand sought mine, and then the faint light from Junean's night eyes rolled along the wall as she shifted her view from one direction to the other.

The next thing I knew Granalis was shaking me lightly and asking me to take my turn. His eyes were glowing in imitation of Junean's. I gently relaxed Coral's grip on my hand and moved myself by feel over to where Junean had been sitting. Granalis languidly stalked over to a place near the wall further in the direction we had been headed and closed his eyes. I quickly worked to recreate the night goggles I had been using before and set to work ensuring the empty tunnel didn't get any more exciting.

Nothing happened for a long while. No sound could be heard save for a light trickle of water joining a deeper pool somewhere far ahead. I could hear every breath from each of my sleeping friends. I was surprised when I thought I saw something move moments before I was going to wake Mikaal. It seemed like a rock had rolled silently out from the wall and down the path. I would have thought I would have heard it before I saw it as far away as it was.

I increased the magnification of my goggles to the limit and could see the rock continuing to roll away, seemingly on its own. A small bit of blurriness around the edges of the rock made me realize that it was covered with this world's version of moss. I was so focused on the silently rolling stone before me that I didn't remember to look behind me. I gasped aloud when I felt something brush by my left hand where it was near the edge of the wall I was leaning against. I quickly reduced magnification to 1x and looked down. An irregularly shaped chunk of wall had wriggled free and landed up against my hand.

Creepy self-propelled masonry didn't seem super threatening, and as I was already touching it I quickly grabbed it and lifted in to where I could examine it more closely. I held it in both hands and turned it slowly, looking for a face or gears or, I don't know what exactly. It appeared to be a chunk of wall and nothing more. Sheepishly I whispered to it, "Are you alive?" and put it up to my ear. Unsurprisingly it did not answer.

I placed it gently before me and watched to see if it moved any more. This quickly became boring, and I stood up and stretched myself, only to hear it roll once I looked away. I decided to keep watching it while I made my way to the sleeping Noran's side and shook him gently.

"Mikaal—wake up quietly. It is your turn to stand guard."

Mikaal sat up and rubbed his eyes muzzily, and once he was alert enough, I pointed to the thing I was watching. He looked at it and at me, back and forth a couple of times, before making a face.

"So, then nothing happened on your watch?" he whispered.

"Until a short time ago, nothing. I thought I saw something very small rolling away from us, but other than that, no," I said quietly, pointing at the wall chunk with a finger.

Mikaal pantomimed me going to sleep and cast two small, dim mage lamps and sent them before and behind us, giving just enough light for me to see after I removed and banished my goggles. Then he walked over and picked up our little friend and carried it to where we would be headed in the morning. I could barely make out his grin as I settled down and tried to sleep. I guess I should have realized by now that I wasn't in Kansas, or Earth, anymore.

I fell asleep to the near silence being broken only by the sound of trickling water and an occasional tap of something shifting. I awoke to Coral's face near my own, lit on the right side by the glow coming from the light I had left in the wall. She told me that it was time to move, and I could tell by the rustling from the others that she had allowed me to sleep until everyone else was up.

We gathered in a circle and had a few bites of food and a swallow or two of water, each making sure that the others were fit to continue before grabbing the light and proceeding on our way. Junean had the best night vision, so we let her lead the way. We walked for a long time through a very boring tunnel, save for the occasional spot where a chunk of the wall had come loose and seemed to roll away down the decline on its own volition, trailing a bit of dust in its wake.

Finally, the way ahead began to lighten and broaden; then we stepped out into an enormous cavern lit by veins of glowing minerals in nearly every pastel shade I could imagine. The site seemed to be both above us and below us as it was reflected in the water of a great still pond, which blocked our further progression. Far across the waters I could almost make out a pillar of some kind which housed a brightly glowing… something.

The water was so still that the reflection was perfect. Nothing moved in this space, and we stood there together in stunned silence looking, peering, straining to capture all the silent beauty before us. It was as if, when we entered the mine, we had begun walking back through Sorra's history and had now reached the dawn of the world's creation. Time seemed to stretch and bend in on itself until we became a part of the overall tableau and locked in this moment in time.

I didn't know how long we stood there speechless, but the weight of the responsibility I had assumed began pressing down on me with exponential force. When I broke through the captivity the vision had asserted on me, it seemed to free my compatriots as well. Without a word, we took a halting step forward and then another until the toes of my boots sent ripples dancing across the surface of the mirror reflection, destroying its residual hold over us.

We spread out again working as a team without need for speech of any kind. We didn't know what we were looking for, but we couldn't imagine this place being at the end of our adventure for the Star Glass without it having a purpose or test involved. This search proved an odd sort of fruitful, for we found the nothing that we sought. The dry part of this awe-inspiring cave was barren of any trigger, trap, or clue as to how we should proceed.

We were walking towards each other again when Granalis flew over the edge of the lake as a shortcut round the curved edge he had earlier searched on foot. The water went from inky stillness to a burst of activity, throwing a plume directly in front of where he was flying. Only quick action and an indignant and uncharacteristic squawk saved him from an unexpected drowning and alerted us to his distress. He began weaving in and out through one burst of spray after another, shaking himself to reduce moisture on his wings as he fought his way back to where we waited.

Coral stepped forward, looking like she was about to dive into the water to fight his attacker, but I threw my arm out to stop her.

We didn't know anything about this place and what lived and moved in the deeps below. She turned to me with a hurt look, but she could see the concern written on my face and she relented. A shock of blue air whizzed by us while I was trying to decide how to help.

Mikaal advanced and threw another blast of icy air toward the water. The first reached its destination, and the surface of the dark pond froze instantly. The second met its target and the freeze grew, allowing Granalis enough of a reprieve to beat his way furiously to land. The ice lasted only a few seconds on the surface as the blue hues in the walls burned brighter, and the ice dissolved almost as quickly as it had formed. Perhaps this then was what had been absorbing Mikaal's spells before. The veins of minerals within the ceiling worked like magic sponges.

Granalis landed with an ungraceful thump and shook his fur dry before we got to him.

"Whatever you do, do not touch the water and do not place yourself above it." He gasped. "The touch of each droplet is like the kiss of the grave. Cold that leeches the strength from your bones and the will from your heart. Had it touched more than the fur of my body, I think I would have died instantly."

Coral shivered and mouthed her thanks to me. I shivered a bit and looked down at my boot. Where my toe had dipped into the water's edge earlier, the leather was eaten away and only the metal toe remained. That was all we had time for before Junean called out a warning. There were bubbles and swirls forming before us, and we all backed toward the tunnel entrance. Only it was no longer there. We put our backs together, as much as that was possible for five people whose bodies were so dissimilar, and prepared to face whatever was roiling the deadly waters.

I kept expecting the disturbance to narrow into a single area and some kind of demented lake creature to thrash out of the depths, but the churning continued at hundreds or maybe a thousand individual points. Just before breaking on the beach, these points turned as one and rolled into view. Rocks, stones, crags, boulders large and small, tumbled over around and through one another out of the froth they themselves had created on a pristine surface. They started as a formless pile just above the boiling lagoon and rolled, scraped, and pushed themselves into higher and higher places within the twisting outline of a man.

Out of the corner of my right eye, I saw Mikaal's gaw weaving the preparations of a magical attack begin to slow and his bright yellow glow dimmed significantly. I briefly chanced a look at his face to see his expression and was taken aback to see a small smile spreading across his features. I looked back to the visitor from the depths just in time to see the outline harden visibly. Each of the parts of the apparition spun in place once or twice and then clicked into place. Everything froze again then, long enough for the ripples to have stilled and the subterranean mirror to reform.

The earth itself seemed to grate out the words. "Greetings Mikaal. It has been some time since we spoke. Greetings to Aaron from another world, Granalis from a world that no longer exists, Junean of Sorra's crust, and Coral of Sorra's depths. We are the Gathering. You are here for the Star Glass, but what makes you believe that you are fit to possess its power?"

I had to take a moment to reconcile what I was seeing to what Mikaal had told me when I first arrived about stones called Critters that appeared inanimate but enough of them became a Gathering like this. The reality was.... Something else.

I was able to make out the movements of a mouth within the bulbous head. I looked to Mikaal again, waiting for him to take the lead as he was the first addressed.

Without stepping forward he said, "Oh, wise Gathering. I know that you know infinitely more than I do even now, but I thought you were mistaken or even crazy when you told me of all that I must do these hundreds of years ago. Yet you were amazingly correct in all that you said. I thank you for allowing me to serve Sorra since then.

Now I will step back and support this man, Aaron, who responded to our call."

Mikaal did as he said he would, moving back and leaving me standing in the forefront. Clips of old movies played in my head briefly, where soldiers stepped back causing others to appear to volunteer. I started to have feelings about this but decided against it.

"I feel like there is a great story that Mikaal will have to tell me another time. It is an honor to meet you, Gathering. I don't understand how you know my name or about me, but you asked me a question, and I'll answer it. I don't believe I am fit to have power on my own. If there is someone stronger, wiser, quicker, or more suited to saving Sorra, I would gladly step aside and let them lead. However, no one has. Along the way I have found these very different individuals who also want to prevent the destruction of this world. Together it is my hope that we can use the power of the Star Glass to save as many others as possible."

"When that work is finished, what of the Star Glass then?" the Gathering rumbled.

"That's a hard question. I don't understand the artifact yet to know of its uses or dangers. Those before us thought it was important to keep it locked away. I don't claim to be wiser than they are, so assuming that we are successful in saving this land, it would probably be best to put it where the power wouldn't tempt people to misuse it."

"You do not wish for power?"

"I didn't have power in my homeland. I was unremarkable. I did occasionally wish that I had more control, but now that I've come to Sorra and have a power of my own, I find that I barely know how to use it and only find it desirable to help those around me. I know that where I came from people have used power to dominate others. Even if it started from a wish to make things better, it almost always ends in disaster."

"As you said, others have sought the Star Glass as a means to help but have been corrupted by its enormous power. It is good that you recognize the danger and should remain vigilant against such desires. We have seen that which attacks our world. We see that which you do not. Something must be done." The individual stones of the form I was speaking with began to spin and vibrate for a time. "We have considered your answers and find you a suitable bearer. We will take you to it."

"How are you able to be within the lake?" I inquired. "You're alive."

"We live, and yet our life is not one of breath and flesh. We remained here to guide and guard because our life is a part of the earth, and we are not harmed by that which unmakes you."

"Can you tell us more of what we face so that we can be more prepared?"

"We can but doing so will cause more hurt than help, and so we will not. You must face each challenge together and grow before you can be ready to know of the next."

I couldn't think of anything else, so I simply replied, "Thank you for entrusting us with the means to help Sorra."

The Gathering became a flurry of motion and vibration, and after a short time steam began to rise from the bulky form. I couldn't figure out what they were doing, but Mikaal pointed out that they were removing the liquid from themselves so that they could safely touch us.

Once dried they began to reform into a small relatively flat surface, which I assumed we would stand on, supported by a frighteningly thin column of rocks. No more explanation was given and so when they grew still, I motioned, and we all squeezed together onto the small area they had created for us. We all held on tightly to them and to each other, not sure how rough the journey across the deadly lake would be.

We began moving towards the lake's surface, but as we got closer there was a subtle bump within the column below us, and we never dropped to less than two hands from the calm, but dangerous waters.

Chapter 19
From Inky Blackness to Unbearable Light

We rode forth in silence save for the irregular bump/grind as the living monolith formed and reformed itself to provide us safe passage where we would never be able to go alone. I remembered how I had been told time and again that it was up to me to save this world; yet without these few companions that I had known less than a week I would have already failed. I had even died! What chance of success did I have? I had already failed to save those I loved once. How could I be a champion?

I was lost in doubt until Coral's arm slipped around me. I looked up from where I had been staring into the waters straight into her eyes and caught there the reflection of the bright light we were slowly approaching. I would die before I lost her, or any of my friends for that matter. Even Granalis, whom I'd known for less than a day, had already saved me and fought alongside us.

Would this artifact be able to turn a nobody from another world with a few new tricks into a force strong enough to save a world? How would I even know how to use it? The questions posed by the Cat-Being also clawed at the edges of my mind. Why was I the one that was summoned?

This contemplation was again brought to a halt as the rack'o'rocks carrying us suddenly thrust forward at an accelerated rate. I barely had time to register that the black waters ended against a perfectly flat vertical surface which protruded sharply up until it squared off to a shiny obsidian floor which was currently above the height of our transport before we bumped up twice more sharply than before and came to a skidding halt.

I was disoriented by the sudden change in pace and by the blinding brilliance of the crystal chest before us. I took a quick look around behind me to ensure that my companions were all safe and that the critters were forming themselves into The Gathering once more. I raised my arms to cover my face from what seemed brighter than my birth world at high noon and tried to see more of my surroundings.

The floor we stood upon was nearly as black as the life-leaching lake behind us and if possible, even more reflective. If I looked directly down behind me, I could see the image of the veins of ore in the jagged ceiling above us, but if I looked anywhere else all I could see was the purest white light radiating from the captive sun, reflected and refracted again and again within the perfectly smooth crystal enclosure. Even closing my eyes didn't sufficiently shield the brightness from my vision.

I heard a hissing noise and realized that it was Junean hissing in pain. Her back was to our prize, and she was seated with her rear limbs covering both sets of her eyes. Coral had her head down and was moaning over her burning eyes as well.

I retreated to the safety of my mind. For the first time since I'd learned to see through my eyes while within my inner chamber, I shuttered those windows. Relief flooded in, and I was able to think again. I created a pair of what I thought solar eclipse glasses looked like, cracked the shutters, and placed them on my face with a non-corporeal hand. It got dark. I un-shuttered the windows and returned to reality. I could now look more or less directly at the chest. Looking away and lifting the glasses, I located my friends and replicated the process with each of them. Junean's glasses had to be modified for twice as many eyes, but in short order we were all able to see when looking in the direction of the chest.

By this time The Gathering had once more become a recognizable form, if smaller. Their voice seemed muted when they spoke again, perhaps because in this location they were fewer in number and insulated from contact with the Sorran soil.

"We are glad you are all unhurt. We were sufficient in number to get you here, but fewer than required to make a softer landing. We have watched and waited these many years for you to take your place in this world. We have stopped those who were unfit to wield this power, yet even now we have fulfilled our purpose. Now it is up to you. We can help you no further. May your actions stay true and your path lead you to a long life for Sorra."

I wasn't really sure how to respond, but by the time I had opened my mouth to speak the figure crumbled into its constituent parts and rolled back into the deeps with a series of varied "plunk" noises. I feel like I opened and closed my mouth a few times trying to recover some equilibrium but shortly turned at the incongruous sound of Mikaal's mirth.

"The first and only time before now that I met The Gathering...." He forced out amongst the chuckles, chortles and guffaws. "They left me the same way. I'm sure I looked just as silly as you do now!" This followed by the thunk, thunk, thunk that I assumed was the Noran equivalent of knee slapping.

I chose to ignore the other assorted sounds of laughter as we stood there together seemingly at the dividing line between the very light of a god and the entrance to the netherworld. I imagined the sound of gears grinding when I remembered I had the key to open this buried treasure around my neck.

I grasped the chain and lifted it carefully over my head. The extreme disparity between the blinding light and equally blinding darkness caused by the glasses we wore to guard against certain blindness made each action more complex. I didn't want to drop the key and risk it falling into the lake where we could not retrieve it. I wasn't able to see a keyhole in the almost oppressive brightness before me, so I reacted by making only slow deliberate movements.

I felt the key with my fingers, silently berating myself for not paying closer attention to its design before now. It felt to me like I remembered an old skeleton key being represented in the cartoons of my youth, so I held the key with the barrel forward and the bit toward the floor in my left hand. I made one, two, three shuffling steps toward the chest with my right hand extended. I couldn't tell how far I was from it, or how far I moved with each step until I brushed its polished surface with my knuckles on the fourth step. I felt my friends, now cured of their fit of situational amusement, coming up behind me.

I ran my fingers over the top surface before me without finding so much as an uneven spot or the slightest blemish. I began fumbling slowly over the side closest to me, feeling for a keyhole. I noticed the thinnest of seams running vertically across the top third, but nothing large enough to be a way in.

I started to get a little concerned at this point but breathed to calm myself before trying to follow the seam around the perimeter of this uncooperative object. I used my index finger to trace the fine line and had my lower hand positioned in the hopes that I would feel an entry point below where the case opened. Even at what felt like a glacially slow pace I still lost my place and had to backtrack a few times before I reached the front of the case again.

Up until this point my compatriots had been standing quietly nearby, assumedly watching me try to crack the case, but at my exasperated sigh Mikaal stepped forward. "What are you doing, Aaron?"

"I am trying to remove a powerful artifact from a glowing box that doesn't seem to give me said artifact," I said crossly.

"Do you remember what I told you of the OrOboid race when you arrived here?"

"They craft incredibly strong objects of crystal."

"Yes and no. I said that they work crystal. When an OrOboid crafts a chest, he crafts it in one piece. The key is made at the same time, and they tell the crystal to give of itself a key. Nothing in this world save that key will open the lid. To ensure the beauty of this creation, this key is typically taken from the bottom face so that it is not visible."

I shook my head in chagrin once again and knelt before the fortress of light. Feeling below it, I found that it was sitting on a stand which was basically like a stool with a hollow seat. Now that I was aware of what I was looking for, I found a long narrow indentation that matched the key I held. I oriented the key carefully by feel to fit it into place. When it was nearly in position it was sucked from my fingers, and with a musical clink the lid popped open.

Chapter 20
... and Back Again?

The Star Glass and its container were gone. The lid opened. One second later I could no longer see it. I heard Coral and Junean gasp in unison. Had this all been a trick?

I removed my glasses now that the source of light was gone, and there it was again. I smacked my forehead and looked again. On the stand was the chest; in the chest was a much less bright spheroid object. When the blinding brightness dropped to merely bright, the solar glasses filtered the light entirely. I collected all the glasses I'd made and banished them while chuckling at my friends' confusion before returning to the task at hand."

I reached out, blinking some to adjust my eyes after the unintended iris exercises, and grasped what I took to be the Star Glass from its crystal prison. I pulled. It didn't move. I pulled harder. The chest shifted on its pedestal. I pulled and twisted. Something groaned and cracked. Then I was holding the Star Glass?

It seemed like a chunk of the chest had adhered to the talisman and broken off. Now the artifact appeared like a glass ball held securely in the grip of two crystal palms whose arm's smooth surface tapered down before flaring out into a heptagonal prism which served as a handle. The base ended with a thick loop. Wait, no… that wasn't right, the loop was actually an endless knot with an open center.

The Star Glass was smaller and more delicate looking than I'd imagined. It was still glowing, but now it resembled the full moon from my home world. It appeared that the illumination from the chamber that had enclosed our prize had faded completely once it was stripped of its contents.

While I stood pondering these things, Mikaal silently came up beside me. "The Legends say," he began.

To which I replied "AAAAAHCK! Don't be creeping around in the dark like that! You'll give me a heart attack."

"Erm, yes, ahem. I apologize….. No one knows for certain, but the Legends say that many years ago Sorra's second Sun unexpectedly vanished in the middle of the day. That evening a bright streak moved slowly across the sky. Its speed increased significantly each hour, and before first light it slammed into the largest mountain in what is now called the Wastelands."

"The closest city to this Star Fall was Adthaamos. This city no longer exists, but then it was bigger than Tiiaan, and some of every Sorran race called it home. An expedition was sent out to investigate. There were two of the strongest Noran magicians, two Moalean far-rangers, two Garanth tinkerers, and a duo of OrOboid crafters. They were expected to return within a fortnight, but after two passed and there was no sign of them, they were given up as lost."

It was about this time that I decided this story was likely to take a fortnight and sat down in front of Mikaal cross-legged. Coral had a similar idea and sat beside me so we could lean against each other.

"Eventually half that number returned, dragging the crystal chest. The survivors recounted that the far-rangers had taken the lead and were the first to reach the crevasse where the heavenly visitor had come to rest. There was no life remaining around the dense, flinty, golden, monument-like structure that had buried itself into the heart of the mountain. They searched for entrances and found none, so they began to scrape away layer after layer of the star stuff until they unearthed its glass heart. One of the far-rangers used

...AND BACK AGAIN?

a magical statuette meant to learn the nature of a thing upon it and was instantly driven mad. None of their efforts at healing were able to restore him.

"They worked to free the seemingly dangerous object. Once they recovered it they began to discuss what to do with it. After losing one of their group to the beautiful device, they decided it was dangerous and that it should be destroyed. The Noran Magicians prepared a complex casting that would attack this unwelcome item with each of the four elements in turn. Within a few ticks of them triggering their spell both were mortally wounded by their attack rebounding at them. Parts of their bodies were frozen, others burned, and others singed and filled with lightning."

I assumed the other Sorrans had heard this story before, but looking at Junean and Coral I could see they were listening intently too. Junean and Granalis now sat to either side of us with intent looks on their faces.

"After the Norans were buried, the remaining group plotted to end their predicament by smashing the seemingly fragile object. They would use no more magic against it. The next plan was to have the strongest of the OrOboid shatter the glass portion with their largest chisel while a Garanth shielded him. When the protective spell was cast the OrOboid was unexpectedly surrounded with a shield so powerful that it was visible to all and much stronger than the caster could normally produce. After the surprise wore off, a cutting tool was put to seemingly defenseless glass. They rained blow after blow on it, but the Star Glass remained unscathed. This at least allowed them to determine that their new charge was indestructible and appeared to amplify magic.

"The members of this search party now tried to determine how the device could be made safe or tamed. They attempted communicating with it with no results. The Garanth tinkerers built a cart meant to keep it safe and allow it to journey easily with them. The Star Glass was ensconced safely in a stone and metal strongbox built into the cart, and so the expedition was set to leave the following morning.

That night the younger of the tinkerers attempted to smooth off a rough edge of their transport using a heat spell. His screams were blissfully short. In the morning when the raging inferno burned down there was nothing left but ash and the pristine artifact. When they looked closer however, they noticed that there was an undamaged area opposite the crystal base holding the glass."

I was glad we weren't here to destroy the artifact. I held it more gingerly now, dangling it in front of me at arm's length. We shared a look between us that my brain translated to, *What have we gotten ourselves into?*

"The remaining party members spent another two days pondering how to proceed in returning with this highly volatile object. Finally, it was the OrOboids' turn to make an attempt. The elder crafter was to take the object out of camp with his apprentice and attempt to use the properties of the object against it. They intended to begin coaxing growth from the crystal at a slow, controlled pace and form a box around it. They carefully oriented themselves beside the crystal foot and away from the glass and began to convince their favored medium to grow away from themselves. Slow and careful as they were, the result of their efforts was the formation of a great razor-sharp crystalline shelf.

"Telling the crystal to break at its original design, they tried again even more slowly. Eventually they made progress. Five days of labor and they had an appropriately sized box roughed out. The elder crafter became weary and decided to call a period of rest. He began preparing to meditate himself into their most restful state.

"His youthful apprentice, emboldened by the first successes they had seen, decided to finish the chest alone. He began calling for small breaks in the lattice, and the chest began to form. The ease with which the crafting took caused yet more confidence to build. In the end, the apprentice finished the chest but perished in attempting to fashion the key. Once the elder crafter returned to full consciousness and mourned the loss of the apprentice, he completed the chest we see before us. The expedition returned, and the Star Glass became a feared and revered ceremonial item. It was held first in Adthaamos for two score years."

Chapter 21
Can We Stop and Ask for Directions?

So now here we were... a merry band of assorted races standing in the near twilight of this incredibly picturesque cavern. We were hale and healthy by and large and had achieved our first goal. We were also surrounded by a deadly lake behind, and a wall of solid mountain ahead. Our little plateau was around the size of my living room in the house I grew up in and would never see again, which is to say, big enough for the few of us to walk around a bit but feeling smaller by the minute.

The Gathering had left us, and all my friends were now looking to me to tell us what our next step should be. I felt much like I imagined a new father felt, taking his first child home. There were no instructions for this thing, and many mistakes could lead to someone dying. Now that we had opened Pandora's box and heard Mikaal's tale, no one wanted to use magic, and few felt comfortable sleeping where they might roll off and drown.

We sat down and discussed options while eating from our dwindling supplies. Junean volunteered to tunnel into the rock wall to see how far into the mountain we were. Other options were brought up and quickly discarded as they all involved magic, or whatever my new gifts were called. Once Junean finished eating, she stepped over to the wall and started clawing through it. I did not want to make her angry....

Can We Stop and Ask for Directions?

Soon she had disappeared from sight. I spent a minute investigating the joint where the platform ended, and the stone began. There was a straight line that seemed to penetrate the mountain as if the strange material was a hot knife and the mountain made of butter.

I looked at this doodad in my hand that we'd gone to so much trouble for and on which all of our future success may well depend. It was beautiful, and yet it also reminded me of a giant baby rattle that had been cast aside by some deity long forgotten. It was much lighter than it appeared it would be, especially to be nearly indestructible. I needed a way to learn how it worked, but without our journey meeting an ignoble end. I needed to think of a way to test the use of magic and my powers safely. Since I and my gifts had not been seen on Sorra before now, it seemed that is where I should focus my efforts.

The Star Glass had never left my hand from the time I grasped it until now, but I needed to visit my inner sanctum, and I didn't want to drop it or lose it if something went wrong. Maybe if I didn't use my skills directly on the object itself, I could avoid activating its defenses. I strung the chain that had held the key through the center of the endless knot at the Star Glass's base. Holding my breath, I let go.

My head didn't fly off, and my face didn't explode. I took a breath. I took a few steps around and then a little jump step just to make sure that the chain and my new "charm" continued to get along. I took another breath. Now I needed a nap.

I rejoined my friends, keeping a little distance in the thought of keeping them safe, but Coral saw my hesitation and wrapped her arm around me, pulling us in close side by side. Junean arrived only a moment later, dripping chunks of glittering ore, sand, and stone.

"I went toward what I sensed to be the surface," she huffed, "but the mountain began to rumble as if it would collapse. I backtracked and went on perpendicular paths. One way the stone became so dense that even I couldn't make much progress. The final path actually did collapse in on me and I had to turn back. There seems no escape that way."

Mikaal suggested that we begin taking turns sleeping while one or two kept watch over the others. Granalis and Junean seemed in the most need of sleep. They each picked a spot against the wall, and we made a barricade of bags around their sleeping forms to keep them from rolling into a murky death. Mikaal, Coral, and I gathered around the chest and sat back-to-back so we could talk and watch.

Coral wondered why we didn't put the Star Glass in the chest since that seemed to make it safe. I could only smack my head at the simplicity of the solution. Mikaal thought it was worth a try. I stood and removed it from my chain and put it back in the box with no hesitation. I closed the lid. The lid popped back open. I closed the lid and pushed harder. The lid stayed closed for a half second and popped back open.

"Is there a trick to this Mikaal?" I asked.

"Normally, no. When the chest is closed the key should drop."

"What if we sit on it?"

Mikaal chuckled. "We could try, but since the chest is not showing signs of life, I fear that it has lost whatever properties it once had."

I sat on it anyways, but Mikaal was right. One by one our options continued to dwindle.

"I don't suppose you have an OrOboid in your bag, do you Mikaal? Apparently, we should have brought one with us," I asked mock hopefully.

Mikaal just shook his head.

I thanked Coral for her idea and sat back down with my side pressed to hers. It was quiet. Even our breathing seemed incredibly loud in a silence that deep. We stayed that way for what seemed like a very long time before I spoke next.

"I will have to try something. To learn how to master it, or at least how to avoid being destroyed by it by mistake. We know at least a few things from your tale. Do you trust me?"

Can We Stop and Ask for Directions?

Coral gave me her reply by squeezing my hand gently. Mikaal responded verbally in the affirmative. I got up and moved away from the chest and the wall, as near as I dared to the deadly lake, keeping my back to them and the Galactic Rattle's business end toward the water. I sat cross legged and retreated inside myself. I could feel the weight on the chain, but even more I could sense a tumult of magic flows whipping around it and now me as its wielder.

I closed my eyes, and I could sense it even more clearly. I listened harder and reached out with my nonphysical senses, not to it but to the flows of magical power. It felt like I was glowing with Sorran energy, but yet, not me.... We.

The flows of power had a rhythm, or a pulse. That was it. It was like a heartbeat. It was not like my heartbeat. I could hear it now more clearly still. A human heart was lub-dub, lub-dub. Point and counter point. This beat was more of a push, push, push, pull. It was steady. With each push pulse the magic grew and intensified. With the pull pulse it calmed. Almost like it was.... Listening.

I had no idea what I was doing. I was merely reacting to some instinct. I didn't even realize it when I spoke. Not with physical words, but via a mental pulse of my own. When it listened, I told it quietly, "light" with words, but also with the image of a mage light like Mikaal had shown me.

A loud hissing sound far out across the water pulled me from mind to body. I opened my eyes and instantly regretted it. I heard Mikaal and Coral cry out in surprise and alarm. Not as bright as the chest had been before, but so large that it filled the cavern, was a ball of yellow very like a sun. Or half a sun. The hissing came from this battle between the water and the celestial body I'd summoned as they were trapped here together. Two eternally opposite elements—fire and water, light and dark—raged on.

The combination of blinding light and icy mist collaborated to steal any meaningful sight from us. Granalis and Junean remained blissfully unaware of any of this with their faces snuggled up to the wall and the fortress of bags behind.

The water was creating great billows of steam, which began to fill the cavern and finally to escape through unseen vents in the ceiling, but not quickly enough for my liking. I did not want to find out what that mist would do to us. I wasn't even sure what I had done, but I needed to un-done it quickly.

I yelled at the Star Glass to stop. I pleaded with it. Finally, I went back inside myself and tried to remember what I'd done. It felt like an eternity before I remembered enough to pulse "cease" at the right moment.

I opened my eyes. The sun was gone. My consciousness followed quickly.

Chapter 22
What Exactly Is This Thing?

I sat up with a start apparently only seconds later and nearly launched a concerned Mikaal into the water and an ignominious end. Thankfully Coral grabbed him as he flew by and dropped to the ground on top of me.

"Ok. I know what I think just happened, but would you tell me what you saw and heard?" I asked.

"Well," Coral began, forehead creased in concentration. "There wasn't a lot to tell. You walked away and sat down in that strange way you have with your legs folded inward in a triangle. You peered into the Star Glass for maybe a half hour. Then the water went from quiet to a frothing, churning mess and gave birth to a growing sphere of gold colored light."

Mikaal jumped in to add, "When the new star stopped moving, the water and the sun hissed and spit like two Tuskerkittys threatening a fight."

"Then you yelled something we didn't understand and took an unexpected nap," Coral finished.

I tried to put my perspective into words and failed utterly. I briefly thought about sending them some mental images, but decided not to chance it lest my new gewgaw decide I was talking to, it? Him? Her? I hadn't detected any signs of awareness or intellect, just an instant response.

After a few false starts trying to explain and being unable to I closed my mouth audibly and allowed myself a half second to growl in frustration.

"I'll have to wait and explain once I understand more about it. Please be patient with me."

Coral gave me a brief brush of a kiss on the cheek, and they walked back to their post.

I turned my back on them again, both to place my body between them and potential danger as well as to keep my magic sight focused on the task at hand. I allowed my vision to shift away from the visible and into the magical while holding the device in my left hand. I flexed my wrist so as to view it from every direction without pointing it at me. I could now see the pulses that I had heard before, but with only my sight there was less evidence of a pattern. It was there, but it was more like an increase in the frenetic swirling of Chaos for three beats followed briefly by a downbeat. I held my breath and looked straight down the barrel of this powerful weapon and saw.... Nothing significantly different.

Ok. "Think, man, think!" I told myself silently. I had no wish to end up with this tiny island as our permanent home, nor to have our existences terminated. "What do you know about this thing?" I continued in my internal dialog.

1. This item is exceedingly powerful. How powerful?

2. Well, if a Sorran attempts to study it by magical means it melts their brain. Great.

3. Trying to attack it with magic results in a rebound effect, and

4. Trying to attack it physically had no impact. No problemo, but no resolvo.

5. Even better, using magic near it can lead to dangerous and unexpected results.

6. However, the Expedition had tried to communicate didn't work for some reason, but I was able to get a response. I wish I knew more about how they tried to communicate.

7. Anything I try is likely to get really dramatic results.

WHAT EXACTLY IS THIS THING?

I had said I would start the test with my gifts, so in the confines of my mind I crafted a mental hand and grasped the globe of the Star Glass. No reaction. I let go with my physical hand and rapped on the glass with a non-corporeal knuckle. The sound it made was so quiet that even in the stillness we were surrounded by I could have imagined it. Great.

Number 8. It made no apparent distinction between my physical being and my mental projections. That could be good or bad. I'd have to experiment more in that vein later as this didn't seem to offer us any hope of escaping our current predicament. I let it drop into my right hand and then retreated into myself.

Once I was alone in my head, I recreated the microscope I had used on Mikaal before and placed it against my right eye before training it on the crystal base. At first glance it looked just like I remember quartz looking under a microscope when I was a kid and had been into geology. Looking a little deeper though, it seemed like the structure of the crystals was weird, like something had been added. Here and there it seemed like the structure of the crystal was buttressed with metal. Not enough for it to have been visible, but it looked like this was engineered for extreme strength. I felt like a Cro-Magnon peering at fire for the first time.

I moved along the side of the handle towards the glass and could clearly see a trail where someone or something had altered this seemingly natural crystal structure. I wasn't sure, since the OrOboid had used this part of the artifact to construct the chest, if this was their doing or something else entirely. I rubbed my eyes briefly before refocusing on the heart of this matter. I had no idea what glass looked like under a microscope, but I couldn't imagine it looked anything like I was seeing. It was like millions of circuits had been embedded into this glass sphere. The size of each trace was smaller than what I knew to be possible in my home world, and we sure didn't have any circuits that could interact with magic. Especially since magic no longer seemed to exist where I came from. I mean, we had stories about magic, but nobody believed it was real.

I increased the magnification and took one more look. I could see faint magical glows centered around octagonal pillars set at defined intervals in the mass of circuits. I could even see markings of some kind on one or two of the components with the magnification at this level. I created a multimeter in my mind and set about measuring voltage between points, holding the leads in mental hands threaded through the microscope lens. The readings were much stronger than I would have expected for a device that was also conducting/controlling/generating magical force as well. Voltages this high would have caused serious heat in anything I was familiar with.

Now I was more puzzled than before. The Star Glass was a device created as the love child of extremely advanced science and Sorran style magic. Couple that with the fact that at least once it had seemed to be able to understand my intent and act on it.

Before I could start mentally spiraling, I caught and redirected my mind like an errant child. *All right now, Aaron.... The why and the wherefore are a thing to be dealt with once the immediate and apocalyptic have been dealt with. How are you going to get you and those who are counting on you back on track?*

Take every thought captive, was part of something my father always repeated to me before the accident took him. It seemed apropos now. This was a puzzle, but it was one I could solve one piece at a time. I had a feeling or a theory that the magical rebound effect was due to the disordered magic pulsing and swirling at the Glass's behest. Could I calm that and restore the magic of my friends?

I threw the enigmatic object over my left shoulder, allowing it to slide along the chain and across the blade of my back so I could look at Mikaal to study the flows of power he utilized.

"Mikaal," I said suddenly.

"Aaargh!" he said, jumping at my voice.

"I need you to use magic..."

"Are you sure that's a good idea?"

"Let me finish the thought. Start the most complex spell you can think of and allow the magic to build up. Hold it as long as possible and then cancel it."

"Hmm. Ok," he said as he stood on four gaw.

The remaining four began weaving in and out in an elaborate pattern. I watched as his limbs began glowing and pulsing violet with power before the glow built up around him. I studied as quickly as I could, but the glow faded as he cancelled the spell before it could take effect. I looked for patterns and flows that I could identify.

"Coral."

"Yes, Aaron?" she said, standing near my right arm. This caused me to jump, not just in fright.

"Can you do the same as Mikaal, but with a different spell you're comfortable with?"

"Of course," she said, moving to where Mikaal had been standing.

I watched as her lovely hands and fingers gracefully performed an elegant ballet and started to shimmer blue, first dimly but increasing steadily. The color leached along her arms until she was bathed in it. I could see similarities and differences now and helped me isolate the variables. This task would be as challenging as repairing Mikaal's DNA had been, but I could use some of what I'd learned from that terrifying episode—compare, contrast, and remove what I didn't understand yet.

"Thank you both."

Their jump told me that I'd been standing silent again for some minutes.

"Mikaal, what was your spell?"

"I was preparing a greater barrier of protection."

"Coral? What about you?"

"I am best at healing, so that's what I did."

I created a canvas on the wall of my mind and began with a photographic reproduction of the Star Glass in the center. I then began adding individual surges of gray and setting them in motion around it. I knew I would have to select a hue to replace the gray, but I wasn't sure what would be most appropriate yet.

My physical eyes finally registered two things. First was that I needed to blink. After that, I noticed that Mikaal and Coral were gone, and Junean and Granalis were standing in front of me.

"Granalis. Can you start a spell, hold it as long as possible and cancel it without finishing the casting?"

"I thought you were just going to stand there staring at us all dead-eyed and never ask."

His motions were quick and tense, and his aura was yellow. He couldn't hold it for long, so I had him repeat it twice until I saw enough.

"What kind of spell was that?"

"I'm a hunter, Aaron. It was a fire attack called flame gout."

"Well, I'm glad you were able to cancel that one, twice."

I altered the arrangement and timing of magic on the canvas, removing any hints of aggressive magic.

"Junean, your turn please"

"How can you stand there so still for so long and then start talking all suddenly like that?" she asked. "It is a bit scary."

"Sorry about that. I'm still learning how to do magic stuff and not be weird while doing it."

"Well, Here goes," she said.

She rocked back and began almost imperceptibly small motions with her nimble toes that were hard to follow, but the orange light sprang up quickly at the ends of her nails and leapt to her head before warping back to cover her body.

Junean saw me moving, and said, "My spell was the creation spell we use to bind a function to a statuette."

"Thank you, Junean."

I made a few more touches to my "painting" and decided to color it a shade I didn't have a name for but in my mind was halfway from blue to violet. I hoped this would work. I prayed that this wouldn't make things worse or cause any of us to spontaneously combust. I studied my creation intently, in an attempt to memorize it. Then I chuckled and created a frame around it and hung it on the wall, thereby affixing it in my mind permanently.

I returned to what we all think of as reality, or as close as I could get since I stepped into this world, and pulled the Star Glass around where I could hold it in front of me. I listened to it until I was synchronized to it, and then I pulsed my image of what it should be into the lull that I thought of as it listening back. I pulsed the image of how I wanted it to be to it as a plea, as a request, and finally as a command. The shifting, swirling shades of sorcerous disarray intensified at the pleas, shattered at the request, and reformed into a perfect replica of the vision I had cast for it.

Success! I almost did a dance of joy until I remembered that random dancing might make my friends think I'd lost my mind.

For good measure I pulsed it again as a command labeled normal/resting/inactive. The flows flexed and hardened, and I realized I had been holding my breath. I had one more change in mind, but I didn't want to put it in place just yet. I wasn't sure how long it had been since I slept, and I distinctly remember feeling like I needed a nap what seemed like a long time ago.

When I looked up my entire party was standing directly in front of me, looking concerned. Apparently to them I had been standing rigid for an hour, breathing erratically and shallowly, and when I suddenly sucked in a blast of air, it brought them near. I was ecstatic that they were safe and that I was still alive to see them safe. We had been in near twilight so long that I decided my first test to see if magic was safe would be a Magelamp. With a quick word/gesture combo, one of my dim creations sprang up on the far side of our jail. Everyone whirled around to look. I took two steps forward, grabbed Coral gently but firmly, twirled, dipped and kissed the girl before lying down and passing out.

Chapter 23
Avante!

Something smelled like bacon. That's what brought me back to consciousness. Alas, it was not bacon. In fact, it was vegetable in origin.

Junean had produced another one of her miniatures which seemed to make or retrieve food from some unknown origin and used it to supplement our few remaining supplies with the fleshy bacontater as I decided to call it. A few of them were cooking on a small heating device I didn't remember seeing. Thankfully bacontaters are salty, filling and delicious. We ate all of our remaining supplies for breakfast, and while we wouldn't starve completely it underlined the fact that it was time for us to move on.

Of course, as soon as I was finished eating everybody circled around to ask about how I had made the Star Glass safe to use magic around. I did my best to explain my thoughts around the Star Glass being a machine that had the ability to act on at least simple directions and generate or control magical power. Since I'd seen no evidence of any form of a computer on Sorra, that was the closest way I could think of to describe it.

I also told them I still wasn't entirely sure how safe it was, but with my limited knowledge and experience of any kind of power I'd done what I could. I still had a long road before saying I had the ability to use its power correctly or understand it fully. After a few more questions, most of which I didn't have satisfactory answers to, we turned our attention to getting the heck out of here.

We moved to the tunnel mouth that Junean had created when trying to find us an escape previously. It didn't seem like a good idea to keep pulling the trigger like this when one false move could bury us or bring the embrace of the life-stealing waters. Junean was our subterranean expert, so I spent a few moments evaluating what could have blocked her.

Her people were able to dig through nearly any kind of soil and rock, so the most likely culprits were dense metals, magical materials, or crafted crystal. The natural mineral formations in the walls surrounding us were beautiful, but Junean said she'd cut through a number of those while searching for a way out. I felt like I needed to get us out of this pit. None of these people would have been here if it weren't for me.

I instructed everyone to stand behind me and to each side of the opening. Within the confines of my mental chamber, I summoned a matched pair of laser drills and pointed them out the windows that were linked to my eyes. I made my body kneel so that my eyes were as near the center of the opening as I was able to manage. I sent an arm with a directional flood light and mounted it at the top of the opening so I could see as far ahead as possible.

The path ahead was relatively straight but much longer than I had expected. I focused my vision at the farthest point I could see and linked the lasers to fire alternating pulses. I needed to break through the side of the mountain, but without sending a flood of molten rock or metal flowing towards us. I said a quick prayer and pushed the big red button marked fire.

The air around us hummed and vibrated briefly before the sound of a thunderclap rolled around us. I hadn't given any thought to how loud drilling through a mountain might be. I spared enough attention to supply myself with hearing protection without stopping, hoping that my friends were covering their ears. I couldn't see how much progress I might be making, but my desire to see the sky overrode my curiosity. Minutes passed and my feet began to tingle from the vibrations.

This went on for what felt like forever before the vibrations changed, becoming a sharper almost ringing sound for another minute. When that change passed and the original thrumming returned, I paused to investigate. I wasn't sure how it was possible, but the temperature in the room in my head seemed high and my non-physical image was glistening with perspiration.

When I stepped back into my body proper and stood up, I decided that that must have been an unconscious representation of what my body was feeling. Far ahead in the newly extended tunnel were the sunset hues of nearly molten rock. Heat was radiating down the passage straight at me. I stepped aside into the cooler air and took a deep breath. Everyone had moved far away from me and seemed to be huddled together looking a bit shell shocked.

"I've never seen a human shoot deadly light from their eyes, nor wield such power," Granalis said shakily.

"I just hope that this will get us back on our way," I gasped back, realizing I was exhausted.

"What did you… how did you… what was that?" Junean asked.

"I was using two drills that use strong pulses of light to tunnel through whatever it was that was in your way."

"You were using the Star Glass's power?" Mikaal queried.

"No. I'm not ready to tap into its power just yet."

"Impressive," Mikaal muttered.

"I wonder how long it will take to cool down," I mused.

Mikaal disentangled himself from the group and peered around the corner. He made some quick motions and muttered some unheard words of power before launching a flurry of ice balls down the tunnel. A loud hissing ensued for a few seconds, and he stepped forward and out of view. When Mikaal broke the huddle, Coral stood up and entwined her arm in mine. We stepped into the shaft, partially blocking the light and casting Mikaal in shadow, just in time to see him cast another barrage of snowballs. A blast of steam and the sound of water changing rapidly from solid to gas assailed us like a one-two punch from a boxer. Coral suggested that Junean accompany Mikaal ahead to determine if I had cut through the blockage so that I could rest. Granalis decided to accompany them.

The trio made a strange sight as they walked away, Junean on the left with her night eyes casting light forward, Granalis on the right mimicking her natural abilities and Mikaal in the middle seeming like a floating head to my human sensibilities. Every so often there would be a yellow flash of building magic followed by a brief shock of cold, steam, and noise.

Coral escorted me back to where our belongings awaited us and sat with her back against the seam where the semismooth rock met the perfectly flat and reflective floor, pulling me down beside her. She kissed me, first on each eye, concern for me written on her face, and then on the mouth, slow and sweet and not nearly long enough for me.

"Watching you wield such power; it is hard to believe that you have only known magic existed and that you had a power of your own for a few days. It also makes me feel hopeful again for the first time since every one of my people was changed. I can almost believe that you could roll back time and undo all the damage that's been done." Her voice was little more than a whisper, but I could hear a deep heart ache warring against hope within it. I wished fervently that I felt worthy of such faith.

"I wish it was as easy for me to have such belief in myself. I only know that being with you makes me want to restore everything that makes you smile and banish everything that makes you weep. I don't have any idea how, but I will gladly spend the rest of my life trying."

She took my face in her hands and kissed me again before patting her hand on her lap and inviting me to rest there. I laid there with her cradling my head and brushing my hair. I wasn't sure if I dozed or not, but I couldn't remember a time in my life when I'd ever felt so at peace.

Laughter echoed down the tunnel, echoing briefly before being absorbed by the stillness of the dead lake. Thankfully the laughter sounded joyful. The laugh and its owners came into view.

"Time to go. You're not going to believe this." Mikaal chuckled as he gathered his pack.

Minutes later we were strolling cautiously down the uneven tube. The view wasn't much, but it felt good to be moving again. We walked only by the lights in my friend's eyes and nearly bumped into them when they slowed and ducked through a narrow opening in the unfinished metal plate barring our path. It looked like it had originally been flat but had resisted to the end. It now had a conical shape like a funnel on its side with a large, ragged hole in the center.

When we stepped through, I could see that there had been another foot or so of rock beyond this obstacle, but we ended up in a well-formed passage. The wall opposite was damaged from my drilling, but this looked oddly familiar. Mikaal, Junean and Granalis were all smiling and striding up the incline to the right.

We followed quietly, holding hands and looking forward to whatever had made our friends so gleeful. The path turned once and became a spiral stairway leading up. When we reached the end of it we made another ninety degree turn and walked maybe five minutes more before our tunnel merged with two others. I thought I was beginning to understand, but I continued to follow without comment as they continued on down the tunnel that was ahead instead of the one that was off to the side. My thought was confirmed a short while later when we saw the stable with our Rhinodons.

By the time we had checked on our mounts, Granalis flew ahead to the exit and found that it was the first hour of the night. Which night we weren't certain yet. We had lost track of the time just as certainly as our sense of direction walking around in the deep passages of the mine. We decided to stay the night near the stables and continue our journey in the morning. Knowing that it was night somehow sapped whatever strength we had remaining. Granalis took the first watch, and soon the rest of us were deep asleep.

Chapter 24
Return to the Land of the Living

Junean woke me for the last watch, informing me sleepily that she had seen and heard nothing in the last two hours. She had not used a light, relying instead on her night eyes, so she was curled up before I magic'd up a Magelamp. I pretended not to hear her sobs as she fell asleep. I was certain that it was excruciating for her to not only be without the one she loved, but also to know that he was no longer human (or Moaleanean or however they spoke of themselves) and be carrying him around in a bag. I wondered for a time as I swung my gaze back and forth down the tunnel if I or anybody else would be able to restore him.

I backed up into the end of the short hall where the walls fell away on either side to form the periphery of the stable. From this vantage point, I could watch the entrance without having to move my eyes, and I grasped the Star Glass. I had no idea how to tackle the challenge of making use of the artifact. The first success that I'd had was purely out of intuition instead of any logic on my part.

I didn't want to do anything that could endanger those who had put their trust in me, but I wanted to make good use of this time. I wasn't even sure how much time I had until the Chaos Cloud would reach Tiiaan. Even if I knew how long we had expended on this quest, after hearing Junean's story there was the possibility that it had begun moving faster or changed course or something I couldn't even fathom.

Return to the Land of the Living

I opened my eye windows, then made and mounted three different types of motion detectors to ensure nothing snuck by me. Before, I had been able to guide the Star Glass by giving orders along with mental images, but it hadn't responded to any other kind of communication. It seemed to only listen for a heartbeat, and that greatly limited the detail I could provide.

I waited for my opening and commanded the artifact to give me a user's manual. A book appeared on the ground where I had envisioned it. Success! I picked it up and began leafing through it. Of course, this would be the first time since my arrival in Sorra that I would come upon another language. There were characters neatly spaced on each page, but not one of them looked like the alphabet I was familiar with. I set it aside. That would have taken a long time anyways.

I tried telling it to explain its capabilities to me by issuing it a mental help command and an image of it sending me an answer mentally. That worked but nearly killed me. Suddenly my mind was flooded with a barrage of thoughts, noises, concepts, which combined to form noise I couldn't process. Thankfully it was very short. It took me a few minutes of panting before I regained my equilibrium. I rubbed my temples and thought. It had responded. That was good. Its response was too much for me to handle. Not good. I needed it to slow down. I wasn't a machine. I created a mental image much like the first, but this time made the response image narrower and indicated a pause between each response. I took a few deep breaths and sent it.

For the rest of my watch, I ended up in a slow deliberate back and forth with it. I saw images of those who had created it. It looked nothing like me or any of the Sorran races I'd seen or heard about. That much was no surprise. It was a bit of a surprise that they seemed to be mostly machines themselves. I saw mental images of three of them. One seemed to have an organic face with only a slit for a nose but very human looking eyes. The other two were machines from the waist down, had the same facial structure, and four three-fingered arms. Two of the arms were large and set high on the shoulder while the remaining two were small and emerged from where a human's nipples would be. I got the impression that they had been the last of their race.

The Star Glass had a designation for itself, but it was unintelligible. It has several modes of operation but was most powerful when commanded to act directly as I had done. It didn't really have a mind, but it seemed capable of rudimentary thoughts and responses. I managed to have it alter its pattern to listen longer so I could issue it more complex commands. I learned to switch modes, which was essentially what I had done by sending it a magical pattern to follow. Now I would be able to do it more easily. I had put it into defend/heal mode, but it also had a direct attack mode, an amplifier/passthrough mode, and a few more I didn't yet understand before my watch ended.

I woke the others, starting with Coral so I could sneak a few moments alone. I couldn't figure out how she could sleep on the ground and wake up looking so flawless. We broke our fast out of the supplies remaining in the Rhinodon's storage. We took very little time to gather our belongings and eat before we moved out.

We stepped out of the mine's entrance and into a misty morning. We didn't mind the fog; the sunlight and air felt glorious after the closeness of the mine. Granalis leapt off his perch upon my pack and soared a high arc around us, surveying the area. He made two passes before making a graceful return and reporting that there were no immediate threats he could see.

Our mounts had been unable to move much in the past few days, so we started out slowly to let them stretch, not that the deadly narrow path on which we had entered gave us much choice. When the path began to broaden, we let the animals go as fast as they felt comfortable with. We moved quickly down the mountain.

I'd forgotten how loud Rhinodon travel was. Mikaal and Coral and I kept a slow conversation going as we rode, with me asking questions about what we were riding past and them taking turns educating me on this world. Occasionally Mikaal pointed out something of interest I'd overlooked, and we kept a friendly conversation up this way for most of the first part of the day.

I asked about why the water in Sorra was so energizing and delicious. Since neither of them had ever been to another world, they didn't have much to offer by way of explanation. This caused me to spend a few minutes trying to describe how flat and boring the water of the world I was from was compared to theirs and how we rarely got to drink it from a natural source due to contamination.

I asked about a huge nest high up on one of the peaks in the distance. Mikaal jokingly instructed that if I see any motion near there we should all become scarce very quickly. Coral explained that he was serious about the danger, but it was mostly a joke because PeakCaps only hatched every fifty years or so and that was a relatively new nest based on its size.

The eggs would continue to grow slowly over the years and stretch the nest out until it was just a taut circle barely holding them aloft. His demeanor transitioned from traveling companion to instructor as he sent me a sequence of mental images showing a beast nearly a quarter of the height of the mountain the eggs were resting on. It had a fearsome face, with a long beak-like muzzle lined with two rows of long needle-sharp teeth. It had pointed ears at the top of its head that were angled forward and could have been mistaken for horns.

Its eyes were overlarge for its head so that they bulged out from below a bony ridge which itself protruded from its forehead. They were bright red with flecks of white and no apparent irises. There was also no evidence of eyelids. The point of its beaky muzzle ended in a four-nostrilled nose. Each nostril was a deep perfectly round orifice which trailed back its face in four aerodynamic grooves. Its head as a whole gave the impression of being carved out of the side of a mountain and then coming to life. This sat atop a long and somewhat serpentine body which was covered in hair.

Due to its immense size, each hair looked much like a young tree rooted in its skin, like a living forest was attacking. Along the back was a series of oddly mismatched wings. The front pair was wide, but not very deep and appeared reptilian and covered with scales. The second and third wing pairs were segmented and leathery like bat wings. Where these joined to the body there was fine hair, and they continued in a line down the body to additional protrusions that I thought of as vertical sails perhaps used for control and gliding. The center of the body had no wings for perhaps a quarter of the overall length before the wing pattern reversed.

There were a set of human bodybuilder arms below the head but scaled up to match the beast's size. The surface of these arms gleamed metallic. The mid-section of the body was propelled by a series of short pincer-tipped insect legs that were more in number than I could easily count. Where these legs ended, just behind the rear wings the body thinned out into a long sinewy tail tipped with a vicious poisonous barb. In one of the images the PeakCap was "standing" up on its coiled tail and using its rear wings for stability. The belly of the beast was covered in overlapping plates of armor. I didn't even want to imagine facing one. I was glad this particular lesson was merely traveling conversation, and not something I could reasonably hope to encounter.

Coral pointed out a waterfall as we descended. It was breathtaking. I could hear its roar echoing off the surrounding mountains. Mikaal told us how a couple of hundred years ago there had been an OrOboid settlement nestled within the fall walls.

Seeing the falls in full sunlight, I was nearly blinded as the sunlight reflected from the lake below and mixed with the crystal in the rock face and then shone through the falling waters.

"This was one of their most prosperous holdings," Mikaal said. "Over time, fewer and fewer OrObabies were born, and those that remained moved to strengthen nearby provinces."

The path narrowed, causing us to ride single file and pass close to an overhang of rock. Coral and Junean were in the lead. Once they drew abreast of the overhang and passed underneath, a keening cry rose from the shadows, and the darkness shattered into four small shapes which speared toward the women. Before anyone could react, blinding bolts stretched out from their necks and met the onrushing attackers. Two times lightning spat forth, and four small bodies bounced off the rock wall and slid down the side of the mountain to our right. I couldn't tell what they were, but I distinctly saw a smoking hole in the torso of one.

I was next in line, so I pulled my sword to be ready, but the daylight seemed to brighten and an unseen oppression lift. I passed beneath safely as did Mikaal. I looked forward and saw both of our female companions holding their Torcs. Mikaal asked me silently what the attacker was, and I could only send back a mental shrug. That image didn't apparently translate well, either due to the lack of such a gesture on Sorra or the fact that Norans didn't really have arms. I explained that I hadn't seen them well enough to know and asked Coral and Junean.

"The response from these neck decorations blinded me, but also probably saved my life despite the ache in my heart," Junean said.

"I couldn't see them at first, but I looked at one of them that was partially in the light as I passed. I've never seen anything like it," Coral added.

When our way broadened, I urged Pakky forward to check on the ladies. They both seemed only slightly rattled and smiled at my concern. We rode three abreast for another hour before we stopped to rest and find something to eat.

III

DEFENSE OF TIIAAN
&
ADVANCE TO BATTLE

Chapter 25
In Time?

We stopped at the first crossroads we'd come to since beginning our trek back to Tiiaan. I tethered our mounts near a stream that probably was fed by the waterfall we had passed based on its flow and direction. There was plenty to forage and drink, and I was glad that these animals had few needs. Granalis began a scouting flight while Junean, Coral, and Mikaal hunted for food of both the animal and vegetable variety as their skills and diets dictated. I took a few minutes to fill up our drinking containers and walked away from our temporary camp on the diagonal so I could try to figure out what I could do against pure Chaos.

I found a flowering plant growing in a crevice between a boulder and the hillock it was resting against and knelt down in front of it. Star Glass in hand, I began crafting a mental image that I hoped would convey what I wanted done. This definitely wasn't on the list of skills that it had given for itself, but I thought it might be worth a try.

I sent an image of the flower, then what it might have looked like younger, then as a seed as I pointed it at the plant and crossed my fingers. A flash of magic surrounded my target, and the plant shrank but remained healthy. A second and third flash and the plant was gone. I tried to roll the boulder away, but I wasn't strong enough. My mental hands didn't have such a limitation, and once the boulder was removed, I was able to locate the seed. It took me a bit longer than I'd hoped as I had guessed wrong as to its appearance. It was good to know that my image didn't have to be perfectly precise, just understandable.

Next, I needed an animal subject on which to test my time reversal process. I looked around for a suitable subject but came up empty. I tried looking around with my magical vision and had no better luck. I was about to give up when Granalis silently dropped onto the recently relocated boulder beside me. His fur-covered wings were nearly silent in flight. He popped a last bit of something into his mouth and chewed, eyeing me appraisingly. "What are you looking for, Aaron?" he asked.

"I need an animal to practice my Chaos plan on." I replied, "Do you think you can find me something?"

Granalis simply leapt back into the air without another word.

While he was gone, I took a moment to think over my observations about the abilities I'd been collecting since arriving on Sorra.

1. I had innate abilities to create objects and bring them into the world. This doesn't seem to cost me much if anything in terms of energy.

2. I can interact with physical objects by creating projections like hands or flat platforms that only I can see. I can do this with very little effort. The cost increases when I use the projections for defense.

3. I can mindspeak. This seems to work differently for me than the natives.

4. Sorran magic is prohibitively hard for me to use for now and uses energies I don't understand.

5. When I learn a new skill, it wipes me out, but as I use it more it becomes easier and less costly to use.

6. I can store my own energy (carefully) and transfer it to objects/people if needed. Too much can also be a problem. I wonder how much I can safely store and what happens after that.

7. The Star Glass can use magic more like a Sorran. If I can master it...

Granalis returned more quickly than I expected, grasping a light-brown rodent in his rear fingers. It was shivering and probably expected to be a meal very soon. I took it gently from him with a non-physical hand and brought it closer. It was smaller than my fist and had rear legs meant for hopping. Its ears were overlong and almost perfectly squared off. It had four sharp top teeth and two wider teeth barely visible under its massive overbite.

I readied my mental image, hoping that it wouldn't hurt this poor creature and that, since I had no idea what it had looked like younger, this would work. I pictured the creature in its current form as well as two smaller younger looking images, then pointed the Star Glass, and waited. Magical flashes started, and then the rodent was smaller and even more defenseless looking. Granalis nodded approvingly. I flashed another image and returned it back to more or less its original form before setting it free.

The top of Mikaal's head became visible, and before long the rest of his person arrived, carrying a bright green stalk of some waxy and flowering vegetation and two fowl. He seemed pleased with his haul, and he and Granalis began starting a fire to cook our meal. Nearby and just up the road, there was a good supply of scrub and deadwood in a small, oddly placed stand of trees. I started toward it, but Mikaal advised caution.

OasisAnts were known to reside in such places, and while he thought this one was empty based on the condition of the trees, there was no need to risk it by walking closer. Instead, I sent a few hands in and grabbed some large logs. There was no response from the tiny grove until I inadvertently hit one of the standing trees as I pulled the firewood towards us. I heard the light 'thunk' of the impact and then the ground around the trees exploded upwards in a flurry of mandibles clacking together on the air. Finding nothing above them, they began receding into the ground, and all was quiet again for a moment.

Then a rumble began with a sound like the very earth was hungry, first heard and then felt. The center of the trees opened up like the doors of a root cellar, throwing trees aside like they were nothing, and then SHE appeared. The Queen.

She was very like the ants I was familiar with save for a few minor details. For one thing, she was nearly half again my height, and her head was adorned with a circlet of some lumpy golden material. She had large mandibles oriented as I would expect, but another slightly smaller set oriented vertically that looked very sharp as they clashed together. The last significant difference was that her abdomen was folded under her rather than behind as I was used to. Then there was the stinger jutting forward from the point of her abdomen. She was also incredibly fast.

I was so startled that only the flaming ball whizzing past my head and slamming into her mouth brought me to action. That slowed her for only a second as she screeched her displeasure and charged. I reached ahead of my body and pulled my spear from my pack while running towards our mounts.

The sound of arrows striking home in the crevices between armored joints announced Coral's arrival to the party. This sound was followed by a hiss-sizzle and a roar from Her Majesty as the acid tips Coral fired began to eat into the less protected joints. I jumped onto one of my platforms and flew ahead just moments before mandibles clacked closed in the space I'd just vacated. Now that I was armed and aloft, it was time to think versus reacting.

"Granalis!" I yelled over the sound of whizzing arrows. "Did you spot any large creatures nearby?" He called back that he had, and when I asked him to draw it here quickly, he shot off. I thought Junean had not returned until the ground erupted near Coral and she appeared. Only Coral's attacks seemed to be having any effect, and I didn't know how many acid arrows she had left. I didn't really want us to destroy an entire colony of creatures, and I assumed that without the Queen all the other ants would die.

Our adversary was closest to me and continued to pursue me. I slowed down and turned to face her, rapping her once sharply on the crown with my spear and then lifting away. She caught me by surprise by jumping up and clipping my foot. I fell backward, thankfully still on my magic surfboard. I had been trying to keep her interested in chasing me, but I hadn't planned to spend the rest of the battle on my back.

I rolled over so I could see where I was going and turned in a slow arc to face her. We were drawing close to her grove. A fireball and an energy bolt slammed into her behind me and she roared her anger.

I caught a flash of white in my peripheral vision to the left, and then Granalis appeared, slaloming through the trees of the Oasis. He looked frightened and harried, but he made it through without so much as brushing the foliage and stirring up the denizens. Once he was clear, he shot up into the sky and did an impressive barrel roll, letting loose a cry like a hawk and drawing the attention of the Queen.

That was when I heard something enormous crash into her home. She apparently heard it too and broke off her pursuit of me to defend her home and her colony. Now that I wasn't being bait, I flew up higher to where I could see what was going on. Once I got high enough, I could see the source of the noise, but I wasn't sure what I was looking at.

There was a "something" standing taller than the trees and swatting them aside as it followed Granalis, who was now circling just below me and just above the height of the creature he brought to the party. It could have been called humanoid, but that was a stretch. It was hard to see as the bulk of it was below the tree line from where I floated. It had a head with a mouth, but neither was well defined, and the entire mass seemed to be shifting and flowing.

It had two long arms with brutish oversized knuckles at the ends which are used to smash aside anything in its way. There was a trail of destruction behind it. An ichor that could be its blood mixed with crushed ant fluids.

Several of the drones that had been hidden underground were crawling around collecting things that could be used to repair their lair and taking them underground, or righting trees in groups. Some slightly larger spiky looking soldiers were skittering in pursuit, and their mandibles were darkened with some material I assumed was from the newcomer. The soldiers did not move as fast as the almost amorphous aggressor. They lost focus on it as the distance increased and noticed first Mikaal, then Junean. Mikaal beat a hasty retreat and stayed on the outskirts of the fight, far enough out to see what was going on, but not close enough to draw the notice of the many combatAnts. Junean also tried to flee but wasn't very fast above ground. Since there were more ants below ground than above, she couldn't go below ground either. Thankfully Granalis swooped her up and out of harm's way before she could take much more than a glancing blow or two.

Roughly in the middle of the copse, the two titans met. Her Majesty was slightly smaller and much faster. She leapt in, cutting deep furrows vertically with her mouthparts while attempting to hold her shifting adversary firmly with her mandibles. Her stinger struck deep into her foe again and again, each wound turning greenish and smoking.

I heard Coral scream behind and below me. She had been hiding behind one of the largest trees on the edge of the Oasis, watching a battle like few had ever seen when her presence was noticed by an army ant. It came after her, catching her off guard. She quickly took a step back and hit it in the head with an arrow from her Tiiaanian bow, making quite a mess. I had to suppress the wave of admiration that washed over me as I watched her react. The exchange drew the attention of other ants.

"Care for a better view?" I asked, dropping down beside her and offering my hand.

"How thoughtful," she replied, grabbing hold and vaulting behind me.

We rose out of range of any unexpected antics, arms around each other as we watched the battle.

It seemed like the Queen was the stronger of the two until the humanoid lost cohesion and began flowing past her hold. One second, she was in control of the situation and the next she was being engulfed. She roared her rage and frustration into its "face" and redoubled her efforts with her stinger. Her head disappeared into the mass, and the activity of her subjects became a frenzy. The ground erupted. All around the battleground ants began tearing chunks from what I was thinking of as the toothpaste monster.

The Ant Monarch's attacks became sluggish, and it seemed like she was in trouble. Slowly the onslaught of tiny bites took effect, and the surge of jelly swallowing her stalled and began to recede. Her head was still mostly inundated, and her minions were tearing their enemy apart piece by piece when she thrust once, harder than before and everything changed.

The jelly-beast let out a roar that faded into a wail. The Queen and all her followers stopped moving. Everything was quiet for one second, and then there was a crack and a sucking noise. The lowest part of the shifting mass, which was perhaps a third the size it had originally been, broke off. The repeated attacks from her sting appeared to have caused it to harden and it left that part of itself behind as it rolled off the Queen's head. She fell to the ground sideways while her assailant rolled away as quickly as the carnage would allow. It swallowed up one of the soldier ants just before it left my sight.

I started to turn away and make sure Mikaal, Granalis, and Junean were well when the resumption of motion from all OasisAnts simultaneously caught my attention. The soldiers surrounded their fallen leader and put their backs to her, forming a ring of protection. The workers walked on, around, and through them and began helping her to stand. They escorted her to where she had first emerged, and she backed slowly down into the ground. The soldiers then scattered themselves around the area, righting and replanting trees forcefully along the way before they buried themselves in the ground using their hind feet in a rotating motion to loosen the soil and slide in backward. The workers busied themselves collecting and storing the bits of enemy and friend alike presumably for food. I didn't turn my back until they had retreated themselves.

Granalis, Junean, Coral, and I hit the ground near the Rhinodons and walked back to our abandoned food and gear, waiting a few minutes for Mikaal to return. Granalis was back to his unruffled self and seemed glad that things had worked out so well. He was explaining to me that the creature he'd drawn into the fight had been lying in wait for us on the path ahead, when Mikaal walked up with the plants and poultry he retrieved on his way back.

Everyone was unharmed, we had enough provisions to make a meal, and the mistake I made that started the battle probably prevented us from having to fight the Sludgemen (as Mikaal told me the beast was called) when we resumed our journey. Junean put a shield sphere up around our mounts and we retreated a bit, putting distance between us and the battleground to prepare our meal. If anything, or anyone tried to get to Pakky and company, Junean would know about it.

Granalis offered to help the ladies turn our finds into something enjoyable to eat after I used my helping hands to recover all the wood as well as the large but delicate mushrooms Coral had gathered and cast aside when danger threatened. Junean pulled the root fruit she'd stowed in her bag before using one of her figures to start a fire. While Mikaal and I stepped away to practice with the Star Glass, Coral was dressing and slicing the birds, Junean the vegetables and fruit, and Granalis was stirring and seasoning two pots over the fire.

In Time?

"Mikaal. I know we left the changed chipchuck you had in Tiiaan. You don't have any more altered animals with you, do you?"

"We have Tibbeus, but I don't think that's what you are looking for."

"We'll get to him eventually, but first I need a target for practice. I don't want my inexperience to hurt anyone. You don't have anything else?"

"No. Well. Hmpf," he said while rustling around in the bag intertwined with his cloak.

A tick or two later and he pulled out a Shadowwormcicle which was encased in ice wrapped in an alarm spell.

I was surprised at this given the amount of pain they'd inflicted on him, but apparently the morning following his encounter with them, he'd found one outside where we'd slept and flash frozen it like he'd done with Tibbeus, and without much thought, put it in his bag for later study. Later during one of his watch shifts he'd remembered it and pulled it out to put the alarm spell on it so that it couldn't free itself and attack him without warning. I asked him to stand back and free it when I told him I was ready.

I prepared myself to send an image of what I imagined a younger worm would look like and nodded to Mikaal to free it. His gaw flashed and the freezing dissipated. The Shadowworm started towards me slowly, and I sent the image and command while pointing the Star Glass at it. A flash of magic and there was the smaller, younger worm. Only, it was still a Shadowworm. It was still corrupting everything it touched and was still crawling toward me.

I took a step back and asked Mikaal to freeze it again. A couple of seconds later it was covered in a verdant glow, and it stopped moving. That's when I noticed the difference in color and flavor between the magic of the Star Glass and what Mikaal had done. I smacked my forehead with the palm of my hand. Communicating with an alien magic computer using images when I couldn't be certain of what images it might understand was challenging.

I jumped into my own head and framed the image I was sending to the Star Glass in another spot on the wall. In the top left I added an analog clock showing 9 p.m. and a second with arrows pointing counterclockwise to the hands reading 1 p.m. In the top right I put a digital clock reading 23:00 followed by another reading 02:00.

I adjusted the image of the Shadowworm to add its current appearance as a corrupted creature and made the target image less young but back in what I imagined its natural state to be and surrounded both with a green aura. Finally, I added a generic looking calendar in the bottom right showing the current year leading back to last year's calendar. Hopefully this would allow the Star Glass to understand that I wanted it to reverse time itself in an area around the target, not de-aging whatever creature I happened to be pointing it at.

With the image locked in my mind, I transferred my consciousness back to my body, held the artifact at the worm thing, and asked Mikaal to release it again. As soon as it moved, I sent my image as a command, and the Shadowworm was swallowed up by another spell. The air crackled and sparks flew from the edges of the pea green aura. Most magic appeared as a transparent field of color, but this effect was brighter and nearly opaque.

I quickly crafted a pair of sunglasses for myself and peered through the aura. The Shadowworm was writhing madly, and the Chaos of the corruption was crawling slowly across the surface of its flesh. I urged the Star Glass to run time back faster. The magical aura intensified, and an electrical arc shot into the sky. Twenty ticks more and the spell stopped. The smell of ozone was thick around us.

I took off the glasses and looked for the worm. Mikaal spotted it first. It was free of the effects of the Chaos cloud, but it wasn't moving. He grew brave and picked it up with his gaw. It hung limp for what seemed an eternity before it twitched once, twice, and then started writhing again.

In Time?

Mikaal began dancing around madly cackling and swinging the worm like a sling. It was hilarious watching a being with eight appendages covered with a cloak appear to slide back and forth along the ground without moving at all. The commotion brought Junean and Granalis to see what was going on. I told them that we'd restored a Shadowworm to its original form, and Junean's face lit up. "So, you can heal Tibbeus?" she asked.

"Maybe, but I've only done this once and that on a worm. I'm not sure how safe it would be for him."

"Please try?" she pleaded.

I nodded, uncertain this was a good idea. I couldn't fault her for grasping hope with both hands and holding tight. She reached into her Tibbeus bag and began to pull him out. I looked to Mikaal to ensure he was ready to do his part. He had stopped dancing and nodded back at me.

"I know you want Tibbeus back to normal as soon as possible, but the food is ready, and I think we stand a better chance of success with full bellies," Coral said carrying two steaming bowls.

Coral held a bowl out to me, and the smell made my stomach growl loudly.

"You are right, of course," Junean said with an unreadable expression.

I took the bowl of food from Coral with a grateful smile, and she handed the other to Junean. My bowl had slices of meat on top while Junean's was vegetarian. Mikaal walked away and reappeared with two bowls, handing one to Coral. The food was delicious, and I thanked them for cooking. Junean was obviously forcing herself to eat, but soon enough the meal was done. Granalis went to clean up. "Here, let me help you Granalis," Coral offered.

"Why don't you stay and comfort Junean. I don't think this will be easy on her." he said quietly to her.

Coral and I helped Junean to get Tibbeus out of the bag and told them to stand behind me. I warned Junean that restoring him would be just as painful for him as it was when the Chaos cloud had touched him in the first place. Before beginning, I asked Mikaal if he had seen the lightning while rewinding the Shadowworm. He had. Everybody took two more steps back before we began.

I asked Junean if she had an image of what he had looked like before. She pulled a rectangle out of her pouch and stretched it out before tapping on a corner. At her touch, the frame was holding a three-dimensional image of her and her mate. I studied it to prepare my mental image and dropped my hand like I was starting a race. Mikaal just looked at me blankly, so I told him to free Tibbeus. Coral crouched behind Junean and gripped her upper arms comfortingly, yet wary of the damage a distraught Moalean's claws could do.

Tibbeus went from motionless to a flurry of activity, but the Star Glass and I reacted before he could get far. His growl of rage disappeared into the same pea green glow that had reverted the Shadowworm to its original form and turned into a howl of pain and despair. It occurred to me that while I struggled to see what was happening through the aura of magic, that my team could probably see everything in detail. This was confirmed for me when a wail of anguish arose from behind me and Junean began a panicked recitation of what was happening to her love.

The size of the field began to expand, and I was confused as to why.

"No Tibbeus! Fight it! He's growing, Aaron! The antler is growing back out!" Junean wailed.

This was taking too long. I ordered the reversal to double speed and then double again.

Junean wailed again, and her recitation became an incoherent string of syllables.

"I know it is hard to watch, but trust that he will be fine." Coral as soothingly as possible over Junean's sobs.

"Let me know when there is no sign of corruption Mikaal."

In Time?

This statement was punctuated by a lightning strike. Suddenly we were surrounded by fingers of electricity arcing first into the sky and then into the ground. I slowed the reversal to keep my friends from being toasted where they stood.

I ordered my arm to stay pointed at the male Moalean and jumped into my mind. I created two giant metal spikes and thrust them into the real world and into the ground on each side of the reversal glow. Once they were planted, I sped the process up again. The arcing returned, but this time leapt directly to the rods and into the ground.

The keening of the lovers went on for what seemed an eternity. Just when I thought I couldn't take it one second longer, it ended. Sparks stopped flying, the ground around the rods had become glass, and the air felt singed. Junean sobbed and ran to the child-sized form lying on the ground. I said a little prayer and walked closer too. I didn't want to have been responsible for the death of someone my friend loved.

I heard a chiming as I walked and looked around. Junean was howling as she held Tibbeus's still form and rocked him. I realized that the sound had been coming from the Star Glass around my neck. I stopped and opened communication with it. It was nearly out of power. I had no idea what its power source was. I inquired what forms of energy it could make use of. It described some things that I didn't understand, but I got the idea that it *could* make use of almost any energy source. However, it had been given instructions by its creator limiting it to recharging from a local source of magic. I could override this by directing it to use specific sources, but it didn't have enough energy to reverse time anymore until it could recharge. That could take hours. I informed it that I would find it a source soon and made sure that it wasn't going to cease functioning.

When I returned to my body, Tibbeus was breathing, and his coloring seemed to be returning to normal. Junean was gently brushing his hair with her back feet and whispering into his ear.

Mikaal told me that he'd tried a healing, but there didn't seem to be anything wrong with him. Coral handed Junean some water and together they dribbled some into Tibbeus's mouth.

In a little over an hour, he stirred on his own and opened his day eyes. He saw Junean's face, and he smiled. Of course, we had to wait for her to stop kissing him before he could speak.

"The last thing I recall, we were running from the malignant storm, and I was trapped. What did I miss?" he said, his voice getting stronger with each word.

Junean spent a few minutes recounting the story from her perspective. He laughed about her carrying him in a magic bag. When she got to the part about how he was restored, she got choked up.

"How are you feeling Tibbeus?" I asked.

"Like I've been reborn! Strong like crystal," he said, standing quickly.

"I don't think so Tib," Junean said, trying to catch him as he toppled over, twisted around, and ended up sitting opposite where he had been originally. Junean helped him get comfortable again, and they put their heads together and just held each other.

Granalis chose this moment to let out an uncharacteristic whoop of joy. Everyone looked around, expecting attack, before looking at the fluffy white being sitting on a boulder nearby.

"Do you realize what you've done? I'll tell you what you've done! The impossible, that's what! In all the years I was imprisoned I don't know of anyone surviving being corrupted."

"He's right," Coral said, "and that means there is hope. It might take time, but there's a chance that lost loved ones might be restored."

"Thank you, Aaron and Mikaal," Junean said, not letting go of Tibbeus.

I got up and motioned for the others to follow me. Mikaal was giddy and hopeful until I informed him that the seemingly limitless

Star Glass did in fact have limits and that we had reached them. Thankfully we didn't have anyone else who needed a Reversing, as I termed it. We needed to get moving soon as we had no idea how much time remained. The Chaos Cloud was still coming, and Tiiaan was still in its path. Even with fresh hope, most of us would die of old age before I could restore an entire city of corrupted.

Chapter 26
Be Careful What You Search For

Stopping for a midday meal had taken much longer than expected. We'd made good progress, but we needed to keep moving if we were going to prevent the Chaos Cloud from destroying Tiiaan. I started readying the Rhinodons while Mikaal and Coral cleaned and packed up the remains of the cookware. Granalis lifted off silently to scout for trouble. When I had the animals ready, we all met where we had left Tibbeus and Junean. I started to offer to fly them along with us when I realized that I could see through them. Junean flickered slightly when she stood and looked in the general direction of where we were standing, but with an unfocused look on her face.

"My friends. I am so grateful that you have done the impossible and brought my husband-to-be back to me. I think that if we had not met, I would have likely died at his hands and my people would not know what had befallen us. We are sorry that we couldn't stay and continue the journey with you, but we were already on a mission for our people that we must see through to the end.

"Tibbeus also needs care that we cannot offer him while we're traveling. I notified my people that we are ready to return, and they provided a Quickness to take us home. We are indebted to you and committed to saving Sorra. Our people will come to pay this debt when we are most needed.

"I have left the Torc that Aaron made for me behind for Granalis since he will be with you. May your way forward be free of barriers and your support of each other strong, until we meet again."

I stood there for a tick longer than I probably should have, processing both the message and the way in which it was delivered before stooping and scooping up the Torc lying on a rock. It was a little big for Granalis and I was going to do… something creative to make it smaller, but I was saved from having to figure out how. Granalis reached out and took the Torc. He made alternating passes with his hands and uttered a low droning sound deep in his throat for a short time before handing it back to me and asking me to put it on for him. I wasn't sure what he'd done, but it was now a perfect fit.

With that out of the way I turned to find Mikaal and Coral already mounted and waiting. I ran the three steps toward Pakky while creating steppingstones below my feet so that I effectively ran onto the animal's back. I got a good hold and felt Granalis settle onto my back before we leapt ahead.

The slap, slap, slap of Rhinodon travel would have caused me to sink inward and become reflective, but the ability to directly mindspeak with the group kept me connected and engaged. We were vigilant against the reappearance of the Gelatin beast or any of its kin but were soon far out of their 'slurping' grounds.

"I'm glad that Junean has Tibbeus back, but I'm going to miss her." Coral sighed.

"I just hope they don't run into the Chaos cloud again on their way." I replied.

"They should arrive safely," Mikaal reassured us. "A Quickness is a magical underground tunnel connecting two points and allowing for travel at a high rate of speed."

It sounded like a great idea to me, and I wondered why we hadn't been using that all along.

The little Norran sighed. "Unfortunately, it takes a significant amount of magic to construct, and given how a traveler would move in darkness and through much loose dirt, only Moaleans use them."

We talked about flows of magic and if there were places of more abundant magic than others. There were. Tiiaan was such a place but most of them were not significantly stronger, and almost all of them had cities built on them. That didn't seem like a worthwhile avenue to follow for providing power to the Star Glass.

With that thought I spent a few moments communicating with the artifact and devised a way for it to communicate its power level to me. I created a watch within my head with two functions. It provided a gauge showing its power level as well as a direction indicator of potential alternate power sources, color coded by the strength of the source. I put it on myself using a mental hand and returned to reality. The watch showed 60% power.

While working with the Star Glass, I had fallen to the rear of the party. When I looked Coral was directly in front of me. I was struck afresh with how attractive she was. Her hair flowing out behind her along with the color variations on her exposed skin tickled my fancy like no other woman ever had. I sent her a gentle wave of love and appreciation while giving her a physical squeeze as closely approximating a hug as I could without the use of my arms. I felt the warmth of her response wash over me. Whatever else befell me, I felt grateful for being able to experience this world. I hoped that if we lived, I could make a home here with these people and this woman especially.

I had always prided myself on being able to judge the time from the position of the sun, but since arriving in Sorra I struggled to read the day. When communicating with the artifact I would probably starve to death if I was alone as I had no sense of time. The sun was now riding low in the sky. Mikaal sent a mental image of the place we should camp and an impression that it was on the downward side of the rise we could make out on the horizon. I wondered as we went how fast Rhinodon travel was as compared to a vehicle from my homeland. We passed the next hour discussing what we might find when we reached Tiiaan and what our chances of success might be.

As we began moving up the last hill, I heard sounds in the distance that sounded like a chime or a gong sounding at irregular intervals. Granalis suddenly shot up from where I'd thought he was napping behind me and flew off ahead of us. Seconds later I heard his mental call. "Trouble. There is a fight ahead on the road."

I was unsure of whether this was something we should get involved in, so I dismounted onto a flight platform to my left and flew myself up to get a better view. In the center of the road stood a corrupted being that I guessed to have been an OrOboid. The mouth atop its head was massive now and rimmed with razor sharp…. Well, Razor blades is what they reminded me of.

Its neck had elongated, making an already tall being even more imposing. The OrObeast's arms now ended in solid crystal points like living spears and behind this the arms were plated in alternating chunks of metal and stone. Its trunk and legs had developed a barklike toughness, and each foot was pointed stone. Every step it took sunk into the ground with a crunch. Metal plates stood out from around its head protecting its sensory membrane. It made no other sound except for a clank and hiss as it struck forward with its mouth like a snake, attempting to remove chunks from its prey.

Facing off with it were three OrOboid wielding spears. One of the sounds I had heard was those crystal spears striking the beast's head plates. OrOboid were unlike anything I could have imagined. Once I took in their initial appearance, which as Mikaal had said was fantastic and majestic, it was the way they fought and moved that was most amazing. They were thrusting and leaping in and out and over and under each other so quickly that I almost couldn't follow. Every time they touched the ground they shifted direction, or sped up, or pressed low to the ground. As they danced through the air they would strike repeatedly with their spears, mostly feints and defense, while twisting and bending in alarming contortions.

I didn't want to contact the OrOboid and distract them, so I informed Mikaal and Coral what I'd seen and asked them to circle left. I asked Granalis to keep low to the ground and try to circle around to the right and confuse the aggressor without becoming a meal. Off he shot to the right while I raced forward overhead. I looked over my shoulder to see what had become of Pakky. He had stopped at the top of the rise when he realized that his passengers were gone. He snorted once and began to graze.

With the rough draft of a plan in motion and those for whom I'm responsible accounted for, I turned my attention back to the rapidly approaching battle. I slowed my descent and saw first a streak of white from the right rake the middle leg joint of the OrObeast, which caused it to abort a strike yet brought no sound except for that of claws on rough hide. A battle is an unnatural event for most people in the time and place that I was from, but when one did occur it would be loud. Between creatures that were completely mute though, the near silence was the most deafening part.

Granalis' effect was short lived. The corrupted OrOboid recovered and struck back, clamping its razor-lined mouth down solidly on the butt of a crystal staff and whipping its owner about wildly. This nearly knocked another OrOboid from the sky, but it twisted in on itself and narrowly avoided impact. One bolt of light followed another slamming into the plating of the head, but the maw did not release its grip. The OrOboid released his spear and backed away from the battle. That was the first time I heard one of them (mind)speak.

"You are here to help?" The voice in my head felt female.

"We are," Mikaal, Coral, and I responded in unison.

I received the impression of acceptance without words, and she turned back to the battle, pulling small slivers of crystal from bands on her arms, which began growing into daggers soundlessly. I was hovering over the battle. Bolts continued to pepper the corrupted being, and two fireballs struck its trunk from the same direction.

The serpentine nature of the combatants inspired me to intervene in a similar manner. Rather than a hand, I created a rope that I could control like one of Mikaal's gaw and dropped it onto the malformed being below. Like a hand, it was still emanating from me, but as soon as it touched down, I began to wrap it around the arms and trunk, being careful to avoid the spearhands veering erratically. Once I had a good grip, I hoisted it and myself up so that it was flailing above the ground. A bolt from Coral hit one of the stone feet, causing it to swing like a pendulum.

I sent a call to all below to back away and asked Mikaal to freeze it. It spit out the spear and began to writhe and swing wildly. The spear flew toward the tallest OrOboid and was deflected at the last moment, but the butt of the spear still struck her and sent her flying, dazed.

Mikaal's spell took effect, and the motion stopped. I lowered my burden to the ground and hurried toward the downed friendly combatant. The OrOboid was struggling to stand and seemed to be reeling, but Coral reached it first. I heard a whisper of her offer to help, and her hands glowed blue as she spoke a healing chant. The glow left her hands and surrounded a gash on its grundel just above its center leg. I arrived in time to hold my hand out to it with a mental offer of help standing. We gripped hands, and I noted that it had two broad fingers and an opposing thumb and a very strong grip. Once it was on its feet, we began introductions.

"I am Kaalesh of Stronghold Waeer, and these are my mates, Kaaden and Kreelen. This creature was one of us. He was sent to investigate disappearances from several of our settlements. He never returned, and this is how we found him. He is an isolationist, and one of our bravest warriors. He has protected our fields from the most dangerous of scavengers and would not have been taken down easily. We do not know what happened to cause him to have changed so."

She stopped speaking and dropped to a knee suddenly, which was doubly unexpected to me as her front leg folded in under her body and hit the ground with her foot still in place and extended toward me. In a flash her mates were beside her, and for the first time I noticed that they were eating and drinking. Kreelen poured a thin liquid that reminded me of green tea into the orifice on top of her head. Her mouth was a perfect circle when opened and contained three rows of small, flat teeth. Kaaden then fed her some small bits of some leafy plant material, and her mouth folded flat and looked human for a second before it opened and closed flat again at a thirty-degree angle. Each time she chewed, her mouth closed in a different position than the last. A few mouthfuls of food and drinks of tea, and she stood up once again, the three of them towering over me.

I asked Mikaal to explain what we knew and turned to examine my patient. He had hit the ground and his sharp feet sunk in a few inches. I heard Mikaal speaking, but it quickly became the sound of an insect buzzing behind me as I turned inward. I used an inner hand to surreptitiously collect a blood sample from the area surrounding the now healed gash on Kaalesh's grundel. I made a small incision in the joint between the metal and stone on the corrupted OrOboid's arm and took a sample here too.

In my mind I placed an electron microscope and a computer to analyze the samples and provide useful output. There were more differences than there were similarities, or at least that's what it seemed like. I needed more samples to be sure. I brought myself back to my body and interrupted Mikaal's explanation with, "I need some of Kaaden and Kreelen's blood."

In retrospect, this was probably not the best way for me to have communicated this. I didn't blame Kaalesh for pressing her spear against my throat. They didn't know me at all and had never seen a human any more than I'd seen an OrOboid. I was glad that I didn't have to speak aloud as that might have punctured my jugular.

"I mean no harm to them or to any of you. I am trying to help your corrupted friend, and I need to understand more about OrOboid bodies to do so." I said with a breathless squeak, trying to project the friendliest tone I could muster under the circumstances.

It is really, really hard to tell what an OrOboid is thinking or feeling since they have no facial expressions or other outward signs. Waiting for her response felt like a lifetime, but the entire encounter probably took only a few seconds. That was probably a good thing, because if it had taken longer Coral would have probably escalated the encounter further by killing Kaalesh. Before that could happen, the spear was pulled away.

"I apologize." She said, "I've never heard of a magic that requires the blood of another for healing. So, I could not imagine that such a statement would indicate anything but an intent to attack."

Mikaal added, "Aaron is from another world and has powers and ideas that nobody from Sorra has ever seen. I assure you he means only good and is here to help save us all."

I turned toward the other two warriors and said aloud and in mindspeak, "Will you allow me to collect a small amount of your blood so I can help your friend?"

Kaalesh was brave and quickly volunteered to give her blood before the others could respond, so I had to sheepishly explain how I already had her blood and had taken it without asking. The other two warriors agreed, and I produced two syringes floating in the air before them. I had no idea how thick their skin was and didn't want to harm them, so I ended up showing Kaalesh how to work the syringes. I asked where on their grundels was the least likely to permanently harm an OrOboid and contained only soft tissue. They pointed, I swiped with an alcohol pad, and the first and second blood draw on Sorra was completed in short order.

Back to my inner room I went with the samples. I marked the three healthy samples as pure and waited to see what came back. The computer quietly whirred away for a few minutes and displayed a color-coded update of the corrupted DNA. Those strands that it was certain of how to repair were surrounded with a green glow, while strands that analysis revealed were probably corrupted but had two or more possibilities for correction were haloed in yellow. There were two strands that were similarly identified as red. It knew these were wrong but didn't have enough data to suggest a correction.

I was hoping that this would have been a more efficient way to restore an individual who had been affected by the Chaos Cloud, but I wasn't sure this would work. I also had no knowledge of the best way to apply the corrections. I shook myself when I returned to my body and the motion caused everyone to turn and look at me. I frowned lightly. This wasn't solely my decision, so I decided to explain the best that I could.

Since I already had everyone's attention, I began to mindspeak to the group. "I'm a novice at using magic or powers, or whatever it is I'm doing. I've had some great successes so far. I have a method that works for restoring those who have been corrupted, but it takes lot of power and may mean that I can't help the next person who needs it. I'm trying to find a new way to reverse this," I waved at the fallen form beside me, "but even with the samples I've collected from each of you there may not be enough information for me to pull it off.

"As I see it, our choices are: First, use the method I've already used and hope I have the power needed. Second, I can attempt to fix your friend the new way, which might work fully, or partially, or kill him. Third, we could carry him with us like an icicle and try to restore him once we've gotten more samples from other OrOboid."

The OrOboid moved close together, which in a human would be huddling up to talk it over. This was similar, but very different. They clasped arms to form a nearly perfect circle. They each had one leg forward and two behind with their front legs curled around one another. Their heads were close but not touching. Their stance seemed intentional and at a glance, shatterproof. The words, "A person standing alone can be attacked and defeated, but two can stand back-to-back and conquer. Three are even better, for a triple-braided cord is not easily broken." popped into my mind.

With no visible or audible cues to show their process I had no idea how long this would take. I wasn't marking the time, but they reached a consensus much more quickly than three of my people would have been able to. They released their stance slowly, almost reluctantly, each of their limbs caressing the others as they broke, and then Kaalesh spoke.

"This is a decision such as a family would make for one of their own, but sadly Andoo has no family. Since there is no one else to decide for him, we speak for him as if he was family. We do not want to weaken you so that you are not ready to help another, but we do need him back. Please try this new way you spoke of."

"Thank you for your vote of trust. I do need to ask two questions before I can begin" I hesitated. It felt a little awkward to ask, but I couldn't be expected to know everything in this new world already. "First, you referred to Andoo as He, but from my examination it seems OrOboid have three genders. I need to understand which he originally was."

Kaaden turn-stepped toward me and spoke somehow sheepishly and boldly at once. "Andoo was a smale like me. Kreelen is an emale and Kaalesh is female. Does that help, or do you need to know more?"

"That helps a great deal. Is there any significant way that Andoo was different from you three? There are two pieces of who he was that appear broken, so I would need to copy those from you, but that may accidentally erase some natural differences. I can do my best to fix that later when I know more."

Kreelen took a turn trying to help. "He is unmated, that is a difference. He was one of our Waeer but lived outside of it. I don't think anyone understood why he did. Aside from that, I can't think of anything significant that we are aware of."

"Thank you—I'll start getting ready." I turned away and then back quickly. Even though I was speaking with only my mind, my mannerisms while speaking were still in place, so I looked at Kaalesh since she was closest. "Oh, uh. One more thing. Do illnesses affecting the other races also affect OrOboid? I realize this seems strange, but it may matter."

Kaalesh responded slowly and thoughtfully. "Not every illness affects us, but the most common ones do, although we often have different symptoms."

I nodded, asked Coral and Mikaal to be ready to cast a healing at Andoo once I began, and turned inward. I copied strands from Kaaden's DNA and replaced all the yellow strands of Andoo's with those. I suspected that the red strands had to do with the bonds of family and/or community ties. I took Kaaden's DNA strand as a starting point and overlaid the other two samples, taking those which were the same from those and replacing them over Kaaden's.

I was going on pure intuition and hopefully I didn't kill or permanently harm Andoo, but it felt like the right move. Something had to be done to save his life. I replaced the red strands on the computer with this modified strand and ran it through the computer again as a sanity check. The computer seemed to think that this DNA chain was whole, so I went with it.

I brought three syringes into existence and began creating and replicating DNA chains as I had done for Mikaal before. I added a virus with the same goal, to replace corrupted DNA chains with the corrected (I hoped) ones. I also added a mental command to the virus that I hoped would work, that when there were no more corrupted DNA to attack, they would die.

Once I had the syringes full, I returned to the world at large and walked toward the frozen OrObeast. I searched for gaps where I could administer each dose. I found only one that seemed like it would work in the joint between metal and stone on one arm. I thought briefly of stabbing into the beasty's one giant eye ring but thought better of it. I inserted the syringe and pushed down hard, hoping that Mikaal's freezing spell wouldn't kill the viruses.

Finding no other openings for my needles, I stepped back and thought. I asked everyone, especially the OrOboid, to step away. I mentally created four huge metal panels like I imagined an old ship might have been made of. I slammed them into the ground as a sort of prison for the unconscious patient and welded them together at the top. This created a smooth wall all the way round it and a few feet higher than I hoped it could jump. I changed one syringe into a nebulizer which I hoped would deliver enough mist for Andoo to breath the virus in. The other I transmuted into an oral syringe.

When I returned to my body again, I realized that I was getting a strong feeling of astonishment from the OrOboid. They hadn't seen me create anything so large and having giant metal plates suddenly slam into the ground would be startling for anyone. Mikaal and Coral were ready to heal, so I lifted them up to hover over the cage and joined them a second later with two hands full of medicine. The astonishment coming from the OrOboid increased. I heard a rustle and saw Granalis land near the OrOboid and attempt to reassure them.

I used a mental hand to place the nebulizer in the corner of the cage and turned it on, before telling Mikaal to break the freezing spell. I readied my rope arm as the corrupted Andoo sprang up suddenly, trying to escape. His leap was thankfully short, and he slid back down the wall with the squeal of crystal on metal. The base of the makeshift pit was rapidly disappearing into mist.

Almost as soon as it touched down, it sprang up again. I lassoed it below the metal plates on its head and held it barely above the ground. Then while it writhed, I used my mental hand to deliver the oral dose straight into its mouth. Once I was certain that it had swallowed, I dropped it to the ground. It jumped one more time. When its body came out of the mist I saw stone, metal and crystal falling away from it.

When it disappeared into the mist again all was silent for an uncomfortable moment before all of us were slammed with a wall of mental anguish. Pain so intense that I nearly lost consciousness raked across our mental barriers. We started to fall due to my lack of foresight and loss of focus, but thankfully I was able to recover and catch us before any damage was done.

"Mikaal or Coral, can you start healing Andoo?"

"Mikaal is knocked out," Coral said. "I'll do it."

I laid Mikaal down carefully across Pakky, hoping that was far enough to keep him safe while Coral started her spell.

When I set him down, I realized that Coral was shouting at me.

"Aaron! I have to see what I'm healing, and this fog is too thick!"

"Sheesh. I should have thought of that. Give me a moment Coral."

Mentally berating myself for not realizing, I reached into the mist with a mental hand and turned the nebulizer off. Having no other idea of how to get rid of the mist safely, I modified the nebulizer with a 'reverse' switch and turned it on. I wasn't sure that was really a thing that could be done, but it didn't stop it from working.

The mist rapidly vanished into the corner, and Coral's delicate fingers flashed blue healing magic. The mental barrage of pain lessened slowly as her spell took hold. A few minutes that felt like forever, and all was quiet again, both physically and mentally. I dropped Coral near the OrOboid and flew over to check on Mikaal. He was rousing and rubbing his head, so I picked him up and brought him over to the group.

"What happened?" they thought in unison at me.

I was about to respond when we all felt a faint "Hello?" skitter across our minds.

We started walking toward the cage, with Kaalesh in the lead and her mates only a pace or so behind. Granalis landed on my shoulder gently as we walked. Before they could get closer, I broke the welds on the rightmost wall and dropped it to the ground with a resounding GONG.

"Careful all. We're still not sure of how well this has worked." I thought to everyone around.

The voice that replied was weak but distinct and new to my mind. "I am not sure what you've done, or how. I'm not sure I'm totally my old self, but I am sane and thankful." Andoo's gratitude was clear, if faint.

When I saw him, he was definitely OrOboid once again. His skin was softer than the others, perhaps like a baby newly born, yet he was covered with a patchwork of lines where foreign materials had been a part of him.

A feeling of joy from all of the OrOboid lasted only a short time before changing to surprise, then alarm with an undertone of anger.

I rushed ahead and asked what was wrong.

"Thank you for restoring me. I am Kandoo," the former OrObeast said.

"That's what's wrong, Aaron. Somehow, he's bonded to all of us. This is not possible. It is against nature." Kaaden bellowed.

It took me a few seconds to process what they were saying to me. It was all so foreign to my way of thinking. I facepalmed and would have banged my head on something in frustration had there been anything suitable near enough.

"We will find a way to fix this. I think once I have examined a few more of your people, especially an unbonded, I should be able to set this to rights." I said sending alarm and chagrin to them.

"I don't want to be fixed. I've never wanted a bond before in my life, but now that I feel it, I can't imagine being without it," Andoo, now Kandoo said.

Kaaden tensed as if to spring, but Kaalesh laid a hand on his arm. "I know this feels wrong to us, but remember, we decided to proceed in this way, knowing it might not be perfect. Aaron has done what nobody else can and thinks he can finish the job. We must be patient and treat him as family as we said we were." Kreelen joined her in placing her hand on Kaaden's other arm, and the tension left him.

We gathered our animals and began to set up camp. By this time, it was already the first watch of the night. Granalis flew in with a few small animals for dinner. I started a fire, and we began to prepare a light meal. The OrOboid were gathered in an uncomfortable circle stance (we could feel their discomfort radiating off of them) with heads together, bringing each other up to date.

Before retiring, Kaalesh told me that they wished to join our party until I was able to complete the restoration of Kandoo to Andoo. They were committed to his safe return and support of him but were also certain that returning among the OrOboid would be disruptive as things stood. We hoped that we might be able to locate some unbonded smales or at least emales in Tiiaan to provide what I needed to correct the restoration.

This decided, we pulled out bedrolls and picked spots to lie down. Coral placed her bedding near mine but not touching. Once I was seated, I looked at our new companions. They were just standing there as if unsure how to proceed.

"Do your people sleep standing up?" I asked (K)Andoo, speaking only to him for the first time.

"No. Those who are bonded sleep lying with their heads together. Those who are not, sleep alone," he responded directly.

"You feel bonded to them because of my mistake, but they don't feel bonded to you? Is that correct?"

"I am not sure how your race works, but this is not just a feeling for us. We were created in such a way that a bond is not only of emotion, but physical, spiritual, and mental. No OrOboid has ever experienced what we are now. Our physiologies... our very nature does not allow what has happened. This would be hurtful to another race, but to them it is like that which was wholesome and pure has been tainted. Every one of those connections is singing out to us that something is very wrong. It is very distracting." His words were earnest, emotion laden, and faded to something akin to a whisper as he ended.

"Is this affected by distance from each other? Is there any way I can help?"

"A lot of distance would help a small amount. I don't know what you would be able to do that would matter until we get the information you need."

I suggested that our new companions eat and drink while I tried to rack my brain for some way to make this better. I talked with Mikaal, Granalis, and Coral, hoping they would have some magical knowledge or experience that would help. In the end, we could only offer to put them into a dreamless sleep by means of magic. Only (K)Andoo accepted, probably thinking that if he was unconscious that it might offer the others some relief. He had no supplies as they had been lost when he was corrupted, so I created a long version of my bedroll and had him lie near Coral and I, with his head towards us. Mikaal's spell knocked him out, and he began setting protective shields so we could sleep.

Looking at the K family, I sensed some but not all the tension roll from them, and they were able to lie down as they would normally have done. Each of them produced a neatly folded woven mat made from some sort of leaves from around one leg. It was dyed the same shade as their skin and so I hadn't noticed it before. Before they spread them out, they each dropped a couple handfuls of crystal dust in a line where they were to lie. With the three of them working in unison, I heard the tickle of a whisper as they instructed the crystal to become three thin pallets directly atop the ground. This provided them a perfectly flat clean surface on which to spread their mats.

A single drop of liquid from a flask produced from I know not where was dripped onto the center of each mat. The mats responded by swelling up from paper thin, to about as thick as one of their fingers. Preparations complete, they laid down. Heads nearly touching, seemingly breathing the same air, two legs on the ground with the topmost leg folded upon itself to lie as neatly as possible on the ground between their groundward legs. It seemed as if they were asleep the moment they were prone.

Chapter 27
Racing the Storm to Tiiaan

I was awakened by the light of a new dawn creeping stealthily toward my face like a cat. When it pounced on my eyes, I woke to my own personal vision of beauty. The SeaWind princess sat on a nearby stone. Her delicate form was outlined by brilliant beams of many-hued light, causing the breath to catch in my throat. Her head turned towards me as the sound of my breathing changed. I could not see her face as she unfolded from her perch, flowing towards me as much as walking.

When she was near enough and my eyes adjusted, I could see her smile, more dazzling than the sunrise. She knelt beside me and brushed my cheek with her lips. I, of course, did the sensible thing, not breathing so she couldn't smell my morning breath. Her smile infected me, and I sat up grinning. I wondered briefly if it was possible to be unhappy in her presence. I hoped we all lived long enough to find out what was possible.

The rest of the camp was waking now, and I heard the sound of Rhinodon grazing; Granalis landing; Mikaal's droning as he released the protective spell he had around us. I stood, pulling Coral along gently by the hand to go check on the OrOboid contingent of our group. I could have probably just reached out with my mind, but I had many more years of living without that ability, and it didn't come naturally yet.

The original three were already awake and had taken up their mats. I wasn't sure where they had put them, but my attention was drawn in by their morning routine. Each OrOboid touched their crystal platform, and it fell instantly into shards. They each grabbed a few pieces and put them in their armbands. Next, they each ingested two mouthfuls of something that I couldn't clearly see. It was as long as they were tall.... They were eating their bedding! When they had enough, they wrang the remainder out and wrapped the thin material around a leg. Finally, they drank once from a small vial they carried and then began to stretch.

They stretched their long legs and crouched low, folding their "knees" in alternating directions. One time up, down, up, followed by down, up, down. Even trying to describe it internally was difficult. The effect was much like a jumping spider, but they contacted the ground first with a foot, then a knee, then a different knee. It was dumbfounding. It amazed me that as different as the Sorran people were, they were able to understand and respect one another.

I gently sent a good morning to them and indicated that we would be waking (K)andoo up so that we could be on our way.

Kreelen spoke for them. "Thank you for the warning. We have gotten over some of the shock of what has happened and are holding on to hope that all will be corrected in time. We should be able to manage better today."

I nodded once, before remembering that the gesture may not mean anything to them. I thanked him and walked away, still holding Coral's hand.

I heard a light rumble from her, and a ripple of darker blue washed across her skin.

"Excuse me, Aaron. I think I'm hungrier than I realized."

I was also hungry, but her needs trumped my own. I had felt love for others before, but nothing like this. I wanted to meet her every need. I had to get control of myself. Now I had some abilities and the Star Glass, and who knows what I could cause to happen if I let my feelings take me over completely.

I thought for a moment, jumping briefly into my inner sanctum, and when I returned to my outer self, I was holding a brown paper bag in my left hand. I pulled Coral gently over to where Mikaal was and opened the bag.

"Have you eaten, Mikaal?"

He turned without moving his feet. "No. I was going to work with you two to get food once I had awakened Andoo."

"I have food to share. Please come join us when you are done."

We walked back to our bedrolls and sat down, side by side. I opened the bag, and the smells of Mama Gigi's café wafted out.

"This was my favorite food for breakfast where I grew up. I thought you might like it as well."

"Where did you get this? How did you get food from another world?" she asked, seeming unusually alarmed.

"I created it, just like I've done with everything else since I arrived here."

"It smells delicious. I was told when I was being taught how to use magic, that you can't make food with magic. I think they said that if you tried, it couldn't be real and wouldn't nourish you."

I smiled sheepishly. "Maybe not knowing what you can't do is a good thing. Maybe it is bad. I'm not sure my power works the same as Sorran magic. I'll understand if you don't want to try it." I said this while placing two steaming ham, cheese, and spinach quiches in front of us.

Her stomach rumbled again, and she picked it up and took a bite. "I think I'll chance it." she said wordlessly. Her eyes and the feeling that was radiating from her told me that Mama Gigi's was just as good as I remembered. I picked up my own and took a bite, savoring the delicate crust and its fluffy, salty filling.

Moments later Mikaal arrived. (K)Andoo was eating with the other OrOboid. He expressed the same concerns as Coral had but soon was halfway through his own quiche.

When everyone had finished eating, we packed up and set out. We rode as before, but with the addition of the four on foot. I was grateful to have them around since they could see in all directions at once. It is very hard to surprise an OrOboid. They run when traveling as they can cover ground quickly with much less effort than jumping.

Kaalesh ran in front, so I had the best view of her. Her foreleg pulled and set the direction of her travel while her trailing legs pushed and steadied. If she needed to change direction by more than a couple degrees, she would lead with another leg. It took me a while watching her to catch it as she never missed a step. Her grundel would twist to keep her two arms always to the left and right of her path of travel. (K)Andoo was in the rear since he was still recovering. Kaaden was on my left and Kreelen on my right.

We hoped to reach Tiiaan before nightfall if there were no more unexpected occurrences. We travelled for three hours uneventfully before the OrOboid needed to stop and eat. This didn't take longer than it took the rest of us to walk around and stretch our legs. We found a nearby stream and filled our water containers. I watched Kreelen fill their tiny vials with water and add a bit of plant dust to it. That solved the mystery of what they drank anyways.

Soon we were mounted and off again. This time we travelled only a half hour before (K)Andoo alerted the group to the fact that we were being followed by a cloud of small birdlike creatures. They were staying directly behind us and gaining speed as they came.

I asked everyone to continue moving forward as if we weren't aware. None of us knew why any group of birds would behave in this way if they didn't intend to attack. At a quick whispered command, Granalis leapt from his perch behind me into the sky, streaking off toward the right at a ninety-degree angle from our direction of travel. He made a broad circle away in the direction we were going. He dropped once to pick up a small snack and headed back towards us. This way he was able to see what was chasing us without it looking like he was.

His 'voice' sounded vaguely predatory when he reported back to all of us. Whatever those creatures had been, they were corrupted now and vile looking. Granalis' eyes in his natural state were very sharp since his people had hunted from the air, and he was able to sharpen them further with his ability to change his body. What he saw, he sent us images of, like mental instant snapshot cameras from when I was a kid.

Very few of the corrupted bird-things looked alike. I wasn't sure if they were all different species, or if they had been changed so completely that they were indistinguishable as to how they began. Some of them looked like they shouldn't be able to fly. Their bodies were distorted and not aerodynamic at all. (Perhaps some Sorran birds flew by magic?) Wings and claws on others were exaggerated and spiked.

All of them had one thing in common—their eyes. Large or small, they all glowed yellow with angry red circles where irises should be. A sub-flock of corruptobirds broke off and headed towards Granalis. We were now traveling on flatlands, and there was no cover or good place to hide or defend ourselves.

I checked my watch to see how much power the Star Glass had. It was reporting eighty-seven percent full, so I decided this was as good a place as any to begin. I prepared my mental commands which would tell it to revert the ones moving towards Granalis as quickly as possible while consuming all the lightning strikes created as a side effect.

"I think this is a good place to make our stand," I said.

Like a group that had been fighting together for years everyone turned right and stopped. Each ally made ready to defend themselves in their own way. Mikaal readied spells, placing shields between our mounts and the onrushing horde. Coral dropped to the ground to stand behind her Rhinodon and readied her bows. The OrOboid formed their circle awkwardly, struggling to cope with one more member than they were used to, and readied spears (where had they had those hidden?) and slivers of crystal which they began growing into throwing daggers. For my part, I picked up the Star Glass from around my neck, held it aloft, and commanded it to begin the de-corruption. I also told it to cancel the spell before it reached critical power levels.

From where I was sitting the horizon was full to my right with avian adversaries. A small space of free sky separated them from the group that had chased Granalis, nearly in front of me now. My view of this group was obscured by the pea soup glow of the time reversal spell. I had never seen lightning abort its strike before. All around the targets of the reversal spell sparks of power would start to leap to ground and then fizzle out as the Star Glass consumed them. The glow and its contents plummeted as the beings were too distracted by pain to fly, much less converge on Granalis. One minute passed and another began. Dimly, I could hear squawks, caws, and bleats of agony, and they were getting too close for comfort.

I glanced at the power meter on my watch. The Star Glass' power was dropping quickly, but with each bolt of lightning it consumed, the rate of decline slowed or even stopped. I instructed the Star Glass to magic faster, told my body to keep my arm pointed, and directed my attention to the big flock of nasties that was close enough for us to see and hear clearly. Raucous screeching assailed our ears, and I thought I caught something that sounded like a child practicing their best evil laugh.

Something heavy landed beside me, between where I stood and the danger. I looked over to see white fur disappearing into the back of something that was in the middle of a transformation. A few breaths later it turned towards me, and I recognized Granalis' orange eyes gleaming from a face that reminded me of a gargoyle. His wings were huge and folded behind his broad back. His limbs were muscular and ended in talons, and his skin had hardened to the appearance of cement. "Granalis in battle mode," I said with a chuckle.

A cry from ahead preceded a streak of obsidian weaving around the OrOboid, between Granalis and me, and over Coral before slamming into the shield in front of Mikaal's mount. With a battle cry of her own, Coral loosed arrows, which flew straight and true taking down a couple of the larger vaguely bird shaped objects. The enemy horde took up their own caws and began strafing runs. As they closed, they were met with lances of light from the Torcs worn by Granalis, Coral, Mikaal, and me. (K)Andoo and Kaaden were at the front of their group and appeared to be competing to see how many foes they could stack up on their spears.

None of my little band had taken any serious damage yet, but this was only the first few of what appeared to be thousands. I heard a tone from the Star Glass alerting me that it had stopped the spell. I chanced a glance at my watch, realizing as I did that, I also held my crystal spear. This time the spell had consumed around twenty-five percent power, so allowing the artifact to suck up lightning helped considerably.

This revelation was cut short by a loud whump sound directly in front of me as Gargoyle-Granalis performed an admirable side tackle on one of the largest assailants in the group. It had been coming right at me and my lack of attention nearly got me badly wounded. There was an ichor dripping from the beak and talons of whatever it was that Granalis dropped on the ground before turning back to battle.

Time for me to earn my keep as the protagonist of this Sorran tale, I thought wryly to myself before taking my mental hands, flattening them out to resemble large flyswatters, and using them to wipe the sky free of great swaths of invaders. Of course, while I was amusing myself by treating this like a swarm of gnats at a picnic, none of my compatriots could see what I was doing. Kaalesh asked all of us what was going on, while throwing crystal darts at a few I'd missed. I responded by sending a mental image of what things looked like through my eyes to everyone.

I felt amusement ripple through my friends before the enemy redoubled its assault. Despite the vast number of crumpled corruptobird bodies strewn on the field, there were many times that number still in the air. Mikaal threw up an electric bolt that jumped from body to body, and a score or more fell to the ground. By this time the sky was darkening as the mass of wings blotted out the sun. Some of the enemy had passed over and began circling back, which we didn't realize until Mikaal cried out. A large weight had slammed into his back, almost knocking him over. Thankfully he wasn't injured. His cloak appeared to be slowly ingesting what ailed it. I hadn't seen this before and from the look on Mikaal's face, he hadn't either. The gift he had been given by the Schoolmasters of Tiiaan proved its value.

Mikaal's original shields protected him from the front, but the attackers were coming from all directions now. He fired his chain energy bolts twice more and then dropped his shield, before starting to cast a bubble of protection over himself. I relayed what was going on to Coral so that she'd be wary of the chink in her armor, before turning and swatting the airspace above and between the little Noran and myself. When his spell completed, Mikaal did the same for me with Granalis covering my back. When I looked to Coral to help him replace her barrier, I saw that she had already done so herself. She was a fierce warrior in her own right. My desire to protect the woman who I was rapidly losing my heart to contended briefly with admiration and respect. Heck, she had already saved me at least a couple times already. I didn't need to be a white knight, just always have her back. If my failing her ever caused her harm I didn't know if I'd ever be able to forgive myself.

I turned slowly, swatting aside foes as I did, trying to even the odds and maybe even gain an advantage. I wondered briefly why Mikaal hadn't tried to provide cover for the OrOboid, but when I saw them fight again, I realized that their acrobatic fighting style wouldn't allow for it. I slapped the sky clean above them to allow them a moment to breathe, but nearly as soon as I would cast the vicious things aside, more would rush in. I wondered how much longer the OrOboid could continue to fight before they needed to eat.

Mad cackling began to echo from the direction that the flight of doom had come from. I continued my spinning defense, keeping one swatter active overhead and one even larger where I could see better what I was hitting. The Torcs around our necks stopped firing their blazing beams and the gems went dark as they expended the energy I had given them. I could recharge them, but not in the middle of this madness.

Finally, I spotted the laughter's source. The mass of flying fighters was high and out of range of most physical attacks, but now came an even stranger sight. Much lower than the others flew four, no, six large fowl things, each with two large forewings and two smaller aft wings. Slowly and laboriously, they advanced, each of them holding their half of a bar that was thrust through the top of a litter... no, as it approached I could see it was more of a cage with tattered cloths flapping along each side. The front was uncovered except for the bars that encased the source of the insane laughter. It pranced, preened, bounded, and bounced around its enclosure, all the while gibbering senselessly. It was a wonder that it didn't knock itself and its bearers to the ground with each pounce.

The attackers parted like a curtain being drawn; the mass of spiraling flight patterns milling round in the direction we had been traveling, cutting off our escape. The foul fowl set down their burden and collapsed on the ground beside it. Each of them seemed like they were wavering from one side of the grave to the other, wheezing and sputtering. If they had stopped moving, I would have assumed from the look of them that they had been decaying for some time. They were corrupted, but somehow controlled, and the corruption seemed to have affected them all in the same way.

The presence inside the cage was the opposite. It was a constant blur of activity. Even when it was directly in front of us, it was hard to focus on as it bounded around. It appeared to have a head that was uncorrupted and unaltered, but each of its limbs and its torso might have been a different being altogether. Its face reminded me of a simian, its torso that of a lizard, legs a mockery of the Garanth, left arm like a squid's tentacles, and right arm like that of a great lion's paw.

Suddenly it stopped moving, gave a long high skreich, squatted down, and bounced on its heels. It looked across us from OrOboid on one side, to Noran on the other, hummed itself a little tune, and said loudly to itself, "Thems as who oppose the master always falls. Soons or lates, they fall." It took two deep ragged breaths before it bounded forward, slamming into the cage. Squid suckers latched on to bars left and right, and as it pressed its face into the space between them it hissed, showing sharply pointed teeth which did not match the apelike mouth. It's one feline claw raked the air wildly as if to rip us to shreds.

"The master tells me to come and see who has set themselves against he." It giggled and gibbered at its cleverness which trailed into a high wail. I had no doubt its mind was even more broken than its body. Every time it spoke it was as if a pool of minds were set into the single head, just as the parts of the bodies were joined. The voice that spoke was the one closest to the surface in that instant.

"Don't fight him." This voice too deep to be coming from this body slurped and burbled as it spoke. "If you give in, he simply destroys what you are. If you fight, he will use you forever, or long enough for it to feel like forever."

"Who is your master?" Kaalesh's voice rang out in mindspace strongly.

An answer came back in a voice ringing just as strong and still inaudible. "Oh, I/we can't tell you that." I stepped forward, keeping my eyes on the interloper but said aloud to Granalis, "Do you know this being?"

"I knew one that it was before it was like this." He replied, nearly in tears. "It was a proud and mighty thing, but it disobeyed once too often. It is good to say its master and not my master though."

Now its eyes shined with fervent hatred and locked onto Granalis. "You have escaped? You have aligned yourself against him? Oh… he will do terrible, awful, unthinkable things to you…"

"I won't allow it," I said before it could continue its threats. "Tell your master to run along home to wherever he came from and take his remaining pets with him."

"So, you are the 'Hero' then?" The giggling voice was back. It made the word hero sound like an epithet.

"Who I am and who we are is no concern of your Master's. At least so long as he stays hidden and sends prisoners to do his bidding," I retorted more bravely than I felt.

It opened its mouth and let out a high keening wail that seemed to come from the bowels of the earth. The wail continued and became the yellow glow of a magical attack. Molten rock seethed in the air in front of it before splitting and launching as lava missiles at each of us at the same time.

They hit the shields Mikaal had cast around the three of us with our Rhinodons and slid to the ground hissing, causing Mikaal to fall to his knees with the blow. Granalis leapt up and back, landing between Coral and Mikaal. The OrOboid sprang to the four points of the compass. The wail did not stop, nor did the missiles. The next volley was a random series. The first went towards (K)Andoo, and I felt him take a glancing hit as he had inadequate time to respond while landing from the first attack.

I sent a command to the Star Glass that magical attacks from this creature could be used as energy and the next two projectiles winked out before they reached their targets. The seething stones that the creature controlled darkened and fell to the ground, crumbling apart on impact.

It blinked at us and cried out in confusion. The reptilian skin of its torso changed to a dark purple and glowed yellow. A rain of acid fell from above us. I heard Granalis yelp and then the rain dried up.

I pointed at the cloud of enemies behind us and commanded the Star Glass to de-corrupt as many of that group as it could safely complete while consuming lightning. The center of the mass disappeared into pea green aura and dropped to the ground while lightning flickered in and out of existence. I had thought to use the reversal on the creatures before us, but if this thing was really made of several other living beings, I would probably only use lots of power and kill it. Instead, I decided to send a message.

"Go back and tell him to begone and trouble Sorra no longer," I said firmly.

"I'm sure you'll be meeting him soon enough." A new voice said from the same twisted body. "Then we'll see who stays and who goes."

It released its grip on the cage and muttered under its breath. The tentacles writhed and danced in the air. Even though its last two attacks had been thwarted, it began another spell. A sound like a waterfall sprang up and a flood sprang forth into being from the suckers and pushed us back a single step before the attack ceased again.

"Hmph." It said in a pouty feminine sigh. "Well. Goodbye."

It said nothing to its transportation crew, but they turned in place, sprang up and dragged the cage across the ground and into the air. They flew around us and on towards Tiiaan.

The doughnut of avian badness slowly played follow the leader, with a few of the stragglers giving halfhearted attacks on Mikaal and

Coral who were closest to them. Coral blasted them from the sky as they came.

This whole ordeal had taken less than two hours. But it seemed that some or all of the storm was going to reach our destination before we did.

Chapter 28
Second Place Finish

Mikaal and Coral took it in turn to heal our injuries, while I recharged our Torcs and evaluated our situation. Everyone had taken a few cuts and bruises including Granalis, whose stony skin was not impervious to the acid and bile that seemed to be the one common weapon among the flock of diversly altered flight crew. Thankfully, none were hurt so badly that they were beyond the help of healing magic. The OrOboid ate and drank quickly while the rest of us worked, and soon we were back in formation and back in the race. We hoped that our arrival wouldn't be too late.

A sense of unease and concern rebounded among our group, threatening to become so strong that it mutated into dread. Thankfully (K)Andoo decided to thrust himself into our reverie and restore hope and purpose.

"I remember what it felt like to be like those things. At least for me, I knew who I had been and what I wanted to do, but I was a prisoner in my own mind. That cage was enmeshed in wildly flickering thoughts of a copy of my mind, fractured nearly beyond recognition. Every person or thing I wanted to save, it wanted to smash, corrupt, or destroy. That mind was the one controlling a body that was mine and yet more destructive and powerful than I could fathom. When I saw my own kind, I rejoiced and thought I was saved."

It struck me as odd as I listened to (K)Andoo speak how passionate his words felt, yet unlike a human he was nearly motionless. I could feel his intensity, but he didn't punctuate his words like I would, with a thrust of a hand when he spoke of action.

"Then watched in horror as this mind and body took my hope and tried to flatten it. Then everything stopped and the agony of change returned. After all that I am sane, I am alive, and that which could not be undone, has been. Please, don't any of you give up. So, there is a powerful force trying to destroy us. I believe we have not yet seen the most amazing things we will accomplish yet."

Now I could see why his people held him in high regard. (K)Andoo was still not himself, but he could in a few words inspire people to keep going. Heck, I was inspired to keep fighting, but also to learn how to influence others like that.

"Most of my life has been striving alone. I believed that the only thing that was worth doing was that which I could accomplish with my own hands and skills. Now, however wrong it may be, I feel a sense of belonging and trust that I knew I would never feel. I believe in every one of you, though I've known you such a short time. Please believe in yourselves or at least believe that all of us, unified in purpose, will do the impossible or die trying. There is nothing more noble than giving one's life to save others."

Our pace increased, even that of the Rhinodons, somehow lifted by the hope and the emotions if not the words. "Thank you." I whispered in return.

We travelled in hopeful stillness, each one lost in their thoughts and preparations to fight another battle. An hour and a half passed before I started seeing flashes of yellow streaking from the ground to the sky and a violet glow spreading along the ground near the horizon line. It seemed that the Avian Army had reached Tiiaan. The battle was underway.

I informed the others of what I saw and asked Granalis to carefully scout ahead again and see if he could learn how things were going. Shortly after he took to the sky, dark clouds began gathering off to our left. Peals of thunder shook the ground, and the air became thick and oppressive with moisture. Once these clouds felt like they were strong enough in number, they struck out toward the battle, moving with speed not often seen in weather patterns.

Granalis reported that he had reached the enemy's rear flank and tried to circle around in both directions. There were too many baddies for him to get around or get a clear view, but he strained his vision to its limits and could see that the city stood and was fighting back with everything they had. He was now returning to us as the storm was making flying dangerous for him.

Lightning leapt from the advancing storm front, moving with the horizon instead of between earth and sky. For a moment, we could all see the thousands of winged bodies illuminated from behind. A significant number of these lit up like bonfires in the air and streaked to earth. A second strike followed and then a third and suddenly the sky was ablaze and raining burning feathers and bird bodies. Slightly below the lightning and mass of combatants I made out a clump of low fliers with their burden of 'The Many Who are One'.

We urged the Rhinodons to maximum speed, and the OrOboid began falling behind. I scooped them up one by one and dropped them on a platform above us. I suggested that they rest and eat so that they had the strength to fight for as long as their kind can. We began having to dodge small numbers of bodies as we drew closer to the battle. Most were enemies; some few were the unlucky denizens of Tiiaan who were caught unawares in the open. I was unsure of the wisdom of racing into battle at all, much less one where we'd already been lucky to survive and even further where the sky itself had joined the battle. That said, my blood began singing like the wind in my ears.

"Try not to draw any attention to us. Defense only for now," Coral suggested. "If we're lucky we can surprise them."

Second Place Finish

Nothing is particularly stealthy about a pack of Rhinodon at full tilt, with a group of floating OrOboid as the cherry on top, but battle is madness when all the participants are sane. This was nearly as chaotic as I imagined the inside of the Chaos Cloud to be. Streaks of light flew in every direction. Some of these were magic attacks, some were physical attacks, while others were burning combatants. Even on the fringe as we were the noise was deafening. The sky was full dark now between the smoke, the avian attackers in the air, and the battle cloud formation.

I heard above it all a stream of insane cackling, the likes of which would have surely done permanent damage to the throat of a normal being. We followed the sound as best we could in the frenzy around us. We were below the enemy forces now, and I was just about to give the order to attack, when I saw the flock split. The sky began to clear of winged forms ahead of us, and we made a beeline for that space. A few of the aerial aggressors noted our presence and made a half-hearted attempt to stop us, but not enough to call attention to our presence. We defended ourselves with only physical attacks. Arrows, crystal daggers and spears were enough for this small task.

The cage touched down at the edge of Tiiaan's outer structures ahead of us, and we slowed our advance to be as quiet as possible. The battle was nearly forgotten in the immediate area, and the enemy Master's herald began his pitch to the Tiiaanians that they should all give up and allow themselves to be destroyed or risk becoming slaves to Its Captor. It brayed on for a few minutes, thankfully never turning around to see us coming. It cycled through a few of its personalities as it alternated from threatening and cajoling those standing by and called for someone in charge to step forward. The sky darkened still further as it spoke as the clouds drew closer.

Suddenly Athious of the Counsel of Three dropped to the ground in front of the creature, seemingly out of nowhere. He was arrayed in form-fitting armor plates of a matte material that I didn't recognize. Each plate was connected by chainmail allowing for freedom of movement and great protection.

"I am Athious. Who are you, and why are you attacking Tiiaan?"

The simian face spoke with the voice of the deep. "We are those who opposed the one we now serve. This, or something equally dreadful, is what happens to those who do not submit to him." There was a deep hissing breath, and another sibilant voice came from the same face. "We attacks because we are told we must. Will you give us the Hero and surrender your lives?"

"Has anybody ever taken you up on that offer before?" Athious laughed deeply.

Keening maniacal cacophony pealed from the creature for far too long in a mockery of the counselor. "Yes. The smart ones do."

The Tiiaanian leader looked surprised and briefly taken aback. "So you say. Yet, no one can win forever, and evil must be defeated. So, we will fight, and we will win."

The misshapen body vibrated with a strange combination of agony and pleasure. "Destroy you." It said loudly, raising a limb towards Athious. It shouted an incoherent stream of syllables in first one voice and then another. Yellow light began playing around the flexing claws of its feline limb. It flexed one last time, burying its claws into its own paw, and a stone missile streaked toward the Garanth leader's chest plate. He raised an arm to defend himself, but the attack broke up into a fine mist before it hit him. I checked my watch, belatedly realizing that it only measured the magic feeding the Star Glass, not other magical activity nearby. The creature howled and attacked again, not realizing what was happening. I stepped toward its back and was deciding what action to take, when it turned toward me. "You. Are you here to give up?" the deep voice spoke.

Startled, I jumped back a half step and shook my head.

"Then you will all learn what will happen to you." It burbled.

When I think back to this time, it always plays back in slow motion, but everything happened so quickly that I could do nothing.

Second Place Finish

It spun around and whipped its tentacle toward Athious. He had a spell at the ready and released a ball of flame back at his attacker. A small decorative glass vial flew one way, narrowly missing the fireball. Both attacks struck home simultaneously. The monster screeched in pain and ran its suckers along its chest but did not fall. The vial struck armor and shattered, leaving a line of wetness down the front of Tiiaan's foremost defender. Purple smoke that stole the remaining light from the world began roiling forth from the spot, curving unnaturally around the man within the armor. He began to howl in intense torment at its caress. Soon he was completely enveloped by a churning mass of mist and only his screams for it to stop, which soon trailed into wordless and guttural growls, indicated that he was still alive within. The cloud grew and pulsed. Everyone who was anywhere nearby took one or more steps back. I was racking my brain as to how I could help him when the cloud pulsed outward once, twice, three times and vanished.

Where a handsome male Garanth had stood was now a grotesque, malformed version of the same. His eyes glowed red with madness, and his face was set in a permanent snarl. His body and armor were fused together, significantly grown and terrifying to look at. His legs were partially melded with the stone that he had been standing on and were reinforcing the knees. Where his hands had been were jutting spikes of bone. He 'grawped' once loudly and looked like he was going to run at me and tear me to pieces but stopped abruptly. A second fog was rising from the ground that made the first feel friendly.

Tendrils of vapor, appearing as disembodied clawed hands, climbed their way up the deformed body, leaving superficial wounds even in the stone and armor. Even this crazed being seemed terrified of it and began trying to slice it away as it advanced. This had no effect on the ephemeral antagonist. Tormenting seconds passed this way until the invader reached his gnarled ears. All of whatever this was forced its way inside his head and then there was a moment of silence.

The creature that was foremost on the Counsel of Three began glowing a violet so deep that it was hard to look at. The red eyes flickered and swirled until the orbs were black with a single purple pinpoint in the center. It looked around and smiled serenely until it spotted me standing behind its forerunner. Its eyes crinkled as it peered intently at my face. Its smile became an unnaturally deep frown. Finally, it spoke, using a body and a voice that had been corrupted and so its speech sounded like dry leaves burning in a bonfire and rusted hinges being opened and closed. "Now isn't this unexpected. You of all people. No matter, this place will soon enough cease to be."

"Why do you think you know me, and why are you trying to destroy this wonderful world?"

"You will learn why I know you in due time. As to the latter question, the answer is simple. Hate. I hate all living things, and I will see them destroyed or unmade. This place will suffer the same fate as all other worlds that have felt my tender mercies."

This wasn't an answer I was prepared for. I could think of ways to convince someone that whatever it is that they want could be found elsewhere, or make it not worth their while to proceed, but how do you convince someone to not wish for the destruction of all they despise? I was mentally rocked, and not having the support of the Tiiaanian leadership when faced with the 'final boss' and defending the city made it worse. But I was not alone. I had good friends with me, which I was reminded of suddenly when Coral's voice rang out beside me.

"How is it possible to hate people you don't know; with lives you have never experienced?"

"Simple. When all that you value in the world is debased and taken from you, there is nothing left but hate."

"That is simply not true. You are deceived. You have taken all that I loved from me…." she gasped, fighting back tears. "And those that I loved most dearly tried to kill me. Yet I have found more people who are worth loving and being loved in turn by."

"Aww. She's sweet, isn't she?" the foe taunted. "You are good. If I still had a heart or a conscience, that might have gotten to me. It is too late now though. All that was good within me has been destroyed and cauterized so that it may never recover. Now I will be merciful to you all, if you will allow me, by ending your existence before others can do even worse to you. If you spurn my mercy, then you will instead receive my wrath."

His voice rose into a banshee song as he finished his pronouncement and made as if to skewer her. This could not be. Action leapt forth from me unbidden. I grabbed the form that was both friend and enemy with a mental hand and slung it back two body lengths to where Athious had originally arrived while simultaneously telling the Star Glass to restore him. A steady green aura obscured him from my view, and the squealing of three beings trapped in one body in indescribable pain began. I urged the process to the quickest reasonably safe pace and turned to the until recently forgotten doomsayer behind me. "Your master is defeated. You are free."

The monstrous being, who spoke with one of many voices, suddenly laughed with many at once. "You think him done? He is barely slowed. You will see him again."

It turned to leave. I wrestled with letting it go. I had proclaimed it free, but if its master remained alive... I had almost decided to slay it when Mikaal placed his gaw on my forearm. He was weaving a spell with two of his other limbs at the departing mishmash of a being. A ball the size and color of an orange fruit from my homeland slowly danced its way from between the little Noran's members, sinking into its back. It appeared to be unaware as it bounced and bounded into its cage and was painstakingly carried aloft in its pannier by its nearly dead pallbearers.

The sounds of forced transformation began to decrease behind me, and we turned to check on Athious. The battle was resuming around us as the two forces sharing the same space began unravelling themselves. The aggressors took the worst of it as they became disinterested in battle, instead orienting themselves on their leader in his retreat. Singed or outright on fire bodies fell from the sky at random. Athious took a deep breath, shuddering on the ground. I kneeled beside him and lifted his hand, feeling for a pulse before realizing that though the Garanth were very similar to humans, they weren't the same. Thankfully they were similar enough that I could feel his heartbeat in his wrist. Eventually his eyes opened, and I called for some water to cool his throat. Someone behind me held out a rudimentary canteen over my shoulder and I poured the contents, drop by drop, into his throat.

Chapter 29
War Counsel of Three Plus

Exhausted as everyone was, both our company and the brave city defenders, we were swiftly escorted through the smoldering streets of Tiiaan to the meeting hall of TownHold. The Mackta and a contingent from the Magic School arrived ahead of us and were being seated in one of the spokes of seats radiating from the massive hexagonal table that anchored the center of the room.

Between the spokes were five brightly colored, carpeted walkways. Magicians sat between the colors of mango and salmon; those who served the Counselors sat between salmon and plum; the Merchant Guild was seated between plum and jade; the Militia or Town Guard sat between jade and pineapple, while the rest of the town sat behind us between pineapple and mango. There were people of nearly every race on Sorra in each group.

I urgently wanted to check on Athious, but there were already enough people buzzing around him, and no few of them seemed to be using healing magic. The room quickly came to order with everyone seated. A spark flew through the room that caused me to shiver, then the Mackta stood. An enlarged image of his face hovered over the table, the apparition somehow looking at each group at the same time.

"For most of you, this is an unprecedented and unforeseen time. There are perhaps only a few living who, like me, are old enough to remember times of war and strife. Now we face extinction at the hands of a being who wants to destroy us purely for the sake of its own animosity. No matter what we face, we must not give up. We must not falter. If we let the darkness take us, who will it go after next? If by our striving we might save not only our own world, but others, we must triumph." A hearty round of affirmations went round the room before he continued.

"Thankfully we have been granted the help of a hero from another world." At this, I shrunk down in my seat as the weight of the expectation of deliverance from an entire world settled on my shoulders. "He and his companions have already quested for and recovered a powerful artifact that should help us." Finished speaking, he nodded once and sat. As he lowered himself the floating head misted out and vanished.

Breauus stood up from beside Athious. I felt the same flicker of current flow through the room again as she reached her full height. "The Counsel would like to suggest a course of action. Normally, our most senior member would speak, but he's feeling a bit weak at the moment from being corrupted and then possessed by something that, even if he were able to speak normally, he could not describe."

I shivered at the memory as the scene replayed in my mind. Guilt rose strong within me. *I should have done something to stop it! I don't know what that would have been, but if I was a real hero... But I can't go back. I can only do better next time.*

"As we discussed before the attack, we have few defenses against the Chaos Cloud and no way of restoring those it has changed. Yet somehow Athious has been restored. We would ask Aaron to share with us how this is possible and what they have learned. If they can instruct us how to resist, then we can partner with them as they seek the enemy and try to thwart its plans. We would also like to understand how the enemy knows Aaron."

This was news that only a very few people were present for, and an unsettling murmur began to grow, especially from the Militia.

WAR COUNSEL OF THREE PLUS

I started to stand in protest that I knew less than anyone else, but I was unable to lift my buttocks from the seat. I tried twice and then gave a mighty heave, which only caused me to slam down harder into my somewhat unforgiving chair with an indignant squawk of protest. Coral sensed my distress and tried to move closer to me and also could not move.

A gaw landed on each of our arms and Mikaal quickly explained that in the meeting hall of Tiiaan, only one person could have the floor at a time. The person standing would be seen and heard by all, and all others would have to remain seated. By this time Breauus resumed her seat and eye began swiveling toward me. Mikaal lifted my arm in a subtle encouragement to attempt standing again.

I rose and was startled to see a bedraggled and much careworn version of my face take shape above the table. I fought down the urge to raise my voice to be heard in such a large room, though everyone present had quieted down as soon as the specter of my face appeared. Despite my urge to talk too loudly, I spoke haltingly at first.

"People of Tiiaan. I have been on Sorra for only a short time, but I have come to love it here. You have been kinder and more welcoming than a stranger might be treated nearly anywhere on the world where I was born. I've made some amazing friends, and I will do everything in my meager power to defend your world. Before I walked through what I now know was a portal in answer to a summons that I felt but didn't understand, I had no powers of any kind."

The murmur from before turned into a gasp of concern.

"I'm not telling you this to scare you or to take away your hope, but to let you understand that I am new to the 'heroing' business and don't have all the answers. We will find them together, just as we," I gestured to both sides of me, "have been doing. In answer to the questions of the Counselors.... We set out to recover the Star Glass and here it is. What it was thought to do, and what it does are a bit different. Between this power growing inside me since I arrived here and this powerful artifact, I now have abilities that are different than your own."

I took a second to look around me in fear that my admission had lost me the audience. I tried to keep my face serious and thoughtful in the hope I would appear to be pausing for dramatic effect.

Wowza. They are hanging on my every word. I guess I'm not so bad at this.

I continued. "I have developed two different ways of restoring those who have been unmade by the cloud. The first is something that only I can do and has some unexpected effects I'm still working through. The second relies on magic that I wield through this sparkly object." I waved the artifact before my face for effect. "And some of you might be able to perform. It takes a LOT of magical power, and it causes lightning storms. Even using this, it takes time and can't be performed forever. This doesn't seem the time and place to try to explain that any further. Regarding the cloud, I haven't even seen it directly myself, unless you count the tiny amount that was used on Athious, but I have a couple of ideas that I plan to try on it."

I took a deep breath before continuing. "Finally, our nameless enemy seemed to know me, but I don't understand how. Where I come from there is no magic, and I've heard of, but never seen, any evil spirits capable of possessing a man…err, Garanth male, especially a noble and strong leader. I have been trying to figure out how such an entity would have any way of knowing a simple man like I have always been. I just don't have an answer for that." I sat down slowly, not knowing what would happen next.

A low babble of a vast number of conversations held all at once sprang up for around two minutes before a new visage was brought to life above the table and a quavering voice spoke up. The face belonged to a youngish-looking Moalean male. It took me some moments to identify the lone standing figure among the Merchant Guild due to his slight stature. He wore clothes that were probably once brightly colorful yet had obviously been through much recently. There were tears and dark stains that were very likely blood.

"I was there when the messenger arrived," the merchant's voice broke as he spoke, trying to keep it together. "I heard what it said. I was in a ditch trying to keep my children from bleeding to death after they were attacked as we returned home from picking up supplies from the village of Nesboth. They don't want us. They want the hero. Maybe if we give him up," he pointed a soil-encrusted claw my way, "they will forget about us and no more of our children will have to lose their lives." He dropped back to his seat then sobbing uncontrollably.

The next face to appear was Mikaal's. "Tinoock. I am very sorry you have suffered the loss of little Tinaak and Timeeck. They were gifted and beautiful children and will be missed by all." He paused but remained standing, forcing a moment of silence. "However, I was there too, both times the emissary gave its ultimatum. The choice it offered is not peace if we hand Aaron over and destruction if we don't. It offers destruction fast or destruction slow. Neither of those options will save any more lives if taken. We must forge our own option. Have faith in each other. Have faith in Aaron, much more than he has on his own. He has grown and accomplished so much so quickly. I will stand beside him and save Sorra or give my last breath trying."

Then the floodgates were opened. Many faces appeared over the table and spoke in favor of giving up, or fighting, or even pretending to give up and then fighting. One ancient and solitary Noran spoke mistrustfully of me since the dark intruder knew me, but he was quickly argued down.

The discussion of how to proceed continued until one elder stood from the military spoke and asked where the adversary was. A young Garanth woman stood and indicated that the 'Flock of Doom' had flown west, but she was immediately followed by an OrOboid female scout that reported they had turned south once they were out of general view of Tiiaan.

I was surprised to hear the second report spoken with an echo. It seemed that the OrOboid's natural mindspeak was picked up by the magic or technology of the meeting hall and presented aloud so that no one was left out of the conversation. It was decidedly odd, as the spoken voice and the mindspeak were very close, but subtly different.

A couple more conflicting reports were given before Mikaal stood and informed the crowd that he had put a tracking spell on the enemy's herald and that if we followed him he was likely to lead us to the 'Spirit Boss'. With this pronouncement hope bloomed once again, and the discussion became a campaign planning session.

Two or more hours later we had reached a consensus. Mikaal, Coral, Granalis, and I would take the lead, supported by a contingent of the strongest mages, half of the remaining lightning lances (which turned out to be what they called their weather platforms), and several dozen assorted foot soldiers. We would leave the morning following next, which we hoped would give us enough time to develop some strategies as to how to deal with the enemy.

Finally, the Mackta stood again. "We have accomplished much this evening. Much remains to be done. We must all draw close together and support one another if we are to succeed. Let us all find what rest we can tonight. Tomorrow our real labors begin." He made a rough coughing sound in the back of his throat, and the room lost the faint orange glow I hadn't even noticed. The room rose as one and began heading towards the various exits.

We also rose before I realized that I had no idea where our Rhinodon were with all our supplies, nor where we would sleep in the Chaos of a city after the first battle of what was to become a war. Thankfully my lack was quickly covered by the ebony gaw of a young Noran tapping my arm. She looked vaguely familiar, which she apparently could read on my face as she addressed it immediately.

"Hi. Jixxey here. I think you met my sister Jixxell when you visited us before. I am the Barracks Master at the magic school. If all of you will please come with me, I'll take you to your rooms. Your mounts are already stabled and fed and getting some much-deserved rest. This way...."

She started away, pointing the way and pulling me along by the wrist. I was again amazed at how the many limbed Norans could move themselves about so smoothly while using their other appendages for other purposes.

I looked back to ensure that my friends were following. They were, of course. Coral slid past Mikaal to get to my side with a fiercely protective and jealous look on her face. She grabbed my left hand and held it tightly as we wound our way through the diverse throngs of people. Mikaal had a bemused look on his face. It seemed that one of the passages Jixxey took us down was a direct passage to the magic school. We stopped at a wide and brightly lit stone archway placed centrally where the paneled hallway ended abruptly in a wall that was a perfect match for the one we had gone through days before.

A female voice came from the bright light before us in the center of the opening. "State your business."

"I told you I'd be back with them quickly, Jixxell, and here we are," my assigned escort huffed. "Please let us through."

"Alright, Jixxey. Have a little patience. There have been so many comings and goings today that I'm stretched a bit thin." Jixxell's voice dripped with weariness. The voice and the light winked out and half a breath later, we were moving again. As soon as the last of us was through, the light flared back to life behind us.

Once through we were in an open courtyard between buildings. To the right appeared to be the stables. At the center of the courtyard, groups of young magicians were working on different projects. One group to the left had a couple of enemy corpses from the battle and was magically studying them. Three Garanth males and a Noran male were weaving intricate orange and green flows in around and through one of the bodies while a Moalean female worked with two multicolored (to my eyes) figurines and another Garanth girl on the other.

The next two groups we passed were in the midst of mock battles, practicing for upcoming conflict. A fireball sprang up from one young mage in the group farthest from us and was deflected by his opponent. It flew towards us before vanishing against a nearly invisible barricade that sprang up from the ground around them as they fought. There was so much magic flowing here that only the strongest magics were visible to me. Like trying to see the beam of a flashlight in the bright sunlight, the weaker ones were hard to see.

The smaller archway Jixxey took us toward had a much more normal door. Of course, where I came from doors had doorknobs, and here they all opened with a spell. I would have to find out the spell before long. We were in the dorm house rotunda, which our little band filled thoroughly.

"The men's dormitory is to the left, and women are right." Jixxey explained, snickering at her turn of phrase.

I was about to protest being separated from Coral, and by her grip increasing on my arm I could tell she was as well. Jixxey continued however, directing us toward the visiting group quarters through the slightly smaller doors across from where we entered. Through these we went into a long wide stone hallway. There were over twenty doors lining the sides, with smaller spaces between doors, increasing the farther along we went.

Several of the rooms were open as we passed, some few were closed. There was a surprising variety in the rooms. Some were traditional rooms for one or two occupants; one was mounds of dirt and moss; one held two rows of stacked beds. She stepped up to one of the open rooms where greenery was growing beside two crystal slabs holding a variety of smaller crystals.

"I hope our OrOfriends will be comfortable here," She offered with a flourish.

I could sense the emotional turmoil from the group as they struggled with the family dynamics that I had accidentally saddled them with. This lasted only a few seconds and before I could offer to do anything useful they walked quietly into the room in single file.

Jixxey turned toward the next room as the door closed behind them. I sent them all a mental message to let me know if they needed me for anything and I would come back to them. Kaalesh responded after a moment that they would be fine and not to worry.

I had been walking as I was pulled without realizing it until we stopped two doors down from the OrOroom. Inside looked a lot like the inn we had stayed at before, but with curtains covering the doors. It was one large room partitioned at head height for privacy purposes with two human sized beds and several pillows piled in a corner. Another room was filled with trees fit for a Noran. The final room was the largest, but the entryway was blocked by a wall of glass or something very like it. When I turned back I saw gaw disappearing into the room of branches and limbs. Only Coral and our guide remained standing with me. Both still had firm grips on my arm, but Jixxey reached out and stroked the dark opening in a wavy motion and then rapped sharply twice on the barrier. The 'room' lit up. I was astonished.

All of the rooms were functional for their intended users and this one was no exception. The dim light showed an idyllic version of the bottom of the ocean or perhaps a lake. There was a variety of plant life of many colors, fish of several species, and an outcropping of rock that looked like a cavern with crenellations reminiscent of a medieval castle that had been submerged unexpectedly. What was even more surprising is that we were looking down into this scene. The area was two to three times my height at least.

Coral gasped excitedly but refused to let go of my arm. Clearly, she wanted to enter but didn't want to leave my side. I smiled as this made me exceedingly happy and kissed her tenderly yet firmly. I explained that I thought I might be able to help the OrOboid further before I rested, and she should take advantage of the hospitality the school had provided. Jixxey told her that her clothes and other belongings were in the room with no pillows, and Coral walked slowly towards that doorway, letting go of my hand grudgingly.

Chapter 30
Guinea Pigs and Dr. Aaron

"Is there anything else you need before I leave you?" Jixxey asked, for some reason still holding my arm.

"I noticed a couple of unattached OrOboid in the council room. I need to examine one of each gender, or as close to that as possible."

"Those two are the only OrOboid in Tiiaan…as far as I know. Neither of them is here in the school since they don't have magic. We'll have to ask after them at the Guard House."

She pulled me along more quickly now that it was just the two of us. We went back out through the rotunda and followed the barracks wall to the right for several minutes until we reached a gate. This was unlike all the other entries into the school. There was no magic here. The barrier that served as a door was made of bricks wrapped with bands of metal at three points. These bands were attached to hinges that looked like they would outlast the end of the world. The rest of the surface I could see was a massive puzzle of gears, switches, and slides surrounding something similar to an old-style clock from my world, but with thirty primary marks around its surface.

Jixxey glanced at the time device briefly before sliding two verticals upward two notches, pushing a catch into one gear thus ceasing its motion, and pushing a switch three times before attempting to turn the handle. A chime sounded above us, and the door swung noiselessly inward.

We stepped through and pulled the door behind us. The opposite side was identical, but everything was in mirror order. We took two steps and stopped. A hissing sound came from directly above us as a brawny Garanth youth was lowered into our path. Steam escaped from the telescoping tubes at his feet, and his hands were clasping twin cudgels that served dual purpose as handles for his personal elevator. He was wearing a guardsman's outfit and had a single pin on his shirt.

"State your business," he snapped sharply.

"Aaron here needs to see Iinndie and Eeaarly. Please have them report to the Improv Suite as soon as possible."

The unnamed guardsman nodded curtly, looked me from head to toe with thinly veiled interest, pulled a lever, and shot upward. Jixxey started off to the left at a slight angle to the unusually smooth wall, taking my wrist with her. The rest of me had to follow or risk dismemberment. We were walking toward an enclosure that bubbled out from the wall made of transparent crystalline columns. Seating of some kind was faintly visible within.

When Jixxey reached the nearest upright and touched it, lights sprang to life within. We walked a few steps further, and she ran her gaw in a swiping motion to the left. At her touch, the columns slid three spaces to the left, leaving an opening wide enough for us to walk through. She pulled me inside, leaving the entry open, and finally released my arm. I was absently running my hand along where she had grasped me (she was stronger than I would have imagined) when she handed me a drink out of a storage area within a cabinet behind me. I gratefully drained it, not caring what it was and surprised at how thirsty I was.

I never even saw the first of our guests arrive. It moved so quickly that only a shadow would have marked his passing if he had not announced, "Eeaarly reporting" loudly into our minds as he arrived. I was trying to decide if I should explain what I needed or wait when I saw the outline of another OrOboid walking our way at a more sedate pace. She moved with obvious grace, placing each step deliberately. I could sense her awareness that I had seen her. In fact, I was certain that I had only seen her because she had intended it so, as if she had been masking her presence before and announced herself without words now.

Once we were all within the Improv room, Jixxey closed the door and I faced the two newcomers, speaking to them mentally and including Jixxey.

"I hope you will be willing to help me. I need to retore my friend Andoo...."

I was going to continue, but as soon as I said his name both Eeaarly and Iinndie reacted visibly.

"He's alive?" and "They found him?" they said over top of one another.

"You know Andoo?" I responded in surprise.

"Well, no. Not exactly," Iinndie said with a blush (which was more of an impression than anything physical), "but every OrOboid has heard of the adventures of Andoo."

"We'd do anything to help you help him," chimed in Eeaarly.

"This will sound strange. Hopefully you react better than the first OrOboid that I asked this of," I continued. "I need a little bit of your blood... both of you."

"Oh." They responded, in unison this time. "Ok."

"My abilities are different than anybody else's on Sorra, and if there was another way to learn what I need to know, I would not ask this."

"I'll go first," Eeaarly said bravely.

"One moment," I said as I retreated into my mind.

I prepared two syringes with alcohol pads and readied my DNA computer with the files from before so it would be ready for work before returning to the outside world. I handed myself the first set of equipment and approached Eeaarly, leaving the second set seemingly floating in the air behind me. I informed him that there would be a little pinch before cleaning the area and retrieving a small sample. I was bemused to 'hear' a small "ah" of surprise when I stabbed him. OrOboid couldn't really look away since their sensory organs were 360 degrees, so I wasn't sure why the small pain surprised him. Finished with the first extraction, I changed out my kit and approached my next 'specimen'. She bravely stepped up to me and extended the midsection of her grundel towards me. A swipe and a poke and I hopefully had what I needed. I thanked them both and returned to my inner room for analysis.

I fed the two new samples into the computer and waited. DNA chains reappeared with red highlighting the same sections as before. This time I could clearly see the mistake I had made in ignorance. Single OrOboid had two specific elements that were different from mated OrOboid. The first seemed to indicate whether they were mated or not. The second just...didn't exist. Like a ladder that was missing a rung there was a gap. I revised the DNA I had applied to Andoo that transformed him from a monster into Kandoo, making him single and blasting the connection that marked him as a part of that family. I created two new full syringes for treatment and returned to the physical room.

I was surprised to see the two OrOboid still present. My earlier 'thank you' had implied an element of dismissal, but either they didn't get the message, or they had decided to stay for another reason.

"Are you going to see him now?" Iinndie said breathlessly (which is a neat trick for someone who doesn't use their lungs at all to speak).

"Assuming he's still awake, yes."

"Can we go with you and meet him?" Eeaarly added, nearly in the same awed tone of 'voice'.

"You can." I paused. "But you should know that my helping him might also cause him a great deal of pain and it might not be fun to watch."

They answered by standing and lining up by the door. Jixxey lead the way, thankfully not retaking her death grip on my wrist. She made a beeline for the gate we had entered through. I laughed under my breath as I had a random thought of how this little parade of people would appear to someone from back home. The nearly human appearance of the Noran girl, contrasted with the very unhuman smoothness of her walk, followed by my road worn appearance, I'd probably have been taken for a prisoner being escorted to my doom. Follow that with two completely silent beings that were so unlike anything ever conceived of… they'd probably be seen as the architects of my destruction.

My idle musing was interrupted by Jixxey opening the door with the mirror action she used on the opposite side. It was amazing to me how the mechanisms made more noise as they were moved than the huge and weighty door did.

Activity in the courtyard of the magic school was diminished now as the sky above us was dark. I hadn't even considered the time and that I might be keeping people awake. I just saw an opportunity to set things right and took it. A couple more turns, and we stopped by the door to the room where my original OrOboid crew were probably sleeping, and I thanked Jixxey for her help. I assured her I'd be fine without her from here on. She would be back in the morning to escort us to breakfast and the day's activities.

I knocked on the wall, seeing as how only a curtain was blocking my entry, and received no answer. Smacking my forehead and calling myself a fool, I called out to (K)andoo mentally, nudging him awake. One gentle mental poke after another and he was up. I stepped backward down the hallway to allow him to exit and almost stepped on the two slender figures behind me.

"Sorry to have wakened you," I said mentally, "but I think I can restore you now. I don't want to wait and have you and the others struggle any longer."

He stretched. "I am tempted to ask you to leave me the way I am. I love the sense of completeness I feel now, but the others are correct. It isn't right or natural."

"Maybe there is good in having gone through the experience. This will probably hurt again, and I'm sorry." I was about to inject him with the first of the syringes when I remembered that we had guests.

"Before we begin though, it seems that 100 percent of the OrOboid population of Tiiaan is greatly interested in meeting you. Since they sacrificed to give me what I needed to hopefully help you, I thought it only fair that I let them." I gestured to each in turn. "This is Eeaarly, and this is Iinndie."

They both stepped up to my right and my left and took a knee on their leading legs, bowing in respect. "We are honored in your presence," they said in unison.

"I am pleased to meet you both. I did not expect any of our people here, much less two strong young warriors like yourselves. If we live long enough, maybe you will share your tales with me."

"Do you think it would be helpful if they were willing to hold on to you as the treatment takes effect?" I asked unsure of whether I was helping or not.

Fierce embarrassment radiated all around me, but with an undercurrent of acceptance.

"Our people do not normally do such things, but if they are willing to comfort me, I would be grateful to not feel alone while I am stripped of this false connection I feel."

Despite the feelings that were pouring off them, neither hesitated to grip his arms. I cleaned my favorite injection spot on his grundel and stabbed him as quickly and gently as possible, pushing the plunger smoothly until it stopped, empty. I repeated with the second dose and stepped back to watch for effect.

It seemed as if I had failed, and nothing was happening until he started to vibrate. It didn't last very long, but he shook with such force that all three of them seemed to be swaying. A sheen of moisture rose on his skin and a high wail of emotional pain shook my insides similarly to how their bodies had been affected.

"It is done. I am Andoo once more and alone again."

"Is there anything else that I can do for you? Will you be ok? Shall I stay with you?"

"No. Thank you, Aaron, my friend. I am weak and weary, but thanks to you I am safe, sane, and no longer abhorrent. Please, go get some rest."

"If you will both allow us, we will watch over him tonight," Iinndie said softly.

I nodded and turned to my room, confident that they were better equipped to support him than I was. Granalis was already asleep on the pillows in the corner when I entered the room. That was the last thing I remembered thinking. I am pretty sure that I fell asleep while I was still falling toward the bed, clothes, and all.

Chapter 31
Night Terrors in the Morning

I had no idea what time it was when I awoke, only that something wet and shrieking landed on top of me. Thankfully I realized it was a sobbing Coral before I flung her away either by strength of arm, mind, or telekinetic ability. Her skin was so cold that on a human would indicate near death, but that didn't seem to be the problem. She was sobbing and shaking and clinging to me. I held her until she calmed a little and asked her to tell me what was wrong.

"I was asleep and having a wonderful dream when I felt a horrible pain in my left arm. I struggled to wake up. When I was able to open my eyes, everything had changed from when I went to sleep. I thought maybe I was still dreaming, but the pain I felt was too real. Something was on my arm eating into me. I pulled it out and threw it, but that damaged my fingers too. All around me the pure, beautiful water and habitat was being destroyed. There were dark eels and dark worms swimming around me, and the water that touched them turned vile. They were spitting darkness at the plants and fish and walls. When I touched the defiled water, it burned me. I had to swim slowly, using mostly my arms and legs to avoid breathing it in and poisoning myself. Finally, I got far enough away to where I could swim faster and climb out."

"Have you tried to heal yourself?"

"Yes, but I'm either too weak, or it just didn't work."

I was starting to hear troubling sounds around us, but I needed to make sure Coral was going to be ok before I looked into that. Since it had been such a short time, I decided to use the Star Glass reversal on her. I held her at arm's length but didn't let her go. Her beautiful skin, normally alive with flowing colors, was a patchwork of burns.... Some looked like chemical burns and others like cold or heat burns. Her clothes, what little there were of them, were torn and frayed.

I pulled her in to comfort her briefly once again and then picked her up and carried her into the hallway where there were fewer flammable objects. I noticed for the first time that Granalis was awake, watching and listening with interest. I told her as I walked that I was going to try to help her. Smoke rolled in from the rotunda. Granalis sniffed once and pounced out in that direction, telling me mentally that he was going to see where he could help and to call him if I needed him.

I sat her down gently against the wall and asked her if she felt strong enough for me to try to help her. She smiled wanly but assured me she'd be fine. I reminded her that this would unfortunately hurt, but it was the best thing I knew to do to heal all the damage she had sustained at once. She nodded and I stepped back.

I brought the artifact up in my right hand and sent it images of Coral yesterday, commanding it to rewind her and pointing it at her simultaneously. I doubt that the pointing was really necessary, but some things are just natural behaviors. She started to shiver and moan, and the smoke coming into the room started to thicken. I didn't want her to hurt, but something else was obviously wrong, so I urged the process to haste. Thankfully the changes weren't as severe as those who had been changed fully. Coral's moans became a thin pained whine and then with an audible 'ding'. It was over.

I rushed to her side and helped her to her feet. She was unsteady and weak, but her skin was restored to the healthy look of clean waters playing in a deep riverbed. She smiled at me, and I could tell she was going to be all right.... At least from this ordeal.

A blast of heat and the smell of someone burning assailed our senses. Six OrOboid burst from the room behind us, silent except for the rustling of fabric as they thrust the curtain aside. I nearly swatted them with a non-corporeal hand before realizing that these were all friends, and thankfully none seemed harmed.

"Do any of you know what's going on?" I asked them.

"We're under attack!" Kaaden said.

"If it wasn't for Iinndie sounding the alarm I think we'd be dead, or at least seriously injured," Kaalesh added.

I stuck my head into their room, still at a loss as to what was going on around me. There were smoking holes nearly covering the floor starting just a couple of paces inside the room. In the gaps between the holes were Shadowworms, Darkfleas, and a couple of Hellsnails, all pinned to the ground by small slivers of silvery crystal.

Something hissed in the corner of the room, and something small, ugly, and mean flew at my face. A flash flew between the door jamb and my head. The thing bounced back across the floor and stopped at the opposite wall, skewered with a crystal shard. I closed the curtain and backed away.

Water in the tank where Coral had been was writhing and churning and spilling out onto the floor in one direction causing Coral to back away toward the smoke and heat from the other end of the hallway. Mikaal was still missing. I called for him mentally once, just before a crash issued from the Tree Suite. I took only one step in that direction before the drape over the doorway billowed outward, hit by something moving fast.

"What was that for?" Mikaal asked plaintively. "I was sound asleep; I heard you yell for me and then my perch dropped out from under me. It sounded like it fell on something, but when I tried to check, it jumped at me."

Satisfied that all my team was alive, I waved him after me and started toward the flaming rotunda, crouching as I went. Through the flames I could see the outline of a vaguely humanoid shape throwing fireballs at multiple targets, but no threats to the sides. I thought about asking Mikaal to use Ice or Water Magic, but I was concerned that doing so would make the person in front of me unable to defend themselves, not to mention anybody else who might be trapped to either side of the doorway. So, I did what I've always done and reacted on instinct.

I created one platform, sized to cover the door and keep smoke and fire out of our hallway. Then I used a mental hand to quickly, but gently, grab the mystery person dancing in the flames, taking care that my hand protected them on all sides, and lifted them back and up in the air in the center of the courtyard.

I yelled to my friends to follow me and then shoved the platform, widening it slightly as it passed the door, through the rotunda, effectively shoving fire, air, enemies, debris, and whatever else that was in my way and unmoving out the opposite door like a cannon. We ran through the parting of the flames and out the door, stopping just to the right against the wall to assess our situation.

I heard a squawk from above, but when I looked up, I only saw my own projected hand.

Coral smacked me on the arm, saying, "Don't be indecent. If you wanted to see that I'm sure she would have shown you if you'd asked." Before turning away.

"I don't understand. What is indecent?"

She looked up and showed me through her eyes. To her Jixxey was held tightly, floating above us, undergarments plain for all to see. Embarrassed and chagrined, I showed her the same sight through my eyes before quickly lowering my accidental captive to the ground and releasing her.

Fighting surrounded us. The ground every few paces was either erupting with flying mini-monsters or collapsing and taking down whomever was unlucky enough to be there. Less common but fiercer were the snails blazing trails of dark slime and zipping up to bite the unwary. Their shells made them difficult to kill.

We weren't certain how widespread the attack was, and where we were standing wasn't safe. Granalis was back in Gargoyle form, pouncing about, gleefully smashing enemies as they arrived like a giant game of Whac-A-Mole, but there was scarring all across his body where his prey had struck back several times.

"Granalis? Are you doing alright?"

"Are you kidding? I feel like a pup again. I haven't had this much fun in decades. Mashing things that go splat and helping others at the same time is the best."

"Ha. I'm glad you're on our side now. If you get into trouble, let us know."

"I promise if things get bad, I'll escape or yell for help."

The area to our right towards the militia barracks was devoid of local life. Only vile crawling and pouncing things could be seen. I created a large platform in the air and slammed it down on the ground. Before anyone had time to ask questions or our invaders pressed the attack, I ran forward onto this safe zone, holding Coral's hand, encouraging the six OrOboid and two Norans along with a large, curved hand.

Once everyone was aboard, I lifted us up above the level of the walls, finally explaining to everyone that I wanted us to get an aerial look at the city to see how we could best help. I got the impression of strong fear from Iinndie and Eeaarly since they couldn't see what they were standing on, just that they were suddenly flying and no idea why. It slowly subsided as I spoke, and they didn't plummet to their doom.

We got high enough up that we could see fresh smoke rising from every part of Tiiaan. Yellow flashes of magic colored the sky and buildings as the town fought to defend itself from an unexpected assault from below. Bolts of fire, lightning, arrows, and darts of

Night Terrors in the Morning

crystal began leaping from those around me to the ground as they sought to keep people alive.

Like always, I couldn't see through my own platform. If I ever got some free time I might work to find a way to resolve that issue, but for now I asked gently to borrow Coral's eyes. That turned out to not be a good idea as she was scanning the ground beneath her, and the rapid eye movements not under my control nearly made me sick and drop all of us.

I withdrew into my mind to think. There seemed to be no end to the creepy crawlies rising from the depths to ravage the people below, and I couldn't exactly go around smashing them one or even many at a time. I needed to see them before they broke through so they couldn't harm anyone else. Once I could see them, then I needed a way to destroy or restore them. Or something like that.

"I need to identify all of the enemies before they come above ground and do more damage." I said apparently thinking aloud.

"Worms are always used as bait for fish, too bad you can't set something out as bait for them." Coral mused in return.

"That's probably a great idea, but I have no idea what would work…. Hmm."

I thought about x-rays or some kind of scanner that could penetrate what I couldn't see, discounting one idea after another. Then I remembered the cousin I used to fish with and the device we used to be able to see fish in a deep lake when fishing. Unable to come up with anything better, I created a burrowing creature scanner modeled after the fish finders I remembered, making it a bit bigger than the one he had.

Back on the platform I went, dropping my new toy in my hands. I turned it on and adjusted it to show me things that were moving underground starting at an inch below the surface and down to the maximum of its range. There were an awful lot of blips on my screen. I wanted to be sure that I was only seeing enemy beings, so I went into a sub-menu and flipped on the "corrupted" setting. I couldn't tell if that had made any difference or not.

I highlighted everything I could see and pulled up the Star Glass for the second time that morning. I fed all the coordinates to it and informed it that it could use them as energy sources. The Chaos, the life, the movement, in whatever ways it could drain them, it should. I started lowering us very slowly, all the while instructing the artifact to heal those Noran, Garanth, and Moalean we came near, starting with the most injured.

I hoped that was enough. I took us to an outer wall of Tiiaan and began flying back and forth in a grid pattern. Where we moved, the tide turned. There were a lot of hurt folks and the flashes of blue healing magic as we went made me hopeful. I shared my vision with my friends twice as healing progressed over large groups of civilians, explaining that the glow was healing. I couldn't stop to look, but I felt a wave of optimism from behind me, and their efforts to pick off enemies above ground redoubled. The Star Glass was burning a lot of magical power, but the blips on my screen were rapidly decreasing in number. The attacks slowed. It seemed like we were flying back and forth raining death on our aggressors and healing on our comrades for hours, but it ended up being only one.

Towards the end of this process I could see that the bad bugs and their wormy brothers had a common point of origin underground. There were gaps between them, but they were all coming from the direction we were to head in tomorrow.

Chapter 32
Preparing Lemonade

We touched down in an open area of the courtyard where we had started out. Mages and non-mages alike ran to meet us. Jixxey removed her gaw from around Mikaal's torso. Her dark skin lightened into a pale green hue, and she alit upon the ground with a grateful sigh. She didn't seem to care for the experience of flight. I banished the platform and turned to face my friends. Coral staggered, and I caught her before she hit the ground.

"Mikaal. Please gather anyone who can use healing magic in the area and lead them in recovery efforts. Have anyone whose injuries don't respond to normal magical healing brought here. Team OrOboid, please refresh yourselves and begin sweeping Tiiaan with the town guard for any stragglers we've missed. Jixxey, where can we get food and a place for Coral to rest?"

She waved us toward a door in the same wall we'd passed several times already. I swear that the door hadn't been there before, but I picked the nearly unconscious SeaWind maiden up and walked that way. I yelled over my shoulder that we'd meet back here in an hour.

Jixxey's color was returning to normal the longer she was on her own gaw on the ground. Each step was perilous due to the sheer volume of damage to the area. Here was a pit, there rocks sharply protruding due to the violence of the attack. After misstepping twice within a few seconds while trying to make the journey easy for my beloved, I ended up creating a platform in front of me, stepping on, and gliding an inch or two off the ground behind the little Noran girl.

We reached the door, and two of her gaw moved in smooth concentric patterns before her. The door clicked ajar and then flew wide when it was smashed into from behind by two Darkfleas. One landed in front of Jixxey, but the other bounded off the inside of the hatch and flew by her face, raking her left cheek with its elongated claws before landing between us. Her scream was delayed by surprise, but she recovered quickly enough to incinerate the one in front of her. My physical hands were full, but I made mental fist and smashed the little bugger that attacked her flat.

The narrow hallway before us was crawling with enemies since both doors had been closed, and the creatures once inside weren't smart enough to get out. Jixxey screamed again, this time a battle cry and threw a barrage of fireballs that torched everything in sight. This was good for ensuring we wouldn't be attacked, but not super helpful for getting us near food and rest.

"Are you ok, Jixxey?"

"I think so, but my face is on fire."

"I imagine it is. There is more than a cut. It looks like your skin is infected by the unbinding. We'll have to get you some help too before it gets too bad. I can't tell how strong the effect is and whether it will stop effecting you or keep going."

"I'll be all right. I'm sure many other people are in worse shape than I am. Let's get her to the mess hall."

"How are we going to get through? You're very good with fire magic."

"I wish I was better with other types. I don't really have anything in my repertoire to put out fires."

"Let me try something."

Coral moaned lightly in my arms. I thought she was just weak from being healed and then having to fight, but I needed to make sure she would be ok. I slammed the door closed and produced a high-flow metal shop vacuum in my mind with a long thin hose attachment. I positioned it across the base of the door, believing that the doors here couldn't be that different from where I came from, and then switched it on. It got very hot as the air from the room was pulled out. I let it run for a full two minutes, figuring between that and the fire, there would be no oxygen left.

I turned it off and asked Jixxey to open the door again. She waved her magic gaw a second time and the door opened, slowly belching black sooty smoke into the sky. The fire was out, but the hallway was reminiscent of hell. I extended the platform I was standing on down the corridor, covering the floor and urged her to proceed. She stepped in, ducking to avoid the worst of the smoke toward the opposite door. I followed, trying to duck and twist to avoid further harming the unconscious lady in my arms. By the time I caught her up, Jixxey had the door open.

The mess hall was extraordinary in size, with three rows of tables running the length of the room. We were at the narrow end. The left wall seemed to be made of machinery. A series of belts driven by large wheels with gears on the inside came out of the wall and then ran off toward the far side of the hall.

Jixxey pointed us to a table and walked to the belt. The table seemed ordinary, and each side had five seat pedestals, which looked lumpy and decidedly uncomfortable. This didn't seem like a good place to rest, but we were here, so I intended to make the most of it.

I walked to the table and shifted Coral in my arms, trying to position her so I could seat her and sit beside her. Her leg was dangling down and touched the vaguely mushroom shaped seat, and it began to change. It lengthened and stretched out, touching the adjacent seat, which began changing too. The two of them flowed into a soft padded bench with a slightly raised rail. A chaise lounge! I laid her gently on it and took a seat behind her head. Without realizing it I must have touched it while I was positioning her, and it had become a highbacked chair with padded arms. I melted into it.

A series of levers and buttons sprang from a panel, or rather a series of panels spaced at regular intervals. Jixxey pressed a button in each of two rows and then push/pulled a lever, followed by two more. The belt closest to her left began spinning slowly, and a whistle spat steam, tooting three times. Gears along the top of the wall whirred and spun in sequence, not driving each other, but almost as if they were passing a message from one to another. First one engaged and spun three clicks outward and made two rotations, and then the last rotation would suddenly catch the next gear over, and so on. While this was distracting, interesting, and entertaining, Coral wasn't getting any better.

A short while later food appeared on the belt, three separate plates with covered cups between them. They reached the end of the first belt and were deposited on the long conveyor running to the front of the room. As soon as the first plate grew close, that belt sprang to life as well, a deep low horn beneath the apparatus announced its motion too.

Jixxey grabbed the three plates and three cups in six of her gaw and brought them over to us. I shook Coral gently, trying to wake her. She stirred but didn't come to. I took the cup closest to me and twisted its top off. I raised her head up and carefully poured the liquid into her mouth. I was very grateful that she swallowed instead of choking. Two more swallows and her eyes fluttered open.

She smiled at me when her eyes focused. "Thank you, Aaron. I'll be fine. I was using the bow they gave me when we left here before and using energy I guess I didn't have to spare. If I eat a bit and rest, I think I'll be ok."

We looked to the plates that had been set before us. They were all identical, and Jixxey was well into hers. She was drinking from hers with the lid on, sucking on the edge with great gusto. I attempted to do the same with limited success, finding the liquid warm but not hot with a bit of acidic bite somewhere between a strong tea and coffee. It was much thicker than either and very invigorating.... Or maybe I was just really thirsty and tired.

Preparing Lemonade

The platter was wide and contained a thin steak, some fresh sliced fruit, and a thick slice of bread with a viscous and salty vegetable paste covering the top surface. I popped a reasonable-sized piece of fruit into my mouth and turned back to Coral. She was sitting up on her wide couch, which took that as its cue to reconfigure itself into a chair close to what I was sitting in, if a bit smaller. Her first bite was delicate, but as she continued her hunger overtook her and soon we were polishing off the last of our meal.

Jixxey asked, "Do you need anything else?"

"I'm sure we both could down another plate, but for now let's bring as much portable food as possible. I'm sure there are a lot more hungry people out there," I suggested.

"Smart," Coral added, sounding stronger.

She approached the panel again, moving a slide at the top before pushing two different buttons and gripping all five levers simultaneously. At that point I became concerned that she was having a fit as she began using the levers like a rowing machine and doing enough reps that I stopped counting. The machinery responded by clicking, whirring, and letting out simultaneous long blasts of noisy steam in both soprano and baritone. She produced a bag from her clothing and flipped a guide bar on the far side of the moving belt, holding the opening directly below the end of the guide. Drink containers with lids and something in bar shape covered with paper twisted at the ends began taking turns dropping into her bag.

We waited a few minutes for the provisions to stop flowing, all the while I was watching the bag to see if it was going to overflow or become too heavy. After watching the bag fill twice over what would've burst a bag from my own world, I decided that magic bags were just the norm for Norrans, or maybe Sorrans in general.

When the barrage of beverages ceased, she turned and offered some to us, taking one of each herself. Before indulging, I asked Jixxey if there were another place in Tiiaan that might be better suited to handle a significantly sized group of people.

"There are likely lots of Chaos affected people, and we'll need to restore them and train others how to do so."

She thought about it briefly and then shook her head. I gestured for her to lead the way and off we went marching back to the magic school main courtyard.

The journey was quick, but when we arrived Mikaal was already waiting for us. He had been busy, and it showed. Fully half of the field was covered with tents filled with beds and magicians and assistants running busily between them. He had a full triage unit up and running. When we walked up, he was taking verbal reports from two assistants and issuing orders. I walked up behind him as he finished, swallowed the bite that was in my mouth in time to say: "Aaron, reporting for duty, SIR!" with a sharp salute. I had never been a soldier, but military efficiency was on display, so I couldn't help myself.

He made a face that showed his confusion and instead gave me a report.

"There are many, many injured and very few that traditional healing spells will effect."

"That's what I figured. How many healers do we have to work with, and how many strong magicians in general?"

"There are nine strong healers, most of whom are already worn thin, and seven strong mages that have light enough wounds to help."

"Jixxey, please provide snacks to Mikaal and the healers and find others to gather more food and drink and distribute them here. Mikaal, collect all of those mages who aren't actively saving a life and bring them here. Please also identify anyone who would be on those lists if their wounds were taken care of."

Coral looked mildly hurt. "I can help!"

"You should be able to join the healers once you're strong enough. Please stay here and rest. You are too important to risk yourself by pushing past your limits."

Preparing Lemonade

Her skin flushed the colors of the deepest ocean, either with pleasure or embarrassment, but she said, "All right," softly and sat against a tent pole.

A blast of wind announced Granalis' arrival, and I turned to him.

"You are well? What have you learned?"

"A few cuts, but nothing serious. There is no part of Tiiaan that is untouched, but the Counsel of Three and the other town leaders are getting organized. There is no other sign of attack that I can see, but that's just like him. He likes to allow time for hope and resistance to organize before he squashes it again."

"Can you tell me who he is and how he knows me now?"

"No. I've tried to say his name even to myself, and I cannot."

"How many worlds has he destroyed?"

"I don't know for certain, but three since my own."

"Do you need to eat before you take on your next mission?"

Granalis got that predatorial look back in his orange eyes. "No. I made time to have a meager snack or two while I worked."

"Please find all the town leaders and ask them to make their way here as soon as possible, so that we can prepare. This is awful, but we may be able to turn this attack to our advantage."

He nodded and took wing. Now that he was back in his natural form, I could see blood and singed fur in several places as he took off. I would need to get someone to look at him when he got back.

There were now three male and two female Garanth under the tent, sitting with heads resting in their top hands while their lower hands were full of Jixxey's quickly disappearing snacks. A Noran male and a Moalean youth were arriving, also munching.

"The rest will be here soon. The runners and assistants have twenty-five more wounded that would be able to join us if they were healed," Mikaal said.

"Are there any that could be brought here?"

"There are one or two too hurt to be of any help, but who are strong enough to be moved. I thought you might ask, so they're on their way, and another tent will be set up beside this one. You plan to try to teach others how to restore them?"

Several witticisms crossed my mind, but none of them would be familiar here so I ended up just saying, "Yes," delivered with a bleak smile.

Jixxey arrived, coaxing food and drink into an elderly Garanth woman's hands, so I waved her over.

"Are there others passing out food?"

"Yes, but there is so much to do. What do you need?"

"Let me see your face."

I took her face in my hands, feeling Coral growing hot behind me. I sent Coral some mental reassurance and continued my examination. The wound was spreading. What had been a quarter inch gash was now nearly double in width, and there were lines of darkness spreading out above and below. It was hot to the touch. I hoped that not every injury we had to deal with was like this. I created a vertical platform in front of me and gently pushed her up against it, turning it horizontally, so as to create a kind of floating operating table.

"I'm going to try to take care of this before it gets worse."

Jixxey sputtered, "Why me? There are others who are hurt worse. I can keep working."

"That is all true, but I haven't seen them. I've seen you, and I don't like how this is spreading. I don't want this to get to your brain. No telling what might happen if it does."

She had nothing else to say except, "Will it hurt?"

"A bit. Can someone knock her out please?"

I had to look around due to the sheer silence around me and the look of horror on her face. Everyone was looking at me like I just offered to eat their children. I shook my head.

"I guess that doesn't translate. Where I come from if we're going to heal someone in a way that might be unpleasant, we give them something to make them go into a deep sleep. Sometimes we'd say that's knocking them out. I guess Sorra doesn't have that."

Mikaal and the others looked a bit relieved, but not entirely for those who didn't know me.

"Let's try this."

I looked her in the eyes and thought 'SLEEP UNTIL I TELL YOU TO WAKE' at her in my most commanding tone. She made a little squawk sound of surprise and then started snoring. I nodded my head. I decided to treat her as I'd treated Mikaal before.

I retreated back into the depths of my mind, using the same microscope as before. *Wait... was that true? If I created something, where did it go when I removed it? If I created it again, was it the same one, or a new thing?*

That train of thought wasn't helpful, so I forced myself to concentrate. I looked at her healthy cheek through the microscope, taking an image of the healthy DNA. I looked at the damaged skin, and just as before, the DNA was nearly completely destroyed. I began repairing chains, and once done, duplicating a virus which targeted (hopefully) only her with corrected DNA as the payload.

I created a needle full of this concoction and placed it and an antiseptic wipe in my physical hands. I cleaned the left side of her face to the best of my ability and began injecting small amounts into multiple points along the darkened edges. As I did, the damage began to retreat. I chased it with the needle, attacking corruption with my tiny rapier. Two dozen or so microinjections and I was done. I stood back, banishing the tools I'd used and looking around.

While I worked, the rest of the people Mikaal had summoned arrived. The sight that greeted them was of a Noran girl floating unconscious in space without the use of magic while a strange alien repeatedly jabbed her in the face with a small blade. Of course, the fact that others seem to think this was ok caused them to stare in amazement.

So, when I looked up, there were nearly twenty people looking at me as if I was a three-headed monster. These are the things you just don't think about when you suddenly walk into another world full of wonderful and scary things you don't understand, and then you find you have your own set of specific skills, and nobody truly understands what you're doing or why.

I couldn't help myself. I lost it. I stood there in the middle of the aftermath of a battle, with wounded all around me after performing minor surgery on a girl I met yesterday, and I wasn't a doctor.... And laughed until my sides hurt. The fact that my laughter made everyone around me even more uncomfortable just made it all the funnier. Eventually I stopped, holding both sides with tears streaming down my face.

"You know. Most of what you here take for granted, I think is amazing, strange, and slightly crazy too." I wiped my eyes with the back of my sleeves and waved my arms over Jixxey's sleeping form. Then I said in my most mysterious voice, "Arise, maiden," while commanding her mentally 'YOU WAKE UP NOW!'.

Dutifully, my patient snorted once and opened her eyes. She rubbed her face gingerly and sat up.

"Better?" I asked.

"It still hurts, but not as much, and it feels like a different kind of pain too."

"Wait an hour or two, and if it still hurts, a healing spell will probably take care of that too."

"Thank you," she said sleepily before hopping down from the hard air and going back to work.

These healers and mages might have found my ways strange, but you can't argue with success. They broke up into small groups and began discussing what they'd seen. About that time a tap on my arm caused me to turn.

Preparing Lemonade

"Why didn't you knock me out?" Coral said trying to hide a bit of hurt and poutiness.

"I didn't have to stab you in the face over and over. Add to that the fact I hoped that you trusted me to know that I was trying to help you, and you wouldn't fight me. Also, I needed to know how you were doing so I knew how fast or slow to make the process go so as not to harm you."

I pulled her aside, as much as an open tent in a field full of Chaos allowed for it.

"You know that there is nobody else that I've ever met that makes me as happy as you, right?"

She blushed again, saying, "I want to believe that. Just so much has happened, and we've known each other such a short time. I can't help being afraid when I see other women that are interested in you."

She had begun looking down as she spoke, and I gently pulled her chin back up so I could look her in the eyes. "When all this is over, and if we win, I'd very much like to know how a SeaWind man asks for a maiden's hand in marriage."

She said nothing more, just buried her face in my chest while I held her close. Even after all the events of today, her hair smelled as clean as the air after a heavy rain or near a waterfall.

We returned to the group, most of which had adjourned to the adjacent tent where the two promised patients were sitting, surrounded by those who would help them. They were obviously in a lot of pain but were talking to those they knew and trying to keep their spirits up. One Garanth man and one Garanth lady were covered nearly head to toe in cuts, burns, bruises, and gashes. Most of the wounds seemed to be laced with unbinding effects. The group parted to allow Coral and I to pass. Mikaal was already in the circle.

"There are two ways that I have found effective in restoring wounds infected with Chaos. The first involves science from my home world that would be very hard to explain here. The other, that

I think some or most of you should be able to perform is rewinding time around the person you wish to restore."

This was met with many gasps and mutters of disbelief in the possibility.

"When we first had to deal with a large, corrupted being, Mikaal froze them. I didn't really think much about it, especially since magic is so new to me. The spell he used forms the starting point for the process I use. How many of you can work such a spell?"

More than half of the hands were raised.

"Can I have two volunteers? One who can cast the spell, and one who cannot, but will allow us to freeze them."

One of the elder ladies stepped forward to cast the spell, but unsurprisingly there were no takers to be frozen. Most had been through enough this morning that even the enticement of learning something new and possibly critical wasn't enough. I thought briefly and looked around. We were near the stables.

"Is there an animal that we might use to practice on?"

One youth on the periphery smiled and ran off. Shortly after, she returned with a beast I'd not seen before. It was about knee high and covered in coarse fur. It had four legs and no discernable face, front, or back.

"Here is a healthy GroundPig. Will this work?"

"That should do nicely. Thank you. For those of you who do not know, I can see magic. What's your name please?" I asked my volunteer.

"Vivine."

"Thank you. Vivine will cast the freezing spell while I watch. I will share with you all an image of what I see. Hopefully seeing what I see when this spell is cast and then when I restore one of our two injured comrades will allow you to develop your own spell that accomplishes the same goal."

There were lots of side conversations, but no one in attendance seemed to have any concerns. I prepared myself to share my vision with everyone nearby and asked Vivine to proceed. Without a word she froze the animal in time, as seen by it disappearing into a dark green light. There were few gasps of amazement, and one young observer spoke up.

"So, you see magic as colored fields. How will this help us to learn how to reverse time?"

"Honestly, I have very little experience in magic. I've only been able to see and do these things since I came to Sorra. This is how I learned to do what I do, and I'm hoping the same will work for one or more of you. If even one of you can learn to replicate what I've done, they can teach it to the rest of you better than I can."

The grumbles and muttering of the group were less hopeful at this news, but we pressed on. I turned to the injured parties.

"I need you to know that this does hurt, probably a good bit. However, it also works. Does either of you want to go first?"

"After you," he said to her.

"Let's get this over with then," she said, "so I can get back to helping out."

I made a platform and helped her climb aboard.

"We're going to have to move her away as this process can cause lightning storms. Stay back."

I floated her out from under the tent and a bit away from anyone. The group dynamic wasn't trending in a good direction. I hoped that seeing her healed would convince them that this was doable. I suggested she close her eyes so she didn't get disoriented by seeing herself through my eyes. I extended the platform and urged her to lie down so she didn't fall over, then I shared my vision again. Now they could all see the platform she was lying on and there were some appreciative sounds from behind me.

I stepped back, pointed the Star Glass, told her we were about to begin, and sent the command to begin to the artifact. Instantly she was bathed in the pea green glow of reversal and began moaning in agony. The Star Glass gathered up the residual energy as lightning began to strike and then vanished all around her. Her wounds were relatively recent, and so the process didn't take long. When the spell finished, I stopped sharing my sight and helped her sit up.

"That was...not enjoyable. But thank you anyways. I'm sure I'll make it now."

We returned to the others, and before the barrage of questions began, I offered, "Remember that we're not trying to de-age the person you're trying to help. We are simply trying to rewind everything that has acted on them. As you can see, it doesn't cause them to lose any memories, for good or for ill. Now, any questions?"

I can't even begin to recall all of the things they asked me, nor how many things I couldn't tell them. There was a lot of back-and-forth discussion, and the few mages that seemed to have some ideas to try were given leave to break off with a small group and try to recreate what I'd done. I suggested that they use plants, or the bodies of the attackers strewn about for testing instead of their fellow townsfolk.

I showed them once more by restoring the man who was sitting waiting to be healed, also mentioning that the faster the reversal, the more electrical energy would be thrown off as lightning. Not one of them had ever heard of capturing lightning to use as energy or had any idea of how to do so.

Around the field small groups practiced trying to bend time to their will. Flashes of magic were going off like fireworks, nearly giving me a headache. I walked from group to group, watching what they were doing and trying to give them feedback that made the color of their magic match what we wanted.

We spent two hours like this, but at midday not one had made a breakthrough. The Counsel of Three and the Mackta had also come to try to learn and make suggestions, but to no avail. Runners began delivering food again, and my team and I sat against a wall eating and thinking.

Preparing Lemonade

"I don't know what made me think this would work," I said, trying to not lose hope entirely. "I've got to think of some way of teaching them. I can't be the only one on all of Sorra who can fight the Chaos."

Coral just snuggled into my side, not knowing what to say that would help and trying to lend comfort by her physical presence.

"Most of us learn spells by having someone show us each step of a spell and practice it over and over. When you cast a spell, you normally just point the Star Glass at your target or stand still as a stone. It isn't easy to learn what you can't see," Coral said, thinking out loud.

"Exactly."

"Could you have the Star Glass take over your body to cast the spells so we could see how it works?" She asked.

"That's a good idea, except I'm not strong enough in that kind of magic. If I could let the artifact use me, instead of me using it, it would probably fry me to a crisp trying to use that much power."

"We don't want that," she said, holding me tighter. "You'll think of something, Aaron. You've done very well up until now."

"If there were just more time." I said, head in hands.

"It's too bad we can't just scoop the spell out of your mind like a matron eating her sour citrus breakfast," Mikaal said, startling me from behind.

At first, I was tempted to snap back with an unkind comment regarding his intelligence, but then the intent sunk in, and I had the beginnings of an idea.

Problem 1, I'm not the one doing the magic. I'm trying to explain something I'm not even doing myself.

Problem 2, I don't know how to interact with Magic the way these people do. Let's tackle these individually. The Star Glass is like a computer. When I needed information from a program at home, I would export the data for use elsewhere. I can inquire with the Star Glass if it can export a spell it's created. Also, even though we speak the same language verbally, the mages all speak the language of Magic, and I do not. Assuming I can get the data, I'll need a translator to make that make sense to the mages.

"Mikaal, you're a genius!" I said as I reincorporated myself and stood.

"I am? Erm. Yes. I'm not sure why you say that, but I'm glad you seem in better spirits."

"Please have all the mages stand side to side with their targets in front of them and wait for me to arrive before they cast any more spells. Coral, please join them. Mikaal, please get Jixxey and any other Noran mages to join you there as well."

Coral gave me a squeeze and a smile and walked away to find something to use as a focal point for casting. Mikaal sputtered twice, completely confused before yelling for an apprentice to call for Jixxey and moving off to deliver orders.

I turned inward to prepare for what I needed to do. The computer I had used for DNA analysis before was going to get a new job. I created a cable connected to both eye/windows and plugged it into the computer, thankful that there were no drivers required for mental projection of a computer for me to have to struggle with.

I needed the computer to process not only video, but also audio. I hadn't created a connection for my ears to the outside world, so I added a set of speakers inset into the wall outside each window and a set of audio/data connections below the left speaker which was right above the computer. I ran a data cable for audio and hoped that would suffice. As luck would have it, the medical analysis software had a module for language learning. I loaded this up and set the language to Magic and the races to Garanth, Noran, and SeaWind.

Preparations completed for Problem Two, I resumed reality and strode boldly up in front of the Mage firing squad. Most of them looked haggard from their efforts and lack of success.

Preparing Lemonade

"I have a new plan that will probably not make much sense to you now, but I ask you to trust me. Each of you will begin casting every type of spell you know at your target, one after the other while I watch. Try to think of the most obscure, varied Magics you have used and use them all. If you're too worn out to keep going, take a break. Rest, get food, but don't wander into the line of fire. I won't be able to respond and help while you're casting, so you'll have to work together to handle anything that goes wrong."

I positioned myself so that I could see every mage at once and locked my body in place. When I returned to my mental command post, I used the computer to identify each mage and their race before telling the program to begin analysis. I sent 'Begin' non-verbally to the group and then turned my attention to the Star Glass. I was dimly aware of the rainbow of magical fireworks that began outside my windows.

I felt the artifact in my hand and thought of the reversal spell, but without a command imperative or target for it to act on. I faintly sensed it responding with a question that felt like 'more parameters needed'. I tried sending a command for it to export the reversal spell to illustrated hard copy, once again giving it an image of a book at my feet. The Star Glass grew warm in my hand and a book appeared in my mind.

I stooped and picked it up to begin leafing through it. It was again in a language I didn't understand, but the pictures gave me some hope that it would in fact be able to provide the details of the spell. I would only have to make sense of what it provided. The images were of hands, seemingly those of its creators based on the metal ports and gadgets pictured, moving through a sequence of hand motions with captions that I hoped were the audible components of the spell.

Checking on the computer showed that an hour and a half had elapsed, and that the computer had gathered a firm, but not unshakeable, grasp of the Language of Magic. I looked out the window and was astonished to see that one of the mages had been replaced by the Mackta. Thankfully the position he replaced was of the same race. If he had replaced someone of another race it might have corrupted the data and caused us to start the process over. I let the program run for another thirty minutes and then returned to my body.

The progress indicator had stopped moving at around ninety one percent and since I had no idea how it had come up with an indicator of the percentage of a language it didn't know in the first place… I figured it would have to be good enough. Hopefully any deficiencies could be cured by the collective knowledge of the School of Magic once I got them close enough. I hoped that cancelling a spell was also part of the language of magic.

"Please stop casting." I said aloud.

My return to life caused one inexperienced mage to lose control of his fireball spell, which thankfully shot upward and didn't endanger anyone. He looked sheepishly at the sky as the flaming missile flew upward before losing cohesion. Two others dropped over onto their sides from exhaustion, an oldster and a young Noran I didn't recognize.

"Everyone take a break and get something to eat. I'll need a few moments to take what I've learned and transform it into something that you can reproduce."

I sat on the ground cross legged and returned to the place inside me. In front of the computer, I again saved the analysis to file so as not to lose the work. I asked the computer to show me how to 'say' (more correctly cast, but the software wasn't written for that) a mage globe since I already knew how to perform that spell. It displayed only the outline of a Garanth making the hand motions.

I instructed it to include both the audio and the 'sign language' in sync and to display all three races side by side. Playing back the 'phrase' was accurate to what I had been taught. Next I had it playback the fireball spell. I had never performed the spell, but it appeared accurate to what I had seen Jixxey do many times.

Preparing Lemonade

I stood and took hold of the Star Glass, both mentally and physically. I instructed the artifact to export the reversal spell to my computer.

Nothing happened.

I felt a query hanging from the Star Glass. It didn't have a path of communication with the computer in my head. I checked and enabled wireless networking on the computer and told it to expect a file. I then repeated my command to the crystal scepter to export the file specifying wireless networking as the recipient in the belief that there was only one such signal on Sorra.

I felt warmth flow over me, and the computer progress indicator zipped from none to done quickly. I went back to the analysis program and told it to import the received file and play it back. The spell took a good three minutes of droning and waving to cast.

It seemed important to also teach the spell to use the Chaos Cloud, and lightning as a battery for the reversal spell. It turned out that these were really two different spells. After export, import, and playback I felt like we had a reasonable chance of success.

Back in my physical form, I stood and noted the position of the celestial bodies in the sky. Coral, Mikaal, and Granalis were by my side nearly at once. They gave me something to eat and drink, which I wolfed down with little thought or taste.

"Please bring those who would learn here and have them all face the wall. Granalis loped off quickly and I heard shouts and runners followed by a flurry of motion."

I popped back into my head and set up a projector for playback of the video data through my left eye and created a speaker at my feet. When I was done, I found there were forty-seven mages of four races aligned to the left and right of me, ten wide and four rows deep.

"Ready?" I shouted aloud.

"We are!" they replied, not nearly in sync, but in one accord.

"The first spell is 'Reversal'. It will reverse the action of Chaos on the body of the target and stop when the influence of Chaos is

The Journals of Aaron the White

gone. The spell is long and will be repeated once. Once we're done with Reversal I'll give you the companion spells. We will take a short break between spells for practice and documentation."

I pressed play, and three two dimensional phantasms were visible even in the bright daylight on the wall. They were twice normal height, and their heads brushed the top of the wall. Garanth four arms, SeaWind two arms, and Norran six gaw variations were worked together in concert with the words laced with Magic.

"Daw, rew, hest, granham, beck, farsuith, zebd." A robotic male voice chanted in slow cadence, repeating the stanza seven times before the 'hand motions' were completed. When the first playback completed, the video/audio played reversed soundlessly, like an old VHS tape rewinding.

"Repeating." The voice said. When it was done the figures vanished, and I relaxed.

Those around me, however, began a flurry of activity. Scribes appeared throughout the group, recording what they had seen and taking corrections from the mages. The Mackta and Glanoot were directly to my right and began having a lively discussion about the power required to cast and sustain such a spell and how the casting might be sped up with some advanced level techniques. They decided their task following the showing of the next two spells was to simplify them so that the time needed to cast was halved.

Mikaal and one other Noran to my left produced frozen specimens they had captured following this morning's attack from their bags and began practicing on them. The young Noran managed to start the spell but couldn't maintain it. His target exploded fantastically, spewing him, the wall, and an unlucky scribe with Chaotic worm guts. Mikaal cast the spell perfectly the first time and held it until the end. When it was done though, so was he. He swooned and landed heavily on the ground, rolled away from me onto his side and started nibbling on something I could only hope was food. I waited fifteen minutes before attempting to move ahead.

Preparing Lemonade

"Are we ready?" I asked again loudly.

This time the answer was incoherent. "One minute please!" a fatigued sounding voice shouted from the back.

"We will wait a short while longer." I hollered back.

This warning seemed to have galvanized these mostly academic mages into preparation to receive the next gift of knowledge. So, when I called for readiness again in five minutes, they were in fact ready.

I repeated the 'Absorb Lightning' spell twice, which was much less time consuming, then gave them twenty minutes to practice again. By the time I had taught them 'Absorb Chaos', I was well and truly beat and completely forgotten by the bulk of the mages. They worked with the scribes long enough to ensure they had an accurate copy of the spells and then splintered into a million pieces, trying to work out how to ensure they could use the weapons I'd provided.

Chapter 33
Ready the Gear of War

This lull did not last long. Athious, looking much stronger than when we'd last seen each other and resplendent in his armor marched up followed by Andoo, Eeaarly, and Iinndie.

"Well done, Aaron," Athious said simultaneously aloud and silently. "I wasn't certain how you would train so many, or anybody at all for that matter. You've improved our chances of success greatly."

"We would like to introduce you to the commander of the Tiiaanian forces that will be accompanying you tomorrow," Eeaarly added.

"I assumed that the good Counselor was filling that role."

"Oh no. I can fight, but I don't give commands. We give only solid Counsel," Athious rejoined.

"Aaron, meet Vaminous." Iinndie spoke into my mind, gesturing behind me.

I turned around, not really expecting anything in particular, but nothing I had seen on Sorra to date prepared me for Commander Vaminous. He was the first Garanth that was significantly taller than I was and more massive to boot. Athious was the hardest, most masculine (to my eyes) man I had seen to date on Sorra. The Commander looked like him, only larger in every respect. Taller, broader, more rugged, and somehow more worn. He had the appearance of someone who life had tried to chew up and spit out, but he was meaner than life and had instead masticated everything thrown at him between his massive molars. He was also the first individual I had noticed sporting any significant facial hair. He had a puffy twirled mustache that made loop-de-loops on each side of his lips before they ended in an upward point.

"So, I finally get to meet the hero man from another world," he began loud enough to almost cause me to step back. He grabbed my hands in the lower of his meaty mitts and my shoulders disappeared into the upper paws. "Let me get a look at you," he continued sternly, picking me up and turning me slightly left and right as easily as if I'd been a baby.

Setting me down, he continued, "Not much to look at, but..." He broke into a smile. "Prettier than me I suppose."

"Good to meet you, Commander," I responded, trying to keep my voice level.

"What do you say we make our way over to the Parade Grounds and ensure you know our warriors and weapons, so we can ensure they're put to good use? We can't let these puny magic slingers have all the fun, eh?"

"Lead the way then, Vaminous." I stepped back and let the much larger man brush past.

The walk wasn't long, but there were a great many mages, scribes, assistants, and onlookers in the area. With the preparations underway, the school doors had been opened wide to keep things moving. There was no way that a single gatekeeper could have kept up with all the comings and goings. The commander didn't seem mean or rude, but he also didn't feel the need to do things like walk around people who were in his way. After he knocked a foursome over like bowling pins, the way cleared before him, and we were through the gate we had gone through last night. (Which at this time felt like a week earlier.)

Even though the door was open, a hissing from above gave us little warning before a soldier dropped, steam blasting every direction, to ask us our business.

"State yo…" He got out before seeing the commander and blasting straight back up in the air and out of the way.

We turned to the right through another gate I hadn't even noticed before and into the Parade Grounds. The ordered Chaos of drilling militia, ceased without a word or an indication from the big man in the lead. Nonetheless, the silence was immediate and deafening. Standing at attention was different for the Garanth, Norans and Moalean. Still, I recognized it immediately when I saw it.

"Warriors of Tiiaan. This is Aaron. He will be leading the charge to go after the source of danger to our City and our World. You are to defend him with your life, so that he can work to keep our families and friends safe. In the absence of direction from me, you are to obey him."

"Yes, sir," the entire field said in sync.

"The warriors before you and the mages behind you are the largest part of the force. We will review the troop types, and then I'll take you to the Cloud Jockeys."

"Good, goo…"

"Form up!" he commanded mentally while I was still finishing my acknowledgement.

Eeaarly vaulted over us to take his place with his squad while Iinndie just seemed to disappear from behind me and reappear among the scouts. It was to her group we went first.

"These are the Rangers. They are normally used for quick strikes as well as reconnaissance, but in a full-scale battle like this, they serve as their name dictates. They strike from a distance using bows and steampistola. Show 'em."

As one, the ranks of Rangers turned, aimed, and fired at a line of targets. The arrows were silent, and every shot was a bullseye. The steampistola whirred and whumped loudly three times per pull. Whatever they were pointed at seemed to be progressively vaporized by the projectiles. Steam rose from the barrel, a port on the right of the sidearm, as well as the target.

I was so focused on the destruction they wrought that I barely registered as they took two steps back, turned, and fired at a second set of targets, repeating the effect again without reloading or missing a beat. This complete, they stepped back a second time, producing spears which they drove into the ground and stood on, squatting low in a defensive posture.

"Efficient and impressive." I offered.

The commander nodded and moved to the next group.

"Breakers. Attack."

This group, which wore armor like Athious, each carried four clubs, with the exception of a single Moalean. They took one pace forward, and life-sized targets hissed up from the ground and into their faces. The bludgeons struck four locations, upper right arm to temple, upper left arm to jaw, lower right to ribs, lower left to abdomen. The targets splintered and fell.

The Breakers advanced again. As they stepped forward, they locked the ends of their clubs together but slightly offset. They took a double handed stance with upper right arm/gaw surrounded by left and lower left surrounded by right. A second step brought them into range of a second set of steam launched targets. They swung their weapons back and forward, and as they did, the weapon bent away from the target and then toward it, doubling the impact of their strikes. The targets were hit so hard that they defied gravity long enough to spin in the air twice before hitting the ground.

"Wow," I said, trying to keep my appreciation brief but appropriate.

A nod and we were moving again, stopping beside the last group.

"Divide. Conquer."

Eeaarly and his crew sprang into motion. 'Hssst-pop' sounded to my left. That was followed by the blur of attackers in flight. They headed right into where the Divide group had been standing, but they were somehow both below and above the attack dummies at the same time. Small blades bisected attackers as the Divide warriors flew past, landing in two distinct piles behind.

"These three-unit types will each contribute to four squads. One will lead, two will flank, and the final will protect our rear and supply train. Any questions?"

"Do these units have any protection from the Chaos cloud?"

"Only what you and the mages can provide. Let's go visit the fliers." Suiting action to word, Vaminous was already moving, throwing the last word over his rapidly departing shoulder.

Athious and I followed quickly. The parade ground ran alongside the outer wall of Tiiaan and ended at a false mountain. It didn't look like stone, but it did rise into the sky at a similar angle. There were no entry points above the gate. The color was a dark, dull grey broken at regular intervals by brass pipes spewing steam into the sky. It wasn't visible from the point we had entered the city, and at first, I didn't know why. Then I looked up.

The steam escaping the mountain stayed close, shrouding the structure in a veil of cloud that reflected the light in a thousand directions. The effect, while magic wasn't involved, was similar to the suggestion field I had used on the door to my room when we first visited Tiiaan. It made an observer uninterested in what was present in this direction. I could only assume that it was intended to serve in that way. We approached the wall and came into the shadow of Steam Mountain.

The wall was rougher than the rest of the structures we'd seen in Tiiaan, and the entryway seemed almost a natural cut into an unnatural surface. We walked down a long, rough-hewn hallway until we reached a dead end. Athious and the commander stopped and waited in the center of the space. Nothing happened. Still nothing happened.

I turned to look behind me as the light seemed to be receding. That's when I realized that we were ascending into the mountain. Once we reached the level which had been the ceiling, there were teeth cut into the wall which seemed to be the source of lift. There was almost no sound as we rose, but when we stopped the pressure driving the machinery vented at all corners with a very audible woosh. Turning around, the way was open again, and the locals were moving ahead into the cavernous room.

I raced to follow, and as soon as my foot left the floor of the elevator it began descending. I turned around in spite of myself as if it was my first time seeing such a thing and continued walking backwards. The roof of the platform was the floor of the two tier (at least) car. I could see many feet, which I assumed belonged to those who worked and lived here. They were surrounding a contraption which was in a state of constant motion.

About this time, I walked into a wall. A wall named Vaminous. They had stopped at a conveyor and were waiting for more of the contraptions to pass in front of them. Each machine had hundreds of moving parts of various sizes and configurations. There was a seat in the center with several levers in front of the cockpit. Each machine had a tender or perhaps a jockey. All wore dark goggles and identical bowler style hats made of metallic weave and emblazoned with a single large lightning bolt. Most were Garanth, but a good number were of the other races. They all wore vests or dresses of thick brown material that looked leatherlike.

They passed and we started to move ahead again until a nearly unbearable clanging started off to our right. This resolved itself into a four-legged walker. Each limb was articulated like a spider's leg. The control cart rode low between the legs but still knee height off the ground. There were half a dozen levers being operated by a bevy of Moalean Mechanics. It strode directly into our path, turned, and a speaking amplifier rose from the front and positioned itself to the lips of the most aged little digger lady I'd seen.

"What are you here for, Commander?" she shouted imperiously in his face.

"Miineux you ol' faker! I told you I was bringing the battle leader to meet you and see your crew."

They shared a blast of laughter as two old friends and rivals who had defended their home for years. Then the walking machine turned completely about, showing us a platform at the back for us to stand on.

"Climb on, groundbound! We'll soon be where we can show you the wonders of Sorran flight."

We jumped aboard the monstrous machine, and it trundled off. Each movement of a joint allowed a jet of moist air to blast forth in one direction or another. I didn't see how this conveyance was efficient with the number of technicians crawling all over it keeping it moving, but when we arrived at the end of the bay right as a flying machine raced off the edge into open air, I lost track of this thought. I found it again moments later when we walked up to the opening and I was looking down at a drop that would absolutely, unequivocally for sure, make me dead if I fell.

Suddenly the floor shot rails up around us, the cart dropped to the floor, and the legs began twisting and grappling around the corner of the leftmost wall beside us. There was an unpleasant lurch, and the machine rose up about a foot and stopped. The left rear leg swung around to the front, above the front left leg, and sought around the corner. Up another stomach lurching foot, then the front right leg reached out and caught on whatever it was gripping. Then it got worse. I was expecting a jolt up. I wasn't expecting the whole contraption to fishtail out over the nothingness below, and THEN shoot us up a foot.

"AaaaaaAAahhoouuuuu!" I bellowed aloud in a very undignified manner.

The right rear leg started moving forward and latched onto a track running up the front of the launch bays.

"Ok. You win." Athious laughed while handing Vaminous ten Patun. "That was funnier than Mikaal's first time up."

I spent the next few minutes inside a crab walking up the side of a mountain with my hand over my mouth to keep from either losing my lunch or repeating my earlier performance. I'm not sure if they could hear me repeating to myself over and over, 'You can't fall. You can catch yourself. You can fly after a fashion.' like a mantra.

Finally, the trip was over. I learned this when we shot suddenly sideways into a bay and thunk, thunked, down to the ground. I gained a new level of respect for all my friends who had entrusted me to fly them aboard something they could not see. I also jumped away from the machine and took several steps away from the open air before I calmed down.

I stood and looked around. The level we were on was several times higher than the one we had left. The entire ceiling was a mass of spinning gears, motorized claws grabbing and moving equipment, drive shafts, and other such mechanical marvels. A layer of misty haze rose up from the machinery, giving everything a dreamlike quality.

The main reason for the ceiling being so high was the ships hanging in their cradles in rows to the left and right. I counted thirty airships within my view. Each ship was a pure white balloon shaped like different kinds of clouds with nearly transparent cabling holding the control pod aloft.

Directly ahead the elevator rose out of the floor, carrying a Garanth pilot and her craft. When the motion stopped and the elevator was even with the floor, the pilot jumped up into her seat and pushed two levers forward. Six narrow rods, three on each side began raising and lowering in sequence, scooting the entire contraption forward like a truncated caterpillar. Together they writhed forward stopping below a deflated cloud hanging from the cradle halfway between the lift and where I stood. She pulled the levers back, turned and cranked on a valve and pushed a button. A loud clang reverberated around the mostly open room and a ladder shot directly upward. As it rose, she grabbed on with three arms and was launched aloft.

It stopped rising and she climbed up two more steps. She put two hands out and grabbed ahold of something not visible from where I stood, pulling it in close to her and attaching it to the top of the ladder. When this was done, she gripped the ladder loosely and slid down into her seat. She pressed another button behind her, and the ladder started descending, pulling a ring of iridescent metal down with the neck of the flat balloon. Jets of steam hsst from both sides as each rung was pulled down into its original place. She grabbed the ring just before the top rung vanished and twisted the neck free.

She slid another lever behind her seat to the right, and a small scorpion stinger shot up the back of the craft stopping a foot away from her face. She pushed the lip and neck of the balloon over the exposed stinger and pulled a rope from somewhere out of view, wrapping it tightly three times around the neck and tying it off. Once more she pressed a button and low whoosh began rising in volume as it progressed. She then turned around and slammed another lever forward. The vehicle reacted by trying to kill her again from several directions at once. Four more scorpion stings shot toward her, thankfully stopping above her head. She turned, looking unconcerned and grabbed the metal ring, shoving it up and latching it to each of these new stings. The balloon was beginning to inflate and now that the two were joined, the spindly legs pushed away from the body and spread out into sails like giant white wings.

Miineux walked up on my left and called out to the pilot. "Creaane! Since you're going out, I'm going to have you show the great hero here how the Lightning Lances fly."

She replied only with a hand signal that I recognized, a thumbs up. Athious and Vaminous appeared on my right.

"If I recall our last conversation, Miineux, she's one of your best Lancers?" Vaminous queried.

"No longer one of our best. Since the first attack, she's shown herself to be the most courageous and capable. It doesn't hurt that she stayed alive."

They continued to talk, but I stopped listening to them and began walking slowly toward the craft I was apparently going to be going for a ride in. I didn't see another seat. I put that aside for now, instead marveling at how quickly the air bladder was filling up and how much it looked like an Altocumulus cloud. Whatever it was made from even had the appearance of motion and fluidity.

Creaane was manipulating levers and controls, and a panel in the airship's bow opened, and two new gadgets extended. The first looked like an open mouth, or maybe a flattened horn, and it turned downward as it extended further, facing toward the back of the craft. Once it stopped moving it began belching a steady stream of fog. Oddly enough, it did not dissipate into the air but continued to collect under and around the cockpit and wings. It continued, getting thicker and thicker until the bottom of the craft could no longer be seen.

The upper doohickey came out and up in an arc until it was directly in front of the Lancer lady. Its motion stopped, and the upper third split in two, becoming an arm on a pivot with a handle at the end nearest the driver and a sharp point pointing at where I stood.

By now the craft was airborne and held in place loosely by the cradle that had originally held the inflatable. She waved to me, and I walked closer.

"Come on," she said, instructing me how to get up. "Grab here and here and put your feet there and there."

"There doesn't seem to be much space where you are."

"You're right. It is a little bit cozy when we give someone a ride, but I think you'll understand why once we get going."

I did as she asked and found myself perched precariously on the lip that ran around the cockpit. There were small ledges on the inside wall, not nearly wide enough for my comfort, but serviceable. She was wearing a harness that I hadn't noticed before, and she briefly removed the latches from the left side ring inset beside her so that she could turn around just enough to instruct me.

The space we were enwrapped in came to just under my armpits where I was standing but was lower towards the front. Creaane handed me half of a second harness, showing me how to put it on by wrestling it onto my left side. As I finished slipping it over my right shoulder, she hooked me into my own set of safety rings and then reclipped herself in place. The floor was just big enough to allow for both of us to stand, but her left foot was against the wall, then my left foot was between hers, then her right foot and mine was pressed up against the right wall. Given how Coral seemed to get jealous if I was near another woman, this was less than ideal, but as I hadn't been asked my opinion, and this young lady was the best, I kept my mouth shut.

The space between us and the giant drop off was now clear of people and equipment. Creaane reached up and released a thin white rope above her head and the cradle set us free. She began moving a lever with each arm in a circular motion and the wings of the craft moved in sync with her motions. We began to move forward slowly. Her top right arm flicked a gear one notch to the right and the wings doubled their speed. We shot out of the side of the faux mountain like nothing I had words for, far faster than I felt comfortable with. I did manage to keep any more undignified sounds from escaping my lips, but only just.

Once aloft and our speed had built up, the ride smoothed out, and after she changed to a higher gear again, her arm motions were slow, and we both began looking around us. There was a lot of wind, and nothing set up to keep it from us. She had pulled her hat down over her eyes. The hat contained a set of dark goggles inset which had been obscured by a fold of the metallic clothlike material.

I tried to speak but only ended up eating a veritable feast of bugs. She heard me gagging and spoke into my mind to keep my mouth shut unless I wanted to sample all the high-altitude insects of Sorra. I quickly crafted a pilot hat and goggles like I remembered from war movies I watched when I was a kid and learned to breathe through my nose. She pointed to the right and mentally informed me that there were practice targets set up for the pilots to use in training exercises. That is where we would be heading.

"Does your ship have a name?"

"Mysterious Lady."

"What powers these airships?"

"Magic."

"You don't talk much, do you?"

"Only if there's something that needs saying."

"So, it is magic steam?"

"We have two primary magic stones per craft. They are recharged in the forge between each flight. One is a heat stone that is immersed in the water tank to create steam. The other is the lightning stone, which you'll see more of just... about... now!"

She grabbed the handle, aimed, and pushed a button with her thumb that was inset into the handle. Electricity flew up from the craft, along the arm and down the point she was aiming before it launched through the air and demolished a 'monster' target on the ground below. She fired off four more shots in rapid succession, each time taking out a 'foe'. She turned to the side and smiled at me. This was the first time I'd seen any emotion from her at all. I smiled back, until we fell.

I can't describe the feeling of riding in a lighter-than-air craft held aloft by an air-filled sack and hearing *POP*. Air started rushing up past us as we fell, but at the same time we were being hammered by air currents from above. Looking up, I could see where something had gashed our floatation device directly above where we sat.

Creaane was good. She reacted immediately. With one hand she turned the wing gear up to maximum and spun her arm levers faster. This caused the wings to buzz like a dragonfly and our downward momentum was turned into forward flight. With her top left hand, she mashed three buttons on the panel in front of her, and a *BLAT* noise came from behind my head. I couldn't turn around, but I could look up. The edges of the tear began thickening and forming together. The rip dripped a sticky white substance onto me. Self-healing balloon! We were going to be ok.

We were moving faster than ever before on the level. The balloon above us began to fill out, and we started to rise. Creaane instructed me to look around and see if I could figure out what had hit us.

At first, I didn't see anything, but then as I looked at the field of what should have been static targets, some of them were moving. A whole herd of Chaos altered beasts was milling about on the practice field. A flash and horn blast from Tiiaan indicated we weren't the only ones who realized we were again under attack. She dodged and weaved as Chaos-infected Spinebeasts threw volley after volley of projectiles at us. She fired back, as she was able, destroying a few.

"The rest of the Lance will be here soon. We just need to hold on and do as much damage as possible before then," she thought at me.

"I'm not used to aerial combat, but I'll do what I can. If you see flashes of lightning around targets, don't fire at them."

I grabbed the Star Glass and held it up over the edge but left it on its chain before instructing it to reverse any Chaos-changed beings on the plain below. I had no idea how many there might be, but there were more than I would have guessed. Across the training field nearly three dozen reversal spells sprang up at once, flashes of aborted lightning making it very hard to see.

The airship dropped down and began moving at high speed again. I couldn't detect a leak, so I wasn't sure why, and I didn't want to distract Creaane by asking more questions. I urged the Star Glass to restore them as fast as possible and was busy looking for other enemies that might not be covered by the spells. Since we were lower now, it was apparent that a large force was en route to the walls of the city. A few of the spells winked out and others started, but it was like splashing water at oncoming waves for all the impact I had.

Suddenly Creaane gasped into my head. "Something is wrong! I have tried to fire again and again but nothing happens!"

Realization dawned quickly, and I aborted the reversal spells with a quick command to the artifact before responding. "I think I know why. Try again."

When I performed a high-speed reversal, lightning resulted. To save power, I'd told the Star Glass it could use lightning. I hadn't thought to instruct it to only eat side-effect lightning caused by the reversal spell. The Lancers attacked with lightning. Now I told the Star Glass to use only the static discharge from the reversal spell. The air was suddenly rent by the sound of multiple nearby thunderclaps as the Lightning Lances began firing again and again into the oncoming horde. Creaane's team were all around us now.

Two of them dropped suddenly as they were struck with flying spikes, but they recovered before hitting the ground. Fireballs and other spells flew from the top of the walls behind us striking here and there, setting horrifying monstrosities on fire or causing them to shatter with their next step. Still, so many came behind them that it seemed all of Sorra's wildlife had been changed into nightmare and sent against us.

I had a brief flash of concern for other smaller settlements and towns and how they might be faring, but the immediacy of my situation made it short lived. My watch told me that I could not rely on the power of the Star Glass for now. I would have to find a new way to contribute to the fight.

I quickly felt sick and vulnerable up in the air as we dodged oncoming projectiles. Something large hurled a tree at us and the Lancers split in two to avoid being hit. The airship in the rear was too slow and a branch caught his wings, spinning him end over end and leaving him aloft, but unable to maneuver. It was around that time that I decided I needed to strike off on my own.

"I'm going to go and fight my way," I told my pilot.

"Are you crazy? You can't jump out of a moving airship in the middle of a battle. You'll either get blasted out of the sky or fall to your death."

"Maybe, but hopefully not," I said back to her before unclipping my harness and jumping overboard.

Of course, I had already created a platform beside the ship and landed directly on it. I wasn't even sure she knew when I was gone. Thankfully my mental projections operated relative to my position, and it stayed in place, ready to catch me. I had my conveyance curl around me for protection from projectiles from below. In this way I was floating in midair in something like a burrito that had a bite taken out from the front. I closed up the space in front of me, leaving just a thin open window for me to see through.

I started flying back and forth close enough to the ground to see the status of the battle. There were hundreds upon hundreds of creatures of varying size and configuration. Some were probably of the same species but had been altered so drastically that it was nearly impossible to tell how they'd started. Some were large and lumbering and scaled with long arms for smashing while others were small and fast with big teeth.

Close to the walls the defenders were vastly outnumbered but fought valiantly. Mages fought from the ramparts, trying to take out the larger attackers before they got close. Everyone was exhausted and it seemed inevitable that Tiiaan would be overrun. There was no promise of help from anywhere.

I flew close to the city and put my back to the wall. The enemy was advancing from where we were supposed to be going in the morning. We needed to clear the road. The enemy was vast, like snowflakes thick on a field. Fine. I'd be the snowplow.

I created the largest platform I could imagine. It covered the field from one side to the other. I curved it up and drove it into the ground in front of our defensive line. Then I started to shove. The ground was irregular but level. Dirt, enemies, trees... all of it went. I pushed until I could no longer go any further. Nightmare creatures crawled over each other at the top, trying to reach Tiiaan. I lifted the bottom of my plow in one quick smooth motion, flinging the contents up and forward, then I dropped it and started again. Three times I plowed the road. Three times I flung.

Half the length of a football field stretched out between the defenders and the rubble pile strewn with Chaos-affected creatures. I wanted to avoid killing anything or anyone, but there were just too many enemies to restore. I hoped that Sorra's ecosystem would recover if we were successful in sending this worldwrecker packing. For now, I needed to do what must be done to ensure the survival of the people in my care.

I flew high and to the extreme south end of the debris pile. Into my mind I went and crafted death from above. I would be a human B-52. I didn't have much wall space left in the room in my head. Another door formed in front of me leading to an armory. It was empty at first but soon was filled with wall-to-wall carpet bombs. A belt delivery system for the bombs ran from the armory to my left eye. As each explosive device was delivered into the physical realm, the straps between each bomb would dissolve, dropping only a steady stream of ordinance.

Satisfied in my creation, even as I was unhappy creating something so destructive, I returned enough of my consciousness to my body to reopen the front of my flying cocoon to drop the bombs. I started my bombing run. I flew slow enough to ensure anything below me would not have a chance. More monstrous creatures were on their way.

I raised a wall of flame and destruction between them and Tiiaan. Once I reached the end of the pile I had raised up and slightly beyond, I turned and went back over the same ground. The whistle and explosion repeated and echoed around me, and I gave myself over to my task. I rained destruction. I was death. Enemies tried to climb over the cratered annihilation and found more of the same. Only once the last bomb fell and detonated did I return to myself.

I wasn't certain if it was my actions or not, but when I looked up, the remaining beasts were scattered and running away. I flew towards the bay we had started out from. The daylight was starting to fail, but soon I was surrounded by the remaining Lightning Lances.

As we approached their home they changed formation into a line with me in the center. One by one they flew into the four open landing bays. They slowed as they entered, sliding onto the waiting cradles, which closed around the balloons and began carrying the ships to their berths. The cradles moved slowly, and it took two minutes once a craft was secured before the landing area was cleared. The craft ahead of me landed in the top bay, then the second bay, then the third, eventually cycling back to the top. I needed no cradle, so when the craft ahead of me landed in the top bay I landed right beside it.

Once on solid ground I dismissed my platform and walked toward the elevator looking around for Creanne.

"What did you do?" Miineux said at my elbow as if she'd been there all along.

"What do you mean?"

"You left here with one of my Lancers and return floating in air. That isn't even to mention all the explosions."

"I did what seemed necessary to allow Tiiaan to still be here to come back to."

"I've never seen anything like it," she said breathing heavier as I continued to walk, and her short legs struggled to keep pace.

"How many did you lose?"

"A lot less than they would have had you not done whatever you did," Athious said gratefully as he and Vaminous pulled alongside us.

"Did Creanne make it back?"

"I haven't seen her yet, but I am sure she did. She has more skill and experience than any three others," Miineux said fondly.

"Is there anything else we need to do here? If not, I'd like to make sure everyone else is safe."

"You've done all you can for us. We'll be ready to fly out with you tomorrow," Miineux said.

I turned to walk away, and my left leg gave out, causing me to inadvertently take a knee.

"Are you hurt?" Miineux asked concernedly.

My stomach complained loudly. *Only my pride.*

"Not hurt, just a bit weak from using a lot of power in a short time."

"Here." Athious held something out for me to take. "These aren't the most appetizing thing, but they are great for getting your strength back after expending a lot of magical energy."

"Thank you," I said as I bit the item. I made a face and nearly spit it out.

"It does taste better if you take it out of the case first." Athious laughed.

He took the bar back, removed a thin layer which was identical in color to the contents, and handed it back to me.

I took a bite. "Well, it's not a lot better, but it is better, and it seems to be helping. Thank you."

I stood and continued on my way, munching the magic snack as I went.

Chapter 34
Roses Amongst the Thorns

Waiting for the elevator felt like an eternity. I was so worried about my friends I almost jumped out of the landing bay. Eventually though we were back at the Parade grounds, Vaminous was yelling orders and checking on his soldiers before he even got through the gate. Athious escorted me back to the Magic School field, where I found Granalis in the tent with the injured. He had been knocked from the sky while he was changing shape after having fought on the ground. The blue glow was just fading from around the hands of a very tired-looking healer as we arrived. I assured myself that he was going to pull through before moving on in search of Coral and Mikaal.

The battle had ended with the mages atop the walls taking down the few invaders that didn't get the message to flee with their brethren. Many mages were still returning. There were so many wounded, and I had so little skill at healing battle wounds. I wanted to be helpful as I searched for those closest to me. Two Norans in the second tent I checked were nearly unrecognizable. They looked as if something large had picked them up and chewed on them. Both were writhing and wailing in torment while a Moalean tried to treat them with his magic statues but kept being flung aside when he got close enough to help. I was able to command them to sleep and wake only when their pain was tolerable.

I saw Mikaal and two of our OrOboid companions and began making my way towards them when I was knocked nearly to the ground by a much-relieved Coral. She scolded me lovingly for causing her to worry. She had been busily working with the Mages, trying to help them learn and improve the spells I'd taught them when I was called away and had no idea where I was when the attack began.

When we arrived to where Mikaal had been, all six OrOboid were there. Mikaal was smiling, which was odd given the circumstances, but as the others saw us arrive, we were included in the conversation, and I understood.

"This is not how things are done," Kaalesh was saying.

"That is true, but this is not exactly an OrOboid enclave, and nothing is normal right now." Eeaarly's retort had a kindly tone but also some frustration as if the conversation had already gone on far too long. "Besides that, we may never have a chance to do it if we don't do it now," Iinndie added.

"There aren't enough of us to complete the ceremony," Kaaden said.

"I'm sure we can find enough people who would be willing to help us," Eeaarly said. "And besides that, it's not like others of our people haven't joined without the ceremony before."

"Am I hearing there is to be a wedding?" I said lightheartedly.

"That's not what we call it, but yes. I have never met two OrOboid like Iinndie and Eeaarly, and they've agreed to become my family," Andoo said proudly.

"That's wonderful." Coral and I said over top one another.

"What is the hold up?" I asked innocently.

"Our traditions are that there be two other families to perform the ceremony of union." Kreelen offered.

"Are you unwilling to be one?" I asked them.

"We are honored to," Kaalesh said, "but we're only one family."

"Does the family have to be three?"

"Sometimes there are more. It isn't unheard of," Kaaden said slowly.

"Could Coral, Mikaal, Granalis and I stand in place of the second family? I know it isn't the same, but I feel like we've become a family." Coral gripped my arm tightly as I said this.

"I would certainly accept it," Andoo offered quickly and brightly. "What say the rest of you?"

One by one each of the other OrOboid voiced their acceptance. Once they had, they asked Mikaal and Coral if they agreed. One could tell by the smiles on their faces that they did.

So, amidst the furor and clamor following the third skirmish in less than two days, we gathered near the healing tent where Granalis lay and learned the flow of an OrOboid joining ceremony. We could only perform the most critical parts of a much longer and more involved process since time, participants, and space were limited, but soon we were ready to begin. It would be the first OrOboid ceremony performed in Tiiaan in over 100 years and word spread quickly throughout the city. Everyone needed the hope that the love of family and commitment to one another brings.

By the time we got started there wasn't room for a single other person to have joined. In fact, there were people lining the walls and sitting on the ledges of buildings. The Lightning Lances that were on patrol even came and hovered above us so that they could watch.

Kaalesh was to officiate. Kaaden took three slivers of crystal and caused them to grow, with Kreelen's help, into three thin pillars that were driven into the ground. Then they caused them to grow towards one another and connect exactly in the center, continuing to grow until they formed a flat disc approximately the radius of my forearm. This served as an arch of sorts under which Kaalesh stood.

The traditional dress for the participants was decorative crystal chainmail, but since this wasn't available and took weeks to craft, they were each adorned with gifts from well-wishers. Eeaarly and Iinndie wore their Divide and Ranger attire, but with sparkly gems, coins, trinkets, and flowers woven in wherever there was room. Andoo had worn little more than a loin cloth all along, so I had quickly fashioned a human-style silver chainmail sheet that Tiiaanians, eager for something good, had fastened to him as best they could with gem studded rings, magic charms which sparkled on their own, and woven thread that reminded me of gold. Needless to say, they were all suitably sparkly if not exactly in the fashion of their tradition.

Granalis sat in his bed, lending his presence if not action to the proceedings. Mikaal escorted Andoo down one path toward the arch, Coral escorted Iinndie, and I brought Eeaarly. We stepped forward in cadence as directed by the sound the archway made when struck by Kaalesh from within and Kaaden and Kreelen from without.

As we stepped to the archway, we released our charges, and they each gripped the columns to their right and to their left, interlacing the fingers of their hands as they did so. They now surrounded Kaalesh who spoke to them, but also to all present.

"You come here as three, but you would all become one?" she said solemnly.

"We do," they said in unison.

"Will you each put the needs of your family above those of yourself?"

"We will."

"Will you strive to bring life to each other, and together, life into the world around you?"

"We shall."

"Such a joining is forever and always. It cannot be broken, save in death. Who stands in favor of your joining?"

"We affirm the joining of these three into one," Coral, Granalis, Mikaal and I said in unison.

The family K then said in response as one. "We join you together now, together always. We link your hands."

Suiting action to words, Kaalesh took Iinndie's right hand in her right, pulling her hand and body forward, while stepping alongside her and out, so that Kaalesh held Iinndie's wrist. Kaaden and Kaalesh took hold of Andoo and Eeaarly's wrists, stepping in, so that six stood closely between the crystal columns. They pushed their charge's hands together, enwrapping the hands of the joinee's with the joiner's hands as they did. The six hands took on a warm and inviting orange hue, that spread across the bodies of the newly betrothed so that they glowed brightly to my sight.

"Here now the three that entered the joining place are gone, and in their place, we call forth Ziinndie, Zandoo, and Zeeaarly. Strength and love to you, family Z!"

At this pronouncement from the raised strong yet silent shout from family K, all Tiiaan broke forth in celebration, shouts, and applause. Family K released family Z and stepped out of the joining place and allowing the newlyweds a moment of bonding, locked hand in hand, and leg in leg, heads together. Food and drink began to appear and flow as if there was no tomorrow to worry about. Hope sprang forth like a bud breaking ground as the party continued. I had a fleeting thought as to what our erstwhile tormentor would have thought about such happiness in the face of their declaration of doom.

This impromptu party lasted until darkness claimed the land and people drifted off to find slumber and comfort in the arms of those they loved. Jixxell came to escort us back to our rooms, explaining that the gates were all to be left open until the final battle was decided, and that Jixxey had fallen asleep after a bit too much frivolity, so she had come to make sure we were safely to bed.

Granalis was sleeping in the tent we had found him in originally and was back in his normal form. I picked him up gently in my left arm, and Coral grabbed my right hand. Jixxell guided us through the thinning throng, back to the school barracks, which had been cleaned of this morning's battle damage and debris. The door on the left just before the room the OrOboid had stayed in last night was now open, showing a second OrOboid room. It was a little rougher than the first room, seemingly put together in haste after the unexpected change in status our friends had gone through. The K family offered to take this room, so that the Z family could stay in the nicest room on the night they became one.

All the OrOboid were settled, and Mikaal waved to us with a tired grin and went into his room, which was repaired enough to be serviceable. Jixxell made as if to walk towards the SeaWind room, but Coral said kindly, but firmly that she could not stand to stay in that room again after what happened last night. Jixxell said that she could find another room for her in the women's dorms, or....

I answered the unspoken question, telling them both that if there wouldn't be too much of a scandal, she would stay in my room. Jixxell smiled appreciatively and asked us if we needed anything further. I thanked her for her help, and we went in to our room so that she could find her bed.

I placed Granalis on his pillows, and he continued sleeping without so much as a start. When I turned around Coral was lying on her traveling blanket on the floor. I told her that she could have the bed. She started to protest, so I picked her up, kissed her firmly, and placed her on the bed. She pulled me down beside her, and we kissed a little longer and fell asleep in each other's arms.

IV

WAR FOR SORRA
&
CONCLUSION

Chapter 35
Marching to the End of Everything

When I awoke, the room was on fire. I tried to scream aloud to check on my friends, but my voice was just a wheeze. I was so weak that I could barely lift my head. In the corner, the pillows where I'd laid Granalis last night to sleep were ablaze, with a small furry corpse smoking in the center. Turning my head, I saw Coral's lovely arm and leg where she hung suspended against the wall, blood dripping from her shoulder and dripping from her fingertips. I tried to use my abilities, but they failed me. My lungs burned and ached, every rasping breath coming harder. My eyes began to close no matter how I willed them to stay open.

I awoke and sat bolt upright, gasping and feeling around for Coral. Of course, this made her jump and squeak aloud as she and Granalis sat in the corner whispering to avoid waking me. I apologized for startling them once I saw that they were fine, and all was well. However, a deep sense of foreboding gripped me, and I felt the dread of not being able to protect the ones I love in return. I felt inadequate, no matter the power I possessed here. How was I supposed to lead these people against an enemy so hell bent on destroying everything he could see?

Coral either read my face, or my emotions were leaking through our link. Either way she came quickly to my side.

"Is something troubling you, Aaron?"

I didn't have the words to explain the feelings, the dream, or my failures in the past. I tried twice to speak, not getting out more than a few words before lapsing into silence. She simply put her arms around me and told me she believed in me. After a few minutes it was enough for me to get my equilibrium and get out of bed.

Once I was standing, the terror and futility faded and my desire to save this world and hopefully not die trying returned. My love for this woman, these people, and this world cast aside my fear.

A good night's sleep had Granalis back on his feet and moving normally. Coral had slept great and woke up ready to fight until I'd scared the bejeebies out of her. We moved to the door, and when it opened, we saw Jixxey standing with her hand poised to knock.

"Breakfast time," she said brightly. "We have to keep up your strength, mighty hero, if we want you to save the day. After all, a hungry hero is no hero at all."

She attempted to latch on to my hand again, but Coral had wrapped herself around my right side and pulled my left hand into her right as soon as she'd seen Jixxey. She 'hmpfhed' briefly and turned and lead the way, knocking briefly on Mikaal's door and both OrOboid rooms.

"Don't you worry dear. You take us to the food, and I'll make sure Aaron has enough to eat to face what's coming."

Mikaal neither answered nor made a sound until we had moved on to the OrOboid rooms. Each family exited their rooms quickly, the newlyweds giving off the sensation of big smiles and serene happiness even though they were all taller than me, and I couldn't see their mouths. Once all the OrOboid had joined us, we started out, Mikaal finally silently creeping up behind us until he announced his presence with a loud yawn.

Back we went into a brilliantly bright Sorran morning, so full of promise and with no hint of impending battle or disaster. We spilled into the Mess Hall, which unlike the last time I was there, was completely full.

Jixxey lead us three-quarters of the way down the long hall to a table and ordering panel that was open. She began working levers, dials, and switches like a madwoman, and soon enough plates began appearing in front of her. She fed the OrOboid first, probably owing to their constant need to eat. This was the first time I'd witnessed any of them sitting on a chair or eating anything other than their moss/mosswater combo. They were served a plate full of vegetation and a small, sliced melon along with a lidded drink like we had received before. All six sat, three on each side of the table by family unit and began feasting. Sounds of appreciation for the variety of foodstuffs leaked out of their conversation with each other and into our general mindspace.

Jixxey returned to the belt as more plates were delivered, bringing a veritable feast back for the rest of us. Each of us got a plate and cup with bread, fruit, and a small pile of noodles that resembled spaghetti squash. Then on her last trip she brought a large platter and placed it between us. It contained eggs, steaks, small bowls of a thick soup or thin pudding, and what I mistook to be sausages, but later turned out to be a very hot pepper that was to be eaten with the steaks. What seemed like mere minutes later and every morsel of food had been demolished.

We cleared the table before Jixxey escorted us back to our rooms to collect whatever items we planned to take with us after getting cleaned up for the day.

"I'll be back in an hour to escort you to the city gates for the muster and sendoff," she said.

True to her word, one hour later she was leading us on our winding way out of the Magic School and through the streets of Tiiaan. We came to the last of the city's large gates that we had not seen, where it seemed the entire remaining population was gathered both inside and outside the city gates. People began to cheer as they saw us. We made an obvious addition to the troops already gathered.

The Journals of Aaron the White

A Noran maiden leading a human holding the hand of a SeaWind lady, followed by a Noran Mage, and the only six OrOboid anywhere nearby. All of this was topped by a fluffy white being sitting on the backpack worn by the human. If Junean was still with us we would have represented all but one of the sentient races in this world.

The cheering continued as we approached the gate itself, and occasionally someone would dart out from the crowd to shake one of our hands, offer encouragement and well wishes, and the occasional small gift. Coral was given a necklace of braided flowers crafted of alternating land and sea flowers by a young girl. The girl's elder brother had imbued it with magic to keep them alive, and also to keep its owner alive by turning one fatal blow.

A large bird buzzed overhead and dropped a charm meant to be worn around the neck with a band that would adjust to the size of the wearer and impart accelerated healing. The properties of this gift were mindspoken to both of us by its giver, but we never saw them. Mikaal was handed a staff with a curved end. It could be used for walking or swinging from branches too far away to reach by gaw. The staff was set to react in the presence of strong Chaos and convert the Chaos energy into Magical energy and feed it to Mikaal.

The gifts and cheering died off for a few minutes as we walked through the thick gates crafted entirely of one piece of stone with a metalwork gate that rolled up and down. The gate was secured to the stone with magically locking clasps, which were supplemented by locking slide bars that slotted into grooves in the gate. A group of mages that were staying behind to defend the city bowed in respect to the OrOboid as they exited the shadow of the gate behind us, handing them each two gloves. These added electrical shock to any crystal held in the hand to add damage with every attack, whether thrown or thrust. They would charge on ambient magic unless a source of Chaos was present for them to feed on. Zandoo was particularly impressed with the thoughtfulness of these gifts as they complemented the natural battle style of his people.

Marching to the End of Everything

Twenty or so steps outside the city proper an impressively sized stage had been erected, covered by a white fabric that was draped down to the ground on all sides. The stage was open on both sides but somehow faced both toward and away from us. An orange shimmering in the air that only I could see highlighted that the front of the stage facing away from the city was being projected towards the city as well. A white painted metal staircase allowed access to the stage on our left. Jixxey lead us to the left where I could make out the edges of the Breaker soldiers, and I was expecting to watch the ceremony with them. To my chagrin, she led us onto the stage and to some comfy looking couches.

The Counsel of Three was already seated on the far end of the stage and was conversing deeply. Miineux and Vaminous were seated behind them, swapping old stories and laughing. They were an amusing pair, she nearly as much smaller than I as Vaminous was larger but treating one another completely as equals.

All but the OrOboid sat on the couches just in time for Glanoot, Notrus, and Maegen from the School of Magic to arrive. They were solemn and quiet, looking all around them.

"This is the first time most of them have been outside of the school walls in years!" Mikaal cackled quietly beside me.

They reached the front of the stage and took a step back and stopped, looking ahead. Only then did I really look at our surroundings. To the left beside the Breakers stood the Rangers and Divide, each in neatly formed rows. There were fewer of them than I remembered, but they were shined and battle ready. Directly in front of us were nearly fifty mages on foot, behind which were the merchants who were following along to bring supplies and the healers to care for any wounded.

Lining the tops of every wall and roofs of buildings were those who were staying behind to defend the city. Finally, to our right were around two dozen Lightning Lances with their agile pilots perched atop the lighter-than-air portion of their crafts, placing them at eye level with those of us on stage. I felt magic building near me and began searching for it. Just then the Mackta winked into existence in front of Glanoot. He turned and looked at me with a twinkle in his eye and mindspoke to me alone.

"I knew you'd feel me coming. Much faster than walking up all those stairs."

Then the amiable little man disappeared as he turned to the crowd with a flicker of an orange aura. His presence loomed large, and his voice boomed, without his raising it while a telepathic echo reinforced the effect.

"People of Tiiaan. Warriors, Mages, and Heroes all. We are threatened. We have done nothing to bring this attack on ourselves save to live happy and quiet lives. This has happened before, and it will certainly happen again. We have been given a chance to stand together against this darkness. A man from another world has been called and come forth. He has taken our welfare as his priority. Not since I was a young man have such momentous events been set in motion. Here and now, I proclaim to you that Aaron is as much of a Sorran as I am. I ask you to join me in calling him brother and friend."

An embarrassingly long cheer rippled across the assembly, and I very much wished for the ability to disappear.

"Today Tiiaan leads the defense of our world, as Aaron leads Tiiaan. Together we will stand or fall. We will hope together for success. To commemorate this day, I hereby commission Aaron as a Mage of the first class; the first in two hundred years." Much more cheering and applause echoed around us and the Mackta waved me forward. I was holding Coral's hand and tried to pull her up with me, but Mikaal gently laid a Gaw on our hands.

"This honor is for you alone, Aaron."

"Go ahead, Aaron. You got this." Coral added, setting his hand free.

He began to wave his hands and chant. His upper hands began to form an orange ball of power that was encircled with rings of violet called forth by his lower hands. With a final word of power, he cast his hands down at my feet and the magic pooled at the floor around me. If I hadn't been sure of the old man's good intentions, I probably would have surfed off the stage and far away.

The magic pulled at the pure white of the fabric on which we stood, and it began to ripple and stretch. As it rose up my body, I felt a compulsion to raise my arms. Soon I could see nothing but white cloth swirling around me as if I was caught in a freak snowstorm. When the casting completed, I was adorned in a robe of pure white, complete with a deep hood. A thin line of deep purple hemmed the arms, hood and feet, which glinted as if it were alive when I looked at it.

"I give you Aaron the White!" he said with a dramatic flourish.

The resultant cheer went on and on. When I thought it was going to finally end, the merchants fired off Sorran fireworks that were visible even in the light of day. At last, the furor receded, and the Mackta exhorted the mages before him.

"You who represent Tiiaanian magic, make us proud. Your willingness to leave the safety of a scholarly life to use your skills to save others is to be commended. I give you my blessing and these words of wisdom. Think fast, cast fast, and if you find yourself in a situation where you don't know what to do, listen to your heart and be bold. That is all any of us can ask of you."

Around this point I realized that I was standing awkwardly with my arms above my head and decided to back slowly and mysteriously toward my couch. I didn't want to detract from others, especially the very powerful and strange Mackta. While I sat, he called Vaminous forward.

The mountain of a man stepped forward and spoke to each of his divisions, giving last minute instructions, but mainly urging them to fight hard, fight smart, and keep each other alive. He also repeated the bit about following me and keeping me alive.

While he was speaking, the Mackta sidled up to me and informed me that as the newly minted White Mage, he would be having me close the ceremony and start the march according to my orders directly from here. Since I had no intention of speaking before arriving on stage, this just caused a giant lump to form in my throat and I hastily tried to gather some encouraging words for an entire city, which represented an entire world.

Rhythmic cheering and banging of weapons announced the end of Vaminous's time on stage. He motioned to Miineux and stepped back. She stood and started advancing, but as she did, she grew. By the time she reached the place he vacated, she was towering over him by a good foot. He hurrumfped behind her but said nothing as she began.

Her team was much smaller than his and more dispersed, but they whooped and yelled to make up for it as she spoke, telling them that they were the finest flyers she'd ever seen and suggesting they all fight like their new Lance Leader, Creaane.

Much sooner than I had hoped I was being called forward to complete the ceremony. I had never been much of a public speaker and was about to shake apart. Fighting didn't seem to scare me, so I couldn't understand why this was making me so nervous. I waved my friends up beside me before I began.

"Never in my life have I been so blessed. Every step in Sorra has been full of life. To see what is being done to it saddens me. It makes me angry. I cannot stand by and do nothing. Mikaal called for someone to come through the portal who could help. I don't know why it was me, but I'm glad. Even if saving this land and all of you costs me dearly, it will be worthwhile. I hope you all feel the same. I don't understand the hatred that this enemy has displayed. I know though that love is stronger than hate. Good is worth fighting for. Friends and family are worth sacrificing for. I am proud to have each of you with me. Where I come from, people don't always treat those who are different from themselves well. Yet I look beside me and see very different people united and made stronger by our differences. We will triumph because we must.

"Mikaal has a tracking spell in place and will direct us to our enemy's location. I expect we will have to deal with both the Chaos Cloud and the Evil One's minions. We must all protect one another. Avoid contact with the Cloud at any cost, except the cost of another's life. Know also that the cloud can surge forward suddenly. Now… Let's bring the light of a bright new day to Sorra and send the dark clouds and vile spirits back into the abyss they crawled out of!"

A cheer went up, but I felt that theatrics were called for at this point to inspire these people to feats of bravery that would likely be needed. I had been racking my brain since the Mackta mentioned I had a speaking part and wasn't coming up with anything that felt right.

The moment nearly passed when a call went up from the back of the Lightning Lance line. Like a sailor at sea sighting land, one of the pilots had extended a mast from his craft and climbed it. In this case, however, he was warning us of severely inclement weather incoming. The Chaos Cloud had arrived and was quickly blocking out sight of everything on the horizon. I grabbed Coral and kissed her briefly but passionately, before running off the front of the stage onto a surfboard shaped mental projection and flying over the heads of the mages and militia in the direction the lookout was pointing.

Chapter 36
Advance Preempted

Flying as fast as my sanity allowed, it took me about four minutes to get close enough to see the cloud as anything more than a shape on the horizon but far enough away that I didn't feel immediately endangered. It was crossing an open plain, roiling and churning as it came on. Before it ran a host of beings both animal and sentient. Screams of horror and all-consuming pain could be heard as the Tiiaanians who had come to send us off fell behind and were caught up by the onrushing tide. I watched the abhorrent thing as this happened and saw it mindlessly and hungrily rushed ahead to capture its prey.

I was hovering about two stories higher than the peaks of destruction and it looked from my perspective like the deep sea troubled from within. I saw it reach out and snatch a bird that flew too close, so I knew it would be more than happy to pull me in if I tried to fly over it.

I called on the Star Glass, pulling it from around my neck and pointing it below. I instructed it to use the Chaos as energy and begin a mass rewinding, reversing the tide. For the first time it responded as if it had a will of its own, suddenly eager to begin this task. The screams of the captured redoubled as their change was halted and they began returning to their own minds and forms. A line of bright green formed in front of the cloud and began chasing the darkness back from whence it came.

I was exultant. The artifact and I could really protect Tiiaan, and eventually Sorra. I whooped and yelled and flew in circles. That was, until I felt the Star Glass getting hot. The dark tide was ebbing. Restored creatures were left behind the green glow lying on the ground weak as newborn babes. Here and there those who had watched their friends and family consumed by the false night and heard their screams turned to reclaim them. They didn't know what had happened, or why, but they were relieved.

I looked at the object I held in my right hand, now nearly glowing with the heat it was radiating. I told it to slow down before it destroyed itself. I had to tell it three times before it responded. It was as if it was enraged and fulfilled, driven to destroy the Chaos no matter the cost to itself or others. It was only when I told it that it would be destroyed before it could finish its objective before it listened to me. Where before I had commanded it, now my command was overridden by its own desire, or programming. It had become so hot that I had to take it off of my neck and hold it by its chain. I was flying to and fro over the edges of the two competing forces, using the rushing wind to cool it. Gently and repeatedly, I coaxed it to slow until it cooled.

Once I felt that I had it back to safe speeds I rose further in the air and tried to communicate with it directly. The heat it was generating was partly due to the amount of power it was converting, and partly also because the Chaos energy it was gathering was more than it needed for even this large of a reversal.

I could do something about this. I created another storeroom in my mind and told it to give the magical energy to me. Once this was done, we were able to drive the darkness back another two miles. At that point my third storeroom was full, and the Star Glass was heating up again. I commanded it to stop, having to add a "for now" behind the command to get it to listen to me.

Quickly as I could, I flew back to Tiiaan and landed on the stage. I had no idea how long I'd been gone. It felt like a long time to me, but this took all of twenty minutes. One of the mages told me later that they heard a Lancer yell about destruction being upon us, then I flew off the stage and took off with a deafening boom. It appeared to them like I flew around like someone fleeing from a flight of stingthings. A great wailing was heard from below me and the wall of darkness fled before me.

"It seems the time has come for our march to begin. Commanders, to your positions!" Then to my friends, "To the Rhinodons!"

Jixxey pointed stage right where Pakky and friends sat. I scooped myself and my eleven companions and all the provisions we had brought on stage and sat us down beside our beasts of burden amongst the merchants. We were packed and at full gallop within minutes, Coral by my side matching my pace perfectly. Mikaal was in the lead. Airships were rising into the air and taking positions in a perimeter around us. I felt a pang of guilt for the foot soldiers that we had left at the rear of the column and wondered how they would catch up.

Our path took us parallel to the line of the Cloud's advance. I hoped that my unplanned attack on it slowed it enough to keep Tiiaan safe until we returned. All I knew was that it was time to take the battle to the enemy.

I was very surprised when mixed divisions of warriors began catching up to us on foot. As long as the path allowed for it, Breakers and Divide ran directly to our left and right. Rangers ran in a fan farther out to watch for attack. Suddenly Vaminous was beside me, laughing at my confusion. He wasn't even winded.

"Neat trick the mages cooked up for us, huh? We have limited time each time we use it, but it will allow us to keep pace with you and not grow tired. It did take us a bit to master it without running into things. Magic does sometimes have its place and uses, but don't look to me to explain it," he said in mindspeak to us.

Advance Preempted

Lancers popped off a few bolts of lightning leading to our left, cloud side. A glance behind and I could see mounted Mages making good time to catch up to us with the trailing group of merchants and warriors bringing up the rear. We kept this pace for an hour before the soldiers started falling behind. I called for the group to reduce pace to a slow walk and asked the scouts to report in.

Rangers had seen a few corrupted creatures which they had either dispatched or for the larger ones, pointed out to the Lancers for air support. Creaane's crew had a less positive report due to their vantage point. They could see the Chaos Cloud advancing towards us along our path, but even more concerning was the solid wall holding steady ahead of us another two hours march. There was also something thrashing a line through the forest beside which we would be passing just before we reached the Cloudwall. We appeared to be walking into a pincer attack.

Vaminous reported that they were ready to resume quickmarch, and we resumed striding boldly toward our objective. I resisted the idea of flying off solo again to deal with whatever was coming. I wanted to protect everyone, but it was unlikely I could do so. They were looking to me for leadership. Even though I knew nothing of such things, they believed in me, so I had to have just as much faith in them.

The number of Chaos-affected creatures coming towards us continued to increase as we closed with the line of destruction. They were coming from the left flank and in our path. Our pace slowed, and lightning began beating a tattoo in a blinding arc toward our attackers. The Lancers rotated their formations above us so that the weight of our defense was borne by all. The changed started including sentient beings, and the mages moved forward to reverse and restore as many of them as possible. A few were so changed that the warriors didn't recognize what they had been. Those were destroyed.

A deep grumbling grew as we approached the edge of the forest, and we prepared to face this new unknown assailant. The trees seemed to ripple and wave as if an unseen wind was churning through the forest in all directions.

All eyes were focused on the many external threats, so when the very ground we walked on rose up and attacked us it caught us by surprise. Nearly the entire center column was thrown to one side or the other. Our Rhinodons were not fans of flying judging by the squeals of alarm. I was thrown off Pakky. Granalis took wing by instinct. Mikaal was pinned under his Rhinodon, but nothing was broken thanks to gaw not having any long bones. Coral's animal had managed to land on its feet, and she was still astride it. I righted Mikaal and his mount with a nearly subconscious hand projection while assessing the damage to our forces.

My eyes darted about, identifying downed warriors and mages amongst the rubble, before tracing upward to the monster rising from the ground. It was broad and flat with long pincers protruding from the edges of its body. I heard Vaminous issuing commands and organizing a defense. A ranger was close to the beast and was sparring with one pincer when another snaked down from above him, grabbing him about the waist and pinning his arms to his sides. He was handed up the beast's body from limb to limb, becoming more wounded each time before being dropped whole into the beast's gaping maw.

I called for everyone to put some distance between them and the beast. Lighting began scoring its flesh from multiple angles. It was then that I noticed the two grounded Lancers that had been struck from the sky when the great Flatworm rose. It roared its dislike of this new turn of events and flicked its body toward the closest of its tormentors, smashing it to bits before the pilot could react. She screamed and was caught by a clacking pincer. She soon shared the ranger's fate.

I tried to communicate with it, but it was either mindless or rejected my contact.

"Mikaal, do you know what this thing is?" I asked.

"I've never seen anything like it. It isn't Sorran and it doesn't seem to be Chaos changed."

One of the mages threw a ball of flames at it and scored a direct hit near its mouth causing it to rear back, roaring its pain and anger. This emboldened our forces, and several Lancers fired into the same area with incredible aim at once. The monster rolled over backward and, in the process, averted its face. It threw those closest to it backward, striking one mage and two warriors with flying rock and dirt. The mage was either unconscious or dead. One of the warriors lost an arm, and the other was quickly back on her feet, bleeding heavily.

It rolled backward end over end twice before compressing itself like a spring and jumping over our forces, landing nearly on top of the merchants and healers. They scattered in all directions. One wasn't fast enough and was caught by a seeking claw. She was prepared though. The little Moalean began growing until she was too big to be lifted and eaten. Soon she was as tall as the enemy and began using her naturally sharp claws to gouge deep furrows in the creature's flesh just as easily as if she were digging through a mountain. Yellow ichor spilt out all over her. She seemed to be getting the best of it until it got hold of her arms. Now it had the advantage. It raised itself up and made to bite her head off. She moved aside enough that it only sank its mouthparts into her shoulder. She screamed in pain and rage but couldn't free herself. Two acid tipped arrows flew from Coral's bow and embedded themselves, hissing and smoking, into the beast on either side of the entrapped Moalean but it was not enough to free her.

Two members of Divide and a Ranger began raking the beast with knives and arrows, but the wounds also weren't deep enough to get its attention. Lancers struck it again and again, shearing off three of its numerous clawed tentacles. The brave Moalean was between her attacker and most of our forces, preventing us from assisting her fully. I saw my spear protruding from Pakky's storage flap as he struggled to his feet and grabbed it with a hand projection.

"Vaminous! Lead the forest side defense. I've got the worm," I shouted mentally.

"Agreed, Aaron!"

"Coral and Mikaal! Get our forces back in order."

"Right." "On it," they replied respectively.

"OrOboids. Let's go."

I created a platform in the dirt below my feet and raised it as I spoke, so they were able to see it. They said nothing, as silent creatures are wont to do, just put action to my words. Seconds later we were hovering over the humongous duo.

Before I could offer any more direction, Zandoo dropped, spear first onto the pincer that held the 20XL Moalean's right arm. He stabbed repeatedly into the joint where it met the tentacle. Before he had struck a third time, the other five joined him, and I stood alone.

Their combined attack caused its jaws to release as it shrieked fury and pain again. I took this as my opportunity and threw my spear toward the largest of what I thought must have been a ring of eyes above its raging orifice. I would have missed with only the strength of my arm, but I gave myself a mental hand, gripping the spear as it flew and plunging it into the orb. The beast didn't fall. It flailed, tossing OrOboid and Moalean aside as it sought to revisit its earlier backflip maneuver. Unfortunately for it, I was still holding the spear in my phantom hand. It backflipped and my spear stayed in place, neatly splitting it down the middle.

The two halves flopped down, side by side, and writhed in what I prematurely hoped was a death spasm. Alas, the split halves began to heal, and it started to rise as two slightly smaller versions of the same beast. Thankfully the mages behind me, led by Coral and Mikaal, were paying attention. A barrage of magical cold struck the healing edges of the worm turning hydra, causing it to freeze from within. It slowed to a fraction of its pace until the next volley, this time of fireballs, caused it to shatter into too many fragments to count.

A cheer went up, and those who were downed began getting up and assessing damage. Tiiaanians helped their comrades up and got ready to march. There wasn't much talk happening, which made the sudden peal of laughter all the more jarring.

"How many times have we seen this, old friend?" The apelike face of the enemy's herald spoke loudly in a basso voice as it and two carrion birds dropped in a spiraling arc from above where the Lightning Lances flew. It let itself go and fell the last few feet, landing heavily and nearly toppling over.

"Seen what you poor soul?" Granalis responded from his perch behind me.

"Why, the heroic march of a world's valiant defenders, heading to the final battle, of course!"

The voice shifted to the formless echo in our minds. "It will ever and always end the same. Their strength will be added to the master's forces. Destruction will come to this world."

"How much you must have seen to have lost all hope like this," I responded to the beast sadly.

Gibbering noises preceded the next words, delivered in a wail. "We has hopes. The master brings the hopes. His breakings are more nicer than what the other baddies do."

Granalis response was a growled. "We never had any proof of that! Just your master's words about the terrors he suffered as he inflicted his own on us. How hopeful is it that you're stuck sharing a body with others?"

The face of the manymonster crinkled up and it let out a high-pitched screech in reply before continuing in a new voice, this time speaking to everyone. "Your bravery will mean nothing in the end. Despair now and give in to your doom!"

It hissed like a serpent and bounded high into the air where it was caught in its cage.

"You've only survived one member of the Master's vast army. Come on then if you dare. It will all be over soon!"

Then they circled round and headed in the direction we had been marching.

Chapter 37
Chasing a Ghost

We had only taken another few steps along our planned route when the noise from the forest ahead rose from a distant thunder and a few shivering trees to a nearly unbearable cacophony accompanied by an earthquake. Trees were uprooted and tossed aside. We kept up our pace, unsure of whether facing the onrushing assailant or the Chaos cloud first was better.

Of course, the answer made itself apparent in short order. The treeline grew dark and was covered with a haze of dust and soil. Large chunks of vegetation flew in many directions, thankfully none of them at us. I was most concerned about the Lancers. A tree thrown in their direction and not avoided in time could cause a catastrophic chain reaction. The dust storm thickened and coalesced closer and closer to us. The Chaos cloud was now visible but was not advancing towards us as I would have expected.

Just before the light of the sun was blocked from our view, the storm halted, and the noise diminished from maddening to merely deafening. Then a column of stone rose into the air and grew in thickness.

"Wait!" the column said, continuing to grow.

When the motion stopped, we were in the presence of the Gathering. That is to say, if what we met before was the Gathering, this was an order of magnitude larger. This would be a gaggle of Gatherings.

"I wasn't expecting to see you again," I said.

"You have done well, Aaron. We are certain you are the right man in the right place to save many. Before you face this adversary, there are a few things that you must know to have the best chance of success," the rocks spoke.

This version of the Gathering, despite its gargantuan size, was somehow the same entity, or enough the same to be able to pick up from where we left off before in the mines as we reclaimed the Star Glass.

I looked behind to see where Coral, Mikaal, and Granalis were and found that most of the Tiiaanians were prostrate or awe stricken where they stood. Those who weren't frozen were looking at me with wonder, that I would talk so with these beings. Did they consider them legends? Or gods? I wondered to myself briefly.

"Vaminous! Creaane! Stay on the lookout. We don't want to let our guard down. We will step aside and listen to what these wise ones have to say before continuing." I nearly shouted mentally, allowing all to hear me in the hope that it would bring everyone back to their senses.

"Yessir, Aaron!" they responded slightly out of phase with one another.

I wasn't certain if what I needed to hear was something that everyone could or should know, or if it was just for me. I also had no idea if such a large being was capable of talking quietly or not but stepping a few paces away from the larger group seemed the right thing to do. I waved Mikaal and Granalis to follow me. Coral enwrapped my arm as I walked around the beneficent behemoth and a bit beyond it. It kept pace with me, which wasn't hard considering its girth, and stopped when I stopped.

"I am listening," I said in as respectful a tone as I possibly could.

"There is a significant difference between you and the people of this world, other than your origin." They began slowly as if still trying to determine how to explain what they knew to someone so different.

I resisted interrupting with questions, though I had many, and by the way Coral was gripping my arm, I thought some of the same questions were running through her mind as well. The Gathering flowed down and reformed into a sitting posture before it continued.

"You may look at us, especially now as we are many more than before, and wonder why we aren't joining you to save Sorra. It is this difference that prevents us. Your people believe that they are possessed of a soul, or spirit, correct?"

"Yes. I would think the same of everyone I've met here."

"We thought that you might believe that. Sorrans have no soul. At least not the way you think of them."

I could only gasp. Looking at Coral and Mikaal, they seemed as confused about what a soul was as I was to learn that they were without one.

"When the people of this world die, they return back to the world. Their life isn't lost. Their memories, thoughts, experiences, and emotions are stored in their bodies and after their passing, they distill into what appears to be a common stone. Mikaal calls them critters, though that's not a very respectful name."

"If I understand correctly, I am now talking to the living embodiment of every life that has ever been on Sorra and their combined knowledge."

"We are a little more complex than that, but at the heart of the matter, yes. Our purpose is to look after our descendants. Most of the time, they don't need our direct intervention. As much as we wish it weren't true, we are unable to directly thwart the actions of those who aren't of Sorra. Those like you who possess a soul… the last time we tried to intervene with one of you, we were greatly damaged. Much that we knew was lost at that time. That is why only a soulbearer can save this world. This enemy is more like you, though he is greatly changed. He was of your world."

"How can that be possible? Is that why he knows me? There are so many people on my world. The odds of someone from my world both being here and knowing of me are unfathomable." I lost a bit of control at this time, grumbling and muttering to myself. The Gathering (Rock God?) and my friends waited for me to collect my calm.

"These things you must learn in order to be victorious. You must discover the who and the why for yourself. They are the key. We do not have this knowledge to give you."

"All right. Not ideal, but all right. I have only one more line of questions."

"You wish to know about how these differences affect your love for this Maiden and desire to be with her?"

"Yes. Well. But…How did you know?" I asked, astonished.

"No matter how different you may be, love leaves a mark on every being of every species we have ever experienced. The love you two share is strong and pure. There is no reason that you cannot be Married and raise a family. Any children you have together might be Sorran or soulbearer. We cannot tell you that detail. At death, you would be parted. She to her way and you to yours. Or you could ask your creator to transform her essence into a soul. HE is able and might be willing."

So, I can spend my life with Coral, if she'll still have me, but wouldn't know about our eternity unless I find and talk to God? Sure! Sounds easy! What could go wrong? Ok. Keep the panic on the inside. You have to live through the first problem to be able to solve the next.

"Thank you."

They began to reform to stand. "Finally… the opposite of Chaos is harmonious order. Logic alone won't suffice. It must be strong, stable, and contain no discord."

Then it took two long strides back into the still-settling dust, lost cohesion, and rolled loudly away.

I wasn't sure how to process much of this new information. I looked to Coral, still wrapped around my arm. I was thankful that this talk of our differences hadn't made her doubt her feelings. I didn't know if my friends knew what a soul was, but that seemed like something that would wait until the present calamity had passed. It occurred to me at this point that I may have another resource of information that remained largely untapped.

"Granalis. I hate to ask this of you, but I think it is time to find out what you might be able to tell us."

He was sitting on the splintered trunk of a tree nearby. His expression indicated that he wasn't looking forward to this, but that he was also not surprised.

"I will share with you what I am able."

"What is your former master's name?"

His mouth opened and he tried to answer but only pained noises escaped from him. Sweat began to run down his temple.

"Ok. Never mind that. What prevents you from answering?"

"A geas was placed on me."

"Who prevents you from speaking?"

Granalis smiled abruptly. "Zeedox the binder. He is or was one of my former master's servants."

"Your master wouldn't have had another do this if he could do it himself. Right" I said this more to myself, thinking aloud, but Granalis took it as a question and nodded agreement.

Coral noticed this and said, "Look! He seemed to be able to agree with you, even if he can't tell you anything directly. Maybe we can learn enough by asking questions that he only needs to confirm or deny."

"Brilliant!" I said with a gentle squeeze of her forearm. "Your master was from my world, so he must have been human at one time."

The shapeshifter nodded again.

"Did anyone ever mention me before he saw me here on Sorra?"

He thought a minute and then said, "He didn't speak of you directly, but now I wonder if one of his stories might have included you."

"Can you tell me the story?"

Again, he opened his mouth and tried to speak, trying to say something that wasn't blocked, but again he shook his head.

It was hard trying to think of questions that could only be answered with a yes or a no that would tell us anything of value. I was thinking, apparently aloud, and was surprised when Granalis answered me when I rhetorically asked, "How would a human leave our world, except by a portal as I had?"

"That's the only way." He seemed as surprised as I was that he spoke.

"So, a human left Earth through a portal and somehow knows me. It couldn't be, could it?" I was muttering aloud to myself.

"Did this person go through the portal alone?"

"No. There was…." Granalis trailed off into pained grunting as his next words fell afoul of the curse.

"I think that's enough for now. We should get moving," I said aloud before continuing to mutter under my breath. "That's not even a possibility, right? I mean, how and why? It doesn't even bear thinking on, even if it is the only idea I have."

The four of us walked back to where our forces were waiting and vigilantly watching for trouble. Everyone was on their feet and repairs and healing were nearly complete. We would move out within fifteen minutes.

Mikaal and Coral were obviously eager to hear who I thought our enemy might be, but even if it was the only thought I had it just couldn't be true. I told them I would tell them everything when I was more certain. The rest of our forces were too awed by meeting The Gathering to inquire what we had learned. Our Rhinodons were standing together, and someone had picketed them for us. We watered and checked our mounts over before mounting.

I looked ahead, and it felt like the biggest obstacle was next. We could weaken the cloud by using it as a source of energy, but even with the Star Glass I wasn't certain that I knew how to destroy a force of destruction. I had just been given a clue, but that wasn't a clear path forward. What was harmonious order and how did I generate it? Or was I supposed to change the nature of the Chaos itself?

I asked Mikaal if he understood what that meant, and he shook his head and looked a bit concerned. He was hoping that I knew. Without giving any context, I mentally requested that if anyone had knowledge of "harmonious order" that they come talk to me. After that, we were on the move again.

The flyers were already aloft and started fanning out first, looking for signs of the enemy, followed quickly by Rangers. All was quiet except for the sounds of a large force on the move. Even the air was still. Exactly the opposite of what one would expect, the closer we got to the inclement weather, the more muted sounds became. There were two points at which random screams or squawks began as some unfortunate creature got too close and was captured and changed. We edged into the forest, and the trees blocked our view, so I began to communicate with the Lancers as to what was ahead.

For the first part of our approach, they didn't have much to share, but as we closed the distance, an unexpected report came in. Roiling clouds of doom covered all Sorra as far as the eye could see at flying height, except that to the right of our course there was a clear gap in the storm. It was as if someone had taken a pie cutter and carved out a large slice in the middle of the pie. The Lady Lancer couldn't see what was at ground level as we were too far away, and we'd still need to break through the field of madness between where we were and the break.

We adjusted our direction to aim for this new and unexpected landmark. More screams sounded to our left, this time from a creature that was sentient. One of our Rangers had gotten close, and the storm reached out and enveloped him. Three mages were sent out to rescue him as we continued along.

"You are the first group of Mages I have asked to restore someone. Please let me know as soon as you are successful, or if you have any trouble. You're not alone out here," I said.

"Yes, First Mage" they said in unison before riding away.

A few minutes later they reported that they were able to perform a reversal spell using the power of Chaos, weakening the storm in that area. Just as they finished updating us, we walked through the last few trees into a glade. We were face to face with our faceless formless foe.

The first time seeing this menace directly I died a little on the inside but tried to keep it from showing. It was a wall of unnaturally dark fog which moved against, not with, any breeze. It was shot through with random flashes of barely perceptible colors. It was clearly demarcated from the surrounding area, and yet the line flexed and pulled as if it was straining against itself to break free of its self-imposed prison. Such a thing is wholly unnatural and paradoxical. Its very existence was a continual contradiction. It felt malignant and unstoppable, and yet brittle as if the impossibility it embodied would tear it apart if struck just so.

A shiver ran across our force as we faced it, which it echoed in reverse. It was a line of anticipation from a thing that had no feelings. Since I had no experience with the Chaos Cloud itself, I didn't have a firm plan. I needed to think and try a couple things. I called for the mage squad leaders to come to me.

They approached silently as we dismounted. There were four troops of a dozen mages, and each troop had four tri's. One would work reversals, one would drain energy from side effect lightning or Chaos, while the other defended the pair. All three could perform each spell and rotate at need. It was a good system, and I was pleased with what they had come up with. The four leaders were Jeen, Darra,

Beele, and Evert. The first two were Norans and the second two Garanth.

"The magic school did well. Did they come up with anything to smash this wall here?" I asked.

"Many, many ideas were presented. Almost all were discarded," Darra spoke. Her voice was softer than her weathered visage.

Evert jumped in, "The Mackta gave us an ancient spell. He gave each of us a grain of sand containing a single immutable truth. The spell directs that truth in a line that is said to cut through confusion and doubt like a sharp knife through sweetmellon. He didn't promise that it would work but was confident enough to give us irreplaceable bits of a broken critter as our focal point."

"My mentor is a healer," Jeen added. "She likened the Chaos Cloud to an infection and created a spell that forces the invader from our world into a fold in space in the same way our endless bags work. If it works properly, it will push the cloud into a place that is said to be the origin point of all destruction in the worlds."

"These spells along with the Chaos drains you taught us were to be backups to the great magic within you," Beele finished.

"I would like you to teach this second spell to Mikaal, Coral, and me. It would be best to be as prepared as possible."

For the next twenty minutes we learned the healer's spell for banishing a chaotic infection into another realm. Once we understood it, I stepped away to communicate with the Star Glass.

In my mind I created a chair and sat in it. Even though the me in my mind didn't have any weight or got tired, there was something comforting about sitting in an easy chair. I opened communication with the magical artifact by inquiring if its creators had given it a spell for destroying a Chaos Cloud.

The response it provided was laced with urgency. It couldn't provide me much in the way of detail, or not in a way that I was able to understand, but it was created to fight against a force of massive destruction. Chaos was such a force. I explained the spell the Tiiaanians provided and planned to attempt it on a large scale.

The Star Glass didn't have any spells or strategies for dealing with bounded destruction fields (as it referred to the phenomenon) nor did it have any understanding of harmonious order. I was able to determine that it had a process for changing the nature of a thing, but it required a pattern to overlay on the target. I filed this away and stepped back to reality.

When I moved, the conversation behind me faded and footsteps fell in behind me. I walked toward the edge of the storm, keeping watch to ensure there were no bursts of movement. Walking towards it made me dizzy and disoriented as what was before me confounded the senses. I stopped and ordered the Star Glass to begin pushing disorder through a rift in time and space.

A line formed directly between my location and the cloud. It wasn't dark so much as an absence of light. It yawned wider like a giant mouth and took a mouthful of storm. My watch dinged, and the rift nearly blinked out as the Star Glass ran low on power. I told it to use the cloud like a battery, and the wall of weird before us shrank back. The rift strengthened and began taking bite after bite of Chaos. It seemed to be working, but progress was agonizingly slow.

I looked over my shoulder and spotted Jeen closest to me.

"Each of you take up a position to my left or my right and use the same spell to widen the gap. Let's see how quickly we can break through."

"Yessir!" a chorus of voices sounded back.

We proceeded in this way for about twenty minutes until we were surrounded on both left and right by the cloud wall. We were advancing at a slow walk. As the rear of our ranks reached the original location the storm had occupied, we noticed it was trying to close in behind us. We had to form a crescent and work on three fronts simultaneously. This wasn't going as well as I'd hoped. The artifact could go on this way for an indeterminate amount of time, but living beings were already sweating with the effort of keeping such a powerful spell active for such a long period.

Creaane reported that we were approximately one third of the way to the passage we sought. I didn't expect this to be easy, but this didn't feel right. I sent a mental command to all to begin a slow retreat while keeping the spells active.

Our forces had been following closely, and it took some time for so many people to reverse course. Once I took a few steps back, I was able to see what I hadn't noticed at first. What was left behind when using this spell wasn't just an absence of the offending weather pattern. The area was just desolate. When we had used the storm as fuel for our magic, causing the storm to cease to be, the landscape left behind was twisted and changed, but there was still something left to save. In this case we were leaving behind nothing. The nothing left behind, assuming that we were banishing not only the Chaos, but also the ground, trees, and possibly twisted animals...there seemed no recovery for the land this way.

"I had the frontline mages stop their spells leaving only mine and those mages working to keep us from becoming trapped active. I was concerned that once we stopped advancing, Chaos would surge forward to retake the space it had occupied and possibly capture our forces. One by one their spells winked out of existence.

The edges of the storm, now uneven and raw from being chomped on held for breathless moments before beginning a slow movement towards us and the original line we had crossed. Thankfully we were moving faster than it was, so we kept the minimum number of mages active to keep the storm at bay until we returned to where we began.

Once back safely in the glade, most of our forces were glad that we had pushed the storm back at all and no one had been harmed. I was crestfallen, partially at the failure, but even more that in our ignorance we might have permanently damaged Sorra, even in a small way.

Coral was able to sense my unease, whether through our connection or by watching me, and came to my side. Vaminous strode up shortly after she took my arm.

"Why did we retreat?" he asked.

"Two reasons. Our progress was too slow to allow our forces to make it all the way through. Couple that with the fact that the method we were using was causing worse harm to the land than the thing we are trying to remove… In my land we would call that the cure being worse than the disease."

This was the first time he listened to every word I said before responding since I'd met him. He gave a curt nod of agreement.

"We will rest and prepare to advance again when you are ready, Aaron," he said, turning as he spoke and throwing my name over his shoulder.

Soon the rest of our forces had withdrawn a respectable distance away, leaving only my original group with me.

"Granalis. In all of your travels with your former master, did anyone ever defeat a Chaos Cloud?"

"No. Even his great enemy is said to have retreated in the face of this threat," he said gravely.

"Hold on. He has an enemy? Perhaps we could work with them," I said, suddenly excited.

"Definitely not." Granalis struggled to add more a few times before he finally was able to continue. "I have heard from more than one source that his enemy is unredeemable."

"Well, well, well. That is interesting, if not as helpful as I'd hoped."

"Excuse me White Mage?" the voice, the speaker, and the form of address all came as a surprise.

A smallish Noran had walked up behind Mikaal from the direction of the support caravan. She was the youngest Noran I'd seen, though I wasn't good at judging the age of one of their race. Her face was small, fair and unlined, and she gave off the impression of a nearly ethereal being. Once I realized that she was addressing me by the title I had been given this morning, I responded.

"Yes, young lady? What can we do for you? What is your name?" I asked as gently as possible.

"I am Deloraa. You asked that if anyone had information on harmonious order to come to you. I am not sure if what I am thinking will help, but I have been thinking of nothing else since I heard your voice."

She seemed uncertain, but I was hopeful. "Go on."

"I am one of the few Noran musicians in Tiiaan and as far as I know, the only musician among our forces. Musical harmony is the intertwining voices of several instruments, supporting each other. Order is when everything is right and correct and the way it should be. So, to me, it seems that harmonious order could be created wherever there are many working together. It sounds silly now that I've said it out loud to you," she said, ducking her head in dismay.

Coral unexpectedly let go of my arm and went to her side. "It makes sense to me. I am glad you were brave enough to come to us."

"You may be onto something," I said. "Give me a second to think." With that, I dropped to the ground to sit and dived back into my mind.

Alone in my mind I paced, wishing that I had some talent for music. It wasn't as if we needed all our forces to sing, and we didn't have instruments. What did we have? We had people. People with minds, hearts, and stories, if not souls. How could we turn people's lives into what we needed?

I thought back to how I'd used colored auras to understand magic. Could I do something similar here? I asked Mikaal mentally if Sorran magic had a way to capture or record thoughts and feelings.

He quickly told me that many had tried to do such a thing, but none had success.

I turned to the computer in my mind and added a new peripheral. I now had a helmet with leads touching my skull, capable of recording what I was receiving telepathically. I set the computer to record both the data as well as a visual representation of the thoughts and emotions.

Crossing my mental fingers, I decided to perform a test. I messaged Deloraa and asked her to do me the honor of sharing with me her most precious memory. I asked her to send me everything she could remember about that moment and how it made her feel. She seemed startled at the contact but agreed.

Thoughts of being at home amongst the trees, traveling to see her family after a long separation. She felt the sun beams peeping through the trees as she swung leaving warm trails across her body. She felt the happy anticipation of reunion with those she held most dear. She felt satisfaction at the work she had accomplished that allowed her to go home. The scene ended as she landed at the door and entered the dwelling where she had grown up, fully embraced in seconds by her parents and sister.

I thanked her for sharing her beautiful thoughts and turned to see the outcome. Data that meant nothing to me was saved in a file and displayed on screen, but it was the visual representation of her thoughts that made me most hopeful. Lines of various colors and intensity swam in motion in a three-dimensional space. I thought the image would be static, but instead it was full of life. Her life.

So far so great. Now the bigger test would be if others could do the same and if the whole would be harmonious. I asked Granalis to be next and started the recording again. For a being who had lost everything, the intensity of his sending caught me off guard.

He was in his roost, holding his wife closely as their first children were born. There was a storm outside, but the place he had made for his new family was warm and strong. He felt his wife's joy as strong as his own and the first hints of budding consciousness from his children. The first little head peeked up and he locked eyes with his eldest daughter just as vertical lightning struck outside, searing the moment forever in his mind.

It appeared that this process was going to be heart wrenching for me. I thanked him for his story and checked to make sure it was recorded too. There was a second pattern joining the first in the faintly outlined box the computer was painting with the life stories of those who shared. Neither brighter nor darker, the starting point of this pattern was from a different direction and ended in a far-off corner of the space, but between those points they came together. They danced and flowed together beautifully. They intertwined and somehow made each other stronger. These two beings from different worlds and different stages of life could with their shared stories make a thing of nearly unending beauty.

One by one I called on friends and strangers, mages and warriors, and all represented sexes to share their best memory or moment. Each time the data meant nothing… but the pattern! The pattern took my breath away afresh with every new addition.

I didn't know how much time had passed when I finished, but it was nearly dark. During this time the camp was attacked by small numbers of corrupted creatures. The Lancers took down an attempted incursion by three large perhaps sentient monstrosities that appeared from behind us. They had been hit with reversal spells, but there had been no effect. Vaminous suggested that they must have been brought here with our enemy and were therefore sent by him to test our strength.

I stood and Coral pressed food into my hands. I ate without thinking and when finished, contacted all our forces and told them that I wanted to share with what we created together. When it seemed we were as safe as an advancing army could be standing outside the enemy's stronghold, I sent them all what I had been seeing. I explained that each part was one of their shared experiences and that this whole was all of us together. When I stopped sending, I could see that they were all impacted as much as I had been.

I didn't want to hesitate any longer. I called to the Star Glass, holding it up on its chain in my right hand and commanded it to take both the image and the data as the pattern to use for its Nature Transformation Spell and told it to apply it to the Chaos Cloud before us. It paused so long that I felt like I'd broken it, and then I saw and felt the magic go out. It was strong and yet subtle. It did not strike the edge so much as overshadow and envelope it. It didn't destroy or create; it altered and shaped. It gave purpose to the Chaos, and life to the void. All the paradox and enigma were spoken to, answered, and resolved. It was set to rights, and the goodness we unleashed was contagious.

The artifact's influence was as tall as the Cloud had been and about as wide as Pakky was long, but within ten minutes of the initial change the impact covered all the cloud we could see. It was our pattern, and yet more. As it took over the Chaos, it restored what it touched. It shimmered in the night like all the lights of a thousand Christmases for a few minutes more, and while it did, it brought balance and restoration. When its work concluded, it faded away.

A collective sigh broke free from those assembled. All the breath that we'd been holding as we faced something so vile for which we had no answer escaped at once. The light of day was no more. There was nothing we could do but wait until the Counter Chaos Cloud overtook and removed the barrier from our path. We decided to set up camp. The orders had just been given when a wail split the still evening air from our right.

Since there was no Chaos cloud in that direction, that was the last direction we would have anticipated an attack from. The Lightning Lancers were still aloft and alert, but they couldn't see anything more than a stirring of the foliage amongst the trees. Unfortunately, my merry little band was the closest to the continued howls and cries, so we prepared to defend ourselves from the unknown once again.

Suddenly the ground in front of us erupted at our faces as a mass of corrupted rodents leapt at us en masse. I had my spear in my hand and my phantom hands at the ready. Instinct saved us from the first attack. I saw things flying at us and swatted the lot of them right to left. Upward of thirty glowing-eyed rat things went flying away, straight into the receding storm. Each of them flickered as chaotic beings flew uncontrollably into an area where normalcy was being restored. Their shrieking trailed off as they hit, but we didn't have time to investigate further as a second volley of cannon rats came flying at our face.

Fireballs and arrows met a few, but a blur in the air obscured the rest for a split second. Bisected enemy vermin fell at our feet, and suddenly Divide was before us. They arrived silently and did their job with blinding efficiency. Still more howls announced the coming of more disorder-enhanced rodents, and it seemed like we might be overrun. Rangers and Breakers broke the next attack with Steampistolas thinning the herd, and the remainder batted away with short staffs.

More were on their way, but I had a second to think now that there were other defenders. Why were these creatures not restored? I nearly hit myself in the forehead as the answer came to me, but instead used the motion to flick a flying devil rat toward the rapidly receding restoration field. These creatures must have been changed but then left the area affected by the Chaos Cloud. The change we made would only affect the evil storm itself and anything currently inside of it. Anything or anyone who left the area would not be changed back.

"Try to fling these things into the Order Storm!" I shouted to those around me. "It should turn them back into whatever they were before."

A chorus of affirmatives sounded back, and fewer bodies hit the ground as a result. One of the not-so-little beasties managed to bound through two Breakers and sink its teeth into the leg of a Ranger while he was reloading. He had the presence of mind to stab it in the head with the arrow in his hand, but the single bite mark showed a strong Chaos infection had been transmitted. Dark splotches began coursing across the man's skin. He tore his pant leg open and was about to stab himself with a fresh arrow as if to remove poison. Before he could damage himself further, I started a reversal spell on him. After he stopped screaming, he was healthy again, if weak.

Lancers began raking the ground with lightning in an attempt to encourage all remaining rodents to turn from their attack and run towards the dueling weather patterns. This was partially successful. Chaos creatures didn't care for self-preservation, but the lightning did blind them and caused them to turn away from the source of light. Granalis was a blur of white, grabbing Chaos vermin that got through and dropping them into the receding storm for deliverance. Mikaal and Coral took my words literally and were nearly dancing around, hands aglow pointing at advancing enemies and where they should go. At the completion of each motion, the advancing creature would fling into the air in an arc towards the restoration field. Their laughter as they worked did serve to lighten the mood.

Between all our efforts, we managed to survive the tide of rodent attack. The whole event was around fifteen minutes long but felt like hours.

The danger passed, Vaminous and Creaane assigned guard rotations, and we slept.

Chapter 38
Great Start.
But How Will the Day End?

The night watch passed with only minimal activity. Morning broke clear and early. Everything was peaceful, sparkling with dew and seemed newly made. Perhaps it was… newly remade. There was almost no evidence of last night's fight. It had either been cleaned up by our forces or carried off as a part of nature's process. The day was fresh with promise, and we'd had our first significant success.

Conversation was friendly and lively as we ate, and it struck me again how everyone seemed to get along and respect each other, regardless of duty, rank, or position. Food was set out in the center of camp, and while we were offered to have it brought to us, we, like all the others, walked to mess.

Food was provided to meet all the needs of each race. It wasn't as delicious as it had been in Tiiaan, but far better than I expected. There wasn't any seating, so people stood or sat together in small impromptu groups and would move from place to place as one conversation ended so they could strike up another.

Creaane had apparently eaten earlier and resumed her duties. Now she contacted me and offered for me to come up and see things from their vantage point. I excused myself with a kiss on the cheek to Coral, who had moved around with me as we ate, and started to platform up to the Lancers. Even then the SeaWind Princess effortlessly stepped boldly beside me though she could not see if my air surfboard was large enough for her. She believed it was and acted on it. As we rose upward, I marveled at her afresh.

One of the airships saw us and made to intercept us. We rose to stand beside her, and Creanne didn't speak but swept her arm to indicate the vista below. There wasn't a cloud in the sky nor destructive fog on the ground. We could tell where the path had been in the storm as it was the only area that wasn't pristine.

We didn't know how or even if we would win this battle, but where we had left our mark Sorra was even more amazing than before. We stood silently appreciating the moment as long as we thought we could, then thanked the Sky Maiden for sharing this with us and headed back down.

The Sorran forces quickly and efficiently struck camp. Orders were given and scouts sent out. We mounted our Rhinodons and sounded the advance. We walked through another short stretch of forest before it gave way to foothills. It was in the foothills that we began seeing signs that the enemy was not gone, nor inactive. We reached the clearly visible line where goodness ended and darkness had yet to be vanquished. In one stretch there was new clean growth and healthy wildlife and the next, everything was withered and desolate. Bodies, both old and new, littered our way. One of the younger mages attempted a reversal spell on one Chaos-covered form that appeared to have been a Garanth. The tarnish of destruction fell away, but life did not return.

We walked onward until we reached a series of mounds that bounded a wide road strewn with debris and the charred remains of many OrOboid. At the sight of so many of their people fallen and left to rot, a collective gasp came from Zandoo and the others. None knew what the mounds were or why they were there, but they had been in place long enough to be covered in a scrubby brown plant life somewhere between grass and moss. While we all wanted to know what had happened here, it didn't seem we could do anything

Great Start. But How Will the Day End?

for these people, so we continued on. A small number of individuals composed of every race and position stopped as we slowly advanced and collected bodies, burying them outside the irregular border of knolls that traced our steps.

Looking ahead, our current course ended at a crystalline edifice jutting from the side of a mid-sized mountain. Based on the descriptions I had heard of OrOboid buildings and the craftsmanship I'd seen from them to date, I was shocked at the sight. Where light should be refracted from the walls and towers making them dazzling to look at, the sunlight seemed weak near this. A faint violet hue was the only light escaping.

We were walking toward a mountain, but unexpectedly our way began to decline sharply and widen. Nothing moved anywhere, and the stench of decay was so strong that some of our support staff were overcome. We reached the lowest point and were about to start up the other side of the earthen bowl we found ourselves in when the stillness we were cloaked in shifted into mayhem.

Around the rim in all directions creatures unlike anything seen in Sorra began bursting forth from the ground. There were an uncountable number of pouncing and spitting feline forms bearing armor, a dozen drakes, and an assortment of turned Sorran wildlife. Each mound of earth we'd passed split in two, issuing flying enemies from within. Some of these were Chaos Converted birds or insects while others were clockwork or reminiscent of dragons.

Vaminous called for healers and support staff to move into the center of our position. Mages and warriors dispersed along the edges to protect the most vulnerable. Creaane and her Lancers were already engaged in dogfights with the aerial enemies but were disciplined enough to keep a reserve positioned back-to-back over our main force.

Lightning split the air, and it began to rain Corruptobirds and automatons. The dragonlike fliers were another story. They were fast and strong. When they were hit it just made them angry. Thankfully they didn't spit fire, or things would have been over quickly. One of our airships was pounced on and the balloon torn to shreds. Dragon and Lancer became hopelessly entangled and fell to the ground in a heap.

Creaane was obviously thinking on her feet. She was being chased by a dragon thing and doing very well considering how much more maneuverable the beast was as compared to her craft. She faked it out, pulling up hard and dropped her repair goop in its face. It went from fierce to hopelessly sticky and unable to fly in a flash. Two more Lancers were dropped by lizardkind, and I decided to focus my efforts on them for now. I reached out with four mental hands, grabbing dragons and pushing them higher and then smashing them together before flinging them away. I did this twice and looked for more of them, but the last two in the air were being dealt with by our air forces. I wanted to help but thought I'd do more harm than good.

Coral and Mikaal were dropping fliers with bow and magic. Granalis was gargoyled up and ready to pounce on anything that got close. The ground forces were about to enter the fray. We were within the circle of fighters, so I continued to look for where I could make the most impact. I looked around, smashing one of the drakes before it ate a Ranger. Several reversal spells were cast on the Sorran animals barreling toward us. We were holding our own so far, but there were twice as many of them as there were of us, and to make matters worse, more aggressors continued to flow from the rim and the mounds.

I turned just in time to see a Catling pounce on Granalis, who was busy pounding on a drake. The look on the feline face made me chortle when it bit into what it thought was flesh and found stone.

Another three bounded over the line of defenders and towards us. One of them was crisped by Lightning courtesy of an observant Lancer. The other two looked like they were going to surprise Mikaal and Coral. I swung my spear like a bat and kept Coral safe with a

Great Start. But How Will the Day End?

home run. She blasted three enemies at the same time it took me to bat away the one. I was going to swat the one coming at Mikaal away, but Divide got to it first.

Six OrOboid roamed the edges, spears flashing and blades flying. They were hungry for vengeance and a desire to keep their families alive. Their fighting style in a free-for-all like this battle was turning into was very effective. They were so fast and nimble that only the Catlings could hope to keep up at all. Kaalesh appeared in my view long enough to land with her spear in the skull of a drake and then leapt away before I knew it.

Despite how strong we were and how well we fought, the weight of numbers bore us backward. I couldn't tell how many, but I knew we had lost more than a few of our group. I had the Star Glass rain down molten rock on the rim, and the rush of attackers there slowed some, but it wasn't enough. I couldn't see the mounds to attack them from where I stood, and there were far too many airborne enemies for me to consider flying. Any highly destructive action I took was likely to do as much damage to those on my side as to the enemy.

Two more Lancers fell, fully engulfed in flames. I was using mental hands and my spear alternately as I dealt with enemies both near and far. Coral and I were standing back-to-back. The battle was so close that I could barely use my spear and had to switch to my sword.

Things weren't looking good for team Sorra. I was pondering taking Coral and flying up when the ground began to tremble again. Four clefts tore the ground apart, one at each cardinal point of the compass. The enemy was in a frenzy, or they were just crazy, and did not notice. A startling number of Moalean emerged from these new openings. These new arrivals tore into the enemies with abandon. A contingent of the Moalean used their magical figurines along with their natural digger aptitude as sappers to block off the enemy's arrival passages.

Three or four Moalean lost their lives in the process, but they were able to prevent any new ground troops from taking the field.

Coral and I returned to the support of our remaining air forces, knocking out dragons and birds. The Lancers had no more reserves, and one quarter of our original airships were down.

A tug at my right sleeve nearly caused me to skewer her until I recognized Junean's voice.

"I told you we'd be there when you needed us, didn't I?"

I nearly scooped her up in a bear hug in my excitement and gratitude, but I fought my reaction down into a big cheesy grin instead.

"Your timing was excellent. Things were not going well. You brought a lot of friends. I'm glad to see you."

"I can't wait to catch up, but for now we have work to do," she said, digging back out of sight.

The battle continued. Now that the trap laid for us was sprung and the tables turned, the Sorrans were driven by a desire to save all they held dear, and they fought savagely. These people who had never known war but had trained and been ready because of the stories passed down from darker times were amazing to me. Not that I really had time to think about it at that moment...

One of the tunnels that our surprise reinforcements had destroyed came alive again with enemies fighting to get free of their unexpected entombment. Even with nearly every combatant fully engaged, only a drake and a Catling broke into the melee before a barrage of magic and projectiles covered their route once again.

The number of aerial combatants had decreased, so I charged Granalis with watching Coral's back and took to the sky using the same flying coffin conveyance as before. This allowed me to circle around the battle and maximize my effectiveness. The Star Glass was fully charged, and I instructed it to reverse all Chaos-laced opponents. Immediately I saw two dozen reversal glows spring up around the battlefield. Next, I turned my attention to the fliers.

Great Start. But How Will the Day End?

The Lancers had fought bravely but were outmatched by the combination of large agile combatants and the unknown quantity of clockwork fliers. The remaining airships were mostly on the defensive. I stayed far enough away so that I wasn't noticed and began smashing dragons out of the air with my non-corporeal fists. I smashed several out of the air as if I was spiking them across a volleyball net, right back into the top of the ridge from where they had emerged.

I got a bit closer so that I could better see the smaller automatons. I grabbed one with two giant hands and broke it in two. Something much smaller than a Moalean seemed to be alive within and dropped to the ground once its ship was destroyed. I crushed any of those surviving enemies like eggs for the next two minutes.

The tide was back in our favor in the skies, so I looked to try to do the same for those that walked below. Unfortunately for me, one of the dragons was heartier than I gave it credit for. I realized that about the time that it pounced on me from on high and bore me to the ground. Since I was encased in a mental projection, I wasn't badly wounded, just shaken like a dog with a bone and dribbled across the field. Once I determined which way was up, I raised my spear as it came to pounce on me again, ending that encounter.

When I stood on the ridge and surveyed the scene below, things were looking much better. No more invaders had appeared. Tiiaanian forces were mopping up stragglers, with here and there an enemy being swallowed alive by the ground, courtesy of the Moalean. I flew back and found Coral, Mikaal, and Junean talking. Granalis was still having too much fun hunting to join them.

Tibbeus walked out of the ground, dripping loose soil from his fur like a human would shed water when walking from the ocean just as I was dropping from the sky.

"We brought every Moalean remaining on Sorra who could fight, save two dozen who we left to protect those who couldn't fight," Junean was saying.

"Every settlement, old or new, has been evacuated or overrun," Tibbeus added.

"How did you know where to find us?" Coral asked.

"We have been getting updates from some of our friends at the Magic School," Junean answered while rubbing a statuette over a cut in her forearm absently.

"We used our Farspeakers," she added, waving a statuette that looked like a mouth and an ear connected by a fine arced line.

Guards were posted from the least wounded of every group. Everybody else began searching for those who could be saved and bringing them to the healers. Enemies were either finished off, or if it appeared they were sentient, frozen and bagged to be addressed later, just as we had done with Tibbeus. He shivered every time a body was shoved into a bag. This was not something the Sorrans had done before, but they found the process amusing and made a game out of "who can bag the most enemies."

Those who could not be saved were taken over the ridge and buried. I helped with this task, partly because I felt guilty for everyone lost, and partly because with my mental projections I could dig a lot of graves quickly and without any adverse effects, like tiredness.

Even though a lot of the Lightning Lancers had been damaged, they did not lose many lives. Creaane's Lancers repaired most of the damaged airships. In the end, they were able to get three quarters of their original numbers back in the air. One more ship than they had pilots.

Food was being prepared and passed around, first to the healers and mages, since they expended the most energy and had to regain their strength to be able to heal or fight. We worked hard for three hours before we could even consider advancing. The Moalean agreed to continue traveling and fighting with us. Vaminous, Coral, Mikaal and I decided to advance out of the bowl trap we were in before

Great Start. But How Will the Day End?

attempting to camp for the night. Not one person wanted to find out the next surprise prepared for us in the darkness.

With only two hours remaining until sundown, we set ourselves in motion again, climbing up over the rim and around collapsed tunnels. One stretch was so demolished that we would have either had to backtrack and find another way or build a bridge. Instead, I placed a platform down large enough for our forces to cross and asked them to step out in faith that the air was solid where I told them to walk. Once everyone was across, I flew back to the front of our group and surveyed for a place to camp.

I mistrusted the obvious clearing we came to along the way to the Darkening Towers which were formerly occupied by the OrOboid. Instead, I played bulldozer and flattened a copse of scraggly trees, only after making sure there weren't any OasisAnts, and directed our forces briefly away from the path to our final destination.

Chapter 39
What Do You Do if the Ghost Catches You?

We rested poorly that night in the shadow of the enemy's fortress. Several other small skirmishes were fought during this time. When I laid down and closed my eyes, I could only recount the battle just completed and replay the loss of many lives. Each one felt as if I had killed them myself. I knew that wasn't so and that they had been here of their own free will, but I was leading them and had brought them into a trap. I wasn't certain that I wouldn't walk them into another even more deadly in the morning.

Coral was exhausted and slept quietly nearby. Mikaal was meeting with the other mages planning for tomorrow. Two stars of OrOboid families head-to-head were on the periphery. Granalis curled up on a tree trunk at my head. After a time lying there, he spoke quietly.

"So, Aaron, you can't sleep." He whispered directly into my ear.

"It seems not," I said reaching up and scratching where his breath caused a tickle.

Granalis' face appeared above mine, peering into my eyes. "You are not lying there feeling guilty over those we lost, are you?"

The eye contact forced me to think about my answer before responding. "Yes. Yes, I am."

"I have heard you say that you'd give your life to save this place. You meant that, right?"

What Do You Do if the Ghost Catches You?

I grabbed Granalis' small form and sat up, placing him in front of me. "Yes. I would."

He stretched himself up to his full height, about as tall as my elbows. "Should all the people of Sorra feel guilty that a man from another world died here in their place if that happens?"

I sighed. "No. I wouldn't want that."

"Each of those people felt the same as you do. They have people that they were willing to die to protect. You didn't kill them, and you can't protect everyone." He jumped sideways onto my backpack to get closer to my eye level. "Besides that, in all the time that I was a prisoner to the master, you have already come further toward stopping him than anyone else. You should celebrate the victories you've won and stay hopeful. This is the first time since I lost everyone that I have had hope."

"Thank you Granalis." I had to stop myself from scratching him behind the ears. He looked like a pet but spoke like a comrade. "You're a good friend. I'm glad you're with us. I wish that I could undo all that was done to your people."

We rose three hours later to wan daylight and the ground shaking. There was no evidence of what was causing it. It went on for a good twenty minutes before stopping abruptly. Since we were all awake, we ate and prepared to meet the day.

The Lightning Lancers set out to scout us a safe way forward. They went all the way to the foot of the mountain, to a vast crevasse within its base without incident. If there were enemies or traps, they weren't detectable from the air.

Those of us on foot or mounted began our march, avoiding anything that looked like a likely trap. Nothing assailed us directly. The ground collapsed suddenly, engulfing a Ranger and two members of Divide when we were halfway to the mountain from where we began. The Moalean were able to recover them before they suffocated. Junean came to report that when they dug to save the

The Journals of Aaron the White

Tiiaanian fighters, they found that the ground ahead was porous, as if something had eaten away at the ground. Moalean warriors would be traveling below ground and reporting to us the safest paths. This would hopefully keep any more of us from being buried alive.

This meant our progress was slower than normal, but by lunchtime we were standing in front of the yawning expanse that reminded me of childhood stories of Dragon hoards. It was wide enough for most of our column to pass through and tall enough to allow six Lancers to fly single file with their wings folded in.

In we went. Six Cloudships that wouldn't be able to enter paired up and began making rounds across the outside of the mountain and toward the dark crystal castle on the rear side. They would look for and alert us to danger as well as take out any enemies they could find. Six more would serve as a rearguard and watch the entrance.

We were as prepared as we could be for anything we could think of. We strode boldly if cautiously into the darkness that deepened more quickly than the lack of sunlight could account for. The Lancers above us lit up their balloons, casting shifting shadows weakly into the path ahead. Columns of stone jutted from the ground like fangs in the jaws of a snaggle-toothed monster. Tremors rose and fell again, and we were concerned that the mountain might fall on us, but aside from a rain of small rocks, the mountain held.

When the shaking ceased a flurry of tiny bodies broke free from the walls and roof ahead and flooded the space between the lit Lancers above us and those of us below. These were the flying DarkRats native to Sorra. Most of them passed us in peace in their natural state, but some number intermingled with the rest were partially corrupted. One of the remaining Lancer's balloons was pierced by their claws and blew sideways into an overhanging ledge, dangling from her deflated balloon into the tide of flying vermin. She didn't take this well. Lightning blinded everyone as she carved a winged rat free path in front of her.

What Do You Do if the Ghost Catches You?

Not a few of the incoming DarkRats, no longer able to see, flew into walls or people, knocking themselves out in the process. Once the wave receded, the pilot climbed up her rigging to assess the damage. The craft was unrecoverable. Creaane messaged that she would be on foot from now on. She pulled the wreckage up out of the way of the rest of her team with a tool I'd not seen before. Minutes later she was among us, carrying her craft's weapon. She reminded me briefly of a four-armed female Rambo holding the gun that was nearly bigger than she was.

Those with Chaos wounds were treated by the mages on the move as best they could, and we pressed onward. Another twenty minutes of creeping through the dark and the way widened. Soon we were in a cavern, the opposite side of which was lit with torches and abuzz with activity.

"They comes!" the screeching voice of the enemy's spliced monster rang out.

"Destroy them by order of the Master!" the burbling voice added.

A barrage of magic came at us from every conceivable angle along with two score projectiles of various types. The Moalean in the vanguard reacted as one before I even saw the danger. Interlocking shields sprang into place between the attack and our people, blocking ninety percent of the damage. A ranger in front of me took an arrow in the knee and fell screaming, ending his adventuring.

Thankfully the Lancers were slightly behind the main group due to the difficulty navigating the narrow cavern and were spared in the first attack. Soon though they came around a bend, one flying as high as possible while a second flew low. Both of them arrived, true to their namesakes, driving forward with their lances made of lightning. Electricity raked the walls and peak, causing hidden attackers to fall screaming from their perches.

Vaminous called a full charge. The front ranks spread out, meeting heavy resistance. Since our arrival was anticipated it didn't seem prudent to make ourselves one large target by keeping ranks. Within ten minutes we were in full melee. The enemy was represented by more Catlings, Dragonlikes, Clockwork metal men, and heart wrenchingly Chaos changed OrOboid.

The glow of magic was everywhere, nearly blinding me. Reversal spells and fireballs were the most popular choices. I ordered the Star Glass to reverse as many OrOboid as quickly as possible, which added aborted lightning strikes to the mayhem. I did remember to instruct the artifact to drain only side-effect lightning so as not to handicap the remaining Lancers.

Granalis the gargoyle bounded over my head, shaking off arrows and magical attacks as he caught sight of the mage that had bound him to the enemy's service. Zeedox the binder was a Dragonman. As hard as the Drakes had been to take down, Zeedox was quite obviously killed upon the impact of Granalis stone body landing on his skull. The look of freedom on my friend's face as the Geas fell away from him and he was well and truly free of all that had bound him was beatific.

I should have known the enemy wouldn't hesitate to attack his own forces, but I didn't foresee the danger. One minute we were holding our own, perhaps even winning, and the next doom struck like a serpent.

A deep violet mist seeped into the cavern. At its touch each being quailed in terror and lost control of their bodies. Pain was etched into their features, and horror that rejected all hope was in their eyes. The vile fog rose along the walls and filled the room. I heard Coral gasp and turned to see her loveliness become a rictus mask, just seconds before I felt the caress of the Devil mist. In the center of the space, the mist coalesced into our quarry, who now became our captor.

"Aaron! Have you no respect for your elders?" His voice and mocking laughter reverberated in the chamber and drove into the core of my being.

Chapter 40
Reunion

All the world was horror. Had we come here to lose in an instant? Was I to blame for this tragedy, both now and in the past? I couldn't save the people I loved before, so why had I thought I could this time? I was powerless against this force. My body wouldn't respond. My mind was spiraling in a funnel of self-doubt and loathing. My lungs would scarcely draw a breath. My eyes were locked on the face of a woman I would give anything for as she wept in agony.

In my physical helplessness my spirit rose within me, and I cried out for help from a source I hadn't thought of since coming to Sorra. Forgotten faith connected me for an instant to my Creator, and the pain and fear became distant as if happening to someone else far away.

A feeling of calm and of being where I was meant to be enwrapped me. I was not only called here. I was also sent. These facts did not mean that it would be easy, nor that success was assured. I could not give up when things were hardest.

I wanted to stay in this moment of surety and purpose, but there was a shadow cast across my life that I had to free myself and everyone else from. I returned to the pain. I forced myself to remember the moment before and that people were counting on me. I turned my head away from the agonized look on Coral's face and toward the voice.

"Oh! You can still move, can you? That's surprising. This combination of effects has never failed before, but neither has the Chaos Cloud."

He continued ruminating to himself, but I decided it was time for action. Regardless of who this used to be, now he was someone who was causing harm. Perhaps if I could knock him out then his power would cease. I called forth a fist and brought it down on his head. Of course, being that he was bodiless it went right through him, making a loud whump sound as it slammed into the cave floor.

"Haven't gotten much brighter, have you? You can't harm me. Oh...but I can harm you!" he shrieked as the pain, especially around my heart intensified.

I struggled to regain control of my faculties. I tried diving into my mind, which did allow me to divorce myself from the agony to some degree. What was I thinking trying to bonk a ghost on the noggin? That was a boneheaded move. Not only should I have known that you can't squash a spirit, but I gave away any chance of surprise I had.

How do you stop a demented soul? Exorcism? I was no priest. What about that movie I watched when I was a kid where they used science to catch ghosts? Would that work? If anything was worth a try, that was.

I created a trap like I remembered it looking and gun like they'd had, a proto something or other. Like I'd done with the laser drill before, I aimed it out the window of my eyes at the poltergeist, threw the trap, and fired.

The erratic beam leapt from my face and straight into his. Boy, was he surprised when suddenly something did affect him. Now it was his turn to scream. He started trying to fly in any and every direction at once, but my weapon acted like an electric lasso, pulling him closer and closer to the waiting trap.

I heard indrawn breath all around as he lost control of the power he was exerting over everyone present. His outline lost cohesion, and it seemed as if he might slip away, but within a few brief seconds he shrieked in a spiral down into my trap. It closed and all was quiet. I walked over and picked up the trap. It was hissing and vibrating, but it was holding. I could hear him cursing me from within.

A cheer went up, from most of those present, friend and enemy alike. A bit anticlimactic perhaps, but I'd take it!

I walked over to check on Coral, holding the trap loosely behind me. She smiled tiredly back at me. Then the laughter began. The high, crazy, too long to be ok laughter. It started with His Herald but then became contagious around the room.

"Oh well done, Aaron! That trick might hold me for a while." Each word was spoken by a different individual in the room, but the cadence never changed.

"But then again, maybe not!"

The speakers of the last two words were nearby and one of them smashed the trap from my hand. It smacked into the ground and spun end over end. When it stopped it began smoking and caught fire.

Then he was there again in front of me.

Time slowed to a crawl as I looked into the face of the man who had known me best. He looked nothing like the too-strong-for-his-age man with eyes crinkled from years of heartfelt smiles that I remembered. It was hard to even look at him. The violet-shot edges of his form pulsed and contracted with no discernable rhythm. For a fraction of a second he looked the age he was when I lost him, but his eyes burned now with hatred and a thirst for vengeance, his "body" distorted as if he had been a body builder his entire life. Then his form contracted, and he was a frail ancient, long hair hanging in sparse tattered strands. The hatred in his eyes blazed brighter in this form. The phantasm swelled and blurred, becoming a face I had only seen in pictures. He was a young man, back straight and strong, shoulders unbent by hard physical labor and emotional pain. His eyes bore not hate, but the avarice and pride of a man driven to make the world his own. I could not imagine what force on earth could have turned such a loving, caring man into the thing before me.

"Aaron. You couldn't save us before. You can't save them now. Despair as I do and give up," it said venomously.

Waves of guilt like I hadn't felt in years crashed onto me. Memory overwhelmed me. I had been 18 for all of two days when it happened. I came home from work and shut off the truck's motor. When the engine noise vanished, it was replaced by terrified screams from behind the house. I burst out of the truck and ran around the building just in time to see my grandfather holding on to my grandmother's ankles. Her legs were disappearing into an angry red hole in the ground beside her garden. I yelled to my grandfather that I was coming. His legs were braced on the ground just outside the crimson breach in the solid earth. I was two steps away from them when the scarlet light flashed and widened, consuming my grandfather's feet. Both of them began sinking into what looked to me like the gateway to hell and I dove for them.

I caught his right arm and locked our forearms together. We had wrestled so many times that I knew this was the strongest hold I had. My head and feet were the only contact I had with the earth and the weight of two people being pulled away from me had me straining every muscle in my body. It wasn't enough. They slipped from my grasp. I was still pushing with all my might, and I went flying back. When I looked up, the vile radiance was fading, and the garden returned to normal. I could still hear their screams. It took me years to forget or convince myself it was a dream and my family had just gone missing, and now it was all back. I staggered at the memory as if struck.

Then the coldness of his words sunk in.

"I. don't. believe. it. Grampa Edward?" I struggled to think "Why? How could this be!? This isn't you!"

REUNION

I heard the gasps of surprise from the Sorrans when they heard who this being was to me and wanted to explain, but this was hardly the time.

"You cretin. Did you think we just stopped existing when you could no longer see us? Just how stupid are you?"

"Stupid? You used to say I was the smartest in the family.... And where is Gramma Betty?"

At the mention of her name, he solidified further and grew. His obvious anger strengthened him.

"Nobody speaks her name to me, least of all you!" he wailed into my face. If he'd been alive, I would have been covered with saliva, he was insane.

"We called to you to save us when the portal opened and we were being pulled through, but you were too weak! Pitiful you were and pitiful you remain! You were the only person who could have saved us! Because of your weakness, the Pinnaclees forced me to watch the only woman I'd ever loved tortured; vivisected in unbelievable agony for years!"

"I am sorry," I gasped, chest tightening in emotion. "I was just a kid. I pulled with everything I had. I tried to keep the ground from swallowing you! I tried to…"

He interrupted in a mimicry of my voice. "I tried. I tried. Well, it wasn't good enough then and it won't be enough now. The irony here is you all rejecting the only kindness I have to give. If you'd just let me destroy you, then you wouldn't have to face THEM later. Regardless, I'll use you just as they would to stop them."

I had no idea what he was talking about, but I had no time to ponder it as some force from him or one of his minions sent me flying backward into a wall. I nearly lost consciousness, but his next words brought me out of my swoon.

"Maybe you'd like to know what it feels like to have your love destroyed before you."

Coral screamed, held captive by some force I couldn't see. Her scream became a wail of intense agony.

Panic nearly caused me to react violently again, but I caught myself, knowing that wouldn't help. But what would? How could I save her and everyone else from a slow torturous death? Maybe unknowingly I'd hit the target before. I reached for the Star Glass and said a silent prayer that this would work. I commanded it, sending a picture of how I remembered Gramma Betty, to cast a glamour over Coral making her look and sound like the woman who raised me.

It was believable enough that if I hadn't caused it, I would have thought my Love had just become my dead Gramma. Within a half second of the change her shrieking stopped, and the ghost of Grampa Edward stammered in confusion and alarm.

"Are you ok?" I asked Coral silently.

"Everything hurts, but I'll live," she answered in the same way.

"I need you to speak only what I tell you and the way I tell you until this is over. Ok?"

"Yes, Aaron."

"Edward!" Coral said in my Gramma's voice.

"Betty! What? How!"

"Never you mind that now. What in the name of all that's holy are you doing?"

"Well, my love. I mean. I'm trying to.... I have to stop those who hurt you from doing the same things to others!"

I think he's buying it! He seemed so broken I didn't know if even this would reach him. I haven't heard Gramma's voice in so many years. What would she say now? Think, think, think, Aaron! Ok Coral, I think she'd say something like this.... And move like this:

"While that is a good and noble goal, do you think this is the way the Good Lord would want you to go about it?" the Coral/Gramma apparition crossed her arms and tapped her right foot.

"Well, no, Betty. But they—"

"Edward. Don't you give me any buts. You know better. You were a good man."

What would Gramma have said to him if she was being tortured and trying to stay true to what she believed? How would she have said what she thought was most important in that moment? Ah! I think I got it. Please let this work!

"Didn't I tell you to keep the faith no matter what they did to me Eddie?"

"Yes, Dear, but I couldn't stand it what they done to you. And…"

"I know, Edward. It was beyond awful. Just don't let them win by becoming just like them! Turn around, ask for forgiveness, and go back where you should be. In the sweet by and by with me and all those who loved you."

"It would seem to be a little late, since I'm already dead."

"Are you now? Well, it seems to me that where we're from, the dead go on to heaven or hell. Not traveling round from place to place causing other folks trouble."

Aaron shivered as he heard the words in his Gramma's voice as if she'd said it again herself. With each phrase he fed Coral he felt close to Gramma Betty's spirit, and he could see it having an effect on the ghost of Grandpa too. The anger and hatred in his eyes were fading. His appearance took on a new form, one between the young brash man and the old strong man. *Is this really working?*

"Maybe there is something else going on here, but I would think doing what we've always done when we've taken a wrong path and asking for forgiveness and grace is worth a try. Don't you?"

Come on, Grandpa! I know you still have to be in there somewhere. Like you used to tell me, sometimes you have to give up the illusion of control and just do the right thing the best way in that moment. I was expecting a fight with an evil enemy, not trying to remember things buried all these years in both of our hearts. This is harder than restoring someone corrupted by the Chaos Cloud, but if I can do it, so can you. Wait. I remember the one thing that Gramma said that stuck with me the most.

"There is no shame in I'm sorry, Eddie."

As he spoke with the faux Betty, Grampa Eddie began to change. He seemed to soften, and the room seemed a bit lighter than before. Now he closed his eyes and was silent for a time. The room held its collective breath.

"Betty. I've been a fool. I don't know how you've put up with me all these years. I can't keep up what I'm doing. I'll try it."

The long awkward silence continued. Nobody dared say a word for fear of interrupting whatever was going on. He shook and wavered for over the next two minutes and then cracked in half, like a crustacean broken to get the meat out. The darkness he had been covered with separated itself from him and dissolved when it hit the floor. What was left behind was a small pale reflection of the man who had taken me in when I was a child after my parents were killed in a plane crash.

"You were right Betty. I'm not sure how or why, but I'm forgiven, and I've been set free from whatever was holding me here. Their power over me is broken. I am whole. I hope I'll see you again soon."

I had the Star Glass banish the glamour.

"I'm sorry that I harmed you, young lady."

Coral looked perplexed but said, "I forgive you."

He turned to me.

"I don't know if you had anything to do with what happened, but I owe you the biggest apology. Of course, you couldn't save us from the most powerful race in existence. I can't believe I fell for the story THEY fed me about you letting go on purpose. They broke my mind, and I was confused. You aren't weak. I am proud of you. Please forgive me."

I ran to him to hug him and embarrassingly, right through him. Picking myself up off the floor with a chagrined look on my face I turned.

"I forgive you. I'm glad you're going to be safe now."

"My time is short. I can feel the pull of eternity. Let me tell you what I can. Your grandmother and I were taken to one of the worlds named Pinnacle. They wanted to turn us both into weapons for them, but for that to happen we would have had to renounce our faith. Betty was strong. Through years of torture and isolation, she was resolute. She never gave in. I wasn't so strong. They turned me into what you saw, but in the end, I was able to turn against them and back to grace. They go from world to world taking and destroying. There is nothing else in all the worlds as wrong and bad as the Pinnaclees. I would tell you more, but I'm out of time."

He was fading consistently as he spoke, and his last words were a whisper carried on the wind from time and places long gone.

Chapter 41
Battle's End

There was another minute of silence as everyone absorbed, or tried to absorb, what had happened. It was broken by the remaining corrupted OrOboid resuming their attack on anyone unlucky enough to be near enough for them to do so. I yelled at Mikaal to look after and heal Coral before striding toward the action. I heard him respond and knew she would be safe.

Only those touched by corruption, or those facing one, continued to fight. Those who had been brought here as a captive part of Grampa's forces were holding their heads, presumably feeling the breaking of whatever influence had been exerted on them.

I sent a strong mental message out before me as I advanced, telling any who no longer wanted to fight against us to throw down their weapons and move toward the entrance. They would not be held responsible for any actions taken while they were controlled by their Master. They should not try to exit the cavern as they might be mistaken for combatants by our forces guarding the exit.

A loud clattering met this pronouncement as weapons and armor of all types hit the floor. I didn't look back, trusting the Sorran forces would ensure that those who surrendered were kept safe from retaliation as I'd promised.

The numbers of OrOboid corrupted were slowly increasing. The back of the cavern was the path to the castle and ever larger and lumbering OrOmonsters were coming from that direction. A Garanth Breaker soldier suddenly flew from behind a bend, back first into the far wall. He hit with a thud and slid slowly down. The floor shook and two of the largest corrupted OrOboid imaginable walked into view. The mountain and all within it shook at their every step.

Nobody stood to face them. I could see reversal spells in progress on many of the lesser enemies. I couldn't imagine that there were any mages still standing that weren't performing reversals.

I looked at my watch to check the power levels. Eighty percent. I hoped it would be enough. I commanded the Star Glass again to cast a high-speed reversal on every corrupted creature within the mountain and Castle, starting with the two mega monsters in front of me.

Magic leapt up from the artifact. My vision of every OrOmonster was obscured by the split pea soup colored aura. There was no pained yelling since these creatures had no voices. I alternated watching the reversal field decrease as my targets were returned to normal and the power meter on my arm. It was decreasing at an alarming rate.

If I ran out of power before the reversal finished, what would happen to those I was trying to help?

I heard the chime notifying me of low power from the Star Glass. There were no more power sources I could safely turn it loose on.

Thinking quickly, I dove into my mind and to the storage rooms I'd prepared. I had three rooms mostly full of magical energy that I rarely pulled from. I created a conveyor belt from the fullest room to my eyes with a chute pointed at the Star Glass. Crossing my fingers, I started feeding my own power into the artifact, just as I had done with Mikaal and the gems in our Torcs before.

The power meter was at ten percent and the chiming was insistent. I told the Star Glass that I was going to supply it with concentrated magic just before the first dollop of "Aaron's magic power goo" fell towards it. The power meter stopped at nine percent.

More power fell and the meter slowly climbed. I emptied the first room and started on the second.

I asked it for a progress report, but with so many targets even something as powerful as this couldn't provide a good estimate. I told it to go as fast as it could manage and to utilize side-effect lightning, but it already was.

I fed it a second room full of power, and still the spell continued. The two giants before me were back to normal, but there were many more within the castle. I had only a half room left of energy to give it, and then I would be nearly defenseless myself. I told it to complete the reversals in progress but begin no more.

I heard Granalis' voice from a faraway distance. He was talking nonsense. Said I was glowing and hot to the touch. I'd have to deal with that later. The chiming of low power was sounding again.

I gave the Star Glass all the power I had. I fell to my knees, weakened. The chime was still sounding, and the spell was still going. Two voices were yelling that I was burning hot. I shrugged, nearly beyond all caring, but maybe the artifact could use that too, so I told it to take the excess heat as energy.

Then I passed out.

When I awoke there were many concerned faces around me.

"I thought I was going to lose you again, Aaron. You laid there barely breathing for half an hour," Coral said through sobs.

"Coral tried to hold you close, but your skin was so hot we started loosening your clothes to cool you," Mikaal added. "Then seconds later you were shivering and cold to the touch."

"The Star Glass did exactly what I told it to, and it nearly killed me. If I have to use it anymore, I hope I get better at it," I half joked.

There were still a few corrupted OrOboid left, but those would be dealt with by our forces. The Moalean were busy creating reversal statuettes to give to the warriors. The battle was effectively over.

Chapter 42
And Then?

I never truly forgot all the lives that were lost under my leadership, but for the first time since I was a teenager, I was able to accept that some losses were beyond my power to control. Many were saved.

Coral was whole and at my side. She and Mikaal, Granalis, and Junean had fought beside me to the very end, and we'd stopped the destruction of Sorra. We now knew that there was an even bigger danger out there somewhere and that it could be coming for us.

We would return to Tiiaan next, but first we had some POWs to deal with. Vaminous had corralled them, humanely as possible, and tried to communicate with them with limited success. We joined him now. There were three distinct people groups. First, the feline humanoids, or Catlings as I'd thought of them, and then the dragonlike race, some who were bipedal, and some walked on all fours or flew. Finally, the clockwork people, who were actually very small and shaped like squid and moved around the world in metal suits for battle.

Each group confirmed that their world had been destroyed by Grampa, and they had nowhere to return to. Some few were willing to try to go back and look for other survivors in the hopes that their race could continue. They would accompany us to Tiiaan and share their stories.

There was one former enemy mage still alive who knew how to open a portal but had little control over what world it connected to and needed other mages to work it with him. It was hoped that with help, he could send those who wanted to go back to their worlds, home.

The being who was many in one was never found, but it was thought that it was only magic that had bound them together in one body. When the master turned and his power was broken, nothing held them together any longer, and they expired quickly and were at last in peace.

Coral and I took some time to talk about what was next for us when we camped that night. We agreed that much of Sorra remained to be explored and restored where possible. This was what we should do next, until her family was restored, and I could ask for her hand in proper fashion. Others could and likely would join us in this work, but it would be our goal. Only when that work was done would we be able to settle in and raise a family.

There was also the matter of the Star Glass. Once Sorra was whole, I would have to find a place for it where its power wouldn't tempt me or others to use it for personal gain.

After Coral and I had a chance to plan, we went to where the rest of the leaders were eating and talking. Mikaal informed us that he would return to Tiiaan. He would report on all that happened and help with the rebuilding of the city. Junean and Tibbeus and the Moalean forces planned to remain for another day, to assist the OrOboid who had been freed and address any still corrupted. Granalis alone had no home to return to. He liked the idea of exploring Sorra and asked to travel with us, but with freedom to come and go as he pleased. His people lived longer than ours and he hoped that one day he would find even a few of his kind.

I am sure that with these Pinnaclees still at large, this life will not get dull or stale, if such a thing was possible on a world like Sorra. I am Aaron the White, and this world and its people are under my protection for as long as I live.

Glossary

<u>Gameball</u>—Sorran sports ball, about the size of an adult human's fist

<u>Chipchucks, Hairs, and Kittles</u>—Sorran small, furry woodland critters, harmless

<u>Star Glass</u>—An artifact of great power. It appears as a glass ball held securely in the grip of two crystal palms, whose arms tapered down and back out into a heptagonal prism and ended with an endless knot with an open center. Appears delicate and glowing like a full moon.

<u>Patuns</u>—Primary unit of the Sorran monetary system, one Patun is the equivalent of one hour of work. Broken into smaller pieces called Hasmut.

<u>Hasmut</u>—Currency of Sorra, worth ten minutes of labor. There are five Hasmut in a Patun.

<u>Spiral Fruit</u>—The tree resembles a barber pole that had sprouted limbs. The fruit is said to be tasty, tart, and sweet at the same time.

<u>Peasant</u>—A rare and utterly tasty bird.

Unbinding—A type of chaos cloud. When it comes into contact with anything living, it will break links inside of the being, both physical and mental. When an unbinding touches non-living items, these things are undone as if they never were, are perverted, or destroyed.

Rockpiper—A small Sorran hunting bird.

Rhinodons—Imposing beasts which are used as transportation and pack animals by the Garanth. Rhinodons have six legs which connect to a body longer and thicker than that of a horse. They are marvelously fast but also noisy as they have large two-toed feet which make slapping noises as they hit the dry earth. The massive neck holds up a head of equally mammoth proportions. Rhinodons have a single tusk protruding from their bony upper lips, which matches the single eye set in a deep socket high on the long head. Rhinodons eat vegetation such as grass, grain, and leaves.

TuskerKitty—To a human they look like a cross between a boar and a wildcat. They are incredibly quick and flexible. TuskerKitties have great furry claws. They are normally vegetarians and so don't have exceptionally sharp teeth. However, their preferred source of food is tree bark, and because of this, they do have very strong jaw muscles.

Gaw—Noran's eight ropelike appendages, instead of jointed arms or legs sprouting from their torsos.

Twinpipe—A small wind instrument that produces two tones at the same time.

Bannam—A stringed instrument with remarkable range, which was alternately strummed and plucked.

GLOSSARY

<u>Grooverfruit</u>—A very hard to find fruit which only grows in high places rich in magic, with very interesting side effects.

<u>Sal Cheese</u>—A strong cheese that tastes like fresh garlic but leaves no noticeable odor.

<u>Rigglewerm</u>—Invertebrate subterranean animals which prey on Moaleans.

<u>Groundpig</u>—Knee high animal covered in coarse fur. It has four legs and no discernable face, front, or back.

<u>OasisAnts</u>—Very like the ants on Earth save for a few minor details. They are nearly half again human height. The Queen bears a circlet of some lumpy golden material that grows from her head. They have large mandibles oriented as one would expect, with another slightly smaller set oriented vertically inside the first. The Queen Ant also has a stinger jutting forward from the point of her folded under abdomen. She is incredibly fast and can walk on her rear legs.

<u>Quickness</u>—A Quickness is a magical underground tunnel connecting two points and allowing for travel at a high rate of speed.

<u>PeakCaps</u>—Enormous beasts that hatch approximately every fifty years. The eggs are laid on the top of a mountain and continue to grow slowly over the years. Their faces are fearsome, with a long beak-like muzzle lined with two rows of long needle-sharp teeth. It has mismatched wings and appendages and hair like tree trunks.

<u>OrOboid genders</u>—3 Sexes exist; Smale—Sperm bearer, Emale—Egg bearer, and Female—Womb bearer.

Main Character List

Aaron—Human Male, called into Sorra to save it. From an Earthlike world with no magic. Learns skills unique to him as he travels.

Mikaal—Noran Male Magician, 1205 years old, prankster, calls for a Hero through the Portal, mentor to Aaron and teacher to many.

Coral—Last SeaWind, Princess, Female Archer and Mage, Love interest of Aaron.

Junean—Moalean Female sent to investigate the Chaos Cloud, Promised to Tibbeus. Daughter of Innean. Carries a bag of magical figurines.

Tibbeus—Moalean Male turned by the Chaos Cloud, Promised to Junean. Originally corrupted and healed by Aaron.

OrOboids: (a three-legged race with an all-purpose sensory organ around their heads who see/hear/interact with the world in 360 degrees and have no true front/back).

Kaalesh—Female OrOboid, sent out to investigate Aandoo's disappearance, Joined to Kaaden and Kreelen.

Kaaden—Smale OrOboid, sent out to investigate Aandoo's disappearance, Joined to Kaalesh and Kreelen.

Main Character List

Kreelen—Emale OrOboid, sent out to investigate Aandoo's disappearance, Joined to Kaalesh and Kaaden.

(Z)Andoo/(K)Andoo/Andoo—Smale OrOboid, Lone Warrior sent out to investigate disturbances in OrOboid settlements.

(Z)Iinndie—Female OrOboid, Ranger class soldier of Tiiaan.

(Z)Eeaarly—Emale OrOboid, Divide class soldier of Tiiaan.

Magic School Headmasters:

Mackta (title)—Senior Headmaster, ancient Garanth man, short but exudes an incredible sense of power.

Glanoot—Garanth. Junior headmaster.

Notrus—Noran. Junior headmaster.

Maegen—Moalean. Junior headmaster.

Counsel of Three:

Athious—Middle-aged and powerfully built Garanth male.

Clanus—Middle-aged and average height Garanth male.

Breauus—Young Garanth woman.

Granalis—Last of his race. Forced into servitude to an evil master, who disfigured him and destroyed his world. Freed and restored by Aaron. In his true form he is covered in the brightest white fur, which is fine and soft as silk, and he has orange pupils. He walks on all fours; the front appendages are furry hands with six fingers and an opposable thumb.

Cairna—Attractive young Garanth clerk in TownHold, obsidian-colored skin.

Jixxell—young Noran woman, keeper of the gate at the Tiiaanian Magic School, acquaintance of Mikaal. Gaw were as black as the metal of the gate. Sister to Jixxey.

Jixxey—Noran Barracks Master at the magic school. Sister to Jixxell.

Creaane—one of the best Lancers. She had her hat pulled down over her eyes. The hat contained a set of dark goggles inset in them which had been obscured by a fold of the metallic clothlike material.

Miineux—Aged Moalean lady. In charge of the Lightning Lancers. Friend of Vaminous.

Vaminous—Massive Garanth Male with a puffy twirled mustache. Friend of Miineux. Commander of Tiiaanian forces.

Pakky—Aaron's Rhinodon.

Deloraa—One of the few Noran musicians in Tiiaan and possibly the only musician among Tiiaanian forces. Suggested a path to Harmonious Order.

Author Bio

Mikel Boland is (hopefully) soon to be known for the Portal Jumpers series of books, stories and novella(s), and assorted other fantasy. He is also trying his hand at modern romance and hopes to be a smashing success in that genre as well. Mikel lives with his beloved wife and three teenagers in Florida. He fed his brain in approximately 25 schools growing up, lived in 7 states, and has moved up to 12 times in a single year. Mikel inherited a love for fiction books from his father and has long since lost count of the worlds he's visited in these pages. Through the process of writing, Mikel has learned that creating is a blast and very therapeutic, editing can cause a need for therapy, and there is much more to learn.

Made in the USA
Columbia, SC
17 June 2025